PENGUIN BOOKS

The Spy

Clive Cussler is the author or co-author of a great number of international best-sellers, including the famous Dirk Pitt® adventures, such as *Crescent Dawn*; the NUMA® Files adventures, most recently *Medusa*; the Oregon Files, such as *The Jungle*; the Isaac Bell adventures, which began with *The Chase*; and the recent Fargo adventures. His non-fiction works include *The Sea Hunters* and *The Sea Hunters II*: these describe the true adventures of the real NUMA, which, led by Cussler, searches for lost ships of historic significance. With his crew of volunteers, Cussler has discovered more than sixty ships, including the long-lost Confederate submarine *Hunley*. He lives in Arizona.

Justin Scott's twenty-four novels include *The Shipkiller* and *Normandie Triangle*; the Ben Abbot detective series; and five modern sea thrillers published under his pen name Paul Garrison. He lives in Connecticut with his wife, the filmmaker Amber Edwards.

Praise for Clive Cussler:

'The guy I read' Tom Clancy

'Clive Cussler is hard to beat' *Daily Mail*

'No holds barred adventure . . . a souped-up treat' *Daily Mirror*

'The Adventure King' *Sunday Express*

'Frightening and full of suspense . . . unquestionably entertaining' *Daily Express*

'All-action, narrow escapes and the kind of unrelenting plot tension that has won Cussler hundreds of millions of fans worldwide' *Observer*

The Spy

CLIVE CUSSLER
and JUSTIN SCOTT

PENGUIN BOOKS

PENGUIN BOOKS

Published by the Penguin Group

Penguin Books Ltd, 80 Strand, London WC2R 0RL, England

Penguin Group (USA) Inc., 375 Hudson Street, New York, New York 10014, USA

Penguin Group (Canada), 90 Eglinton Avenue East, Suite 700, Toronto, Ontario, Canada M4P 2Y3
(a division of Pearson Penguin Canada Inc.)

Penguin Ireland, 25 St Stephen's Green, Dublin 2, Ireland
(a division of Penguin Books Ltd)

Penguin Group (Australia), 250 Camberwell Road, Camberwell, Victoria 3124, Australia
(a division of Pearson Australia Group Pty Ltd)

Penguin Books India Pvt Ltd, 11 Community Centre, Panchsheel Park, New Delhi – 110 017, India

Penguin Group (NZ), 67 Apollo Drive, Rosedale, Auckland 0632, New Zealand
(a division of Pearson New Zealand Ltd)

Penguin Books (South Africa) (Pty) Ltd, 24 Sturdee Avenue, Rosebank, Johannesburg 2196, South Africa

Penguin Books Ltd, Registered Offices: 80 Strand, London WC2R 0RL, England

www.penguin.com

First published in the United States of America by G. P. Putnam's Sons 2010
First published in Great Britain by Michael Joseph 2010
Published in Penguin Books 2011

001

Printed in England by Clays Ltd, St Ives plc

Except in the United States of America, this book is sold subject
to the condition that it shall not, by way of trade or otherwise, be lent,
re-sold, hired out, or otherwise circulated without the publisher's
prior consent in any form of binding or cover other than that in
which it is published and without a similar condition including this
condition being imposed on the subsequent purchaser

ISBN: 978-1-405-93270-7

www.greenpenguin.co.uk

For Amber

The Gunner's Daughter

I

March 17, 1908 Washington, D.C.

The Washington Navy Yard slept like an ancient city guarded by thick walls and a river. Old men stood watch, plodding between electric time detectors to register their rounds of factories, magazines, shops, and barracks. Outside the perimeter rose a hill of darkened workers' houses. The Capitol Dome and the Washington Monument crowned it, glittering under a full moon like polar ice. A whistle moaned. A train approached, bleeding steam and clanging its bell.

U.S. Marine sentries opened the North Railroad Gate.

No one saw Yamamoto Kenta hiding under the Baltimore and Ohio flatcar that the locomotive pushed into the yard. The flatcar's wheels groaned under a load of fourteen-inch armor plate from Bethlehem, Pennsylvania. Brakemen uncoupled the car on a siding, and the engine backed away.

Yamamoto eased to the wooden crossties and stone ballast between the rails. He lay still until he was sure he was alone. Then he followed the tracks into the cluster of three-story brick-and-iron buildings that housed the Gun Factory.

Moonlight lancing down from high windows, and the ruby glow of banked furnaces illuminated an enormous cavern. Traveler cranes hulked in shadows overhead.

Colossal fifty-ton dreadnought battleship guns crowded the floor as if a fiery hurricane had leveled a steel forest.

Yamamoto, a middle-aged Japanese with threads of gray in his shiny black hair and a confident, dignified manner, wove a purposeful route through the watchmen's prescribed paths, examining gun lathes, machines for rifling, and furnaces. He paid special attention to deep wells in the floor, the brick-lined shrinking pits where the guns were assembled by squeezing steel jackets around fifty-foot tubes. His eye was sharp, refined by similar clandestine 'tours' of Vickers and Krupp – the British and German naval gun factories – and the Czar of Russia's ordnance plants at St. Petersburg.

An old-style Yale lock secured the door to the laboratory storeroom that dispensed supplies to the engineers and scientists. Yamamoto picked it open quickly. Inside, he searched cabinets for iodine. He poured six ounces of the shiny blue-black crystals into an envelope. Then he scrawled 'crystal iodine, 6 ounces' on a requisition sheet with the initials 'AL' for the Gun Factory's legendary chief designer, Arthur Langner.

In a distant wing of the sprawling building, he located the test caisson where armor experts simulated torpedo attacks to measure the awesomely magnified impact of explosions underwater. He rummaged through their magazine. The sea powers locked in the international race to build modern dreadnought battleships were feverishly experimenting with arming torpedoes with TNT, but Yamamoto noted that the Americans were still testing formulations based on guncotton propellants. He stole a silk bag of Cordite MD smokeless powder.

As he opened a janitor's closet to filch a bottle of ammonia water, he heard a watchman coming. He hid in the closet until the old fellow had shuffled past and disappeared among the guns.

Swift and silent, Yamamoto climbed the stairs.

Arthur Langner's drawing loft, which was not locked, was the workshop of an eccentric whose genius spanned war and art. Blueprints for stepped-thread breeches and visionary sketches of shells with smashing effects as yet unheard of shared the workspace with a painter's easel, a library of novels, a bass violin, and a grand piano.

Yamamoto left the Cordite, the iodine, and the ammonia on the piano and spent an hour studying the drafting tables. 'Be Japan's eyes,' he preached at the Black Ocean Society's spy school on the rare occasions that duty allowed him home. 'Take every opportunity to observe, whether your ultimate mission is deception, sabotage, or murder.'

What he saw frightened him. The 12-inch guns on the factory floor could throw shells seven miles to pierce ten inches of the newest face-hardened side armor. But up here in the drawing loft where new ideas were hatched, the Americans had preliminary sketches for 15-inch guns and even a 16-inch, seventy-foot-long monster that would hurl a ton of high explosives beyond the curve of the Earth. No one knew yet how to aim such a weapon when the distances were too great to gauge range by 'spotting' the splashes of near misses. But the bold imagination that Yamamoto saw at work warned him it was only a matter of time before America's 'New Navy' invented novel concepts for fire control.

Yamamoto stuffed a wad of paper money in the gun

designer's desk – fifty twenty-dollar U.S. gold certificates – considerably more than what one of the arsenal's skilled workmen earned in a year.

Already the U.S. Navy was third only to England's and Germany's. Its North Atlantic Fleet – brazenly rechristened the 'Great White Fleet' – was showing the flag in a swaggering voyage around the world. But Britain, Germany, Russia, and France were not America's enemies. The true mission of the Great White Fleet was to threaten the Empire of Japan with naked steel. America aimed to command the Pacific Ocean from San Francisco to Tokyo.

Japan would not allow it, Yamamoto thought with a prideful smile.

It was only three years since the Russo-Japanese War spawned in blood a new master of the Western Pacific. Mighty Russia had tried to strong-arm Japan. Today the Empire of Japan occupied Port Arthur. And Russia's Baltic Fleet lay under three hundred feet of water at the bottom of the Tsushima Strait – thanks in no small part to Japanese spies who had infiltrated the Russian Navy.

As Yamamoto closed the drawer on the money, he had the eerie sensation of being watched. He looked across the desk into the bold gaze of a beautiful woman whose photographic portrait stood in a silver frame. He recognized Langner's dark-haired daughter and admired how faithfully the photographer had captured her compelling eyes. She had inscribed it in a flowing hand 'For Father, the "gunner" who "dreads nought"!'

Yamamoto turned his attention to Langner's bookshelves. Bound volumes of patent applications vied with novels for the space. The applications filed recently had been written on a typewriter. Yamamoto pulled volume after volume, working his way back to the last year that applications were submitted in longhand. He spread one on the designer's desk, then chose a sheet of paper from a side drawer and a Waterman fountain pen with a gold nib. Referring repeatedly to the sample of handwriting, he forged a brief, incoherent letter. Ending it with the words 'Forgive me,' he scrawled Arthur Langner's signature.

He took the iodine and the ammonia into the gun designer's washroom. With the butt of his Nambu pocket pistol he crushed the iodine crystals on the marble wash-stand and brushed the resultant powder into a shaving mug. He wiped the gun clean with the washroom towel, leaving a purplish smear on the cloth. Then he poured ammonia onto the iodine powder, stirring with Langner's toothbrush until he had a thick paste of nitrogen iodide.

He propped open the lid of the grand piano, reached into the narrow end farthest from the keyboard, and smeared the paste on the closely bunched strings. After it dried, the explosive concoction would become unstable and extremely sensitive to impact. A gentle vibration would set off a loud bang and a flash. Alone, the explosion would damage little beyond the piano. But as a detonator, it would be deadly.

He placed the silk sack on top of the cast-iron frame, immediately above the strings. The sack contained enough Cordite MD smokeless powder to propel a twelve-pound shell two miles.

Yamamoto Kenta left the Gun Factory the way he had entered, his eyes still stinging from the ammonia. Suddenly, things went wrong. The North Railroad Gate was blocked by an unexpected burst of late-night activity. Switch engines were huffing gondola cars in and out, attended by a horde of brakemen. He retreated deeper into the arsenal, past the powerhouse, through a maze of roads, buildings, and storage yards. Orienting himself by the powerhouse smokestacks and a pair of experimental radio-antenna towers silhouetted against the moonlit sky, he crossed a park and gardens bordered by handsome brick houses in which slept the families of the commandant and officers of the yard.

The ground rose higher here. To the northwest he glimpsed the Capitol looming over the city. He saw it as yet another symbol of America's fearsome might. What other nation could have erected the largest cast-iron dome in the world at the same time they were fighting a bloody Civil War? He was almost to a side gate when a sentry surprised him on a narrow path.

Yamamoto had just enough time to back into a hedge-row.

His capture would disgrace Japan. He was ostensibly in Washington, D.C., to help catalog the recent contribution of the Freer Collection of Asian art to the Smithsonian Institution. The front allowed him to mingle with the Diplomatic Corps and powerful politicians, thanks to their wives who fancied themselves artists and hung on his every word about Japanese art. Genuine experts at the Smithsonian had caught him off base twice already. He had blamed gaps in his hastily learned knowledge on a poor command of English. So far, the experts accepted the excuse. But there would be absolutely no plausible explanation for a Japanese curator of Asian art caught prowling the Washington Navy Yard at night.

The watchman came up the path, boots crunching on gravel. Yamamoto backed in deeper, drawing his pistol as a last resort. A gunshot would rouse Marine guards from their barracks at the main gate. Deeper he pushed, feeling for an opening in the branches that would lead out the other side.

The watchman had no reason to look into the hedge-row as he plodded by. But Yamamoto was still pushing backward against the springy branches, and one snapped. The watchman stopped. He peered in the direction of the sound. In that instant the moon bathed both their faces.

The Japanese spy saw him clearly – a retired sailor, an 'old salt,' supplementing his meager pension with a night watchman's job. His face was leathery, his eyes bleached by years of tropical sunlight, his back stooped. He straightened up at the sight of the slender figure hiding in the hedge. Suddenly galvanized, the pensioner was no longer an old man who should have called for help but was hurled back to his time as a long-limbed, broad-shouldered 'blue jacket' in the full tide of life. A strong voice that once carried to the mast tops demanded, 'What the devil are you doing in there?'

Yamamoto wormed out the back of the hedge and ran. The watchman pushed into the hedge and got tangled in it and roared like a bull. Yamamoto heard answering shouts in the distance. He changed course and raced along a high wall. It had been raised, he had learned while preparing for his 'tour,' after looters invaded when the Potomac River flooded the yard. It was too high to scale.

Boots pounded on gravel. Old men shouted. Electric flashlights flickered. Suddenly he saw salvation, a tree standing near the wall. Digging his india-rubber crepe soles into the bark, he shinnied up the trunk to the lowest branch, climbed two higher, and jumped onto the wall. He heard shouts behind him. The city street below was empty. He jumped down and cushioned a hard landing with flexed knees.

At Buzzard Point, near the foot of 1st Street, Yamamoto boarded an eighteen-foot motorboat powered by a two-horse Pierce 'Noiseless.' The pilot steered into the current and down the Potomac River. A shroud of surface mist finally closed around the boat, and Yamamoto exhaled a sigh of relief.

Huddling from the cold in the cubby under the bow, he reflected upon his close call and concluded that his mission had suffered no damage. The garden path where the night watchman had almost caught him was at least a half mile from the Gun Factory. Nor did it matter that the old man had seen his face. Americans were contemptuous of Asians. Few could distinguish between Japanese and Chinese features. Since immigrants from China were far more numerous than those from Japan, the watchman would report an intrusion by a despised Chinese – an opium fiend, he thought with a relieved smile. Or, he chuckled silently, a nefarious white slaver lurking to prey on the commandant's daughters.

Five miles downriver, he disembarked in Alexandria, Virginia.

He waited for the boat to depart the wooden pier. Then he hurried along the waterfront and entered a dark warehouse that was crammed with obsolete naval gear deep in dust and spiderwebs.

A younger man whom Yamamoto had labeled, scornfully, 'The Spy' was waiting for him in a dimly lit back room that served as an office. He was twenty years Yamamoto's junior and ordinary-looking to the point of being nondescript. His office, too, held the outdated paraphernalia of earlier wars: crossed cutlasses on the walls; a Civil War–era Dahlgren cast-iron, muzzle-loading cannon, which was causing the floor to sag; and an old 24-inch-diameter carbon arc battleship searchlight propped behind his desk. Yamamoto saw his own face mirrored in its dusty eye.

He reported that he had accomplished his mission. Then, while the spy took notes, he related in precise detail everything that he had seen at the Gun Factory. 'Much of it,' he said in conclusion, 'looks worn out.'

'Hardly a surprise.'

Overworked and underfunded, the Gun Factory had produced everything from ammunition hoists to torpedo tubes to send the Great White Fleet to sea. After the warships sailed, it forwarded trainloads of replacement parts, sights, firing locks, breech plugs, and gun mounts to San Francisco. In another month the fleet would recuperate there from its fourteen-thousand-mile voyage around South America's Cape Horn and refit at the Mare Island Naval Shipyard to cross the Pacific.

'I would not underestimate them,' Yamamoto retorted gloomily. 'Worn-out machines are replaceable.'

'If they have the nerve.'

'From what I saw, they have the nerve. And the imagination. They are merely catching their breath.'

The man behind the desk felt that Yamamoto Kenta was possessed – if not unhinged – by his fear of the American Navy. He had heard this rant before and knew how to change the subject by derailing the Jap with lavish praise.

'I have never doubted your acute powers of observation. But I am awed by the range and breadth of your skills: chemistry, engineering, forgery. In one fell swoop you have impeded the development of American gunnery and sent their Congress a message that the Navy is corrupt.'

He watched Yamamoto preen. Even the most capable operative had his Achilles' heel. Yamamoto's was a self-blinding vanity.

'I've played this game a long time,' Yamamoto agreed with false modesty.

In fact, thought the man behind the desk, the chemistry for the nitrogen iodide detonator was a simple formula found in *The Young Folks' Cyclopaedia of Games and Sports*. Which was not to take away from Yamamoto's other skills, nor his broad and deep knowledge of naval warfare.

Having softened him up, he prepared to put the Jap to the test. 'Last week aboard the *Lusitania*,' he said, 'I bumped into a British attaché. You know the sort. Thinks of himself as a "gentleman spy."'

He had an astonishing gift for accents, and he mimicked, faultlessly, an English aristocratic drawl. '"The Japanese," this Englishman proclaimed to all in the smoking room, "display a natural aptitude for espionage, and a cunning and self-control not found in the West."'

Yamamoto laughed. 'That sounds like Commander

Abbington-Westlake of the Admiralty's Naval Intelligence Department, Foreign Division, who was spotted last summer painting a watercolor of the Long Island Sound that just happened to contain America's latest Viper Class submarine. Do you suppose the windbag meant it as a compliment?'

'The French Navy he penetrated so successfully last month would hardly call Abbington-Westlake a windbag. Did you keep the money?'

'I beg your pardon?'

'The money you were supposed to put in Arthur Langner's desk. Did you keep it for yourself?'

The Jap stiffened. 'Of course not. I put it in his desk.'

'The Navy's enemies in Congress must believe that their star designer, their so-called Gunner, was guilty of taking a bribe. That money was vital to our message to the Congress to make them wonder what else is rotten in the Navy. Did you keep the money?'

'I should not be surprised that you would ask such a degrading question of a loyal associate. With the heart of a thief you assume that everyone is a thief.'

'Did you keep the money?' the spy repeated. A physical habit of maintaining utter stillness masked the steely power of his compact frame.

'For the last time, I did not keep the money. Would you feel more secure if I swore on the memory of my old friend – your father?'

'Do it!'

Yamamoto looked him full in the face with undisguised hatred. 'I swear on the memory of my old friend, your father.'

'I think I believe you.'

'Your father was a patriot,' Yamamoto replied coldly. 'You are a mercenary.'

'You're on my payroll,' came the even colder retort. 'And when you report to your government the valuable information you picked up in the Washington Navy Yard's Gun Factory – *while working for me* – your government will pay you again.'

'I do not spy for the money. I spy for the Empire of Japan.'

'And for me.'

'Good Sunday morning to all who prefer their music minus the sermon,' Arthur Langner greeted his friends at the Gun Factory.

Rumpled in a baggy sack suit, his thick hair tousled and bright eyes inquisitive, the Naval Ordnance Bureau's star designer grinned like a man who found interest in all he saw and liked the strange bits most of all. The Gunner was a vegetarian, an outspoken agnostic, and devoted to the theories of the unconscious mind put forth by the Viennese neurologist Sigmund Freud.

He held patents for an invention he named the Electrical Vacuum Cleaning Machine, having hitched his fertile imagination to a heartfelt notion that science-based domestic engineering could free women from the isolation of housework. He also believed that women should have the right to vote, work outside the home, and even practice birth control. Gossips smirked that his beautiful daughter, who ran with the fast set in Washington and New York, would be a prime beneficiary.

'A one-man lunatic fringe,' complained the commandant of the navy yard.

But the chief of Naval Ordnance, having observed Langner's latest 12-inch/.50 caliber gun shoot up his Sandy Hook Atlantic Test Range, retorted, 'Thank God he works for us instead of the enemy.'

His Sunday-morning chamber musicians, a ragtag mix of Gun Factory employees, laughed appreciatively when Langner joked, 'Just to assure any eavesdropping blue noses that we're not complete heathens, let's start with "Amazing Grace." In G.'

He sat at his grand piano.

'May we please have an A first, sir?' asked the cellist, an expert in armor-piercing warheads.

Langner lightly tapped middle A, to which note the strings could tune their instruments. He rolled his eyes in mock impatience as they fiddled with their tuning pegs. 'Are you gentlemen cooking up one of those new atonal scales?'

'One more A, if you can spare it, Arthur. A little louder?'

Langner tapped middle A harder, again and again. At last the strings were satisfied.

The cellist began the opening notes of 'Amazing Grace.'

At the tenth measure, the violins – a torpedo-propulsion man and a burly steamfitter – took up 'once was lost.' They played through and began to repeat.

Langner raised his big hands over the keys, stepped on the sustain pedal, and lofted 'a wretch like me' on a soaring G chord.

Inside the piano, Yamamoto Kenta's paste of nitrogen iodide had hardened to a volatile dry crust. When Langner fingered the keys, felt hammers descended on G, B, and D strings, causing them to vibrate. Up and down the scale, six more octaves of G, B, and D strings vibrated sympathetically, jolting the nitrogen iodide.

It exploded with a sharp *crack* that sent a purple cloud pouring from the case and detonated the sack of Cordite. The Cordite blew the piano into a thousand slivers of wood and wire and ivory that riddled Arthur Langner's head and chest, killing him instantly.

2

By 1908, the Van Dorn Detective Agency maintained a presence in all American cities of consequence, and its offices reflected the nature of each locality. Headquarters in Chicago had a suite in the palatial Palmer House. Dusty Ogden, Utah, a railroad junction, was served by a rented room decorated with wanted posters. New York's offices were in the sumptuous Knickerbocker Hotel on 42nd Street. And in Washington, D.C., with its valuable proximity to the Department of Justice – a prime source of business – Van Dorn detectives operated from the second floor of the capital city's finest hotel, the new Willard on Pennsylvania Avenue, two blocks from the White House.

Joseph Van Dorn himself kept an office there, a walnut-paneled den bristling with up-to-date devices for riding herd on the transcontinental outfit he commanded. In addition to the agency's private telegraph, he had three candlestick telephones capable of long-distance connections as far west as Chicago, a DeVeau Dictaphone, a self-winding stock ticker, and an electric Kellogg Intercommunicating Telephone. A spy hole let him size up clients and informants in the reception room. Corner windows overlooked the Willard's front and side entrances.

From those windows, a week after Arthur Langner's tragic death at the Naval Gun Factory, Van Dorn watched apprehensively as two women stepped down from a streetcar, hurried across the bustling sidewalk, and disappeared inside the hotel.

The intercommunicating phone rang.

'Miss Langner is here,' reported the Willard's house detective, a Van Dorn employee.

'So I see.' He was not looking forward to this visit.

The founder of the Van Dorn Detective Agency was a heavily built, bald-headed man in his forties. He had a strong Roman nose, framed by bristling red whiskers, and the affable manner of a lawyer or a businessman who had earned his fortune early and enjoyed it. Hooded eyes masked a ferocious intelligence; the nation's penitentiaries held many criminals gulled into letting the big gent close enough to clamp on the handcuffs.

Downstairs, the two women riveted male attention as they glided through the Willard's gilt-and-marble lobby. The younger, a petite girl of eighteen or nineteen, was a stylishly dressed redhead with a vivacious gleam in her eyes. Her companion was a tall, raven-haired beauty, somber in the dark cloth of mourning, her hat adorned with the feathers of black terns, her face partially veiled. The redhead was clutching her elbow as if to give her courage.

Once across the lobby, however, Dorothy Langner took charge, urging her companion to sit on a plush couch at the foot of the stairs.

'Are you sure you don't want me to come with you?'

'No thank you, Katherine. I'll be fine from here.'

Dorothy Langner gathered her long skirts and swept up the stairs.

Katherine Dee craned her neck to watch Dorothy pause on the landing, turn back her veil, and press her forehead against a cool, polished marble pillar. Then she straightened up, composed herself, and strode down the hall, out of Katherine's sight and into the Van Dorn Detective Agency.

Joseph Van Dorn shot a look through the spy hole. The receptionist was a steady man – he would not command a Van Dorn front desk were he not – but he appeared thunderstruck by the beauty presenting her card, and Van Dorn noted grimly that the Wild Bunch could have stampeded in and left with the furniture without the fellow noticing.

'I am Dorothy Langner,' she said in a strong, musical voice. 'I have an appointment with Mr. Joseph Van Dorn.'

Van Dorn hurried into the reception room and greeted her solicitously.

'Miss Langner,' he said, the faintest lilt of Irish in his voice softening the harder tones of Chicago. 'May I offer my deepest sympathy?'

'Thank you, Mr. Van Dorn. I appreciate your seeing me.'

Van Dorn guided her into his inner sanctum.

Dorothy Langner refused his offer of tea or water and got straight to the point.

'The Navy has let out a story that my father killed himself. I want to hire your detective agency to clear his name.'

Van Dorn had prepared as much as possible for this difficult interview. There was ample reason to doubt her father's sanity. But his wife-to-be had known Dorothy at Smith College, so he was obliged to hear the poor woman out.

'I am of course at your service, but –'

'The Navy says that he caused the explosion that killed him, but they won't tell me how they know.'

'I wouldn't read too much into that,' said Van Dorn. 'The Navy is habitually secretive. What does surprise me is they tend usually to look after their own.'

'My father deliberately established the Gun Factory to be more civilian than naval,' Dorothy Langner replied. 'It is a businesslike operation.'

'And yet,' Van Dorn ventured cautiously, 'as I understand it, civilian factories have recently taken over many of its duties.'

'Certainly not! Fours and 6s, perhaps. But not the dreadnought guns.'

'I wonder whether that shift troubled your father.'

'Father was accustomed to such shifts,' she answered drily, adding with a faint smile, 'He would say, "The slings and arrows of my misfortunes are the tugs and pulls of Congress and local interests." He had a sense of humor, Mr. Van Dorn. He knew how to laugh. Such men don't kill themselves.'

'Of course,' Van Dorn said gravely.

The Kellogg rang again.

Saved by my Bell, Van Dorn thought to himself. He stepped to the wall where the instrument was mounted, picked up the earpiece, and listened.

'Send him in.'

To Dorothy Langner he said, 'I asked Isaac Bell, my best operative, to step down from an important bank robbery case in order to look into the circumstances of your father's death. He is ready to report.'

The door opened. A man in a white suit entered with

an economy of motion unexpected in one so tall. He was well over six feet, leanly built – not more than one hundred seventy-five pounds – and looked to be about thirty years old. The full mustache that covered his upper lip was gold, as was his thick, neatly trimmed hair. His face had the robust appearance of an outdoorsman who was no stranger to sun and wind.

His large hands hung still at his sides. His fingers were long and precisely manicured, although an observer keener than the grieving Dorothy Langner might have noticed that the knuckles of his right hand were red and swollen.

'Miss Langner, may I present chief investigator Isaac Bell?'

Isaac Bell assessed the beautiful young woman with a swift, penetrating glance. Mid-twenties, he estimated her age. Intelligent and self-possessed. Desolated by grief yet extraordinarily attractive. She turned to him beseechingly.

Bell's sharp blue eyes softened in an instant. Now they were tinged violet, his inquiring gaze veiled with tenderness. He took off his broad-brimmed hat in deference to her, saying, 'I am so sorry for your loss, Miss Langner,' and swept a drop of blood from his hand with a pure white handkerchief in a motion so graceful as to be invisible.

'Mr. Bell,' she asked. 'What have you learned that will clear my father's name?'

Bell answered in a voice pitched low with sympathy. He was kindly yet direct. 'Forgive me, but I must report that your father did indeed sign out a quantity of iodine from the laboratory store.'

'He was an engineer,' she protested. 'He was a scientist.

He signed for chemicals from the laboratory every day.'

'Powdered iodine was an essential ingredient of the explosive that detonated the smokeless powder in his piano. The other was ammonia water. The porter noticed a bottle missing from his cleaning closet.'

'Anyone could have taken it.'

'Yes, of course. But there are indications that he mixed the chemicals in his private washroom. Stains on a towel, a volatile powder on his toothbrush, residue in his shaving mug.'

'How can you know all this?' she asked, blinking away angry tears. 'The Navy won't let me near his office. They turned away my lawyer. They even barred the police from the Gun Factory.'

'I gained admittance,' said Bell.

A male secretary wearing a vest, bow tie, banded shirt-sleeves, and a double-action Colt in a shoulder holster entered urgently. 'Beg your pardon, Mr. Van Dorn. The commandant of the Washington Navy Yard is calling on the telephone, and he's hopping mad.'

'Tell the operator to switch the line to this telephone. Excuse me, Miss Langner . . . Van Dorn here. Good afternoon, Commandant Dillon. How are you today? . . . You don't say?'

Van Dorn listened, casting Miss Langner a reassuring smile.

'. . . Well, if you'll forgive me, sir, such a general description could fit half the tall men in Washington . . . It could even describe a gentleman right here in my office as we speak. But I assure you that he does not look like he's been at fisticuffs with the United States Marines – unless the Corps turns out a lesser breed of Leatherneck than in my day.'

Isaac Bell put his hand in his pocket.

When Joseph Van Dorn next replied to the caller, it was with a benign chuckle, though if the commandant had seen the chill in his eyes he might have retreated hastily.

'No, sir. I will not "produce" an employee of mine on your sentries' assertion that they caught a private detective red-handed. Clearly the man in my office was not "caught" as he is standing here in front of me . . . I will register your complaint with the Navy Secretary when we lunch tomorrow at the Cosmos Club. Please convey my warmest regards to Mrs. Dillon.'

Van Dorn replaced the earpiece on its hook, and said, 'Apparently, a tall, yellow-haired gent with a mustache knocked down some navy yard sentries who attempted to detain him.'

Bell displayed a row of even white teeth. 'I imagine he'd have surrendered quietly if they hadn't tried to beat him up.' He turned back to Dorothy Langner, his expression gentler. 'Now, Miss Langner. There is something I must show you.'

He produced a photographic print, still damp from the developing process. It was an enlarged photograph of Langner's suicide note. He had snapped it with a 3A Folding Pocket Kodak camera that his fiancée – a woman in the moving-picture line – had given him. Bell shielded most of the photograph with his hand to spare Miss Langner the deranged raving.

'Is this your father's handwriting?'

She hesitated, peered closely, then reluctantly nodded. 'It looks like his handwriting.'

Bell watched her closely. 'You seem unsure.'

'It just looks a little . . . I don't know! Yes, it is his handwriting.'

'I understand that your father was working under great strain to speed up production. Colleagues who greatly admired him admit he was being driven hard, perhaps beyond endurance.'

'Nonsense!' she snapped back. 'My father wasn't casting church bells. He ran a gun factory. *He* demanded speed. And if it were too much for him he would have told me. We've been thick as thieves since my mother died.'

'But the tragedy of suicide,' Van Dorn interrupted, 'is that the victim can see no other escape from the unbearable. It is the loneliest death.'

'He would not have killed himself in that manner.'

'Why not?' asked Isaac Bell.

Dorothy Langner paused before she answered, noting despite her grief that the tall detective was unusually handsome, with an air of elegance tempered by rugged strength. That combination was a quality she looked for in men but found rarely.

'*I* bought him that piano so he could take up music again. To relax him. He loved me too much to use my gift as the instrument of his death.'

Isaac Bell watched her compelling silvery blue eyes as she pleaded her case. 'Father was too happy in his work to kill himself. Twenty years ago he started out replicating British 4-inch guns. Today his gun factory builds the finest 12s in the world. Imagine learning to build naval guns accurate at twenty thousand yards. Ten miles, Mr. Bell!'

Bell cocked his ear for a change of tone that might express doubt. He watched her face for telltale signs of uncertainty in her lyrical description of the dead man's work.

'The bigger the gun, the more violent the force it has to tame. There is no room for error. You must bore the tube straight as a ray of light. Its diameter can't vary a thousandth of an inch. Rifling demands the artistry of Michelangelo; shrinking the jacket, the precision of a watchmaker. My father *loved* his guns – all the great dreadnought men love their work. A steam-propulsion wizard like Alasdair MacDonald loves his turbines. Ronnie Wheeler up in Newport loves his torpedoes. Farley Kent his faster and faster hulls. It is joyous to be devoted, Mr. Bell. Such men *do not kill themselves*!'

Joseph Van Dorn intervened again. 'I can assure you that Isaac Bell's investigation has been as thorough as –'

'But,' Bell interrupted. 'What if Miss Langner is right?'

His boss looked at him, surprised.

Bell said, 'With Mr. Van Dorn's permission, I will look further.'

Dorothy Langner's lovely face bloomed with hope. She turned to the founder of the detective agency. Van Dorn spread his hands wide. 'Of course. Isaac Bell will get right on it with the full support of the agency.'

Her expression of gratitude sounded more like a challenge. 'That is all I can ask, Mr. Bell, Mr. Van Dorn. An informed appraisal of all the facts.' A sudden smile lit her face like a sunbeam, suggesting what a lively, carefree woman she had been before tragedy struck. 'Isn't that the least I can expect of a detective agency whose motto is "We never give up. Never!"'

'Apparently you've investigated us, too,' Bell smiled back.

Van Dorn walked her out to the reception room, repeating his condolences.

Isaac Bell went to the window that faced Pennsylvania Avenue. He watched Dorothy Langner emerge from the hotel with a slender redhead he had noticed earlier in the lobby. In any other company the redhead would be rated beautiful, but beside the gunner's daughter she was merely pretty.

Van Dorn returned. 'What changed your mind, Isaac? How she loved her father?'

'No. How she loved his work.'

He watched them hurry to the stop as a streetcar approached, pick up their long skirts, and climb aboard. Dorothy Langner did not look back. The redhead did, casting an appraising glance up at the Van Dorn windows as if she knew where to look.

Van Dorn was studying the photograph. 'I never saw such a clear picture from film. Near as sharp as a proper glass plate.'

'Marion gave me a 3A Kodak. Fits right in my overcoat. You ought to make them standard equipment.'

'Not at seventy-five dollars each,' said the parsimonious Van Dorn. 'They can make do with Brownies for a buck. What's on your mind, Isaac? You look troubled.'

'I'm afraid you had better assign the accounting boys to look into her father's financial affairs.'

26

'Why is that?'

'They found a wad of cash in his desk thick enough to choke a cow.'

'A *bribe*?' Van Dorn exploded. 'A bribe? No wonder the Navy's playing it close to the vest. Langner was a government employee empowered to choose from which foundry to buy steel.' He shook his head in disgust. 'Congress hasn't forgotten the clamor three years ago when the steel trust fixed the price of armor plates. Well, that explains why she had to relax him.'

'It looks,' Isaac Bell admitted, 'like a clever man did something stupid, couldn't face getting caught, and killed himself.'

'I'm surprised you agreed to look further.'

'She is a passionate young lady.'

Van Dorn looked at him curiously. 'You are engaged, Isaac.'

Isaac Bell faced his boss with a guileless smile. For a man who was worldly in the many ways he would have to be to be a scourge of criminals, Joe Van Dorn was remarkably prim when it came to affairs of the heart. 'The fact that I am in love with Marion Morgan does not render me blind to beauty. Nor am I immune to passion. What I meant, however, is that the strikingly attractive Miss Langner's belief in her father is immense.'

'Most mothers,' Van Dorn retorted astringently, 'and all daughters profess disbelief when their sons or fathers engage in criminal acts.'

'Something about that sample of his handwriting struck her oddly.'

'How'd you happen to find the suicide note?'

'The Navy had no clue how to proceed. So they left everything in place except the body and padlocked the door to keep the cops out.'

'How'd you get in?'

'It was an old Polhem.'

Van Dorn nodded. Bell had a way with locks. 'Well, I'm not surprised the Navy had no clue how to proceed. In fact, I imagine they're paralyzed with fear. They may have President Roosevelt hell-bent on building forty-eight new battleships, but there are plenty in Congress scheming to rein them in.'

Bell said, 'I hate to leave John Scully in a lurch, but can you keep me off the Frye Boys case while I look into this?'

'A lurch is where Detective Scully likes to be,' Van Dorn growled. 'The man is too independent for my taste.'

'And yet, a clairvoyant investigator,' Bell defended his colleague.

Scully, an operative not famous for reporting in regularly, was trailing a trio of violent bank robbers across the Ohio-Pennsylvania border. They had made a name for themselves by leaving notes written in the blood of their victims: 'Fear the Frye Boys.' They had robbed their first bank a year ago in New Jersey, fled west, robbing many more, then laid low for the winter. Now they were rampaging east from Illinois in a string of bloody assaults on small-town banks. As innovative as they were vicious, they employed stolen automobiles to cross state lines, leaving local sheriffs in the dust.

'You will remain in charge of the Frye case, Isaac,' Van Dorn said sternly. 'Until Congress gets around to funding some sort of national investigation bureau, the Justice

28

Department will continue to pay us handsomely to capture criminals who cross state lines, and I don't intend to let a maverick like Scully disappoint them.'

'As you wish, sir,' Bell replied formally. 'But you did promise Miss Langner the full support of the agency.'

'All right! I'll shift a couple of men Scully's way – briefly. But you're still in charge, and it should not take you long to confirm the veracity of Langner's suicide note.'

'Can your friend the Navy Secretary get me a yard pass? I want to powwow with the Marines.'

'What for?' the boss smiled. 'A rematch?'

Bell grinned back but sobered quickly.

'If Mr. Langner did *not* kill himself, someone went to a lot of trouble to murder him and besmirch his reputation. The Marines guard the gates of the navy yard. They must have seen that someone leave the night before.'

3

'More limestone!' yelled Chad Gordon. Greedily watching his newest torrent of molten iron gush like liquid fire from the taphole into its ladle, the Naval Ordnance Bureau metallurgist muttered a triumphant, 'Hull 44, here we come!'

'All canvas and no hull' was a charge regularly leveled at Chad Gordon for running risks with three-thousand-degree molten metal that no sane man would.

But no one denied that the brilliant star deserved his own blast furnace in a remote corner of the steel mill in Bethlehem, Pennsylvania, where he experimented eighteen hours a day to create low-carbon pig iron to process into torpedo-resistant armor plate. The company had to assign him two separate crews of workmen, as even poverty-stricken immigrants accustomed to working like dogs could not keep up with Chad Gordon's pace.

On this snowy March night, his second shift consisted of an American foreman, Bob Hall, and a gang that Hall regarded as the usual bunch of foreigners – four Hungarians and a gloomy German who had replaced a missing Hungarian. As near as Bob Hall could make out from their jabbering, their missing pal had fallen down a well or been run over by a locomotive, take your pick.

The German's name was Hans. He claimed to have worked at the Krupp Werke in the Ruhr Valley. That was fine with foreman Hall. Hans was strong and seemed to know his business and understood more English than all four Hungarians combined. Besides, Mr. Gordon wouldn't give a damn if the German had come straight from Hell as long as he worked hard.

Seven hours into the shift, a 'hang' of partly solidified metal formed near the top of the furnace. It threatened to block the uptake that vented volatile hot waste gases. Foreman Hall suggested clearing it before it got any bigger. Chad Gordon ordered him brusquely aside. 'I said, "More limestone."'

The German had been waiting for such an opportunity. Quickly, he climbed the ladders to the top of the furnace where barrows were standing by with fresh stock. Each contained a twelve-hundred-pound load of iron ore, or coke, or the dolomitic limestone with an unusually high content of magnesia that the hard-driving Chad Gordon was counting on to strengthen the metal.

The German grabbed a barrow of dolomitic limestone and rolled the two-wheel cart to the mouth of the furnace.

'Wait for the boil!' the foreman bellowed from down at the base where melted impurities were tumbling from the slag notch. The molten iron and slag in the bottom of the furnace were roaring at a full three thousand degrees Fahrenheit. But the ore and coke on top had barely reached seven hundred.

Hans didn't seem to hear him as he dumped the limestone into the furnace and hurriedly descended the ladders. 'You lunatic,' yelled the foreman. 'It's not hot enough. You blocked the uptake.'

Hans shouldered past the foreman.

'Don't worry about the hang,' Chad Gordon shouted without bothering to look up. 'It'll drop.'

The foreman knew better. The hang was trapping explosive gases inside the furnace. Hans's dump had only made it worse. A lot worse. He shouted to the Hungarians, 'Get up there and clear the uptake!'

The Hungarians hesitated. Even if they couldn't fully understand English, they knew the danger of flammable gases accumulating above the batch. Hall's clenched fist and angry gestures at the ladder sent them scrambling to the top of the furnace with bars and picks. But just as they started to break up the hang it dropped on its own accord in one solid piece. Just like Mr. Gordon had predicted. Except the barrow of limestone heaped on the cool surface had also blocked the uptake. When the hang dropped, the sudden burst of outside air into the furnace combined with the heat below to ignite the trapped waste gases.

They exploded with a roar that lifted the roof off the building and threw it onto a Bessemer converter fifty yards away. The blast blew boots and clothing off the Hungarians and incinerated their bodies. Tons of fiery debris splashed down the sides of the furnace. Like a burning waterfall, it drenched the foreman and Chad Gordon in flames.

The German ran, gagging from the stink of cooked flesh. His eyes were wide with horror at what he had set off and terror that the boiling metal would catch up with him, too. No one took notice of one man running when suddenly every man in the giant mill was running. Workers from the other blast furnaces raced to the scene of death, driving wagons and carts for makeshift ambulances to carry the injured. Even the company thugs guarding the gate ignored Hans as they gaped in the direction from which he ran.

The German looked back. Flames were shooting into the night sky. The buildings around the blast furnace were wrecked. Walls had collapsed, roofs tumbled to the ground, and everywhere he saw fire.

He cursed aloud, astonished by the immensity of the destruction he had wrought.

The next morning, changed from his workman's clothing into a somber black suit and exhausted from a sleepless night of brooding on how many had died, Hans stepped off a train at Washington, D.C.'s National Mall Station. He scanned the newsstands for headlines about the accident. There were none. Steelmaking was dangerous business. Workmen were killed daily. Only local newspapers in the mill towns bothered listing the dead – and often then only the foremen for their English-speaking readers.

He took a ferry to Alexandria, Virginia, and hurried along the waterfront to the warehouse district. The spy who had sent him to the steel mill was waiting in his curious den of obsolete weapons.

He listened intently to Hans's report. He asked probing questions about the elements that Chad Gordon had introduced into his iron. Knowledgeable and insightful, he drew from Hans details that the German had barely noticed at the time.

The spy was lavish in his praise and paid in cash what he had promised.

'It is not for the money,' said the German, stuffing it in his pocket.

'Of course not.'

'It is because when war comes the Americans will side with Britain.'

'That is beyond any doubt. The democracies despise Germany.'

'But I do not like the killing,' Hans protested. Staring morbidly into the lens of the old battleship searchlight behind the spy's desk, he saw his face reflected like a decaying skull.

The spy surprised Hans by answering in northern-accented German. Hans had assumed that the man was American, so perfect was his English. Instead, he spoke like a compatriot. 'You had no choice, *mein Freund*. Chad Gordon's armor plate would have given enemy ships an unfair advantage. Soon the Americans will launch dreadnoughts. Would you have their dreadnoughts sink German ships? Kill German sailors? Shell German ports?'

'You are right, *mein Herr*,' Hans answered. 'Of course.'

The spy smiled as if he sympathized with Hans's humane qualms. But in the seclusion of his own mind he laughed. God bless the simple Germans, he thought. No matter how powerful their industry grew, no matter how strong their Army, no matter how modern their Navy, no matter how loudly their Kaiser boasted *'Mein Feld ist die Welt,'* they always feared they were the little guy.

That constant dread of being second best made them so easy to lead.

Your field is the world, Herr Kaiser? The hell it is. Your field is full of sheep.

4

'It was a Chinaman,' said Marine Lance Corporal Black, puffing smoke from a two-dollar cigar.

'If you believe the Gramps Patrol,' puffed Private Little.

'He means the night watchmen.'

Isaac Bell indicated that he understood that the 'Gramps Patrol' were the pensioners employed as night watchmen to guard the navy yard inside the gates, while the Marines manned the gates themselves.

He and the husky young leathernecks were seated at a round table in O'Leary's Saloon on E Street. They had been generous sports about their previous encounter, offering Bell grudging respect for his fighting skills and forgiving black eyes and loosened teeth after only one round of drinks. At Bell's urging they had polished off a lunch of steaks, potatoes, and apple pie. Now, with whiskey glasses at hand and Bell's Havanas blueing the air, they were primed to be talkative.

Their commandant had ordered a list of everyone who had passed through the gates the night that Arthur Langner had died, they told him. No names had aroused any suspicion. Bell would get Joe Van Dorn to wangle a peek at that list to confirm the commandant's judgment.

A night watchman had reported an intruder. The report had apparently not even reached the commandant, rising no higher up the chain of command than the sergeant of the gate guard, who had deemed it nonsense.

Bell asked, 'If it were true, what the Gramps Patrol reported, why do you suppose a Chinaman would break into the navy yard?'

'Looking to steal something.'

'Or after the girls.'

'What girls?'

'The officers' daughters. The ones who live in the yard.'

Private Little looked around to make sure no one was listening. The only patron close enough was curled up on the floor, snoring in the sawdust. 'Commandant's got a couple of lovelies I wouldn't mind getting to know better.'

'I see,' said Bell, suppressing a smile. The idea of an amorous Chinese infiltrating an American Navy base by scaling a ten-foot wall guarded by Marines at every gate and watchmen inside did not suggest a productive path of investigation. But, he reminded himself, while a detective had always to be skeptical, the wise skeptic dismissed no possibility without first considering it. 'Who,' he asked, 'was this old night watchman who told you this?'

'He didn't tell us. He told the sergeant.'

'His name is Eddison,' said Black.

'Big John Eddison,' Little added.

'How old is he?'

'Looks a hundred.'

'Big old man. Nearly as tall you, Mr. Bell.'

'Where would I find him?'

'There's a rooming house where the salts hang out.'

Bell found Eddison's rooming house on F Street within

a short walk of the navy yard. It had a front porch filled with rocking chairs, empty this cold afternoon. He went in and introduced himself to the landlady, who was laying her long table for supper. She had a thick Southern accent, and a face still pretty despite the lines acquired in years of hard work.

'Mr. Eddison?' she drawled. 'He's a good old man. Never a bit of trouble like certain of his shipmates I could name.'

'Is he in?'

'Mr. Eddison sleeps late, being as how he works at night.'

'Would you mind if I waited?' Bell asked with a smile that flashed his even teeth and lighted his blue eyes.

The landlady brushed a wisp of gray hair from her cheek and smiled back. 'I'll bring you a cup of coffee.'

'Don't trouble yourself.'

'No trouble, Mr. Bell. You're in the South now. My mother would spin in her grave if she heard I let a gentleman sit in my parlor without a cup of coffee.'

Fifteen minutes later, Bell was able to say without stretching the truth too far, 'This is the finest coffee I have had since *my* mother took me to a pastry shop in Vienna, Austria, when I was only knee-high to a grasshopper.'

'Well, you know what I've a mind to do? I'll put on a fresh pot and ask Mr. Eddison if he'd like to have a cup with you.'

John Eddison would have been even taller than Bell, the detective saw, had age not bent his back. He had big hands and long arms that must have been powerful in his day, a shock of white hair, pale runny eyes, the enormous

37

nose that old men often grew, and a firm mouth set in sagging jowls.

Bell extended his hand. 'I'm Isaac Bell, Van Dorn investigator.'

'You don't say,' Eddison grinned, and Bell saw that the slow movement of age masked a sprightly manner. 'Well, I didn't do it. Though I might have when I was younger. How can I help you, sonny?'

'I was speaking with Lance Corporal Black and Private Little of the Marine guard, and –'

'You know what we said about the Marines in the Navy?' Eddison interrupted.

'No, sir.'

'A sailor had to accidentally bang his head four times on a low beam to demonstrate that he was qualified to join the Marines.'

Bell laughed. 'They told me that you reported you had surprised a prowler in the navy yard.'

'Aye. But he got away. They didn't believe me.'

'A Chinese?'

'Not a Chinaman.'

'No? I wonder where Black and Little got the idea the prowler was Chinese?'

'I warned you about the Marines,' Eddison chuckled. 'You laughed.'

'What sort of man did the prowler look like?'

'Like a Jap.'

'Japanese?'

'I told those fools' sergeant. Sounds like their sergeant had Chinamen on the brain. But like I said, I don't think the sergeant believed I saw anyone at all – Chinaman, Jap

– he didn't believe me, period. Thought I was a stupid old man having visions. The sergeant asked me if I was drinking. Hell, I haven't had a drink in forty years.'

Bell couched his next question carefully. He had met very few Americans who could distinguish Japanese from Chinese. 'Did you get a close look at him?'

'Aye.'

'I was under the impression it was dark.'

'The moon shone square in his face.'

'How near were you to him?'

Eddison held up his large, wrinkled hand. 'Any closer, I'd have wrapped these fingers around his throat.'

'What was there about him that seemed Japanese?'

'His eyes, his mouth, his nose, his lips, his hair,' the old man fired back.

Again, Bell framed his skepticism cautiously. 'Some people say they have trouble telling the two races apart.'

'Some people ain't been to Japan.'

'And you have?'

Eddison straightened up in his chair. 'I sailed into Uraga Harbor with Commodore Matthew Perry when he opened Japan to American trade.'

'That's sixty years ago!' If this wasn't an ancient mariner's tall tale, Eddison was even older than he looked.

"Fifty-seven. I was a main topman on Perry's steam frigate *Susquehanna*. And I pulled an oar in the commodore's launch. Rowed the Old Man into Yokosuka. We had Japs coming out of our ears.'

Bell smiled. 'It does sound as if you are qualified to distinguish Japanese from Chinese.'

'As I said.'

'Could you tell me where you caught the prowler?'

'Almost caught him.'

'Do you recall how far that was from the Gun Factory?'

Eddison shrugged. 'Thousand yards.'

'Half a mile,' Bell mused.

'Half a *sea* mile,' Eddison corrected.

'Even farther.'

'Sonny, I'll bet you're speculating if the Jap had something to do with the explosion in Mr. Langner's design loft.'

'Do you think he did?'

'No way of knowing. Like I say, the Jap I saw was a full thousand yards from the Gun Factory.'

'How big is the navy yard?' Bell asked.

The old sailor stroked his chin and looked into the middle distance. 'I'd imagine that between the walls and river, the yard must take up a hundred acres.'

'One hundred acres.' Nearly as big as a northeastern dairy farm.

'Chockful of mills, foundries, parade grounds. Plus,' he added with a meaningful look, 'mansions and gardens – where I intercepted him prowling.'

'What do think he was doing there?'

John Eddison smiled. 'I don't think. I *know*.'

'What do you know he was doing there?'

'He was right close by the officers' mansions. The commandant's daughters are comely young ladies. And your Japs, they like the ladies.'

5

There were days when even a boy genius like Grover Lakewood was glad for time off from the laboratory to clear his
head of the intricacies of aiming a gun at a moving target
from a moving ship. The fire-control expert spent most
days and many nights inventing myriad calculations to
counter the effects of roll, pitch, yaw, and trajectory curves.
It was absolutely fascinating work, made all the more
intense by the fact that Lakewood had to devise ways for
ordinary minds to apply his calculations in the midst of
battle when guns were thundering, seas breaking, and steel
splinters howling through the smoke.

In his spare time he toyed with futuristic formulas to
tackle the challenges of cross-rolling – where he imagined
his ships firing ahead instead of broadside – and tried to
take into account the ever-increasing ranges of big guns
and the ever-flattening trajectories of high-velocity shells.
Sometimes he had to turn himself upside down like a salt-
shaker to empty his brain.

Rock climbing offered such a break.

A day of rock climbing started with the train ride to
Ridgefield, Connecticut, then a drive across the New York
state line in a rented Ford auto to Johnson Park in the
Westchester estate country, then a two-mile hike to a remote
hill called Agar Mountain, all leading to a slow, hard climb
up a rock wall to the top of a cliff. The train ride was a

chance to just stare out the window for two hours and watch the land change from city to farm. Driving the auto required his full attention to the rutted roads. The hike filled his lungs with fresh air and got his blood going. The climb demanded complete concentration to avoid falling off the cliff and landing a long, long way down on his skull.

This unusually warm weekend for early spring had brought walkers to the park. Striding purposefully in his tweed jacket, knickers, and boots, Lakewood passed an old lady on her 'constitutional,' exchanged hearty 'Good morning!'s with several hikers, and observed, longingly, a couple holding hands.

Lakewood was quite good-looking, sturdily built, with a ready smile, but working six and seven days a week – often bunking on a cot at the lab – made it hard to meet girls. And for some reason, the nieces and daughters that the older engineers' wives marched in to meet him were never that appealing. It usually didn't bother him. He was too busy to be lonely, but now and then when he saw a young couple he thought, One day I'll get lucky, too.

He hiked deeper into the park until he found himself alone on a narrow path through dense forest. When he saw movement ahead, he was disappointed because he was hoping to have the cliff to himself and concentrate on climbing in peace and quiet.

The person ahead stopped and sat on a fallen log. When he drew closer, he saw it was a girl – and a petite and very pretty girl at that – dressed for climbing in trousers and lace-up boots like his. Red hair spilled from her brimmed hat. As she turned her head abruptly toward him, her hair flashed in the sunlight, bright as a shell burst.

She looked Irish, with paper-white skin, a small, upturned nose, a jaunty smile, and flashing blue eyes, and he suddenly remembered meeting her before . . . Last summer . . . What was her name? Let's see, where had they met . . . Yes! The 'company picnic,' hosted by Captain Lowell Falconer, the Spanish-American War hero to whom Lakewood reported his range-finder developments.

What was her name?

He was close enough to wave and say hello now. She was watching him, with her jaunty smile, and her eyes were lighting up with recognition. Though she looked as puzzled as he felt.

'Fancy meeting you here,' she called, tentatively.

'Hello,' said Lakewood.

'Was last time at the shore?'

'Fire Island,' said Lakewood. 'Captain Falconer's clambake.'

'Of course,' she said, sounding relieved. 'I knew I knew you from somewhere.'

Lakewood searched his memory, goading himself: *Lakewood!* If you can land a 12-inch, five-hundred-pound shell on a dreadnought steaming at sixteen knots from a ship rolling in ten-foot seas, you ought to be able to remember the name of this Gibson Girl lovely who is smiling at you.

'Miss Dee,' he said, snapping his fingers. 'Katherine Dee.' And then, because his mother had raised him properly, Lakewood doffed his hat and extended his hand and said, 'Grover Lakewood. How very nice to see you again.'

When her smile spread into one of delighted recognition, the sunlight of her brilliant hair seemed to migrate into her eyes. Lakewood thought he had died and gone to

43

Heaven. 'What a wonderful coincidence!' she said. 'What are you *doing* here?'

'Climbing,' said Lakewood. 'Climbing the rocks.'

She stared in what appeared to be disbelief. 'Now, that *is* a coincidence.'

'How do you mean?'

'Well, that's why I'm here. There's a cliff up that path that I'm going to climb.' She cocked an eyebrow that was so pale as to be almost invisible. 'Did you follow me here?'

'What?' Lakewood flushed and began to stammer. 'No, I –'

Katherine Dee laughed. 'I'm teasing you. I didn't mean you followed me. How would you even have known where to find me? No, it's a perfect coincidence.' Again she cocked her head. 'But not really . . . Do you remember when we talked at the clambake?'

Lakewood nodded. They hadn't talked as much as he would have liked to. She had seemed to know everybody on the captain's yacht and had flitted from one person to another, chatting up a storm. But he remembered. 'We decided we both liked to be out of doors.'

'Even though I have to wear a hat for the sun because my skin is so pale.'

More pale skin had been visible that summery day. Lakewood remembered round, firm arms bared almost to her shoulders, her shapely neck, her ankles.

'Shall we?' she asked.

'What?'

'Climb the rocks.'

'Yes! Yes. Yes, let's.'

They started along the path, brushing shoulders where

it narrowed. Every time they touched, he felt an electric shock, and he was thoroughly smitten by the time she asked, 'Do you still work for the captain?'

'Oh, yes.'

'I seem to recall that you told me something about cannons.'

'They call them guns in the Navy. Not cannons.'

'Really? I didn't know there was a difference. You said "they." Aren't you in the Navy?'

'No, I work in a civilian position. But I report to Captain Falconer.'

'He seemed like a very nice man.'

Lakewood smiled. '"Nice" is not the first word that comes to mind for Captain Falconer.' Driven, demanding, and daunting came closer to the mark.

'Someone told me he was inspiring.'

'That, he is.'

She said, 'I'm trying to remember who said that. He was very handsome, and older than you, I think.'

Lakewood felt a hot stab of jealousy. Katherine Dee was talking about Ron Wheeler, the star of the Naval Torpedo Station at Newport who all the girls fell over. 'Most of them are older than me,' he answered, hoping to get off the subject of the handsome Wheeler.

Katherine put him at ease with a heartwarming smile. 'Well, whoever he was, I remember that he called you the "boy genius."'

Lakewood laughed.

'Why do you laugh? Captain Falconer said it, too, and he was a hero in the Spanish-American War. Are you a Boy Genius?'

'No! I just started young, is all. It's such a new field. I got in at the beginning.'

'How could guns be new? Guns have been around forever.'

Lakewood stopped walking and turned to face her. 'That is very interesting. But, no, guns have not been around forever. Not like they are now. Rifled guns can fire tremendous ranges no one ever imagined before. Why, just the other day I was aboard a battleship off Sandy Hook and –'

'You were on a *battleship*?'

'Oh, sure. I go out on them all the time.'

'Really?'

'On the Atlantic Firing Range. Just last week the gunnery officer said to me, "The new dreadnoughts could hit Yonkers from here."'

Katherine's pretty eyes grew enormous. 'Yonkers? I don't know about that. I mean the last time I sailed into New York on the *Lusitania* it was a clear day, but I couldn't see Yonkers from the ocean.'

The *Lusitania*? thought Lakewood. Not only is she pretty but she's rich.

'Well, it's hard to see Yonkers, but at sea you can spot a ship that far. The trick is, hitting it.' They resumed walking, shoulders bumping on the narrow path, as he told her how the invention of smokeless powder allowed the spotters to see farther because the ship was less shrouded in gun smoke.

'The spotters range with the guns. They judge by the splashes of shot whether they've fallen short or overshot. You've probably read in the newspaper that's the reason for all big-guns ships – all the guns the same caliber – so

46

firing one in fact aims all.' She seemed much more interested than he would expect of a pretty girl and listened wide-eyed, pausing repeatedly to stop walking and gaze at him as if mesmerized.

Lakewood kept talking.

Nothing secret, he told himself. Nothing about the latest range-finding gyros providing 'continuous aim' to 'hunt the roll.' Nothing about fire control that she couldn't read in the papers. He did boast that he got interested in rock climbing while scrambling up a hundred-foot 'cage mast' the Navy was developing to spot shell splashes at greater distances. But he did *not* say that the mast builders were experimenting with coiled lightweight steel tubing to make them immune to shell hits. He did *not* reveal that cage masts were also intended as platforms for the latest range-finding machines. Nor did he mention the hydraulic engines coupled to the gyro for elevating turret guns. And certainly not a word about Hull 44.

'I'm confused,' she said with a warm smile. 'Maybe you can help me understand. A man told me that ocean liners are much bigger than dreadnoughts. He said that *Lusitania* and *Mauritania* are 44,000 tons, but the Navy's *Michigan* will be only 16,000.'

'Liners are floating hotels,' Lakewood answered, dismissively. 'Dreadnoughts are fortresses.'

'But the *Lusitania* and *Mauritania* steam faster than dreadnoughts. He called them "greyhounds."'

'Well, if you think of *Lusitania* and *Mauritania* as greyhounds, imagine a dreadnought as a wolf.'

She laughed. 'Now I understand. And your job is to give it teeth.'

'My job,' Lakewood corrected proudly, 'is to sharpen its teeth.'

Again she laughed. And touched his arm. 'Then what is Captain Falconer's job?'

Grover Lakewood considered carefully before he answered. Anyone could read the official truth. Articles were devoted daily to every aspect of the dreadnought race, from the expense to the national glory to gala launchings to flat-footed foreign spies nosing around the Brooklyn Navy Yard claiming to be newspapermen.

'Captain Falconer is the Navy's Special Inspector of Target Practice. He became a gunnery expert after the battle of Santiago. Even though we sank every Spanish ship in Cuba, our guns scored only two percent hits. Captain Falconer vowed to improve that.'

The steeply sloped face of Agar Mountain loomed ahead. 'Oh, look,' said Katherine. 'We have it all to ourselves. No one's here but us.' They stopped at the foot of the cliff. 'Wasn't that crazy man who killed himself blowing up his piano involved with battleships?'

'How did you hear about that?' asked Lakewood. The Navy had kept the tragedy out of the papers, admitting only that there had been an explosion at the Gun Factory.

'Everyone in Washington was talking about it,' said Katherine.

'Is that where you live?'

'I was visiting a friend. Did you know the man?'

'Yes, he was a fine man,' answered Lakewood, staring up the rocks, surveying a route. 'In fact, he was on the captain's yacht for the clambake.'

'I don't believe I met him.'

'It was a darned sad thing . . . Terrible loss.'

Katherine Dee turned out to be a strong climber. Lakewood could barely keep up. He was new to the sport, and noticed that her fingers were so strong that she would raise her entire weight by the grip of one hand. When she did, she was able to swing her body to reach high for the next grip.

'You climb like a monkey.'

'That's not a very nice compliment.' She pretended to pout as she waited for him to catch up with her. 'Who wants to look like a monkey?'

Lakewood figured he better save his breath. When they were eighty feet off the ground and the tops of the trees looked like feathers far below, she suddenly pulled farther ahead of him.

'Say, where'd you learn to climb like that?'

'The nuns at my convent school took us climbing on the Matterhorn.'

At that moment, Grover Lakewood's hands were spread wide, gripping crevices to either side, as he felt for his next toehold. Katherine Dee had reached a position fifteen feet directly above him. She smiled.

'Oh, Mr. Lakewood?'

He craned his neck to see her. It looked like she was holding a giant turtle in her strong white hands. Except it couldn't be a turtle this early in the year. It was a large rock.

'Careful with that,' he called.

Too late.

It slipped from her hands. No it didn't! She *opened* her hands.

6

Langner's suicide note kept tickling the back of Isaac
Bell's mind.

He used his pass from the Navy Secretary to reenter
the Gun Factory, opened the Polhem padlock on the
design-loft door again, and searched Langner's desk. A
stack of special hand-laid stock that Langner apparently
reserved for important correspondence matched the
paper on which the suicide note was written. Beside it was
a Waterman fountain pen.

Bell pocketed the pen, and stopped at the chemist's laboratory where Van Dorn maintained an account. Then he
took a streetcar up Capitol Hill to Lincoln Park, a neighborhood that was flourishing as Washingtonians moved
up the Hill from the congested swampy areas around the
Potomac River, which turned foul in the summer heat.

Bell found the Langner home directly across the street
from the park. It was a two-story brick row house with green
shutters and a wrought-iron fence around a small front yard.
The Van Dorn auditor investigating Arthur Langner's financial affairs had uncovered no evidence of a private income.
Langner would have had to purchase this new house on his
Gun Factory salary, which, the auditor had noted, equaled
that of top managers in private industry.

The house looked newly built – as did all but a handful
of old wooden structures on the side streets – and boasted

tall windows. The brickwork was typically ornate, flaring skyward to an elaborate dentated cornice. But inside, Bell noted in a glance, the house was anything but typical. It was decorated in a spare, modern manner, with built-in cabinets and bookshelves, electric lamps, and ceiling fans. The furniture was up-to-date, too, and very expensive — airy yet strong pieces made by the Glaswegian Charles Rennie Mackintosh. Where, Bell had to ask, did Langner get the money to pay for Mackintosh furniture?

Dorothy was no longer dressed in black but in a silvery gray color that complemented her eyes and her raven hair. A man trailed her into the foyer. She introduced him as 'My friend Ted Whitmark.'

Bell pegged Whitmark as a hail-fellow-well-met salesman sort. He looked the picture of success, with a bright smile on his handsome face, an expensive suit of clothes, and a crimson necktie speckled with Harvard College's insignia.

'More than a friend, I'd say,' Whitmark boomed as he shook Bell's hand with a hearty grip. 'Closer to a fiancé, if you get my drift,' he added, tightening his grip emphatically.

'Congratulations,' said Bell, squeezing back.

Whitmark let go with an easy smile, and joked, 'That's some shake. What do you do in your spare time, shoe horses?'

'Would you excuse us for a moment, Mr. Whitmark?' Bell asked. 'Miss Langner, Mr. Van Dorn asked me to have a word with you.'

'We have no secrets here,' said Whitmark. 'At least, none that are any business of a detective.'

'That's all right, Ted,' said Dorothy, laying a hand on his

arm and giving him a kind smile. 'There's gin in the kitchen. Why not mix us cocktails while Mr. Bell reports?'

Ted Whitmark didn't like it but he had no choice but to exit, which he did with a grave 'Don't be keeping her too long, Bell. The poor girl is still recovering from the shock of her father's death.'

'This will just take a minute,' Bell assured him.

Dorothy slid the pocket doors shut. 'Thank you. Ted gets flatteringly jealous.'

'I imagine,' said Bell, 'he has many good qualities to have captured your hand.'

She looked Bell straight in the face. 'I am not rushing into anything,' she informed him in what the tall detective could not help but interpret as a blunt and flattering statement of interest from a very appealing woman.

'What line is Ted in?' Bell asked, diplomatically changing the subject.

'Ted sells foodstuffs to the Navy. In fact, he's leaving soon for San Francisco to get ready to provision the Great White Fleet when it arrives. Are you married, Mr. Bell?'

'I am engaged.'

An unreadable smile danced across her beautiful lips. 'Pity.'

'To be perfectly honest,' said Bell, 'it is not a pity. I am a very lucky man.'

'Perfect honesty is a fine quality in a man. Are you visiting today for more important reasons than to *not* flirt with me?'

Bell took out the fountain pen. 'Do you recognize this?'

Her face clouded. 'Of course. That's my father's pen. I gave it to him for his birthday.'

Bell handed it to her. 'You may as well hold on to it, then. I took it from his desk.'

'Why?'

'To confirm that he had used it to write his letter.'

'The so-called suicide letter? Anyone could have written that.'

'Not quite anyone. Either your father or a skillful forger.'

'You know my position on that. It is not possible that he killed himself.'

'I will keep looking.'

'What about the paper the letter was written on?'

'It was his.'

'I see . . . And the ink!' she said, suddenly eager. 'How do we know it was written with the same ink as in his pen? Perhaps it wasn't this pen. I bought it in a stationer's shop. The Waterman Company must sell thousands.'

'I've have already given samples of the ink in this pen and on the letter to a chemistry laboratory to ascertain whether the ink is different.'

'Thank you,' she said, her face falling. 'It's not likely, is it?'

'I'm afraid not, Dorothy.'

'But if it is his ink, it still doesn't prove he wrote that letter.'

'Not beyond all doubt,' Bell agreed. 'But I must tell you frankly that while each of these facts must be investigated, they are not likely to give us a definitive answer.'

'What will?' she asked. She seemed suddenly bewildered. Tears glinted in her eyes.

Isaac Bell was touched by her suffering and confusion. He took her hands in his. 'Whatever it is, if it exists, we will find it.'

'The Van Dorns never give up?' she asked with a brave smile.

'Never,' Bell promised, although in his heart he had less and less hope that he could lay her pain to rest.

She clung to his hands. When she finally let them go, she stepped closer and kissed his cheek. 'Thank you. That's all I can ask.'

'I'll keep in touch,' said Bell.

'Would you stay for a cocktail?'

'I'm afraid I can't, thank you. I'm expected in New York.' As she walked him to the door, Bell glanced into the dining room and remarked, 'That is a splendid table. Is it a Mackintosh?'

'It sure is,' she answered proudly. 'Father used to say if buying a piece of art that he could not afford meant eating beans for supper, he would eat beans for supper.'

Bell had to wonder if Langner had gotten tired of beans and accepted a bribe from a steel mill. As he stepped through the gate he looked back. Dorothy was standing on the step, looking for all the world, he thought, like a fairy princess locked in a tower.

The B & O Railroad's Royal Limited was the fastest and most luxurious train from Washington to New York. As night darkened the lead crystal windows, Isaac Bell used the quiet journey to review the hunt for the Frye Boys. The state line–jumping bank robbers that Van Dorn detectives had been tracking through Illinois, Indiana, and Ohio had vanished somewhere in eastern Pennsylvania. As had Detective John Scully.

Dinner aboard the Royal, the equal of Delmonico's or the new Plaza Hotel, was served in a mahogany-paneled dining car. Bell had Maryland rockfish and a half bottle of Mumm, and reflected upon how much Dorothy Langner reminded him of his fiancée. Clearly, were she not grieving for her father, Dorothy would be a quick-witted, interesting woman, much like Marion Morgan. The women had similar backgrounds: each lost her mother young and had been educated more than most women thanks to doting fathers who were accomplished men and wanted their daughters to exercise their talents fully.

Physically, Marion and Dorothy could not be more different. Dorothy's hair was a glossy black mane, Marion's a gleaming straw blond; Dorothy's eyes were a compelling blue-gray, Marion's an arresting coral-sea green. Both were tall, slim, and lithe. And both, he thought with a smile, could stop traffic by merely stepping into the street.

Bell checked his gold pocket watch as the Royal pulled into its Jersey City terminal. Nine o'clock. Too late to visit Marion at her hotel in Fort Lee if she was shooting pictures tomorrow. The laugh was on him. Marion was directing a two-reel moving picture about imaginary bank robbers while he was chasing real ones. But a movie drama, he had already learned from observing her at work, took as much planning and detail work as the real thing. And for that, a girl needed her sleep.

He scanned the newsstands and the papers that boys were hawking when he got off the train. Headlines dueled for attention. Half proclaimed a fantastic variety of Japanese threats to the Great White Fleet if — as was rumored — President Roosevelt ordered it close to the Japanese

Islands. Half blamed the murder of a New York school-teacher on Chinese white slavers. But it was the weather banners Bell was searching, hoping for a bad forecast.

'Excellent!' he exclaimed aloud. The Weather Bureau predicted clouds and rain.

Marion would not have to rise at dawn to catch every available ray of sunlight.

He hurried from the terminal. The sixteen-mile trolley ride to Fort Lee would take at least an hour, but there might be a better way. The Jersey City Police were experimenting with a motor patrol like New York's across the river and, as he expected, one of their six-cylinder Ford autos was sitting in front of the terminal manned by a sergeant and patrolman formerly of the Mounted Division.

'Van Dorn,' Bell addressed the sergeant, who looked a little lost without his horse. 'It's worth twenty dollars to get me to Cella's Park Hotel in Fort Lee.'

Ten would have done it. For twenty, the sergeant cranked the siren.

The rain started as the racing police Ford crested the Palisades. Flinging mud, it tore down Fort Lee's Main Street, skidded along the trolley tracks, and whisked past a movie studio whose glass walls glittered in its feeble headlamps. Outside the village, they pulled up to Cella's, a large white two-story frame building set in a picnic grounds.

Bell bounded across the front porch with a big grin on his face. The dining room, which turned into a bar at night, was still open and doing a roaring business as the actors, directors, and cameramen conceded that without sunlight to film by, tomorrow was a lost day. A gang of pitch-perfect singers was grouped around the piano har-monizing,

> *'You can go as far as you like with me*
> *In my merry Oldsmobile.'*

He spotted Marion at a corner table, and his heart nearly stopped. She was laughing, deep in conversation with two other women directors whom Bell had met before: Christina Bialobrzesky, who claimed to be a Polish countess but whose accent sounded to Bell's ear like New Orleans, and the dark-haired, dark-eyed Mademoiselle Duvall of Pathé Frères.

Marion looked up. She saw him standing in the door-way and jumped to her feet with a radiant smile. Bell rushed across the room. She met him halfway, and he picked her up in his arms and kissed her.

'What a wonderful surprise!' she exclaimed. She was still in her working clothes – shirtwaist, long skirt, and a snug jacket. Her blond hair was heaped up in back, out of her way, exposing her long, graceful neck.

'You look lovely.'

'Liar! I look like I've been up since five in the morning.'

'You know I never lie. You look terrific.'

'Well, so do you. And then some . . . Have you eaten?'

'Dinner on the train.'

'Come. Join us. Or would you rather we sit alone?'

'I'll say hello first.'

The hotel proprietor approached, beaming with fond memories of Bell's last visit and rubbing his hands. 'Champagne, again, Mr. Bell?'

'Of course.'

'For the table?'

'For the room!'

'Isaac!' said Marion. 'There are fifty people in here.'

'Nothing in my grandfather Isaiah's will says I can't spend a portion of his five million dollars on a toast to the beauty of Miss Marion Morgan. Besides, they say that Grandfather had an eye for the ladies.'

'So five million was not all you inherited.'

'And when they get drunk, they won't notice us slipping upstairs to your room.'

She led him by the hand. Christina and Mademoiselle Duvall were also still in their work clothes, though the flamboyant Frenchwoman wore her usual riding pants. She kissed Bell's cheeks and called him 'Eee-zahk.'

'This week we all three are each shooting about bank row-bears, Eee-zahk. You must give me inspector tips.'

'She wants more than tips,' Marion whispered with a grin.

'Are bank row-bears not the symbol of *Americain* freedom?' Mademoiselle Duvall demanded.

Bell returned a grim smile. 'Bank robbers are symbols of death and terror. The trio I'm chasing at the moment routinely shoot everyone in the building.'

'Because they fear to be recognized,' said the French director. 'My bank row-bears will shoot no one because they will be of the poor and known by the poor.'

Christina rolled her eyes. 'Like Row-ben Hoods?' she asked acerbically.

'Just so the audience knows who's who,' Marion suggested, 'you better make them wear masks.'

'A mask can only mask a stranger,' said Mademoiselle

Duvall. 'Were I to don a mask' – she demonstrated with her scarf, drawing the silk across her Gallic nose and sensual mouth so that only her eyes were visible – 'Eee-zahk will still recognize me by my gaze.'

'That's because you're making eyes at him,' laughed Marion.

Isaac Bell's expression changed abruptly.

'Is not my fault! Eee-Zahk is too handsome to contain myself. For that, I would have to pull the wool over my eyes.'

Now they noticed his features harden. He appeared remote and cold. Mademoiselle Duvall reached out and touched his arm. *'Chéri,'* she apologized. 'You are too serious. Forgive my behavior if I was *inapproprié.'*

'Not at all,' Bell said, patting her hand distractedly as he gripped Marion's tightly under the table. 'But you have given me a strange idea. Something to think about.'

'No more thinking tonight,' said Marion.

Bell stood up. 'Excuse me. I have to send a wire.'

The hotel had a telephone that he used to call the New York office and dictate a wire to be sent to John Scully care of every Van Dorn post in the region where the detective had last been heard from.

NAME CHANGED FRYES HEADED HOME NEAR
FIRST JOB IN NEW JERSEY

Marion was smiling in the lobby next to the stairs. 'I said good night for you.'

7

'Get down to Greenwich Village and bring back Dr. Cruson,' Isaac Bell ordered an apprentice when he rushed into Van Dorn's Knickerbocker office early the next morning. 'You are authorized to take a taxi both ways. On the jump!'

Dr. Daniel Cruson was a handwriting expert.

The apprentice raced off.

Bell read his telegrams. The laboratory in Washington confirmed that the ink on Arthur Langner's note was the same ink in Langner's pen. He was not surprised.

A wire from Pennsylvania demonstrated the shortcomings of John Scully's lone-wolf approach to detecting. The operatives who Joe Van Dorn had assigned to assist Scully while Bell investigated the Arthur Langner death had sent:

CAN'T FIND SCULLY.

STILL LOOKING.

RETURN C/O WESTERN UNION SCRANTON AND

PHILADELPHIA.

Bell growled a mild oath under his breath. They had split up to increase their chances of finding Scully. If they didn't find him by noon, it would fall to him to inform the boss that the detectives assigned to help Scully track the Frye Boys were instead tracking Scully.

Bell called for the research operative he had brought into the case. Grady Forrer was a grizzly bear of a man with an immense chest and belly. He looked like a fellow you would want on your side in a barroom brawl. But his greatest strengths were a ferocious determination to track down the minutest details and a prodigious memory.

'Have you found out where home was for these hydrophobic skunks?' Bell asked. 'Where did they grow up?'

The research man shook his head. 'I've been beating my brains out, Isaac. Can't find any set of three Frye brothers anywhere in New Jersey. Tried cousins. No go.'

Bell said, 'I have an idea about that. What if they changed their name at the time of their first unauthorized withdrawal? That original robbery was in the middle of the state, if I recall. East Brunswick Farmers' Mutual Savings.'

'Hick-town bank about halfway to Princeton.'

'We always ascribed their gunning down the teller and the customer to viciousness. But what if those three were stupid enough to rob the nearest bank to home?'

Grady Forrer stood up straighter.

'What if they murdered witnesses because they were recognized – even while wearing masks. Maybe the witnesses knew them as local boys. Little Johnny down the road grew up and got a gun. Remember their first note in blood? "Fear the Frye Boys."'

'So maybe they weren't so stupid, after all,' marveled the research man. 'From then on everyone called them the "Frye Boys."'

'Just like they wanted us to. Find a family near that East Brunswick bank with three brothers or cousins who suddenly disappeared. Even two brothers and a next-door neighbor.'

Bell wired the operatives sent to help Scully, and Scully himself, instructing them to head for East Brunswick.

Merci, Mademoiselle Duvall!

And who else has been steering my thoughts?

Which brought him straight back to his photograph of Arthur Langner's suicide note. He laid it next to the snapshot he had taken yesterday morning of one of Langner's handwritten patent applications. He pored over them with a magnifying glass, searching for inconsistencies that might suggest forgery. He could see none. But he was not an expert, which was why he had summoned the handwriting expert from Greenwich Village.

Dr. Daniel Cruson preferred the high-sounding title 'graphologist.' His white beard and bushy eyebrows fit a man who spouted lofty theories about the European 'talking cure' of Drs. Freud and Jung. He was also prone to statements like 'The complex robs the ego of light and nourishment,' which was why Bell avoided him when he could. But Cruson possessed a fine eye for forgery. So fine that Bell suspected that 'Dr. Graphology' made ends meet by cobbling up the occasional bank check.

Cruson inspected the photograph of the suicide note with a magnifying glass, then screwed a jeweler's loupe into his eye and repeated the process. At last he sat back in his chair, shaking his head.

Bell asked, 'Do you see inconsistencies in that handwriting that might suggest it was penned by a forger?'

Cruson said, 'You are a detective, sir.'

'You know I am,' Bell said curtly to head off a windy discourse.

'You are familiar with the work of Sir William Herschel?'

'Fingerprint identification.'

'But Sir William also believed that handwriting exposes character.'

'I am less interested in character than forgery.'

Cruson did not hear. 'From this mere sample, I can tell that the man who wrote this note was eccentric, highly artistic, and very dramatic, too. Given to the grand gesture. Deeply sensitive with powerful feelings that could be overwhelming.'

'In other words,' Bell interrupted, bleakly conceding he would have to report the worst to Dorothy Langner, 'the emotional sort likely to commit suicide.'

'So tragic to take his own life so young.'

'Langner wasn't young.'

'Given time, with psychological analysis, he could have investigated the sources of his sorrow and learned to control his self-destructive impulses.'

'Langner was not young,' Bell repeated.

'He was very young.'

'He was sixty years old.'

'Impossible! Look at this hand. See the bold and easy flow. An older man's writing cramps – the letters get smaller and trail off as the hands stiffen with age. This is beyond any doubt the handwriting of a man in his twenties.'

'Twenties?' echoed Bell, suddenly electrified.

'No older than thirty, I guarantee you.'

Bell had a photographic memory. Instantly he returned

in his mind's eye to Arthur Langner's office. He saw the bookshelves lined with bound volumes of Langner's patent applications. He had had to open several to find a sample for his camera. Those filed before 1885 were handwritten. The more recent were typed.

'Arthur Langner played the piano. His fingers would have been more supple than those of the average man his age.'

Cruson shrugged. 'I am neither musician nor physiologist.'

'But if his fingers were not more supple, then this could be a forgery.'

Cruson huffed, 'Surely you didn't summon me here to analyze the personality of a forger. The more skillful the forgery, the less it would tell me about his personality.'

'I did not summon you here to analyze his personality but to confirm whether this is a forgery. Now you are telling me that the forger made a mistake. He copied Langner's hand from an early sample of his handwriting. Thank you, Dr. Cruson. You've opened a new possibility in this case. Unless his piano playing made his handwriting like that of a young man, this is a forgery, and Arthur Langner was murdered.'

A Van Dorn secretary burst in waving a sheet of yellow paper. '*Scully!*'

The telegram from loner John Scully that he thrust into Isaac Bell's hand was typically terse.

GOT YOUR WIRE. HAD SAME THOUGHT.
SO-CALLED FRYES SURROUNDED WEST OF EAST
BRUNSWICK.

64

LOCAL CONSTABULARY THEIR COUSINS.
CARE TO LEND A HAND?

'"Surrounded"'? asked Bell. 'Did Mike and Eddie catch up with him?'

'No, sir. All by himself, like usual.'

It looked like Scully had found the Fryes' real names and trailed them home only to discover that the bank robbers were related to a crooked sheriff who would help them escape. In which case even the formidable Scully had bit off more than he could chew.

Bell scanned the rest of the telegram for directions.

WILLIARD FARM.
CRANBURY TURNPIKE TEN MILES WEST OF STONE CHURCH.
LEFT TURNOFF FLAGGED.
MILK TRUCK ONE MILE.

Middle of nowhere in the Jersey farm country. It would take all day to get there connecting to local trains. 'Telephone the Weehawken garage for my auto!'

Bell grabbed a heavy golf bag and raced down the Knickerbocker's stairs and out to Broadway. He jumped into a taxi and ordered the driver to take him to the pier at the foot of 42nd Street. There he boarded the Weehawken Ferry to New Jersey, where he had parked his red Locomobile.

8

Commodore Tommy's Saloon on West 39th Street hunched like a fortress in the ground floor and cellar of a crumbling brick tenement a quarter mile from the pier where Isaac Bell's ferry cast off. Its door was narrow, its windows barred. Like a combination Congress, White House, and War Department, it ruled the West Side slum New Yorkers called Hell's Kitchen. No cop had laid eyes on the inside of it in years.

Commodore Tommy Thompson, the saloon's bullet-headed, thick-necked proprietor, was boss of the Gopher Gang. He collected tribute from criminals in the drug trade, prostitution and gambling, pickpockets and burglars, passed along a portion to bribe the police, and delivered votes to the Democratic political machine. He also dominated the lucrative business of robbing New York Central freight cars, his nickname testifying to a level of success in his field that rivaled railroad tycoon Commodore Cornelius Vanderbilt's in his.

But that business was about to come to a bloody end, Commodore Tommy suspected, as soon as the railroad got around to organizing a private army to run his train robbers out of New York. So he was planning ahead. Which was why, as Isaac Bell's ferry sped across the Hudson River, Commodore Thompson was shaking hands on a new deal with a couple of 'queueless' Chinese – Americanized high-tone Chinamen who had chopped off the long pigtail worn by their immigrant countrymen.

Harry Wing and Louis Loh were hatchet men for the up-and-coming Hip Sing tong. They spoke good English, were duded up in snappy suits, and were, Thompson took for granted, deadly behind the mild expressions on their well-scrubbed pusses. He had recognized kindred spirits the instant they approached him. Like his Gophers, the Hip Sing profited by controlling the vice rackets with muscle, graft, and discipline. And like Tommy's Gophers, the Hip Sing were driving out rivals and getting stronger.

The deal they had brought him was irresistible: Tommy Thompson's Gopher Gang would allow the Chinese gangsters to open opium dens on Manhattan's West Side. For half the take, the Commodore would protect the joint, supply the girls, and pay the cops. Harry Wing and Louis Loh would gain for the Hip Sing tong white middle-class customers with money to spend – the casual 'ice cream users' afraid to venture into the back alleys of Chinatown. A square deal, as President Teddy Roosevelt would say. Done squarely, Sophie Tucker would sing.

The Newark, New Jersey, auto patrol tried to catch Isaac Bell in a Packard.

His 1906 gasoline-powered Locomobile race car was painted fire-engine red. He had ordered the color from the factory to give slower drivers a better chance of seeing him in time to get out of the way. But the color, and the Locomobile's thunderous exhaust, did tend to draw the attention of the police.

Before he reached East Orange he had left the Newark cops in the dust.

In Elizabeth they came after him on a motorcycle. Bell lost sight of the machine long before Roselle. And now the countryside was opening up.

The Locomobile had been built for the speedway and held many records. Attaching fenders and lights for street driving had tamed it not at all. In the hands of a man with nerves of steel, a passion for speed, and the reflexes of a cat, the big sixteen-liter machine cut a fantastic pace on New Jersey's farm roads and blasted through sleepy towns like a meteor.

Clad boot to chin in a long linen duster, his eyes shielded by goggles, his head bare so he could hear every nuance of the four-cylinder engine's thunder, Bell worked the shifter, clutch, and horn in relentless tandem, accelerating on straights, sliding through bends, warning farmers, livestock, and slower vehicles that he was coming through. He would have enjoyed himself immensely were he not so worried about John Scully. He had left the lone-wolf detective in a lurch. The fact that Scully had fallen into the lurch on his own meant nothing. As case boss, he was responsible for looking after his people.

He drove with his big hands low on the spoked steering wheel. When he had to slow in towns, it took both hands to lever the massive beast into turns. But when he poured on the speed on the farm roads, she grew beautifully responsive. One hand was enough, as he repeatedly reached out to pump up the fuel pressure and blow the horn. He rarely touched the brakes. There was little point. The men in Bridgeport, Connecticut, who built the Locomobile had supplied a stopping system that relied on squeezing the chain shafts – a halfhearted afterthought amounting to little more than no brakes at all. Isaac Bell didn't care.

As he roared out of Woodbridge, a one-twenty-horsepower Mercedes GP roadster tried to give him a run for his money. Bell pressed the Locomobile's accelerator pedal to the floor and kept the road to himself.

9

'What's this?' asked Commodore Tommy Thompson.

'He says he got a proposition fer yer.'

Tommy's bouncers, two broken-nosed fighters who had murdered his numerous rivals over the years, were standing close on either side of a refined gentleman they had escorted into his backroom office.

In cold silence, Tommy Thompson sized up what appeared to be a genuine Fifth Avenue swell. He was a medium-built man about his own age, thirty. Medium height, expensive gold-headed cane, expensive long black coat with a velvet collar, costly fur hat, kid gloves. Heat was pouring from the coal stove, and the man quietly removed his gloves, revealing a heavy ring studded with jewels, and unbuttoned his coat. Under his coat, the Gopher Gang leader could see a solid-gold watch chain thick enough to hold a brewery horse and a dark blue broadcloth suit of clothes. Tommy could have entertained three chorus girls for a week in Atlantic City for what the swell had paid for his boots.

The swell said not a word. He stood utterly still after removing his gloves and opening his coat, except for when he lifted a hand to smooth the tip of his narrow mustache with his thumb, which he then hooked in his vest pocket.

A cool customer, Commodore Tommy decided. He also decided that if all the cops in New York chipped in they still could not afford to disguise a detective in such an outfit. Even if they could raise the dough, there wasn't a cop in the city who could paint that born-with-a-silver-spoon-in-his-mouth expression on his mug. So the gang boss asked, 'What do you want?'

'Can I assume,' the swell asked, 'that you are indeed the leader of the Gopher Gang?'

Commodore Tommy grew wary, again. The swell was not a complete stranger to Hell's Kitchen. He had pronounced the gang's name correctly – as 'goofer.' Not like the newspapers spelled it for Fifth Avenue readers. Where had he learned to say goofer?

'I asked you what do you want?'

'I want to pay you five thousand dollars for the services of three murderers.'

Tommy Thompson sat up straight. Five thousand dollars was a *hell* of a lot money. So much money that he forgot all about goofer and gopher and threw caution to the winds. 'Who do you want murdered?'

'A Scotsman named Alasdair MacDonald needs killing in Camden, New Jersey. The murderers must be adept with knives.'

'Oh, must they, now?'

'I have the money with me,' said the swell. 'I will pay you first and trust you will deliver.'

Tommy Thompson turned to his bouncers. The bruisers were grinning mirthlessly. The swell had just made a fatal mistake in admitting he had the dough on him.

'Take his five thousand dollars,' Tommy ordered. 'Take his watch. Take his ring. Take his gold-headed cane and his coat and his fur hat and his suit and his boots, and throw the son of a bitch in the river.'

71

They moved as one, surprisingly fast for big men.

The swell's coat and tailored suit concealed a powerful frame. The stillness of his stance masked blinding speed. In the space of a heartbeat, one bouncer was sprawled on the floor, stunned and bloodied. The other was pleading for mercy in a high-pitched squeal. The swell had clamped his head under one arm, while he pressed his thumb to the bouncer's eye.

Commodore Tommy gaped in astonished recognition.

Fitted over the swell's thumbnail gleamed a razor-sharp gouge. The tip pressed the corner of the bouncer's eye, and it was clear to the pleading gangster – and to Commodore Tommy – that with a flick of his thumb the swell could scoop the man's eye out of his head like a grape.

'Jaysus, Jaysus, Jaysus,' breathed Tommy. 'You're Brian O'Shay.'

At the sound of that name the bouncer, whose eye was a fraction of an inch from being extracted from its socket, began to weep. The other, still struggling for breath on the floor, gasped, 'Can't be. Eyes O'Shay is dead.'

'If he was,' said Commodore Tommy, 'he's back from it.'

The Gopher Gang leader stared in wonder.

Brian 'Eyes' O'Shay had vanished fifteen years ago. No wonder he knew goofer. If Eyes hadn't vanished, they'd still be battling each other to boss Hell's Kitchen. Barely out of childhood, O'Shay had mastered the gang weapons – slingshot, lead pipe, brass knuckles, and axheads in his boots – and even gotten his mitts on a police revolver. But O'Shay had been most feared for gouging out rivals' eyes with a specially fitted copper thumbnail.

'You've moved up in the world,' said Tommy, getting over his shock. 'That gouge looks like it's pure silver.'

'Stainless steel,' said O'Shay. 'Holds an edge and don't corrode.'

'So you're back. And rich enough to pay people to do your killing for you.'

'I won't offer twice.'

'I'll take the job.'

Eyes O'Shay moved quickly, raking the bouncer's cheek even as he released him. The man screamed. His hands flew to his face. He blinked, removed his hands, and stared at the blood. Then he blinked again and smiled with gratitude. Blood was streaming from a slice that traversed cheekbone to jaw, but his eyes were intact.

'Get up!' Commodore Tommy ordered. 'Both of ya. Go get the Iceman. Tell him to bring Kelly and Butler.'

They hurried out, leaving Tommy Thompson alone with O'Shay. Tommy said, 'This ought to put an end to the rumors that I killed you.'

'You could not on your best day, Tommy.'

The Gopher Gang boss protested the insult and the contempt behind it. 'Why you talking like that? We was partners.'

'Sometimes.'

They stood in silence, old rivals taking each other's measure. 'Back,' Tommy muttered. 'Jaysus Christ, from where?'

O'Shay did not answer.

Five minutes passed. Ten.

Kelly and Butler sidled into the Commodore's office, trailed by Iceman Weeks.

Brian O'Shay looked them over.

Typical new-breed Gopher, he thought, smaller, compact men. And wasn't Progress a wonderful thing? Tommy was a throwback to the old days when bulk and muscle ruled. Now clubs and lead pipe were giving way to firearms. Kelly, Butler, and Weeks were built more like himself but dandified in the latest gangster fashion – tight-fitting suits, bright vests, florid ties. Kelly and Butler wore polished yellow shoes with lavender socks. Weeks, the Iceman, stood out in hose of sky blue. He was the cool one who would hang back, let the hotheads take the chances, and then swoop in for the prize. In his dreams, the Commodore would die of something quick, and Iceman Weeks would own the Gophers.

O'Shay took three butterfly knives from his coat and handed one to each. They were German made, exquisitely balanced, quick to open, and sharp as razors. Kelly, Butler, and Weeks hefted them admiringly.

'Leave them in the man when you do the job,' O'Shay ordered with a glance at the Commodore, who seconded the order with a blunt threat. 'If I ever sees youse with them again, I'll break your necks.'

O'Shay opened a bulging wallet and removed three return tickets to Camden, New Jersey. 'MacDonald,' he said, 'will be hanging out in Del Rossi's Dance Hall soon after dark. You'll find it in the Gloucester district.'

'What does he look like?' asked Weeks.

'Like an avalanche,' said O'Shay. 'You can't miss him.'

'Get going!' Commodore Tommy ordered. 'Don't come back 'til he's dead.'

'When do we get paid?' asked Weeks.

'When he's dead.'

The killers headed for the railroad ferry.

O'Shay pulled a thick envelope from his overcoat and counted out fifty hundred-dollar bills on Tommy Thompson's wooden desk. Thompson counted it again and stuffed the money in his trousers.

'Pleasure doing business.'

O'Shay said, 'I'll have use for those tong hatchet men, too.'

Commodore Tommy stared hard. 'What tong hatchet men would you be wondering about, Brian O'Shay?'

'Those two highbinders from the Hip Sing.'

'How in Christ's name did you know about them?'

'Don't let the fancy duds confuse you, Tommy. I'm still ahead of you and always will be.'

O'Shay turned on his heel and stalked out of the saloon.

Tommy Thompson snapped his fingers. A boy named Paddy the Rat appeared at a side door. He was thin and gray. On the street, he was almost as invisible as the vermin he was named for. 'Follow O'Shay. Find out where he hangs and what moniker he goes by.'

Paddy the Rat followed O'Shay east across 39th. The man's fine coat and fur hat seemed to glow as he cut a path through the shabbily dressed poor who thronged the greasy cobblestones. He crossed Tenth Avenue, crossed Ninth, where he neatly sidestepped a drunk who lurched at him from the shadow of the elevated train tracks. Just past Seventh he stopped in front of an auto-rental garage and peered in the plate-glass window.

Paddy crept close to a team of dray horses. Shielded by their bulk, stroking their bulging chests to keep them calm, he racked his brain. How could he follow O'Shay if he rented an automobile?

O'Shay turned abruptly from the glass and hurried on.

Paddy got uncomfortable as the neighborhood changed. New buildings were going up, tall offices and hotels. The grand Metropolitan Opera House reared up like a palace. If the cops saw him, they would run him in for invading the Quality's neighborhood. O'Shay was nearing Broadway. Suddenly he disappeared.

Paddy the Rat broke into a desperate gallop. He could not return to Hell's Kitchen without reporting O'Shay's address. There! With a sigh of relief he turned into an alley beside a theater under construction. At the end of the alley he saw the tail of the long black coat twirl around a corner. He raced after it and skidded around that corner, straight into a fist that knocked him to the mud.

O'Shay leaned over him. Paddy the Rat saw a glint of steel. A needle burst of pain exploded in his right eye. He knew instantly what O'Shay had done to him and he cried out in despair.

'Open your hand!' said O'Shay.

When he did not, the steel pricked his remaining eye. 'You'll lose this one, too, if you don't open your hand.'

Paddy the Rat opened his hand. He quivered as he felt O'Shay press something round and terrible into his palm and close his fingers around it almost gently. 'Give this to Tommy.'

O'Shay left the boy whimpering in the alley and retraced his steps to 39th Street. He stood in the shadows, still as a statue, until he was sure the little weasel didn't have a partner watching. Then he continued east under the Sixth

Avenue El, checked his back, walked to Fifth Avenue, and turned downtown, still studying reflections in windows.

A mustachioed Irish cop directing traffic shouted at a freight wagon to stop so the well-dressed gentleman could cross 34th Street. Doormen – whose blue-and-gold uniforms would have done an all-big-gun dreadnought's captain proud – scrambled when they saw him coming.

O'Shay returned their crisp salutes and marched into the Waldorf-Astoria Hotel.

IO

Isaac Bell spotted John Scully's red handkerchief tied to a hedge. He swung the Locomobile into the narrow road it marked, eased up on the accelerator pedal for the first time since he left Weehawken, and closed the cutout, which quieted the thunderous exhaust to a hollow mutter.

He steered up a steep hill and drove a mile through fallow farm fields that awaited spring planting. The resourceful Scully had procured a milk-can collection truck somewhere, exactly the sort of vehicle that would not look out of place on New Jersey's farm roads. Bell eased quietly alongside it so the Locomobile could not be seen from the road. Then he heaved his golf bag off the passenger seat and carried it to the hillcrest where the Van Dorn detective lay flat on brown grass.

The laconic loner was a short, round man with a moon face who could pass for a trusted colleague of preachers, shopkeepers, safecrackers, or murderers. Thirty pounds of fat disguised slabs of rock-hard muscle, and his diffident smile concealed a mind quicker than a bear trap. He was training field glasses on a house down the hill. Smoke rose from the kitchen chimney. A big Marmon touring car was parked outside, a powerful machine covered in mud and dust.

'What's in the bag?' Scully greeted Bell.

'Couple of five irons,' Bell grinned, removing a pair of

78

humpback twelve-gauge Browning Auto-5 shotguns. 'How many in the house?'

'All three.'

'Anyone living there?'

'No smoke before they drove up.'

Bell nodded, satisfied that no innocents would be caught in a cross fire. Scully passed him the field glasses. He studied the house and the automobile. 'Is that the Marmon they stole in Ohio?'

'Could be another. They're partial to Marmons.'

'How'd you get a line on them?'

'Played your hunch about their first job. Their real name is Williard, and if me and you was half as smart as we think we are, we'd have tumbled to it a month ago.'

'Can't argue with that,' Bell admitted. 'Why don't we start things off by putting their auto out of action.'

'We'll never hit it from here with these scatter guns.'

Bell pulled from the golf bag an ancient .50 caliber Sharps buffalo gun. John Scully's eyes gleamed like ball bearings. 'Where'd you get the cannon?'

'Our Knickerbocker house dick separated it from a Pawnee Bill Wild West Show cowboy who got drunk in Times Square.' Bell levered open the breech, loaded a black-powder cartridge, and aimed the heavy rifle at the Marmon.

'Try not to set it on fire,' Scully cautioned. 'It's full of their loot.'

'I'll just make it hard to start.'

'Hold it, what's that coming?'

A six-cylinder K Ford was bouncing up the lane that lead to the farmhouse. It had a searchlight mounted on the radiator.

'Hell's bells,' said Scully. 'That's Cousin Constable.'

Two men with sheriff stars on their coats climbed out of the Ford carrying baskets. Scully studied them through the glasses. 'Bringing them supper. Two more makes five.'

'Got room in your milk truck?'

'If we stack 'em close.'

'What do you say we give them time to get distracted filling their bellies?'

'It's a plan,' said Scully, continuing to observe the house.

Bell watched the lane to the house and turned around repeatedly to be sure that no more relatives came up the back road he had taken.

He was wondering where Dorothy Langner got the money to buy her father a piano when Bell remembered that she had given it to him only recently.

Scully got uncharacteristically talkative. 'You know, Isaac,' he said, gesturing toward the farmhouse below and the two automobiles, 'for jobs like this wouldn't it be nice if somebody invented a machine gun light enough to tote around with you?'

'A "sub" machine gun?'

'Exactly. A *sub*machine gun. But how would you lug all that water to cool the barrel?'

'You wouldn't have to if it fired pistol ammunition.'

Scully nodded thoughtfully. 'A drum magazine would keep it compact.'

'Shall we start the show?' Bell asked, hefting the Sharps. Both detectives glanced at the woods near the house where the Frye Boys would run when Bell disabled their autos.

'Let me flank 'em first,' said Scully. Putting words to action, he waddled down the hill, looking, Bell thought, like a bricklayer hurrying to work. He waved when he was in place.

Bell braced his elbows on the crest, thumbed the hammer to full cock, and sighted the Sharps on the Marmon's motor cowling. He gently squeezed the trigger. The heavy slug rocked the Marmon on its tires. The rifle's report echoed like artillery, and a cloud of black smoke spewed from the muzzle and tumbled down the hill. Bell reloaded and fired again. Again the Marmon jumped, and a front tire went flat. He turned his attention to the police car.

Wide-eyed constables boiled out of the house waving pistols. The bank robbers stayed inside. Rifle barrels poked from the window. A hail of lever-action Winchester fire stormed at the black-powder smoke billowing from Isaac Bell's Sharps.

Bell ignored the lead howling past his head, methodically reloaded the single-shot Sharps, and shot the Ford's motor cowling. Steam spurted from the hot radiator. Now their quarry was on foot.

All three bank robbers darted from the house, rifles blazing.

Bell reloaded and fired, reloaded and fired. A long gun went flying, and the man staggered, clutching his arm. Another turned and ran toward the woods. Rapid fire bellowed from Scully's twelve-gauge autoload and caused him to change his mind. He skidded to a stop, looked around frantically, and flung his weapon down and threw his hands in the air. The constables, gripping pistols, froze. Bell stood up, aiming the Sharps through the black smoke. Scully sauntered from the woods, pointing his shotgun.

'Mine's a twelve-gauge autoload,' Scully called

conversationally. 'Fellow up the hill's got a Sharps rifle. About time you boys got smart.'

The constables dropped their pistols. The third Frye boy levered a fresh cartridge into his Winchester's chamber and took deliberate aim. Bell found him in his sights, but Scully fired first, tipping the barrel of his shotgun high to increase the range. The slugs spread wide at that distance. Most tore past the bank robber. Two that did not peppered his shoulder.

Neither shot man was mortally wounded. Bell made sure that they would not bleed to death and handcuffed them with the others in Scully's milk truck. They started downhill, Scully driving the truck, Bell in his Locomobile bringing up the rear. Just as they reached the Cranbury Turnpike, Mike and Eddie, the Van Dorns assigned to help Scully, appeared in an Oldsmobile, and the caravan headed for Trenton to turn the bank robbers and the crooked cops over to the State's Attorney.

Two hours later, nearing Trenton, Bell saw a road sign that jogged his photographic memory. The sign was a stack of town and road names lettered on white arrows that pointed south: the Hamilton Turnpike, the Bordentown Road, the Burlington Pike, and the Westfield Turnpike to Camden.

Arthur Langner had written appointments on a wall calendar. Two days before he died he had met with Alasdair MacDonald, the turbine-propulsion specialist who had been contracted by the Navy's Steam Engineering Bureau. MacDonald's factory was in Camden.

Her father loved his guns, Dorothy Langner had pleaded. As Farley Kent loved his hulls. And Alasdair MacDonald his turbines. A wizard, she had called Mac-Donald, meaning he was her father's equal. Bell wondered what else the two men had in common.

He squeezed the Locomobile's horn bulb. The Olds-mobile and milk truck skidded to a dusty halt. 'There's a fellow I ought to see in Camden,' Bell told Scully.

'Need a hand?'

'Yes! Soon as you turn this bunch in, could you get to the Brooklyn Navy Yard? There's a naval architect in the draw-ing loft named Farley Kent. See if he's on the up-and-up.'

Bell turned the Locomobile south.

'ON CAMDEN'S SUPPLIES, THE WORLD RELIES,'

a billboard greeted Isaac Bell as he entered the industrial city, which occupied the eastern shore of the Delaware River across from Philadelphia. He passed factories that made everything from cigars to patent drugs to linoleum and terra-cotta and soup. But it was the shipyard that dominated. The incongruously named New York Ship-building Company lined the Delaware and Newton Creek with modern covered ways and gigantic gantries thrusting at the smoky sky. Across the river sprawled Cramp Ship Builders and the Philadelphia Navy Yard.

Evening was falling before Bell found the MacDonald Marine Steam Turbine Company inland from the riverfront in a warren of smaller factories that supplied the shipyard with specialty items. He parked the Locomobile at the gates and asked to see Alasdair MacDonald. MacDonald was not in. A friendly clerk said, 'You'll find the Professor down in Gloucester City – just a few blocks from here.'

'Why do you call him the Professor?'

'Because he's so smart. He was apprenticed to the inventor of the naval turbine, Charles Parsons, who revolutionized high-speed ship propulsion. By the time the Professor emigrated to America, he knew more about turbines than Parsons himself.'

'Where in Gloucester City?'

'Del Rossi's Dance Hall – not that he's dancing. It's more saloon than dance hall, if you know what I mean.'

'I've encountered similar establishments out west,' Bell said drily.

'Cut over to King Street. Can't miss it.'

Gloucester City was just down the river from Camden, the two cities blending seamlessly. King Street was near the water. Saloons, quick-and-dirties, and boardinghouses hosted workingmen from the shipyards and the bustling river port. Del Rossi's was as unmissable as MacDonald's clerk had promised, boasting a false front mocked up to look like a proscenium arch in a Broadway theater.

Inside was bedlam, with the loudest piano Bell had ever heard, women shrieking with laughter, perspiring bartenders knocking the necks off bottles to pour faster, exhausted bouncers, and wall-to-wall sailors and shipyard hands – five hundred men at least – determined to win the race to get drunk. Bell studied the room over a sea of flushed faces under clouds of blue smoke. The only occupants of the saloon not in shirtsleeves were himself, in his white suit, a handsome silver-haired gent in a red frock coat whom he guessed was the proprietor, and a trio of dandified gangsters tricked out in brown derbies, purple shirts, bright waistcoats, and striped ties. Bell couldn't see their shoes but suspected they were yellow.

He plowed through broad shoulders toward the frock coat.

'Mr. Del Rossi!' he shouted over the din, extending his hand.

'Good evening, sir. Call me Angelo.'

'Isaac.'

They shook hands. Del Rossi's were soft but bore the long-healed burns and cuts of ship work in his youth.

'Busy night.'

'God bless our "New Navy." It's like this every night. New York Ship launches the *Michigan* next month and just laid the keel for a twenty-eight-knot destroyer. Across the river, the Philadelphia Navy Yard is building a new dry dock, Cramp launches *South Carolina* come summer, plus they've already nailed a contract for *six* 700-ton destroyers – six, count 'em, *six*. What can I do for you, sir?'

'I'm looking for a fellow named Alasdair MacDonald.'

Del Rossi frowned. 'The Professor? Follow the sound of fists cracking jaws,' he answered with a nod toward the farthest corner from the door.

'Excuse me. I better get over there before someone floors him.'

'That's not likely,' said Del Rossi. 'He was heavyweight champ of the Royal Navy.'

Bell sized MacDonald up as he worked his way across the room, and he took an immediate shine to the big Scotsman. He looked to be in his forties, tall, with an open countenance and muscles that rippled under a shirt soaked with perspiration. He had several boxing scars over his eyebrows – but not a mark on the rest of his face, Bell noticed – and enormous hands with splayed-out knuckles. He cupped a glass in one, a whiskey bottle in the other, and as Bell drew close he filled the glass and stood the bottle on the bar behind him, his eyes fixed on the crowd. It parted suddenly, explosively, and a three-hundred-pound bruiser lumbered at MacDonald with murder in his eye.

MacDonald tracked him with a wry smile, as if they were both in on a good joke. He took a swig from his glass and then, without appearing to rush, closed his empty hand into an enormous fist and landed a punch almost too fast for Bell to see.

The bruiser collapsed to the sawdust-strewn floor. MacDonald looked down at him amiably. He had a thick Scots accent. 'Jake, me friend, you are a purrfectly fine laddie 'til the drink riles your noggin.' Of the group around him, he asked, 'Would someone see Jake home?'

Jake's friends carried him out. Bell introduced himself to Alasdair MacDonald, who, he surmised, was drunker than he looked.

'Do I know you, laddie?'

'Isaac Bell,' he repeated. 'Dorothy Langner told me that you were a particular friend of her father.'

'That I was. Poor Artie. When they made the Gunner they broke the mold. Have a drink!'

He called for a glass, filled it to the brim, and passed it to Bell with the Scottish toast, '*Slanj*.'

'*Slanj-uh va*,' said Bell, and he threw back the fiery liquor in the same manner as MacDonald.

'How is the lass bearing up?'

'Dorothy is clinging to the hope that her father neither killed himself nor took a bribe.'

'I don't know about killing himself – mountains shade dark glens. But I do know this: the Gunner would have shoved his hand in a punch press before he'd reach for a bribe.'

'Did you work closely together?'

'Let's just say we admired each other.'

'I imagine you shared similar goals.'

'We both loved dreadnoughts, if that's what you mean. Love 'em or hate 'em, the dreadnought battleship is the marvel of our age.'

Bell noticed that MacDonald, drunk or not, was dodging his questions artfully. He backtracked, saying, 'I imagine you must be following the progress of the Great White Fleet with keen interest.'

Alasdair snorted scoffingly. 'Victory at sea goes to ordnance, armor, and speed. You've got to shoot farther than the enemy, survive more punishment, and steam faster. By those standards, the Great White Fleet is hopelessly out-of-date.'

He splashed more liquor in Bell's glass and refilled his own. 'England's HMS *Dreadnought* and the German dreadnought copies have longer range, stronger armor, and dazzling speed. Our "fleet," which is simply the old Atlantic Squadron tarted up, is a flock of *pre*-dreadnought battleships.'

'What's the difference?'

'A pre-dreadnought battleship is like a middleweight fighter who learned to box in college. He has no business

in the prize ring with heavyweight Jack Johnson.' Mac-
Donald grinned challengingly at Bell, whom he outweighed
by forty pounds.

'Unless he did graduate studies on Chicago's West Side,'
Bell challenged him back.

'And put on a few pounds of muscle,' MacDonald
acknowledged approvingly.

Impossible as it seemed, the piano suddenly got louder.
Someone banged on a drum. The crowd made way for
Angelo Del Rossi to mount a low stage opposite the bar.
He drew from his frock coat a conductor's baton.

Waiters and bouncers put down trays and blackjacks
and picked up banjos, guitars, and accordions. Waitresses
jumped onto the stage and cast off their aprons, revealing
skirts so short that police in any city with more than one
church would raid the joint. Del Rossi raised his baton.
The musicians banged out George M. Cohan's 'Come On
Down,' and the ladies danced what appeared to Bell to be
an excellent imitation of the Paris cancan.

'You were saying?' he shouted.

'I was?'

'About the dreadnoughts that you and the Gunner . . .'

'Take the *Michigan*. When she's finally commissioned,
our newest battleship will have the best gun arrangement
in the world – all big guns on superimposed turrets. But
tissue-thin armor and rattletrap piston engines doom her
to be a *semi*-dreadnought at best – target practice for German and English dreadnoughts.'

MacDonald drained his glass.

'All the more terrible that the Bureau of Ordnance lost
a great gun builder in Artie Langner. The technical bureaus

hate change. Artie forced change . . . Don't get me started on this, laddie. It's been an awful month for America's battleships.'

'Beyond the death of Artie Langner?' Bell prompted.

'The Gunner was only the first to die. One week later we lost Chad Gordon, our top armorer at Bethlehem Iron Works. Horrible accident. Six lads roasted alive – Chad and all his hands. Then last week that damned fool Grover Lakewood fell off the hill. The cleverest fire-control expert in the business. And a hell of a fine young man. What a future he'd have given us – gone in a stupid climbing accident.'

'Hold on!' said Bell. 'Are you telling me that *three* engineers specializing in dreadnought battleships have all died in the last month?'

'Sounds like a jinx, doesn't it?' MacDonald's big hand passed over his chest in the sign of the cross. 'I would never say our dreadnoughts are jinxed. But for the sake of the United States Navy, I hope to bloody hell Farley Kent and Ron Wheeler aren't next.'

'Hulls at the Brooklyn Navy Yard,' said Bell. 'Torpedoes at Newport.'

MacDonald looked at him sharply. 'You get around.'

'Dorothy Langner mentioned Kent and Wheeler. I gathered they were Langner counterparts.'

'Counterparts?' MacDonald laughed. 'That's the joke of the dreadnought race, don't you see?'

'No I don't. What do you mean?'

'It's like a shell game, with a pea under every shell and every pea packed with dynamite. Farley Kent devises watertight compartments to protect his hulls from torpedoes.

But up in Newport, Ron Wheeler *improves* torpedoes — builds a longer-range torpedo that carries heavier explosives, maybe even figures out how to arm it with TNT. So Artie has to — had to — increase gun range so the ship can fight farther off, and Chad Gordon had to cast stronger armor to take the hits. Enough to drive a man to drink . . .' MacDonald refilled their glasses. 'God knows how we'll get along without those lads.'

'But speed you say is also vital. What about you in Steam Engineering?' Bell asked. 'They say you're a wizard with turbines. Wouldn't Alasdair MacDonald's loss be as devastating to the dreadnought program?'

MacDonald laughed. 'I'm indestructible.'

Another fistfight broke out across the dance hall.

'Excuse me, Isaac,' said MacDonald, and he waded cheerfully into it.

Bell shouldered after him. The flashily dressed gangsters he'd seen when he came in were hovering around the impromptu ring of cheering men. MacDonald was trading punches with a young heavyweight who had the arms of a blacksmith and admirable footwork. The Scotsman appeared slower than the younger man. But Bell saw that Alasdair MacDonald was allowing his opponent to land punches as a way of gauging what he had. So subtle was he that none of the blows scored any damage. Suddenly Alasdair seemed to have learned all he needed to. Suddenly he was fast and deadly, throwing combinations. Bell had to admit they outclassed the best he had thrown when he boxed for Yale, and he recalled with a grateful smile Joe Van Dorn steering him into 'graduate study' in Chicago's saloons.

The blacksmith was weaving. MacDonald finished him

off with an upper cut that was no harder than it had to be to do the job, then helped him to his feet, slapped his back, and bellowed for all to hear, 'You did good, laddie. I just got lucky ... Isaac, did you note this fellow's foot-work? Don't you think he's got a future in the ring?'

'He'd have floored Gentleman Jim Corbett in his prime.'

The blacksmith accepted the compliment with a glassy-eyed grin.

MacDonald, whose own eyes were still restlessly scanning the crowd, noticed the gangsters coming purposefully his way. 'Oh, here's another contender – two more. No rest for the weary. All right, lads, you're runts, but there's two of ya. Come and get it.'

They weren't quite runts, although MacDonald out-weighed them handily, but they moved with assurance and held their hands well. And when they attacked, it was clearly not the first time they had teamed up. Talented street fighters, Bell assessed them, tough slum kids who had fought their way into the upper ranks of a gang. Full-fledged gangsters now, out for a night of mayhem. Bell moved closer in case things got out of hand.

Hurling filthy curses at Alasdair MacDonald, they attacked him simultaneously from both sides. There was a viciousness to the concerted assault that seemed to anger the Scotsman. Face flushed, he feinted a retreat, which drew them forward into a powerful left jab and a devastating right. One gangster staggered backward, blood spurting from his nose. The other crumpled up, holding his ear.

Bell saw steel flash behind Alasdair MacDonald.

Isaac Bell whisked his over-under, two-shot derringer out of his hat in a blur of motion and fired at the third gangster, who was lunging at Alasdair MacDonald's back with a knife. The range was close, nearly point-blank. The heavy .44 slug stopped him in his tracks, and the blade fell from his hand. But even as the roar of gunfire sent patrons stampeding for cover, the dandy with the bloody nose was thrusting another knife at the Scotsman's belly.

MacDonald gaped, as if astonished that a friendly brawl would turn deadly.

Isaac Bell realized that he was witnessing a premeditated attempt at murder. A fleeing spectator blocked his vision. Bell slammed him out of his way and fired again. Above MacDonald's bloody nose, the knife wielder grew a red hole between the eyes. His knife fell inches short of Alasdair MacDonald's belt.

Bell's derringer was empty.

The remaining killer, the one floored, rose behind Mac-Donald with a fluid ease that showed him neither hurt nor slowed by the blow he had taken to his ear. A long-bladed knife flipped open in his hand. Bell was already pulling his Browning No. 2 semiautomatic from under his coat. The killer thrust his knife at MacDonald's back. Tucking the pistol to his body to shield it from the running men, Bell fired. He knew that he would have stopped the killer dead with a shot to the brain. But someone crashed into him just as he pulled the trigger.

He did not miss by much. The shot pierced the dandy's right shoulder. But the Browning's pinpoint accuracy was gained at the cost of stopping power, and the killer was left-handed. Although the .380 caliber slug staggered him, momentum was on the killer's side, and he managed to sink his blade into Alasdair MacDonald's broad back.

MacDonald still looked astonished. His eyes met Bell's even as the detective caught him in his arms. 'They tried to kill me,' he marveled.

Bell eased the suddenly dead weight to the sawdust and knelt over him. 'Get a doctor,' Bell shouted. 'Get an ambulance.'

'Laddie!'

'Don't talk,' said Bell.

Blood was spreading rapidly, so fast that the sawdust floated on it instead of absorbing it.

'Give me your hand, Isaac.'

Bell took the huge splayed hand in his.

'Please give me your hand.'

'I've got you, Alasdair – *Get a doctor!*'

Angelo Del Rossi knelt beside them. 'Doc's coming. He's a good one. You'll be O.K., Professor. Won't he, Bell?'

'Of course,' Bell lied.

MacDonald gripped Bell's hand convulsively and whispered something Bell could not hear. He leaned closer. 'What did you say, Alasdair?'

'Listen.'

'I can't hear you.'

But the big Scotsman said nothing. Bell whispered into his ear, 'They came after you, Alasdair. Why?'

MacDonald opened his eyes. They grew wide with sudden recognition, and he whispered, 'Hull 44.'

'What?'

MacDonald closed his eyes as if falling asleep.

'I'm a doctor. Get out of my way.'

Bell moved aside. The doctor, youthful, brisk, and apparently competent, counted MacDonald's pulse. 'Heartbeat like a station clock. I have an ambulance on the way. Some of you men help me carry him.'

'I'll do it,' said Bell.

'He weighs two hundred pounds.'

'Get out of my way.'

Isaac Bell cradled the fallen boxer in his arms, stood to his feet, and carried MacDonald out the door to the sidewalk, where Bell held him while they waited for the ambulance. Camden cops were holding back the crowds. A police detective demanded Bell's name.

'Isaac Bell. Van Dorn operative.'

'Nice shooting in there, Mr. Bell.'

'Did you recognize the dead men?'

'Never saw 'em before.'

'Out-of-town? Philadelphia?'

'They had New York train tickets in their pockets. Care to tell me how you got mixed up in this?'

'I'll tell you everything I can – which isn't much – as soon as I get this fellow to the hospital.'

'I'll be waiting for you at headquarters. Tell the desk sergeant you want to see Barney George.'

A motor ambulance mounted on the new Model T

chassis pulled up in front of the dance hall. As Bell laid MacDonald inside, the boxer clutched his hand again. Bell climbed in with him, beside the doctor, and rode to the hospital. While a surgeon worked on the Scot in the operating room, Bell telephoned New York with orders to warn John Scully, who was watching hull designer Farley Kent, and to dispatch operatives to the Naval Torpedo Station at Newport to guard the life of Ron Wheeler.

Three men central to the American dreadnaught program had died, and a fourth was at death's door. But if he had not witnessed the attack on Alasdair MacDonald, it would have been reported as a likely event in a saloon brawler's life instead of attempted murder. There was already a possibility that Langner had been murdered. What if the Bethlehem foundry explosion MacDonald had told him about wasn't an accident? Was the Westchester climbing accident murder, too?

Bell sat by the man's bed all night and into the morning.

Suddenly, at noon, Alasdair MacDonald filled his mighty chest with a shuddering breath and let it slowly sigh away. Bell shouted for the doctor. But he knew it was hopeless. Saddened, and deeply angry, Bell went to the Camden Police headquarters and reported to Detective George his part in failing to stop the attack.

'Did you retrieve any of their knives?' Bell asked when he had finished.

'All three.' George showed them to Bell. Alasdair Mac-Donald's blood had dried on the blade that killed him. 'Strange-looking things, aren't they?'

Bell picked up one of the two others not stained and examined it. 'It's a Butterflymesser.'

'A who?'

'A German folding knife, modeled on a Balisong butterfly knife. Quite rare outside the Philippine Islands.'

'I'll say. I've never seen one. German, you say?'

Bell showed him the maker's mark incised on the tang of the blade. 'Bontgen and Sabin of Solingen. Question is, where did they get them . . . ?' He looked the Camden detective full in the face. 'How much money did you find in the dead men's pockets?'

Detective George looked aside. Then he made a show of flipping through the pages of his handwritten case notes. 'Oh, yeah, here it is – less than ten bucks each.'

Eyes cold, voice grim, Bell said, 'I am not interested in recouping what might have gone astray before it was recorded as evidence. But the correct number – the actual amount of cash in their pockets – will indicate whether they were paid to do the killing. That amount, spoken privately between you and me, will be an important clue for my investigation.'

The Camden cop pretended to read his notes again. 'One had eight dollars and two bits. The others had seven bucks, a dime, and a nickel.'

Isaac Bell's bleak gaze dropped to the Butterflymesser he was holding. With a peculiar flick of his wrist, he caused the blade to fly open. It glinted like ice. He appeared to study it, as if wondering what use to put it to. Detective George, though deep in the confines of his own precinct, nervously wet his lips.

Bell said, 'A workingman earns about five hundred dollars a year. A year's pay to kill a man might seem the right amount to an evil person who would commit such an act for money. Therefore, it would help me to know whether those two killers who did not escape were carrying such a large sum.'

Detective George breathed a sigh of relief. 'I guarantee you, neither packed such a roll.'

Bell stared at him. Detective George looked happy he had not lied.

Finally Bell asked, 'Mind if I keep one of these knives?'

'I'll have to ask you to sign for it – but not the one they killed him with. We'll need that for the trial if we ever catch the son of a bitch – which ain't likely if he don't come back to Camden.'

'He's coming back,' Isaac Bell vowed. 'In chains.'

'"Guts" Dave Kelly – the one you put a hole in his head – and "Blood Bucket" Dick Butler took their orders from a brain named Irv Weeks – the "Iceman," on account of he's got cold blue eyes like ice, heart and soul to match. Being that Weeks is smarter than Kelly and Butler was by a long shot, and seeing how you described him hanging back waiting for his chance, I'll lay money it was Weeks who got away.'

'With my bullet in his shoulder.'

'The Iceman is a tough customer. If it didn't kill him, you can bet he's hopped a freight train back to New York and paid a midwife to dig it out.'

Harry Warren, Van Dorn's New York gang specialist, had come down on the train in response to Bell's telephone call and gone straight to the Camden city morgue, where he identified the murderers Bell had shot as members of the Hell's Kitchen Gopher Gang. Warren caught up with Bell at the police station. The two Van Dorns conferred in a corner of the detectives' bull pen.

'Harry, who would send these Bowery Boy hellions all the way to Camden?'

'Tommy Thompson, the "Commodore," bosses the Gophers.'

'Does he traffic in hired killings?'

'You name it, Tommy does it. But there was nothing to

stop these guys from hiring out on their own – so long as they paid Tommy his cut. Did the Camden cops find big money on the bodies? Or should I ask, did they *admit* to finding big money on the bodies?'

'They claim they didn't,' Bell replied. 'I made it clear that we are after bigger fish than thieving cops, and from the answer I got back I am reasonably certain that the amounts were small. Perhaps they would be paid afterward. Perhaps their boss kept the bulk of it.'

'Both,' said Harry Warren. He thought hard. 'But it's strange, Isaac. These gang boys usually stick close to home. Like I say, Tommy would do anything for dough, but Gophers and the like tend not to venture out of their own neighborhoods. Half of them couldn't find Brooklyn, much less cross state lines.'

'Find out why they did this time.'

'I'll try and brace Weeks soon as I learn where he's recuperating and –'

'Don't brace him. Send for me.'

'O.K., Isaac. But don't count on much. No one's keeping books on a deal like this. For all we know, it could have been personal. Maybe MacDonald poked one too many guys in the snoot.'

'Have you ever heard of a New York gangster using a Butterflymesser?'

'You mean the Philippine flip-open knife?'

Bell showed him the Butterflymesser.

'Yeah, there was a Duster who joined the Army to get away from the cops, ended up fighting in the Filipino insurrection. He brought one back and killed a gambler with it who owed him money. At least, that's what they said, but I bet it was the cocaine. You know how "dust" makes 'em paranoiac.'

'In other words, the Butterflymesser is not common in New York.'

'That Duster's was the only one I ever heard of.'

Bell raced to New York.

He hired a driver and mechanic to drive his Locomobile back while he took the train. A police launch, provided by Detective George, who was delighted to help him leave Camden, ran him across the Delaware River to Philadelphia, where he caught a Pennsylvania Railroad express. When he arrived at the Knickerbocker Hotel, light in the afternoon sky still glowed on the green copper roof, but nearer the street the red brick, French renaissance façade was growing dim.

He telephoned Joseph Van Dorn long-distance in Washington.

'Excellent job on the Frye Boys,' Van Dorn greeted him. 'I just had lunch with the Attorney General, and he is tickled pink.'

'Thank John Scully. I only held his coat.'

'How much longer to wrap up the Langner suicide?'

'This is bigger than Langner,' Bell retorted, and he told Van Dorn what had transpired.

'Four murders?' Van Dorn asked incredulously.

'One for sure – the one I witnessed. One likely – Langner.'

'Depending upon how much credence you put in that crackpot Cruson.'

'And the other two we have to investigate.'

'All connected by battleships?' Van Dorn asked, still sounding incredulous.

'Every victim worked in the dreadnought program.'

'*If* they're all victims, who's behind it?'

'I don't know.'

'I don't suppose you know why either.'

'Not yet.'

Van Dorn sighed. 'What do you need, Isaac?'

'Van Dorn Protection Services to guard Farley and Wheeler.'

'To whom do I bill those services?'

'Put it on the cuff 'til we figure who the client is,' Bell answered drily.

'Very amusing. What else do you need?'

Bell issued instructions to the crew of operatives Van Dorn put at his call – temporarily, as his call with the boss had made clear. Then he took the subway downtown and a trolley across the Brooklyn Bridge. John Scully met him in a Sand Street lunchroom a stone's throw from the fortresslike gates of the Brooklyn Navy Yard.

The cheap restaurant was starting to fill up as day shifts ended at the yard and surrounding factories, and boilermakers, drop forgers, tank testers, reamers, and patternmakers, machinists, coppersmiths, pipe fitters, and plumbers rushed in for supper.

Scully said, 'Near as I can discover, Kent's on the up-and-up. All he does is work and work some more. Devoted as a missionary. I'm told he hardly ever leaves his drawing table. He's got a bedroom attached to his drawing loft, where he stays most nights.'

'Where does he stay the rest of the nights?'

'Hotel St. George when a certain lady from Washington comes to town.'

'Who is she?'

'Well, that's the funny thing. She's the daughter of your exploding-piano guy.'

'Dorothy Langner?'

'What do you think of that?'

'I think Farley Kent is a lucky man.'

The Brooklyn Navy Yard surrounded a large bay of the East River between the Brooklyn Bridge and the Williamsburg Bridge. Designated a 'battleship yard,' and officially named the New York Navy Yard, its factories, foundries, dry docks, and shipways employed six thousand ship workers. Tall brick walls and iron gates enclosed twice the acreage of the Washington Navy Yard. Isaac Bell showed his Navy pass at the Sand Street Gate, which was flanked by statues of eagles.

He found Farley Kent's drawing loft in a building dwarfed by enormous ship sheds and gantry cranes. Night had blackened the high windows, and the draftsmen worked by electric lamps. Kent was young, barely out of his twenties, and deeply shaken by Alasdair MacDonald's murder. He mourned that MacDonald's death would cripple America's development of large-ship turbines. 'It will be a long while before the United States Navy will be able to install advanced turbines in our dreadnoughts.'

'What is Hull 44?' Bell asked.

Kent looked away. 'Hull 44?'

'Alasdair MacDonald implied that it was important.'

'I'm afraid I don't know what you are talking about.'

'He spoke freely about Arthur Langner and Ron Wheeler and Chad Gordon. And about you, Mr. Kent. Clearly, you five men worked closely. I am sure you know what Hull 44 means.'

'I told you. I do not know what you are talking about.'

Bell regarded him coldly. Kent looked away from his stern face.

'"Hull 44,"' the detective said, 'were your friend's dying words. He would have told me what it meant if he had not died. Now it's up to you.'

'I can't – I don't know.'

Bell's features hardened until they looked like they had been cut from stone. 'That powerful man held my hand like a child and tried to tell me why he was murdered. He could not get the words out. You can. *Tell me!*'

Kent bolted into the hallway and yelled loudly for the sentries.

Six U.S. Marines escorted Bell out the gates, their sergeant polite but unmoved by Bell's pass. 'I recommend, sir, that you telephone for an appointment with the commandant of the yard.'

Scully was waiting in the lunchroom. 'Have yourself some supper. It's a swell grub station. I'll watch for Kent.'

'I'll spell you in fifteen minutes.'

Bell could not remember when he had last eaten. He was just raising a sandwich from his plate when Scully dashed back and motioned him to the door. 'Kent broke from the gate like the favorite at the Kentucky Derby. Heading east on Sand. Wearing a tall-crowned black derby and a tan topcoat.'

'I see him.'

'That's the direction of the Hotel St. George. Looks like the lady's back in town. I'll cut over to the St. George on Nassau in case you lose him.' Without waiting for Bell's response, the independent Scully disappeared around the corner.

Bell followed Kent. He lay back half a block, screened by the crowds pouring in and out of the saloons and eateries, and passengers hopping on and off streetcars. The naval architect's tall bowler was easy to track in a neighborhood where most men wore cloth caps. His tan coat stood out among dark coats and pea jackets.

Sand Street passed through a district of factories and storehouses on its route between the navy yard and the Brooklyn Bridge. The damp evening chill carried the scents of chocolate, roasting coffee, coal smoke, harbor salt, and the sharp, pungent aroma of electrical shorts sparking from the trolley wires. Bell saw enough saloons and gambling halls to rival San Francisco's 'Barbary Coast.'

Kent surprised him at the enormous Sand Street Station where streetcars, elevated railway trains, and a trolley line under construction converged on the Brooklyn Bridge. Instead of passing under the station and continuing on to the Heights and the Hotel St. George, the naval architect suddenly darted through an opening in the stone wall that supported a ramp to the Brooklyn Bridge and hurried up the stairs. Bell dodged a trolley and tore after him. Hordes of people were streaming down the steps, blocking his view. He pushed his way to the top. There he caught sight of Farley Kent walking toward Manhattan on the wooden promenade in the center of the bridge. So much for a lady at the Hotel St. George.

The wooden walkway was flanked by elevated rail and trolley tracks and crowded with an evening rush of men walking home from work in Manhattan. Trains and street-cars hurtled past. They were packed with humanity, and Bell – who had spent many years tracking criminals on horseback in the open spaces of the West – understood those who preferred to walk in the cold, even assaulted by the constant shriek and rumble of train wheels.

Kent shot a glance over his shoulder. Bell removed his distinctive broad-brimmed white hat and moved side to side to be shielded by the crowds. His quarry hurried against the foot traffic, head down, staring at the boards and ignoring the dramatic panorama of New York's sky-scraper lights and the twinkling carpet of red, green, and white lanterns shown by the tugboats, schooners, steam-ers, and ferries plying the East River two hundred feet under the bridge.

The stairs on the Manhattan side led down to the City Hall district. The instant Kent hit the pavement he spun on his heel and hurried back toward the river he had just crossed. Bell followed, wondering what Kent was up to as they neared the waterfront. South Street, which passed under the bridge and paralleled the East River, was bor-dered by a forest of ship masts and bowsprits. Finger piers and warehouses thrust into the stream, forming slips in which moored three-masted sailing ships, tall-funneled steamers, and railroad barges.

Kent turned uptown, away from the Brooklyn Bridge. He hurried for several blocks, walking fast, not bothering to look back. When he reached Catherine Slip, he turned toward the water. Bell saw trading vessels rafted side by side. Deck cranes swung pallets of freight from ship to shore. Longshoremen trundled them into the warehouses. Kent passed the ships and headed for a long and unusually narrow steam yacht, which had not been visible from South Street.

Bell observed from the corner of a warehouse. The narrow yacht, which was fully one hundred feet long, had a sleek knife blade of a steel hull painted white, a tall steering bridge amidships, and a tall smokestack aft. Despite its businesslike appearance, it was luxuriously finished with brass fittings and varnished mahogany. Moored incongruously among the grimy trading vessels, it was, Bell thought, well hidden.

Farley Kent dashed up a gangway. Lighted portholes gleamed from the low cabin. Farley Kent pounded on the door. It opened, spilling light, and he disappeared inside and yanked it shut. Bell followed immediately. He put his hat on his head and crossed the pier with quick, firm strides. A deckhand on one of the trading vessels noticed. Bell gave him a grim stare and a dismissive nod, and the man looked away. Bell confirmed that the yacht's decks were still empty of sailors, stepped quietly across the gangway, and pressed his back to the bulkhead that formed the cabin.

Removing his hat again, he peered in a porthole cracked open for ventilation.

The cabin was small but luxurious. Brass ship lamps

cast a warm glow on mahogany paneling. In a swift glance, Bell took in a sideboard with crystal glasses and decanters secured in racks, a dining table set within a horseshoe banquette with green leather upholstery, and a voice pipe for communicating throughout the vessel. Hanging over the table was a Henry Reuterdahl oil painting of the Great White Fleet.

Kent was shrugging out of his coat. Watching him was a short, stocky, athletic-looking Navy officer with an erect posture, a puffed-out chest, and a captain's bars on his shoulder boards. Bell could not see his face, but he could hear Kent shout, 'Damned detective. He knew exactly what to ask.'

'What did you tell him?' the captain asked calmly.

'Nothing. I had him thrown out of the yard. Impertinent busybody.'

'Did it occur to you that his visit concerned Alasdair MacDonald?'

'I didn't know what the hell to think. He gave me a case of the rattles.'

The captain seized a bottle from the sideboard and poured a generous glass. As he thrust it at Kent, Bell finally saw his face – a youthful, vigorous face that ten years ago had been splashed reverently on every newspaper and magazine in the nation. His exploits in the Spanish-American War had rivaled those of Teddy Roosevelt's Rough Riders for coolheaded bravery.

'Well, I'll be . . .' said Bell, half aloud.

He shoved open the cabin door and strode inside.

Farley Kent jumped. The Navy captain did not, but merely regarded the tall detective with an expectant gaze.

'Welcome aboard, Mr. Bell. When I learned the terrible news from Camden, I hoped you'd find your way here.'

'What is Hull 44?'

'Better to ask *why* Hull 44,' answered Captain Lowell Falconer, the Hero of Santiago.

He offered a hand that had lost two fingers to shell splinters.

Bell closed it in his. 'It is an honor to make your acquaintance, sir.'

Captain Falconer spoke into the voice pipe. 'Cast off.'

13

Feet pounded on deck. A lieutenant appeared at the door, and Falconer engaged him in urgent conversation. 'Farley,' he called. 'You might as well get back to your loft.' The architect left without a word. Falconer said, 'Please wait here, Bell. I won't be a minute.' He stepped outside with his lieutenant.

Bell had seen the Reuterdahl painting of the Great White Fleet on the cover of *Collier's* magazine last January. The fleet lay anchored in the harbor of Rio de Janeiro. A native boat was rowing toward the bright white hull of the anchored flagship *Connecticut*, waving an advertisement that read:

American Drinks. SQUARE DEAL at JS Guvidor

Smoke and shadow in a dark corner of the sunny harbor scene obscured the sleek gray hull of a German cruiser.

The deck moved under Bell's feet. The yacht began backing out of her slip into the East River. When she engaged her propellers ahead and wheeled downstream, Bell felt no vibrations, nor even the faintest throbbing of the engines. Captain Falconer stepped back into the cabin, and Bell gave his host a curious glance. 'I've never been on such a smooth-running steam yacht.'

Falconer grinned proudly. 'Turbines,' he said. 'Three of them, linked to nine screw propellers.'

He pointed at another painting, one which Bell had not seen from the porthole. It depicted *Turbinia,* the famous experimental turbine-powered vessel Alasdair MacDonald's mentor had raced through an international gathering of naval fleets at Spitshead, England, to dramatize turbine speed.

'Charles Parsons left nothing to chance. In the event that something went wrong with *Turbinia,* he built *two* turbine racers. This one's named *Dyname.* Do you remember your Greek?'

'The result of forces acting together.'

'Very good! *Dyname* is actually *Turbinia*'s big sister, a trifle beamier, modeled after the torpedo boats of the nineties. I had her refitted as a yacht and converted her boilers to oil, which opened up a lot of space in the former coal bunkers. Poor Alasdair used her as a test craft and modified the turbines. Thanks to him, even though she's beamier than *Turbinia,* she burns less fuel and goes faster.'

'How fast?'

Falconer laid an affectionate hand on *Dyname*'s varnished mahogany and grinned. 'You would not believe me if I told you.'

The tall detective grinned back. 'I wouldn't mind a trick at the helm.'

'Wait 'til we're out of congested waters. I don't dare open her up in the harbor.'

The yacht steamed down the East River into the Upper Bay and increased her speed dramatically. 'Quite a clip,' said Bell.

Falconer chuckled, 'We rein her in until we reach the open sea.'

The lights of Manhattan Island faded astern. A steward appeared bearing covered dishes and spread them on the table. Captain Falconer bid Bell sit across from him.

Bell stood where he was, and asked, 'What is Hull 44?'

'Please join me for supper, and while we head to sea I will tell you the secret of *why* Hull 44.'

Falconer began by echoing Alasdair MacDonald's lament. 'It's ten years since Germany started building a modern Navy. The same year we captured the Philippine Islands and annexed the Kingdom of Hawaii. Today, the Germans have dreadnought battleships. The British have dreadnought battleships, and the Japanese are building, and buying, dreadnought battleships. So when the U.S. Navy embarks on distant service to defend America's new territories in the Pacific, we will be outclassed and out-gunned by the Germans and the British and the Empire of Japan.'

Brimming with such zeal that he left his beefsteak untouched, Captain Falconer regaled Isaac Bell with the dream behind Hull 44. 'The dreadnaught race teaches that change is always preceded by a universal conviction that there is nothing new under the sun. Before the British launched HMS *Dreadnaught,* two facts about battleships were engraved in stone. They took many years to build and they had to be armed with a great variety of guns to defend themselves. HMS *Dreadnaught* is an all-big-guns ship, and they built her in a single year, which changed the world forever.

'Hull 44 is my response. America's response. I recruited

the best brains in the fighting-ship business. I told them to do their damnedest! Men like Artie Langner, the "Gunner," and Alasdair, whom you met.'

'And saw die,' Bell interrupted grimly.

'Artists, every one of them. But like all artists, they're misfits. Bohemians, eccentrics, if not plain loony. Not the sort that get along in the regular Navy. But thanks to my misfit geniuses hatching new ideas and refining old ones, Hull 44 will be a dreadnought battleship like none that sail the seas – an American engineering marvel that will overwhelm the British *Dreadnought* and the German *Nassau* and *Posen,* and the worst Japan can throw at her – Why are you shaking your head, Mr. Bell?'

'That's too big a deal to keep secret. You're obviously a wealthy man, but no individual is rich enough to launch his own dreadnought. Where do you get your funds for Hull 44? Surely someone high up must know.'

Captain Falconer answered obliquely. 'Eleven years ago I had the privilege of advising an Assistant Secretary of the Navy.'

'Bully!' Bell smiled his understanding. That explained Lowell Falconer's independence. Today, that Assistant Secretary of the Navy was none other than the nation's fiercest champion of a strong Navy – President Theodore Roosevelt.

'The President believes that our Navy should be footloose. Let the Army defend ports and harbors – we'll even build them the guns. But the Navy must fight at sea.'

'From what I've seen of the Navy,' said Bell, 'first you will have to fight the Navy. And to win that fight you would have to be as clever as Machiavelli.'

'Oh, but I am,' Falconer smiled. 'Though I prefer the word "devious" to clever.'

'Are you still a serving officer?'

'I am, officially, Special Inspector of Target Practice.'

'A wonderfully vague title,' Bell remarked.

'I know how to outfox bureaucrats,' Falconer shot back. 'I know my way around Congress,' he continued with a cynical smile and raised his maimed hand for Bell to see. 'What politician dares deny a war hero?'

Then he explained in detail how he had planted a cadre of like-minded younger officers in the key bureaus of Ordnance and Construction. Together, they were angling to overhaul the entire dreadnought-building system.

'Are we as far behind as Alasdair MacDonald claimed?'

'Yes. We launch *Michigan* next month, but she's no prize. *Delaware, North Dakota, Utah, Florida, Arkansas,* and *Wyoming,* first-class dreadnoughts, are stuck on the drawing boards. But that's not entirely a bad thing. Advancements in naval warfare pile up so quickly that the later we launch our battleships, the more modern they will be. We've already learned the shortcomings of the Great White Fleet, long before it reaches San Francisco. First thing we'll fix when they sail home is to paint them gray so enemy gunners can't spot them so easily.

'Paint will be the easy part. Before we can turn our new knowledge into fighting ships, we have to convince the Navy Board of Construction and Congress. The Navy Board of Construction hates change, and Congress hates expense.'

Falconer nodded at the Reuterdahl. 'My friend Henry's got his tail in a crack. The Navy invited him along to paint pictures of the Great White Fleet. They did not expect him to also fire off articles to *McClure's Magazine* informing the world of its shortcomings. Henry will be lucky to find his way home on a tramp steamer. But Henry's right, and I'm right: It's O.K. to learn by experience. O.K. to learn by failure, even. But it is *not* O.K. not to improve. *That is why I build in secret.*'

'You've told me why. You've not told me what.'

'Don't be impatient, Mr. Bell.'

'A man was murdered,' Isaac Bell replied grimly. 'I am not patient when men are murdered.'

'You just said *men*.' Captain Falconer stopped bantering and demanded, 'Are you suggesting that Langner was murdered, too?'

'I rate his murder increasingly likely.'

'What about Grover Lakewood?'

'Van Dorn operatives in Westchester are looking into his death. And in Bethlehem, Pennsylvania, we are investigating the accident that killed Chad Gordon. Now, are you going to tell me about Hull 44?'

'Let's get topside. You'll see what I mean.'

Dyname had continued to increase her speed. There was still no trembling from the engines, despite a powerful drone of rushing sea and wind. The steward and a sailor appeared with seaboots and oilskins. 'You'll want these on, sir. She's no yacht, once she gets moving. More like a torpedo boat.'

'Torpedo boat, hell,' muttered the sailor. 'She's a submarine.'

Falconer handed Bell a pair of goggles with smoked

glass so dark it seemed opaque and looped another pair over his own head.

'What's this for?'

'You'll be glad you have them when you need them,' the captain answered enigmatically. 'All set? Let's get up to the bridge while we can.' The seaman and steward wrestled the door open, and they stepped on deck.

The slipstream hit like a punch in the face.

Bell pushed forward on the narrow side deck less than five feet above the rushing water. 'She must be doing thirty knots.'

'Still loafing along,' Falconer yelled over the roar. 'We'll get moving once we pass Sandy Hook.'

Bell glanced back. Fire was flickering from the smoke funnel, and the wake was so frothed that it glowed in the dark. They climbed onto the open bridge, where thick slabs of glass screened the helmsman, who was clinging to a small spoked wheel. Captain Falconer shouldered him aside.

Ahead in the dark, an intermittent white light blinked every fifteen seconds.

'Sandy Hook Lightship,' said Captain Falconer. 'Last year we'll see it. They're moving the light to mark the new Ambrose Channel.'

Dyname bore down on the fifteen-second blinker. In its back glow, Bell glimpsed the white-lettered 'Sandy Hook' and 'No. 51' on the side of the black vessel as it fell rapidly behind them.

'Hang on!' said Captain Falconer.

He laid the hand with the missing fingers on a tall lever.

'Bowden cable connection direct to the turbines. Same as flexible-cable brakes for bicycles. I can increase steam from the helm without ringing the engine room. Like the throttle on your auto.'

'Alasdair's idea?' asked Bell.

'No, this is mine. You're about to feel Alasdair's.'

14

Bell gripped a handhold as *Dyname*'s bow lifted from the water. The drone of sea and wind grew explosive. Spray battered the glass screen. Captain Falconer switched on a searchlight mounted in front, and the reason for her knife-shaped narrowness was immediately apparent. The light revealed eight-foot seas sweeping under them at fifty knots. A hull of any other shape would have smashed against the water so hard it would wreck itself.

'Did you ever drive anything this fast?' Falconer shouted.

'Only my Locomobile.'

'Care to try her?' Falconer asked casually.

Isaac Bell grabbed the helm.

'Steer around the bigger seas,' Falconer recommended. 'If you bury the bow, those nine propellers will drive us straight to the bottom.'

The helm was remarkably responsive, Bell thought, capable of whisking the hundred-foot yacht left and right with a twitch of the spokes. He dodged big seas repeatedly, getting a feel for how she handled. In half an hour they were more than twenty-five miles from land.

Bell saw a flicker of light in the distance. A deep rumbling noise began rolling in the night.

'Are those guns?'

'Twelves,' said Falconer. 'See the flash?'

Orange-and-red flames lanced the dark ahead.

'Those higher-pitched sounds are 6s and 8s. We're inside the Sandy Hook Atlantic Test Range.'

'Inside? While they're shooting?'

'While the cat's away the mice will play. The senior captains are circumnavigating the world with the Fleet. My boys are right there, learning their trade.'

Powerful beams of light bristled into the sky.

'Searchlight exercise,' said Falconer. 'Battleships hunting destroyers, destroyers hunting battleships.'

Sweeping sky and water, the searchlights suddenly converged on a battleship, previously invisible in the dark, and lit bright as noon a low-slung white hull hurling spray.

'Look! That's just what I've been telling you about. That's *New Hampshire*. She wasn't yet commissioned when the Fleet sailed. Just finished her shakedown. Watch what happens to her foredeck.'

The searchlights showed seas breaking over the battleship's bow and deluging her forward guns.

'Decks awash in light seas! Guns underwater! Told you paint will be the easy part. We need higher freeboard and flared bows. Our newest capital ship has a *ram* bow, for God's sake, like we're going to war with Phoenicians!'

Bell saw a wave strike her anchor billboard and scatter in blinding clouds.

'Now, watch her on the roll. See that armor belt rising? ... Now, watch it disappear as she rolls back and submerges it. If we don't extend our armor to protect the ships' undersides when they roll, the enemy will draft small boys to sink them with peashooters.'

A searchlight swung their way, probing the dark like an angry white finger.

'*Goggles!*'

Bell covered his eyes with the black goggles just in time. An instant later the light that caught *Dyname* would have blinded him. Through the blackened glass he could see clear as day.

'Searchlights are as powerful as big guns,' Falconer shouted. 'They'll completely disorient every man on the bridge and blind the spotters.'

'Why are they aiming at us?'

'It's a game we play. They try to catch me. Good practice. Though once they get your range it's impossible to shake them loose.'

'Oh, really? Hang on, Captain!'

Bell yanked back on the throttle. *Dyname* stopped as if she had hit a wall. The searchlight beam soared ahead in the direction they had been steaming. Bell spun the helm with both hands. The light was coming back for him. He nudged the throttle lever as he steered the yacht at a right angle, waited for the propellers to bite, then rammed it forward.

Fire belched from the stack. *Dyname* took off like an Independence Day rocket, and the searchlight beam skittered away in the wrong direction.

'O.K., Captain. You've told me why and you've shown me why. But you still haven't shown me *what*.'

'I'll lay a course for the Brooklyn Navy Yard.'

A new day was lighting the tops of the Brooklyn Bridge towers as *Dyname* sliced into the East River. Bell was still at the helm, and he steered under the bridge and bore right, toward the navy yard. From the water he could see numerous ships under construction on the ways and in the dry docks. Falconer pointed to the northernmost way, which was isolated from the others. He called down the voice pipe to the engine room to disengage the propellers. The tide was slack. *Dyname* drifted on her momentum to the foot of the way, where its rails angled into the water. Above her soared a gigantic skeletal frame partially sheathed in steel plate.

'Hull 44, Mr. Bell.'

Isaac Bell drank in the noble sight. Even with her frames awaiting more armor, there was a majesty to her flaring bow, an eagerness to join the water, and a promise of power as yet unleashed.

'Keep in mind she doesn't even officially exist yet.'

'How can you hide a six-hundred-foot ship?'

'It resembles a hull that Congress authorized,' Captain Falconer answered with an almost imperceptible wink. 'But, in fact, from her keel to the top of her cage mast she will be chockful of brand-new ideas. She will have all the latest in turbines, guns, torpedo protection, fire control. But most important, she is uniquely designed to continue improving by swapping new innovations for old. Hull 44 is far more than one ship. She's the model for entire classes to be built, and the inspiration for ever-more-innovative, ever-more-powerful *super*-dreadnoughts.'

Falconer paused dramatically. Then he intoned in a hard, grim voice, 'And that is why Hull 44 is targeted by foreign spies.'

Isaac Bell raked Captain Falconer with a cold eye.

'Are you surprised?' he asked curtly.

Isaac Bell had had it with Falconer's attempts to lead him in circles. As inspiring a sight as the great ship was, and as much as he had relished driving a fifty-knot race yacht he would have better spent the night combing Hell's Kitchen for the man who murdered Alasdair MacDonald.

Falconer backed off when he heard Bell's cold retort.

'Of course everyone spies,' the captain admitted. 'Every nation with a naval shipyard or a treasury to buy a warship spies. How far ahead are their friends and enemies in guns, armor, and propulsion? What new next invention will make our dreadnought vulnerable? Whose gun is longer range? Whose torpedo goes farther? Whose engines are faster, whose armor stronger?'

'Vital questions,' Bell concurred. 'And it is normal — even for nations at peace — to seek the answers.'

'But it is *not* normal,' Falconer shot back, 'and certainly not right for nations at peace to commit sabotage.'

'Hold your horses! *Sabotage?* There's no evidence of sabotage in these murders — no destruction, with the possible exception of the foundry accident in Bethlehem.'

'Oh, there is destruction, all right. Terrible destruction. I said sabotage and I meant sabotage.'

'Why would a spy kill when killing is sure to draw attention to his spying?'

'They fooled me, too,' said Captain Falconer. 'I feared that Artie Langner had accepted bribes and killed himself out of guilt. Then I thought, What awful luck that poor young Grover Lakewood fell on his head. But when they killed Alasdair MacDonald, I knew it had to be sabotage. And didn't he, too? Didn't he whisper, "Hull 44"?'

'As I told you,' Bell admitted.

'Don't you see, Bell? They're sabotaging Hull 44 by murdering *minds*. They're attacking the minds that imagine the vital guts of that warship – guns, armor, propulsion. Look past the steel and armor plate. Hull 44 is no more than the minds of the men still working on it and the minds of those who died. When saboteurs kill our minds, they kill unborn thoughts and new ideas. When they kill our minds, they sabotage our ships.'

'I understand,' Bell nodded thoughtfully. 'They sabotage our ships not yet launched.'

'Or even dreamed of!'

'Which enemy do you suspect?'

'The Empire of Japan.'

Bell recalled immediately that old John Eddison had claimed to have seen a Japanese intruder in the Washington Navy Yard. But he asked, 'Why the Japanese?'

'I know the Japs,' Falconer answered. 'I know them well. I served as an official observer aboard Admiral Togo's flagship *Mikasa* when he destroyed the Russian Fleet at the battle of Tsushima – the most decisive naval battle since Nelson beat the French at Trafalgar. His ships were tip-top, his crews trained like machines. I *like* the Japs, and I certainly admire them. But they are ambitious. Mark my words, we will fight them for the Pacific.'

Bell said, 'The murderers who attacked Alasdair Mac-Donald were armed with Butterflymessers manufactured by Bontgen and Sabin of Solingen, Germany. Isn't Germany a leading contender in the dreadnaught race?'

'Germany is haunted by the British Navy. They'll fight tooth and claw for the North Sea, and Britain will never let them near the Atlantic. The Pacific is our ocean. The

Japanese want it, too. They are designing ships for distant service across the wide Pacific, just as we are. The day will come when we'll fight them from California to Tokyo. For all we know, the Japs will attack this summer when the Great White Fleet approaches their islands.'

'I've seen the headlines,' Bell said with a wry smile. 'In the same newspapers that inflamed the war with Spain.'

'Spain was a cakewalk!' Falconer retorted. 'A stumbling relic of the Old World. The Japs are new – like us. They've already laid down *Satsuma,* the biggest dreadnought in the world. They're building their own Brown-Curtis turbines. They're buying the latest Holland submarines from Electric Boat.'

'Nonetheless, early in an investigation it pays to keep an open mind. The saboteurs could serve any nation in the dreadnought race.'

'Investigation is not my department, Mr. Bell. All I know is that Hull 44 needs a man with gumption to protect her.'

'Surely the Navy is investigating –'

Falconer interrupted with a sarcastic snort. 'The Navy is still investigating reports that the battleship *Maine* sank in Havana Harbor in 1898.'

'Then the Secret Service –'

'The Secret Service has its hands full protecting the currency and President Roosevelt from fiends like the one who shot McKinley. And the Justice Department will take years to launch any sort of national bureau of investigation. Our ship cannot wait! Dammit, Bell, Hull 44 demands an outfit that's got steam up and is itching to cast off.'

By now Bell knew that the Special Inspector of Target

Practice was manipulative, if not underhanded, and devious by his own admission. But he was a true believer. 'As an evangelist,' Bell told him, 'the Hero of Santiago would give Billy Sunday a run for his money.'

'Guilty,' Falconer admitted with a practiced smile. 'Do you suppose Joe Van Dorn would allow you to take the job?'

Isaac Bell fixed his gaze on the bones of Hull 44 rising on the ways. As he did, a yard whistle started the workday with a deep-throated bellow. Steam cranes chanted full-throttle. Hundreds, then thousands, of men swarmed onto the a-building ship. Within minutes, red-hot rivets were soaring like fireflies between 'passer boys' and 'holders-on,' and soon she echoed the din of hammers. These sights and sounds thrust Bell's memory back to Alasdair MacDonald mourning his dead friend, Chad Gordon. *'Horrible. Six lads roasted alive — Chad and all the hands working beside him.'*

As if a shooting star had swept the last strands of darkness from the morning sky, Isaac Bell saw the mighty dreadnought for what she could be – a lofty vision of living men and a monument to the innocent dead.

'I would be amazed if Joe Van Dorn didn't order me to take the job. And if he doesn't, I'll do it myself.'

Armoured Coffins

15

April 21, 1908 New York City

The spy summoned the German Hans to New York, to a cellar under a *Biergarten* restaurant at Second Avenue and 50th Street. Barrels of Rhine wine were half submerged in a cold underground stream that flowed through the cellar. The stone walls echoed the musical sound of tumbling water. They sat face-to-face over a round wooden table illuminated by a single lightbulb.

'We plot the future beside a buried remnant of pastoral Manhattan,' the spy remarked, gauging Hans's response.

The German, who appeared to have put a dent in the Rhine wine supply, seemed moodier than ever. The question was, had Hans's brain become too congested by wine and remorse to make him useful?

'Mein Freund!' The spy fixed Hans with a commanding gaze. 'Will you continue to serve the Fatherland?'

The German straightened visibly. 'Of course!'

The spy concealed a relieved smile. Listen closely, and you could still hear Hans's heels click like a marionette's. 'I believe your many experiences include working in a shipyard?'

'Neptun Schiffswerft und Maschinenfabrik,' Hans answered proudly, obviously flattered that the spy remembered. 'In Rostock. A most modern yard.'

'The Americans' "most modern yard" is in Camden, New Jersey. I think that you should go to Camden. I think you should establish yourself quickly in the city. You can draw on me for whatever you need, be it operating funds, explosives, false identification, forged shipyard passes.'

'To what end, *mein Herr*?'

'To send a message to the United States Congress. To make them wonder whether their Navy is incompetent.'

'I don't understand.'

'The Americans are about to launch their first all-big-guns battleship.'

'*Michigan*. Yes, I read in the papers.'

'With your experience, you know that the successful launch of a 16,000-ton hull from land into water demands balancing three powerful forces: gravity, drag on the slip-way, and the upthrust of the stern's buoyancy. Correct?'

'Yes, *mein Herr*.'

'For a few fraught seconds as the launch begins – when the final keel and bilge blocks are removed and the tumbler shores fall away – the hull is supported by nothing but the cradle.'

'This is correct.'

'I ask you, could strategically placed sticks of dynamite, exquisitely timed to detonate the instant she starts to slide down the ways, derail her cradle and tumble *Michigan* onto dry land instead of the river?'

Hans's eyes lighted with the possibility.

The spy let the German fix his imagination upon the avalanchine crash of a 16,000-ton steel vessel falling on its side. Then he said, 'The sight of a five-hundred-foot-long dreadnought hull sprawled on the ground would make a laughingstock of the United States' "New Navy." And surely destroy the Navy's reputation with a Congress already reluctant to appropriate the money to build more ships.'

'Yes, *mein Herr.*'

'Make it so.'

Commodore Tommy Thompson was listening, calculatingly, to Brian 'Eyes' O'Shay's scheme to send his Hip Sing partners to San Francisco, when a boy ran into his 39th Street saloon with a note from Iceman Weeks.

The Commodore read it. 'He's offering to kill the Van Dorn.'

'Happen to say how?'

'Probably still thinking it through,' Tommy laughed, and passed the note to Eyes.

In a strange way, he thought, they had picked up their old partnership. Not that Eyes dropped in regular. This was only his third visit since the five thousand dollars. Nor did Eyes want in on the take, which was a big surprise. Just the opposite. Eyes had lent him money to open a new gambling joint under the El Connector on 53rd, which was raking in dough already. Add that to his deal with the Hip Sing, and he was sitting pretty. Besides, when he and Eyes talked, Tommy found he trusted him. Not with his life, Jaysus knew. Not even with his dough. But he trusted Eyes' good sense, just like when they were kids.

'What do you think?' he asked. 'Should we take him up on it?'

O'Shay smoothed the tip of his narrow mustache. He hooked his thumb in his vest pocket. Then he sat still as stone, legs stretched out, heels in the sawdust, and when he finally spoke he stared at his feet as if addressing his fine boots. 'Weeks is tired of lying low. He wants to come home from wherever he's hiding, which is probably Brooklyn. But he's afraid you'll kill him.'

'He's afraid I will kill him on your say-so,' Tommy corrected acidly. 'And you will say so.'

'I already have,' Eyes O'Shay answered. 'Your so-called Iceman –'

'*My* so-called Iceman!' Commodore Tommy erupted in tones of wrathful indignation.

'*Your* so-called Iceman, who *you* sent to Camden when I paid you five thousand dollars, allowed the only credible witness in that dance hall – a Van Dorn Agency detective, for the love of Mary – to witness him committing murder. When the Van Dorns catch up with him – and we know they will – or the cops nail him for some other transgression, the Van Dorns will ask, "Who'd you do murder for?" And Weeks will answer, "Tommy Thompson and his old pal Eyes O'Shay, who we thought was dead but ain't."'

O'Shay looked up from his boots, expression noncommittal, and added, 'Frankly, if I didn't insist, you'd be screwy not to kill him on your own. You've got more to fear than I do. I can disappear, just like I done before. You're stuck here. Everyone knows where to find the Commodore – on 39th in Commodore Tommy's Saloon – and pretty soon the word will get around on your new joint on 53rd. Don't forget, Van Dorns aren't like cops. You can't pay Van Dorns to look any other way than at you. Down a gun barrel.'

'So what do you think about Weeks offering to kill the witness?'

Eyes O'Shay pretended to ponder the question.

'I think Weeks is brave. Sensible. Practical. Maybe he has something up his sleeve. If not, then he's firmly possessed by delusions of grandeur.'

The Gopher Gang boss blinked. 'What does that mean?'

'"Delusions of grandeur"? It means Weeks will have to get damned lucky to pull it off. But if he does kill the Van Dorn, your troubles are over.'

'The Iceman is tough,' Tommy said hopefully. 'And he's smart.'

O'Shay shrugged. 'With a little luck, who knows?'

'With a little luck, the Van Dorn will kill him, and that'll be it for witnesses.'

'Either way, how can you lose? Tell him to give it a whirl.'

Thompson scrawled a cryptic reply on the back of Weeks's note and shouted for the kid. 'Get in here, you little bastard! Take this to wherever that scumbucket is hiding.'

Brian O'Shay marveled at the sheer depths of Tommy's stupidity. If Weeks did manage to kill the Van Dorn – who was not just any Van Dorn but the famously deadly Chief Investigator Isaac Bell – Iceman Weeks would be the Hero of Hell's Kitchen, which would make him a prime candidate to take over the Gophers. How surprised Tommy would be by Weeks's shiv in his ribs.

Tommy's brand of stupidity reminded O'Shay of the Russian Navy in the Russo-Jap war. Clueless as the Baltic Fleet, when old-fashioned warships and ancient thinking bumped into the modern Japanese Navy. Ahoy, bottom of the Tsushima Strait, here we come!

'Now, could we get back to the business at hand, Tommy – the journey of your Chinamen to San Francisco?'

'They're not exactly *my* Chinamen. They're Hip Sing.'

'Find out how much money they will require to make them *your* Chinamen.'

'What makes you think they want to go to San Francisco?' Tommy asked. The Gopher Gang boss could not figure out what O'Shay was up to.

'They're Chinamen,' O'Shay answered. 'They'll do anything for money.'

'You mind me asking how much you can afford?'

'I can afford anything. But if you ever ask me for more than something is worth, I will regard it as an act of war.'

Commodore Tommy changed the subject. 'I wonder what the Iceman has up his sleeve.'

DEADLY SNAKE HERE;
SERUM USEFUL IN INSANITY
POISON FROM THE LANCE-HEAD'S BITE WILL KILL
AN OX WITHIN FIVE MINUTES
Lachesis Muta Called 'the Sudden Death'
by the Natives of Brazil

The wind plucked the sheet of newspaper out of the Washington Park grandstand just as Brooklyn came to bat in the eighth inning. Iceman Weeks watched it float across the infield, past Wiltse on the mound, past Seymour in center, straight toward where he was holed up – cuffless and collarless in drab flannel, disguised as a sorry-looking plumber's helper – on the grass behind centerfield, where he wasn't likely to run into any fans from New York.

If the Iceman were capable of loving anything, it was baseball. But he couldn't risk being spotted in New York at tomorrow's home opener at the Polo Grounds, so he was making do in the wilds of Brooklyn where no one knew him. His favorite Giants were lambasting the sorry Superbas. The Giants were hitting hard, and the cold wind blowing cinders, hats, and newspapers had no effect on Hooks Wiltse's throwing arm. His left-handed twisters had dazzled the Brooklyn batters throughout the game, and by the bottom of the eighth New York was ahead 4 to 1.

Weeks's ice-blue eyes locked on the juicy headline as the newspaper blew overhead.

Poison from the Lance-head's Bite Will Kill an Ox Within Five Minutes

He leaped off the grass and caught the paper in both hands.

Ball game forgotten, he read avidly, tracing each word with a dirty fingernail. The fact that Weeks could read at all put him miles ahead of most of the Gopher Gang. New York's daily newspapers were packed with opportunities. The society pages reported when rich men left town for Newport or Europe, leaving their mansions empty. The shipping news gave notice about cargo to be plundered from the docks and Eleventh Avenue sidings. Theater reviews were a guide to pickpockets, obituaries a promise of empty apartments.

He read every word of the snake story, galvanized by hope, then started over. His luck had turned. The snake would recoup his losses from the worst hand ever dealt: Van Dorn detective Isaac Bell turning up in Camden the night they killed the Scotsman.

133

A lance-headed viper from Brazil, the most deadly of all known reptiles, will be exhibited tomorrow tonight before the Academy of Pathological Science at its monthly meeting at the Hotel Cumberland in 54th Street and Broadway.

The paper said that the sawbones were interested in the snake because a serum made from the lance-head's deadly venom was used to treat nervous and brain diseases.

The Iceman knew the Cumberland.

It was a twelve-story, first-class hotel billed in the ads as 'Headquarters for College Men.' That and the $2.50-a-night room fee ought to keep out the riffraff. But Weeks was pretty sure he could dress like a college man, thanks to his second advantage over ordinary gangsters. He was half real American. Unlike the full-blooded Micks in the Gophers, only his mother was Irish. The time he had met his father, the Old Man had told him that the Weekses were Englishmen who had landed here before the *Mayflower*. Wearing the right duds, why couldn't he march into the lobby of the Hotel Cumberland like he belonged?

He figured that the Cumberland house dicks could be got around by twisting the arm of a bellboy to run interference for him. Weeks had one in mind, Jimmy Clark, who had a sideline distributing cocaine for a pharmacist on 49th, which had become a riskier business since the new law said that dust had to be prescribed by a doctor.

A human lives only one or two minutes after the poison enters the system. The viper's venom seems to paralyze the action of the heart, and the victim stiffens and turns black.

He already had a setup. It wasn't like he'd been hiding out doing nothing. Soon as he had learned where Isaac Bell slept when he was in town, he had finagled a laundress he knew into a job at the Yale Club of New York City, betting she could sneak him into the detective's room.

Jenny Sullivan was fresh off the boat from Ireland and deep in hock for her fare. Weeks had bought her debt, intending to put her to work on the sheets instead of ironing them. But after Camden, he had persuaded people who had reason to do him a big favor to wangle Jenny a job at Bell's club. That was when he wrote Commodore Tommy, offering to kill the detective. But he hadn't yet managed to screw up the courage to hide under Bell's bed with a pistol and tangle with him man-to-man.

Weeks was tough enough to have gouged Bell's .380 slug out of his own shoulder with a boning knife rather than let some drunken doctor or midwife tip off Tommy Thompson as to his whereabouts. Tough enough to pour grain alcohol into the wound to stop infection. But he had already seen Bell in action. Bell was tougher – bigger, faster, and better armed – and only a mug got in a fight he could not win.

Better to match Bell with 'the Sudden Death.'

The paper said that the curator of the Bronx Zoo reptile house would deliver the animal in a box made of thick glass.

'"He can't get out,"' the curator promised the Pathology Society doctors who were invited to view the reptile.

Weeks reckoned that with a bullet hole in his shoulder, a box made of thick glass big enough to hold a four-foot-long poisonous snake would be too heavy for him to carry alone. And if he dropped it trying to carry it under one arm and the glass broke, look out! A bum shoulder would be the least of his problems. He needed help. But the boys he could trust to lend a hand were both dead – shot by the blazing-fast Van Dorn dick.

If he tried to recruit anyone to carry the glass box, the word would flash to Tommy Thompson that Iceman Weeks was back in town. Might as well tie his own hands behind his back and jump in the river. Save Tommy the trouble. Because you didn't have to be a brain to figure out that Eyes O'Shay would order the Commodore to kill the man who'd been spotted by a Van Dorn dick while doing the killing Eyes had paid for. Weeks could swear until he was blue in the face that he would never squeal. O'Shay and Tommy would kill him anyway. Just to be on the safe side.

At least Tommy had written back that he approved of him killing Isaac Bell. Of course he didn't offer to help. And it went without saying that if Tommy and Eyes saw a chance to kill him first, they wouldn't wait for him to take a crack at Bell.

Wiltse bunted in the ninth and Bridwell doubled. When the inning ended New York had two more runs, Brooklyn did not, and Weeks was leading the rush for the Fifth Avenue Elevated with a fair notion of how to transport the snake to the Yale Club.

He needed a suit of 'college man' clothes, a steamer trunk, a pane of glass, a bellboy with a luggage cart, and directions to the fuse box.

16

'Who is that officer?' Isaac Bell demanded of the Protection Services operative assigned to guard Farley Kent's drawing loft in the Brooklyn Navy Yard.

'I don't know, Mr. Bell.'

'How did he get in here?'

'He knew the password.'

Van Dorn Protection Services had issued passwords for each of the Hull 44 dreadnought men it was guarding. After getting past the Marines guarding the gates, a visitor still had to prove he was expected by the individual he claimed to be visiting.

'Where is Mr. Kent?'

'They're all in the test chamber working on that cage-mast model,' the Protection Services operative answered, pointing across the drawing loft at a closed door that led to the laboratory. 'Is there something wrong, Mr. Bell?'

'Three things,' Bell answered tersely. 'Farley Kent is not here, so he does not seem to have expected that officer to visit. The officer has been studying Kent's drawing board since I walked in. And in case you haven't noticed, he is wearing the uniform of the Czar's Navy.'

'Them blue uniforms look all the same,' the operative replied, reminding Bell that few PS boys possessed the brains and moxie to climb the ladder to full-fledged Van Dorn detective. 'Besides, he's carrying them rolled-up drawings like they all do. You want I should question him, Mr. Bell?'

'I'll do it. Next time someone walks in unexpected, assume he's trouble until you learn otherwise.'

Bell strode across the big loft past rows of drawing boards that were usually occupied by the naval architects testing the cage mast. The man in the Russian officer's uniform was so engrossed in Farley Kent's drawing that he gave a startled jump and dropped the rolls he had tucked under his arm when Bell said, 'Good morning, sir.'

'Oh! I do not hear approach,' he said in a heavy Russian accent, scrambling to pick them up.

'May I have your name, please?'

'I am Second Lieutenant Vladimir Ivanovich Yourkevitch of His Majesty Czar Nicolas's Imperial Russian Navy. And to whom do I have the honor –'

'Have you an appointment here, Lieutenant Yourkevitch?'

The Russian, who looked barely old enough to shave, bowed his head. 'Sadly, no. I am hoping to meet with Mr. Farley Kent.'

'Does Mr. Kent know you?'

'Not yet, sir.'

'Then how did you get in here?'

Yourkevitch smiled, disarmingly. 'With entitled demeanor, impeccable uniform, and crisp salute.'

Isaac Bell did not smile back. 'That might get you past the Marines guarding the gate. But where did you get the password to go to Kent's drawing loft?'

'In bar outside gates, I meet Marine officer. He tells me password.'

Bell beckoned the Protection Services operative.

'Lieutenant Yourkevitch will sit on that stool, away from this drawing board, until I return.' To Lieutenant Yourkevitch he said, 'This gentleman is fully capable of knocking you to the floor. Do as he tells you.'

Then Bell crossed the loft and pushed open the door to the test chamber.

A dozen of Kent's staff were circled around a ten-foot-tall model of an experimental battleship cage mast. The young naval architects held wire snips, micrometers, slide rules, notepaper, and tape measures. The round, free-standing structure, which stood on a dolly, was made of stiff wires that spiraled from base to top in a counterclockwise twist and were braced at intervals by horizontal rings. It represented, in miniature, a one-hundred-twenty-foot-high mast made of lightweight tubing and was correct in every detail down to the mesh platforms within some of the rings, electric leads and voice pipes running from the spotters' top to the fire director's tower, and tiny ladders angling up the interior.

Two of Kent's architects held ropes attached to opposite sides of the round base. A tape measure strung between the walls passed next to the top. An architect on a stepladder watched the tape closely. Farley Kent said, 'Portside salvo. Fire!'

The architect on the left side jerked his rope, and the man watching the tape called out how much the tower had swayed. 'Six inches!' was recorded.

'At twelve-to-one, that's six feet!' said Kent. 'The spotters on top better hold on tight when the ship fires her main turrets. On the other hand, a tripod mast will weigh one hundred tons, while our cage of redundant members will weight less than twenty – a huge savings. O.K., let's measure how she sways after being hit by several shells.' Wielding a wire snips, he severed at random two of the spiraled uprights and one of the rings.

'Ready!'

'Wait!' An architect sprang up the ladder and propped a sailor doll with red cheeks and a straw hat in the spotting top.

The test chamber rang with laughter, Kent's the loudest of all.

'Starboard salvo. Fire!'

The rope was jerked, the top of the mast swayed sharply, and the doll flew across the room.

Bell caught it. 'Mr. Kent, may I see you a moment?'

'What's the matter?' asked Kent as he snipped another vertical wire and his assistants watched carefully to see the effect on the mast.

'We may have caught our first spy,' Bell said in a low voice. 'Could you come with me, please?'

Lieutenant Yourkevitch jumped from the stool before the Van Dorn Protection Services operative could stop him and grabbed Kent's hand. 'Is honor to meet, is great honor.'

'Who are you?'

'Yourkevitch. From St. Petersburg.'

'Naval Staff Headquarters?'

'Of course, sir. Baltic Shipyard.'

Kent asked, 'Is it true that Russia is building five battle-ships bigger than HMS *Dreadnought*?'

Yourkevitch shrugged. 'There is hope for super-dreadnoughts, but Duma perhaps say no. Too expensive.'

'What are you doing here?'

'The idea is that I meet legend Farley Kent.'

'You came all the way here just to meet me?'

'To show. See?' Yourkevitch unrolled his plans and spread them over Kent's table. 'What do you think? Improvement of form for body of ship?'

While Farley Kent studied Yourkevitch's drawings, Bell took the Russian officer aside, and said, 'Describe the Marine officer who gave you the password.'

'Was medium-sized man in dark suit. Old like you, maybe thirty. Very neat, very trim. Mustache like pencil. Very . . . what is word – precise!'

'Dark suit. No uniform?'

'In mufti.'

'Then how did you know he was a Marine officer?'

'He told me.'

Isaac Bell's stern expression grew dark. He spoke coldly. 'When and where are you supposed to report back to him?'

'I don't understand.'

'You must have agreed to report to him what you saw here.'

'No. I do not know him. How would I find him?'

'Lieutenant Yourkevitch, I am having difficulty believing your story. And I don't suppose it will do your career in the Czar's Navy any good if I turn you over to the United States Navy as a spy.'

'A spy?' Yourkevitch blurted. 'No.'

'Stop playing games with me and tell me how you learned the password.'

'Spy?' repeated the Russian. 'I am not spy.'

Before Bell could reply, Farley Kent spoke up. 'He doesn't need to spy on us.'

'What do you mean?'

'I mean that we should spy on him.'

'What are you talking about, Mr. Kent?'

'Lieutenant Yourkevitch's "improvement of form for body of ship" is a hell of a lot better than it looks.' He gestured at various elements of the finely wrought drawing. 'At first glance it appears bulky amidships, fat even, and weirdly skinny fore and aft. You could say it resembles a cow. In fact, it is brilliant. It will allow a dreadnought to toughen its torpedo defense around machinery and magazines, and increase armament and coal capacity even as it attains greater speed for less fuel.'

He shook Yourkevitch's hand. 'Brilliant, sir. I would steal it, but I would never get it approved by the dinosaurs on the Board of Construction. It is twenty years ahead of its time.'

'Thank you, sir, thank you. From Farley Kent, it is great honor.'

'And I'll tell you something else,' said Kent, 'though I suspect you've already thought of it yourself. Your hull would make a magnificent passenger liner – a North Atlantic greyhound that will run rings around *Lusitania* and *Mauritania*.'

'One day,' Yourkevitch smiled. 'When there is no war.'

Kent invited Yourkevitch to have lunch with his staff, and the two fell into a discussion of the just-announced building of the White Star liners *Olympic* and *Titanic*.

'Eight hundred forty feet!' Kent marveled, to which the Russian replied, 'I am thinking idea for one thousand.'

Bell believed that the earnest Russian naval architect had wanted nothing more than the chance to commune with the famous Farley Kent. He did not believe that the self-proclaimed officer who approached Yourkevitch in a Sand Street bar was a Marine.

Why did he give the Russian the password without demanding he report on Kent's drawings? How had he even known to approach the Russian? The answer was chilling. The spy – the 'saboteur of minds,' as Falconer called him – knew whom to target in the dreadnought race.

'This foreign-spy stuff is new to us,' said Joseph Van Dorn. The boss was puffing agitatedly on a quick after-lunch cigar in the main lounge of the Railroad Club on the twenty-second floor of the Hudson Tunnels Terminal before catching a train to Washington.

'We hunt murderers,' Isaac Bell retorted, his tone grim. 'Whatever their motive, they are first and foremost criminals.'

'Still, we'll be making decisions on horseback.'

Bell said, 'I had the research boys draw up a list of foreign diplomats, military attachés, and newspaper reporters who might double as spies for England, Germany, France, Italy, Russia, Japan, and China.'

'The Navy Secretary just sent me a list of foreigners the Navy suspects could be engaged in espionage.'

'I'll add it to mine,' said Bell. 'But I want an expert to look them over and save us wild-goose chases. Don't you have an old pal still in the Marines who pulls wires at the State Department?'

'That's putting it mildly. Canning's the officer who arranges for Marine Corps Expeditionary Regiments to storm ashore at State's request.'

'He's our man – tight with our overseas attachés. Soon as he goes through our lists of foreigners with a fine-tooth comb, I recommend that we observe them in Washington, D.C., and New York, and around navy yards and factories building warships.'

'That will require an expensive corps of detectives,' Van Dorn said pointedly.

Bell had his answer ready. 'The expense can be written off as an investment in friendships forged in Washington. It can't hurt to have the government rely upon the Van Dorn Agency as a national outfit with efficient field offices across the continent.'

Van Dorn smiled pleasedly, his red whiskers spreading wide and bright as a brush fire at that happy thought.

'In addition,' Bell pressed, 'I recommend that Van Dorn Agency specialists listen in the various immigrant neighborhoods of the cities that have navy yards – German, Irish, Italian, Chinese – for talk of spying, rumors about foreign governments paying for information, and sabotage. The dreadnought race is international.'

Van Dorn considered that with a hollow chuckle. 'We could be looking for more than one spy. Told you this is beyond our usual.'

'If not us,' retorted Isaac Bell, 'who?'

17

Twice that afternoon Iceman Weeks administered beatings notable for their viciousness and the fact that neither left marks not covered by clothing. He was an expert, exercising skills he had honed since boyhood shaking down peddlers and collecting debts for loan sharks. Compared to longshoremen and carters, a skinny bellboy and a frightened little laundress were pieces of cake. The pain grew worse as the day wore on. As did the fear.

Jimmy Clark, the bellboy at the Cumberland Hotel, received the first seemingly endless flurry of fists in the alley behind the pharmacist where he went to exchange last night's take for tonight's cocaine. Weeks emphasized that his problems would be nothing compared to Jimmy's problems if the bellboy didn't do exactly what he was told. Any sort of double cross would make this event a happy memory.

Jenny Sullivan, the apprentice laundress at the Yale Club, caught hers in an alley half a block from the Church of the Assumption, where she had gone to pray for relief of her debt.

Weeks left her vomiting with pain. But so important was her role in his plan that when Weeks stopped hitting the girl, he promised that if she did as he ordered her entire debt was canceled, paid in full. As she dragged her aching body to work, her pain and her fear were unexpectedly mingled with hope. All she had to do was stand lookout at the club's service door at a late hour when no one was around and steal a key to unlock a third-floor bedroom.

18

Isaac Bell and Marion Morgan met for dinner at Rector's. The lobster palace was as famous for its mirrored green-and-gold interior, its lavish linens and silver, its revolving door – the first in New York – and its glittering patrons as it was for its crustaceans. Situated on Broadway, it was two blocks from Bell's office in the Knickerbocker. He waited out front under a gigantic statue of a gryphon ablaze in electric lights and greeted Marion with a kiss on her lips.

'I'm sorry I'm late. I had to change clothes.'

'I was, too. I just got done with Van Dorn.'

'I have to at least try to compete with the Broadway actresses who eat here.'

'When they see you in that getup,' Bell assured her, 'they will run back to their dressing rooms and blow their brains out.'

They pushed around the revolving door into a brilliant room that held a hundred tables. Charles Rector gestured frantically to the orchestra as he rushed to greet Marion.

The musicians broke into 'A Hot Time in the Old Town Tonight,' the title of Marion's first two-reeler about a detective's girlfriend who stopped the villain from burning down a town. At the sound of the music, every woman flashing diamonds and every gent dressed to the nines looked up to see Marion. Bell smiled as an appreciative buzz rippled across the restaurant.

'Miss Morgan,' Rector cried, seizing her hands in his. 'When last you honored Rector's you were making news-reels. Now everyone is talking about your moving picture.'

'Thank you, Mr. Rector. I thought the musical accompaniment was reserved for beautiful actresses.'

'Beautiful actresses are a dime a dozen on Broadway. A beautiful moving picture director is as rare as oysters in August.'

'This is Mr. Bell, my fiancé.'

The restaurateur squeezed Bell's hand and pumped heartily. 'My congratulations, sir. I can't imagine meeting a more fortunate gentleman on the Great White Way. Would you like a quiet table, Miss Morgan, or one where the world may see you?'

'Quiet,' Marion answered firmly, and when they were seated and the Mumm was ordered she said to Bell, 'I am astonished he remembered me.'

'Perhaps he read yesterday's *New York Times*,' Bell smiled. She was so pleased by her reception, and there was lovely high color in her face.

'The *Times*? What do you mean?'

'They sent a fashion reporter to the Easter Parade last Sunday.' He unfolded a clipping from his wallet and read aloud:

'"One young woman, who strolled after tea from Times Square to the Fifth Avenue parade, caused a sensation. She wore lavender satin and a black, plume-laden hat, the size of which caused men to step aside to give her room to pass. This dazzling creature walked as far as the Hotel St. Regis, and then departed toward the north in a red Locomobile motorcar."

'And speaking of red, your ears are.'

'I am mortified! They make it sound as if I were sashaying up Fifth Avenue seeking attention. Every woman there was dressed up for Easter. I only wore that hat because Mademoiselle Duvall and Christina bet me ten dollars I didn't have the nerve.'

'The reporter got it all wrong. You were *attracting* attention. Had you been *seeking* it, you would not have skedaddled in that red Locomobile but would have sashayed up and down the avenue until dark.'

Marion reached across the table. 'Did you see this strange article on the other side?'

Bell turned it over. '*Lachesis muta?* Oh, yes. He's a doozy of a snake. Dripping deadly venom and mean as a hanging judge. You know, the Cumberland Hotel is only ten blocks up Broadway. I'll bet I can talk my way into a Pathology Society meeting with a pretty girl on my arm, if you want to go see him.'

Marion shuddered.

When the champagne arrived, Bell raised his glass to her. 'I'm afraid I can't say it better than Mr. Rector. Thank you for making me the most fortunate gent on the Great White Way.'

'Oh, Isaac, it's so good to see you.'

They sipped the Mumm and discussed the menu. Marion ordered Egyptian quail, declaring she had never heard of such a bird, and Bell ordered a lobster. They would start with oysters, 'Lynnhavens from Maryland,' their waiter assured them, 'big ones sent up special for Mr. Diamond Jim Brady. If I may recommend, Mr. Bell, Mr. Brady usually follows his lobsters with some ducks and a steak.'

Bell demurred.

Marion took his hand across the table. 'Tell me about your work. Will it keep you in New York?'

'We've landed a spy case,' Bell answered in a low voice no one else could hear over the stir of laughter and music. 'It's tangled up in the international dreadnought race.'

Marion, accustomed to him revealing case details to her to hone his own thoughts, replied in the same level tone. 'Rather different than bank robbers.'

'I told Joe Van Dorn: international or not, if they kill people they are first and foremost murderers. At any rate, Joe will fort up in Washington, and he's given me the New York office and carte blanche to dispatch operatives around the country.'

'I presume it has to do with the naval gun designer whose piano blew up.'

'It's looking more and more that it was not a suicide but a diabolical murder deliberately staged to appear to be suicide. And in such a bizarre way as to discredit the poor man and the entire gun system he developed. Of course, the hint of bribery taints everything he touched.'

Bell told her his doubts about Langner's suicide note, and his conviction that the Washington Navy Yard prowler seen by old John Eddison had indeed been Japanese. He told her how the deaths of the armor expert and the fire-control expert had been originally presumed to be accidents.

Marion asked, 'Did anyone see a Japanese man in the Bethlehem Iron Works?'

'The men I sent out there report that someone was seen running off. But he was a big fellow. Over six feet. Pale. Fair-haired. And thought to be German.'

'Why German?'

'Apparently as he ran for it he was heard to mutter, *"Gott im Himmel!"*'

Marion cocked an exquisitely skeptical eyebrow.

'I know,' said Bell. 'It's thin stuff.'

'Was either a pale, fair-haired German or a Japanese seen with Grover Lakewood, who fell off the cliff?'

'The Westchester County coroner told my man that no witness saw Lakewood crash to the ground. Lakewood had told friends he was spending the weekend practicing rock climbing, and his fatal head injuries were consistent with a climbing accident. Poor devil fell a hundred feet. They buried him in a closed coffin.'

'Was he climbing alone?'

'An old lady said she saw him shortly before the accident with a pretty girl.'

'Neither German nor Japanese?' Marion asked with a smile.

'A redhead,' Bell smiled back. 'Presumably Irish.'

'Why Irish?'

Bell shook his head. 'Her features reminded the old lady of her Irish maid. Again, thin stuff.'

'Three different suspects,' Marion observed. 'Three different nationalities ... Of course, what could be more international than the dreadnought race?'

'Captain Falconer is inclined to blame Japan.'

'And you?'

'There is no question that the Japanese are practiced at spying. I learned that, before the Russo-Japanese War, they thoroughly infiltrated the Russian Far East Fleet with spies who pretended to be Manchurian servants and laborers.

When the fighting started, the Japanese knew more about Russian Navy tactics than the Russians did. But I'm keeping an open mind. It really could be any one of them.'

'A tall, handsome detective once told me that skepticism was his most valuable asset,' Marion agreed.

'It's a big case that keeps getting bigger. And because the dreadnought program is so large and widespread, the scope of the case – the links – might have gone unnoticed quite a while longer if it weren't for Langner's daughter insisting that her father didn't kill himself. Even then, if she hadn't managed to get to Joe Van Dorn through her old school chum, then I would not have personally witnessed poor Alasdair's murder. His death would have been written off as a saloon brawl, and who knows how many more they might have killed before anyone got wise.'

Bell shook his head. 'Enough talk. Here come the oysters, and we've both got early starts tomorrow.'

'Look at the size of these!' Marion tipped an enormous oyster off its shell into her mouth, let it slide down her throat, and asked with a smile, 'Is Miss Langner as beautiful as they say?'

'Who says?'

'Mademoiselle Duvall met her in Washington. Apparently there isn't a man on the East Coast over nineteen who hasn't fallen for her.'

'She is beautiful,' said Bell. 'With the most extraordinary eyes. And I imagine were she not grieving she probably would be even lovelier.'

'Don't tell me you've fallen for her, too.'

'My falling days are over,' Bell grinned.

'Do you miss them?'

'If love was gravity, I would be in free fall. What was Mademoiselle Duvall doing in Washington?'

'Seducing an Assistant Secretary of the Navy into hiring her to shoot movies of the Great White Fleet steaming through the Golden Gate into San Francisco. At least, that's how she got the job filming the fleet's departure from Hampton Roads last winter, so I assume she's using the same tactics. Why do you ask?'

'This is strictly between us,' Bell replied seriously. 'But Mademoiselle Duvall has had a long affair with a French Navy captain.'

'Oh, of course! Sometimes when she's being very eye-battingly mysterious she'll hint about *"Mon Capitaine."*'

'*Mon Capitaine* happens to specialize in dreadnought research – which is to say, the Frenchman is a spy, and she is likely working for him.'

'A spy? She's such a flibbertigibbet.'

'The Navy Secretary gave Joe Van Dorn a list of twenty foreigners who've been poking around Washington and New York on behalf of France, England, Germany, Italy, and Russia. Most look like flibbertigibbets, but we've got to investigate each of them.'

'No Japanese?'

'Plenty. Two from their embassy – a naval officer and a military attaché. And a tea importer who lives in San Francisco.'

'But what could Mademoiselle Duvall possibly film for the French Navy that the rest of us can't?'

'Filming could be her excuse to get close to American Navy officers who might talk too much to an attractive woman. What did you mean, "the rest of us." Are you filming the Fleet, too?'

'Preston Whiteway just got in touch.'

Bell's eyes narrowed slightly. The wealthy Whiteway had inherited several California newspapers. He had expanded them into a powerful chain of the yellowest yellow journalism type, and a movie newsreel company that Marion had started up for him before she came east to make moving pictures.

'Preston asked me to shoot the Fleet arriving in San Francisco for *Picture World*.'

'Preston's newspapers are predicting war with Japan within the week.'

'He'll print anything to sell a newspaper.'

'Is this a one-time job?'

'I would not be working for him as an employee, you can be sure, but as a highly paid contractor. I could squeeze it in between the movies I'm shooting here. What do you think?'

'I have to hand it to Whiteway. He is certainly persistent.'

'I don't think he sees me that way anymore – Why are you laughing?'

'I believe he is still male and in possession of his eyesight.'

'I mean that Preston knows that I am not available.'

'By now that should have sunk in,' Bell agreed. 'If memory serves, the last time he was in our company you threatened to shoot him. When do you leave?'

'Not before the first of May.'

'Good. They're launching the *Michigan* next week.

Captain Falconer will throw a big party. I was hoping you could come with me.'

'I'd love to.'

'It's my chance to observe the foreign flibbertigibbets in a room full of Americans who might talk too much. You'll provide cover and a second pair of eyes and ears.'

'What do you suppose ladies wear to a battleship launching?'

'How about that hat men step aside for?' Bell grinned. 'Or you can ask Mademoiselle Duvall. Even money, she'll be there, too.'

'I don't like that she knows you're a detective. It could put you in danger if she really is a spy.'

Ten blocks up Broadway, things were going like clock-work for Iceman Weeks.

First, he managed to make it the four blocks from the subway to the Cumberland Hotel without being spotted by anybody who'd squeal to Tommy Thompson. Crossing Broadway, he passed right under the noses of Daley and Boyle – Central Office pickpocket detectives who were hurrying down to their regular station at the Metropolitan Opera – and they didn't even notice him in the sack suit he'd found airing on a Brooklyn fire escape.

Then in the lobby, the Cumberland's house detectives were distracted while changing shifts. Neither dick gave Weeks's duds a second glance. Even if his boots did not compare to the polished shoes on the college men, the Academy of Pathological Science doctors rushing to their meeting weren't watching his feet.

Jimmy Clark, dressed up like an organ-grinder's monkey in his purple bell-hopper uniform, looked right through him, doing a good job of acting like they had not had a 'conversation' earlier in the day.

'Boy!'

Jimmy hurried over, ducking his head to conceal the fear and hatred in his eyes. 'Yes, sir.'

Weeks handed him a luggage ticket for the battered old steamer truck he had had delivered earlier to the hotel and tipped him a nickel. 'Put my trunk on your cart and wait for me by the side door of the Academy meeting. I have a steamship to catch and I don't want to disturb the members when I leave early.'

Jimmy Clark said, 'Yes sir.'

Weeks was luckier than he knew. Between out-of-town guests swaggering out for a night on the Great White Way and Pathological Academy doctors pouring in to view the lance-headed viper, the hotel lobby was too busy for anyone to take note of a queer accent. While dressed like a college man, Weeks still spoke like a lifelong citizen of Hell's Kitchen, and anyone who listened would have heard, 'Dun wanna destoib de members wen I leave oily.'

The other piece of good luck – and this one he knew about – was that the hotel fuse box in the cellar was at the bottom of the same stairs that led to the side door of the lobby-level ballroom where the doctors were meeting the snake. Weeks put his hat on the chair nearest the door to reserve it and milled around a little so he didn't have to talk to anyone before the meeting started. When it did, he took his seat and caught a last glimpse of the sticker-plastered steamer trunk on Jimmy's cart as the door closed.

He listened impatiently as the speaker gassed on about welcoming the members and dispensing with reading the minutes. Then the head doctor talked about how they would milk the snake's deadly poison and turn it into a serum to cure lunatics. And the good thing about this particular species of snake was that it had a lot more venom that most. Christ knew how many loonies it would cure, but for Isaac Bell it meant that even if the snake missed its first shot it'd hit him again fully loaded.

The zookeepers came in with the snake. The room got real quiet.

The glass box, Weeks saw, would fit in the trunk. That was a relief. He had had no way of knowing for sure until now. Two men were carrying it, and they placed it on a table up front.

Even from halfway across the ballroom, the snake looked wicked. It was moving, coiling and uncoiling, its surprisingly thick, diamond-patterned body gleaming in the lights. It seemed to flow, moving around the box like one long, powerful muscle, flicking a forked tongue and investigating the seams where the glass sides met the glass top. It took particular interest in where the hinges attached, and Weeks figured that a little air got in there, and the snake could sense movement. The doctors were muttering, but no one seemed that inclined to have a closer look.

'Do not worry, gentlemen,' called the medico running the show. 'The glass is strong.' He dismissed the men who had carried it. Iceman Weeks was glad to see them go because they might make more trouble than the doctors. 'And thank you, sir,' he said to the curator, who left, too. Better and better, thought Weeks. Just me and the snake and a bunch of sissies. He looked to the door. Jimmy Clark had opened it a crack. Weeks nodded. *Now.*

It did not take long. Just as the first row rose and tentatively approached the glass box, the lights went out, and the room was suddenly pitch-black. Fifty men shouted at once. Weeks sprang to the door, wrenched it open, and felt in the dark for the trunk. He heard Jimmy pounding up the steps, trusting the banisters to guide him. Weeks opened the streamer trunk, felt for the pane of glass, tucked it under his arm, and pushed back into the ballroom where the shouts were getting loud.

'Keep your heads!'

'Don't lose your nerve!'

A couple of quick thinkers lit matches, which cast weird, jumpy shadows.

Weeks hadn't a moment to lose. He rushed up the side of the ballroom, hugging the wall, and then cut across the front. When he was six feet from the snake, he shouted at the top of lungs, 'Look out! Jaysus, don't drop it!,' and smashed the window glass on the wooden floor.

Shouts turned to screams, followed immediately by the pounding of hundreds of feet. Before Weeks could yell, 'He's loose. He's out. Run! Run! Run!,' many panicky voices did it for him.

Jimmy Clark deserved a place in Heaven for how quickly he wheeled up the trunk.

'Careful,' muttered Weeks. 'Let's not drop it.'

Feeling in the dark, they lifted the glass box into the trunk, shut the lid, got it back on the cart, and wheeled it out the side door of the ballroom. They were almost to the alley when the lights came on.

'House dick!' Clark hissed a warning.

'Keep going,' Weeks said coolly. 'I'll deal with the dick.'

'Hey! Where you going with that?'

Dressed like a college man, Weeks blocked the way so Jimmy could roll his cart out the door, and answered, 'Out of here, before I miss my steamer.'

The house dick heard, 'Outta her, 'fer I miss me steamer,' and drew his pistol.

By then Weeks had his fingers firmly inside his brass knuckles. He brought the bigger man down with a lightning-fast, bone-smashing blow between the eyes. He caught the pistol as it dropped, pocketed it, and found Jimmy in the alley. The bellboy looked scared stiff.

'Don't go rattly on me, now,' Weeks warned him. 'We still got to get across town.'

19

There appeared to be a commotion up Broadway when Isaac Bell and Marion Morgan stepped out of Rector's. They heard clanging fire bells and police whistles and saw crowds of people milling in every direction and decided the best way to Marion's ferry was to take the subway.

Uptown in twenty minutes, they walked to the pier holding hands. Bell escorted her aboard the boat and lingered on the gangway. The whistle blew.

'Thank you for dinner, darling. It was lovely to see you.'

'Shall I come across with you?'

'I have to get up so early. So do you. Give me a kiss.'

After a while, a deckhand bawled, 'Break it up, lovebirds. All ashore that's goin' ashore.'

Bell stepped off, and called as the water widened between the boat and dock, 'They say it may shower on Friday.'

'I'll do a rain dance.'

He rode the subway downtown and stopped at the Knickerbocker to check in with the Van Dorn night watch, who asked, 'Did you hear about the snake?'

Lachesis muta.

'He escaped.'

'From the Cumberland?'

'They think he made it down to the sewer.'

'Bite anybody?'

'Not yet,' said the nightman.

'How'd he get loose?'

'I've heard fourteen versions of that since I came on tonight. The best one is they dropped his box. It was made of glass.' He shook his head and laughed, 'Only in New York.'

'Anything I should know before morning?'

The nightman handed him a stack of messages.

On top was a cablegram from Bell's best friend, Detective Archie Abbott, who, in return for an extended European-honeymoon leave, was making contacts in London, Paris, and Berlin to establish Van Dorn field offices overseas. Socially prominent and married to America's wealthiest heiress, the blue-blooded Archibald Angell Abbott IV was welcome in every embassy and country estate in Europe. Bell had already cabled him with instructions to use that unique access to get an inside perspective on the dreadnought race. Now Archie was coming home. Did Bell prefer he take the British *Lusitania* or the German *Kaiser Wilhem der Grosse*?

'Rolling Billy,' Bell cabled back, using the popular name for the grand but lubberly German liner. Archie and his beautiful bride would spend their Atlantic crossing in the first-class lounges, charming high-ranking officers, diplomats, and industrialists into speaking freely on the subjects of war, espionage, and the naval race. Neither the stiffest Prussian officer nor the worldliest Kaiser's courtier would stand a chance when Lillian started batting her eyes. While Archie, a confirmed bachelor until he had fallen head over heels for Lillian, was no slouch in the wife-beguiling business.

John Scully had left an enigmatic note: 'The PS boys are babysitting Kent. I got a mind to nose around Chinatown.' Bell tossed it in the wastebasket. In other words, he'd hear from the detective when Scully felt like it.

Reports from the Van Dorn agents in Westchester and Bethlehem offered no new news about the climbing accident and the steel mill explosion. Neither had gotten a line on their possible suspects, the 'Irish' girl or the 'German' mill worker. But the agent in Bethlehem warned against jumping to conclusions. It seemed that no one who knew Chad Gordon was surprised by the accident. The victim was an impatient, hard-driving man, casual about the safety rules and known to take terrible risks.

There was disturbing news from Newport, Rhode Island. The Protection Services agent assigned to Wheeler at the Naval Torpedo Station reported chasing off, but failing to capture, two men who tried to break into the torpedo expert's cottage. Bell ordered up extra PS boys, fearing it had not been an ordinary burglary attempt. He also wired Captain Falconer recommending that Wheeler be instructed to sleep in the well-guarded torpedo station barracks instead of his own place.

The middle telephone, the one marked with a chorus girl's rouge, rang, and the nightman snapped it up. 'Yes, sir, Mr. Van Dorn! . . . As a matter of fact, he's right here.' The nightman passed Bell the telephone, mouthing: Long-distance from Washington.

Bell pressed the earpiece to his ear and leaned into the mouthpiece. 'You're working late.'

'Setting an example,' Van Dorn growled. 'Anything I should know before I turn in?'

'Archie's coming home.'

'About time. Longest honeymoon I ever heard of.'

Bell filled him in on the rest. Then he asked, 'How did you make out with your pal at the State Department?'

'That's why I'm telephoning,' Van Dorn said. 'Canning crossed off most of our list's foreigners and added a couple he's got suspicions about. One that catches my eye is some kind of visiting art curator at the Smithsonian Institution. Named Yamamoto Kenta. Japanese. Just like Falconer says. Might be worth getting a line on him.'

'Have you got someone down there you can send to the Smithsonian?'

Van Dorn said he did, and they rang off.

Bell stifled a yawn as he shrugged into his coat. It was well past midnight.

'Watch your step passing sewers,' said the nightman.

'I imagine by now Mr. Snake is swimming in the Hudson River.'

The men's clubs on West 44th Street shared the block between Sixth and Fifth avenues with stables and parking garages, and Isaac Bell was too busy sidestepping manure and dodging town cars to worry about snakes. But when he arrived at the limestone-and-brick, eleven-story Yale Club of New York City, he found the entrance blocked by three ruddy-faced, middle-aged men, considerably worse for wear from a night on the town, swaying arm in arm on the front steps.

Clad in blazers and Class of '83 reunion scarves, the Old Blues were singing 'Bright College Years' at the top of their lungs. Isaac Bell lent a sleepy baritone to the chorus and tried to get around them.

'We're taller than the Harvard Club,' they cried, gesticulating derisively at a squat clubhouse across the street.

'Come up to the roof with us!'

'We'll hurl bouquets down upon the Crimsons.'

The doorman came out and cleared a path for the tall detective. 'Out-of-town members,' he marveled.

'Thanks for the escort, Matthew. Never would have made it inside without you.'

'Good night, Mr. Bell.'

There was more Yalesian song coming from the Grill Room in back, though not as loud as the revelers out front. Bell took the stairs instead of the elevator. The grand, two-story lounge was typically empty this late at night. He lived on the third floor, which contained twelve spartan bachelor rooms, six on each side of the hall, with the bathroom at the end. A steamer trunk sat in the hall, partly blocking his door.

Apparently a member had just got off the ship from Europe.

Yawning sleepily, Bell reached to push the trunk out of his way as he stepped around it. He was surprised it felt light – already empty. The staff usually cleared trunks the instant they were unpacked. He gave it a closer, second look. It was a battered old trunk, with faded labels from the Hotel Ritz in Barcelona and Brown's of London and the Cunard liner *Servia*. He could not recall the last time he had seen that name; the ship had probably been out of service since the turn of the century. Among the faded luggage check labels, a bright new one caught his eye. The Cumberland Hotel, New York.

Funny coincidence, last-known residence of Mr. Snake. He wondered why a member of the Yale Club of New York would stay at the Cumberland before moving to the private but austere bachelor quarters. Most likely a decision to stay long-term in New York, as the rates were considerably lower at the club, even counting the cost of dues.

He unlocked his door and took a step into his room. An odd odor tweaked his nostrils. It was so faint, it was almost indiscernible. He paused, his hand already outstretched, feeling for the wall switch to turn on the overhead light. He tried to identify the gamy aroma. Almost like a sweaty pigskin fencing suit. But his was around the corner on 45th Street, hanging in his locker with his foils and saber at the Fencers Club.

The light from the hall spilled over this shoulder. Something on the bed glinted.

Isaac Bell was suddenly wide awake. He bounded sideways into the room so at not to present a silhouette in the open door. Flattened against the wall with all his senses on high alert, he whipped his Browning pistol from his shoulder holster and hit the light switch.

On the narrow bed was a box made of glass, so heavy that it pressed deep into the chenille spread. It was cube-shaped, about twenty-four inches on each side. Even the lid was glass. It was open. It dangled from sprung hinges as if whoever had opened it had hastily dropped the heavy slab, which had bent the metal hinges, and run for his life.

Bell felt the hairs rise on the back of his neck.

He shot a swift look around the small room. The dresser top was empty but for a box of his cuff links. On the night table was a reading lamp, a *Pocket Guide to New York*, Mahan's *The Influence of Sea Power Upon History*, and Burgoyne's *Submarine Navigation*. The door to the closet was closed and the small safe in the corner where he stored his weapons locked. Still pressing his back to the wall, Bell peered again at the glass box itself. The interior was mostly obscured by reflections on the glass. Slowly, he moved his head to view it from different angles.

The box was empty.

Bell stood still as a hunter. There was only one place the snake could be hiding and that was under the bed in the dark space hidden by the overhanging bedspread. Suddenly he saw movement. A long, forked tongue flickered from under the bedspread, testing the air for motion at which to strike. Tight against the wall, moving in minute increments, Bell eased toward the door to get out of the room and lock the reptile inside. Chloroform poured under the door would put it out of action.

But before he had moved half a foot the viper's tongue began flickering faster as if it were about to make its move. He braced to hurl himself out the door in one jump. Just as he was about to spring, he heard the elevator door open. The Old Blues tumbled into the hall bellowing:

'Where'er upon life's sea we sail:

For God, for Country and –'

Isaac Bell knew he had no choice. If he shouted for the alums to run, the old boys weren't sober enough to understand even if they heard him. At the same time, his warning would either spook the creature into striking him or send it slithering out the door, straight at them.

He reached to the side with the barrel of his pistol and used it to swing the door shut. The air it stirred aroused the lance-head. In a sudden blur of motion, it shifted position under the bed and flew at his leg.

Bell had never moved so fast. He kicked out at the pointed head blazing toward him. The snake smashed against his ankle with an astonishingly muscular impact, staining his trouser cuff with a splash of yellow venom. Only his own animal reflexes and the fact that his boot covered his ankle saved Bell's life. In the space of a breath, the animal spun itself into a tight coil and struck again. By then Bell was airborne. Diving for the bed, he grabbed the pillow and threw it at the snake. The snake struck, spraying the pillow yellow and leaving two deep holes in the cloth. Bell ripped the spread off the bed, twirled it like a toreador, and flung it over the snake to trap it in the cloth.

The snake slithered out from under, coiled again, and tracked Bell with malevolent eyes. Bell raised his pistol, aimed carefully at its head, and fired. The snake attacked at the same instant the gun roared, striking so swiftly that Bell's bullet missed and smashed the dresser mirror. As glass flew, the snake's needle-sharp fangs struck Bell in the chest, directly over his heart.

20

Bell dropped his gun and closed his hand around the snake's neck.

The animal was shockingly strong. Every inch of its four-foot length writhed with spasmodic, sinewy power as it squirmed to break his grip and strike him again. Its fangs were cocked inside its arrow-shaped head. Yellow venom dripped from its wide-open jaws. Bell imagined that he could see in its eyes a gleam of triumph, as if the serpent were sure that its deadly poison had already won the battle and that its prey would die in minutes. Gasping for breath, Bell reached with his free hand for the knife in his boot. 'Sorry to disappoint you, Mr. Snake. But you made the mistake of sinking your fangs into my shoulder holster.'

An Old Blue threw open the door. 'Who's shooting guns in here?'

At the sight of the headless snake still twitching in Bell's fist, he turned white and pressed both hands to his mouth.

Bell pointed commandingly with his bloody knife. 'If you are going to be sick, the facilities are down the hall.'

Matthew the doorman stuck his head in the room. 'Are you —'

'Where did that steamer trunk come from?' demanded Bell.

'I don't know. It must have arrived before I came on.'

'Get the manager!'

The club manager arrived minutes later in his night-clothes. His eyes widened at the sight of the broken mirror, the headless snake twitching on the floor, its head resting on the dresser, and Isaac Bell wiping his knife with a ruined pillowcase.

'Assemble your staff,' Bell told him. 'Either *Lachesis muta* here was *not* blackballed by the Membership Committee, or one of your people helped him into my room.'

Iceman Weeks was hoofing it across town, having watched from a stable until Isaac Bell entered the Yale Club and waited to make sure he didn't come out again. At Eighth Avenue he turned up several blocks, walked under the connector line that linked the Ninth Avenue and Sixth Avenue Els, and knocked on an unmarked door to a house just inside 53rd Street where Tommy Thompson had opened a gambling hall on the second floor. The Gopher guarding the door said, 'What the hell are you doing here?'

'Tell Tommy I got good news for him.'

'Tell him yourself. He's on the third floor.'

'Figured he'd be.'

Weeks climbed the stairs, passed the gambling hall, guarded by another guy who looked surprised to see him, and headed for the third floor. One of the steps sagged a little under his foot, and he guessed it was rigged to dim the electric light in Tommy's room above the gambling hall to warn him someone was coming.

Weeks waited, bouncing from leg to leg, while they sized

him up through the peephole. Tommy himself opened the door. 'I guess you did it,' he said. 'Or you wouldn't be here.'

'Are we square now?'

'Come on in. Have a drink.'

Tommy was drinking Scotch highballs. Weeks was so excited that the booze went straight to his head. 'Wanna hear how I did it?'

'Sure. Just wait 'til we're done here. Shut that light.'

Tommy's bouncer pushed the switch, plunging the room into near darkness. He hinged open a trapdoor, and Weeks saw that they had cut a square hole in the floor down through the ceiling below and filled it with a smoky pane of glass. 'Latest thing,' chuckled Tommy. 'One-way mirror. We see down. All they see in the ceiling is their own mugs.'

Weeks peered down at the gambling floor where six men were seated around a high-stakes poker table. One of them Weeks recognized as the best card mechanic in New York. Another, Willy the Roper, specialized in rounding up players to be fleeced. 'Who's the mark?'

'The swell in the red necktie.'

'Rich?'

'Eyes O'Shay says that necktie means he's a Harvard.'

'What's his line?'

'Selling food to the Navy.'

Selling food to the Navy sounded to Iceman Weeks like a way to get rich. The Navy business was booming. That Commodore Tommy was engaged in separating so exalted a dude from his money by rigging a high-stakes poker game sounded like Tommy had moved up several notches from robbing freight cars. 'What are you taking this Harvard for?' he asked casually.

'Eyes said to take him for all he's got and lend him dough to lose more.'

'Sounds like Eyes wants to have something on him.'

'Won't be hard. Ted Whitmark is a gambling fool.'

'What do you get out of it?' Weeks asked, pouring himself another highball.

'Part of our arrangement,' Tommy answered. 'Eyes has been mighty generous. If he wants Mr. Whitmark to lose his dough at poker and get in hock to lose some more, it's a pleasure to help him.'

As Weeks poured his third drink, it occurred to him that Commodore Tommy Thompson was normally more tight-lipped. He wondered what made him so talkative all of a sudden. *Jaysus!* Was Tommy inviting him to share in the Gophers?

'Want to hear how I did Bell?'

Tommy shut the trapdoor and gestured for his bouncer to turn on the light. 'You see that over there on the table? You see what that is?'

'It's a telephone,' Weeks answered. It looked brand-new, all shiny, the candlestick type you saw in the best joints. 'You're getting up-to-date, Tommy. Didn't know you had it in ya.'

Tommy Thompson grabbed Weeks by his lapels, effortlessly picked the smaller man off the floor, and threw him hard against the wall. Weeks found himself on the carpet, his head ringing, his brain squirming. 'What?'

Tommy kicked him in the face. 'You didn't kill Bell!' he roared. 'That telephone tells me that right now Bell is grilling everybody who works in that club.'

'What?'

'The telephone says the Van Dorn's alive. You didn't kill him.'

Iceman Weeks pulled the pistol that he had taken from the Cumberland Hotel house dick. Tommy's bouncer stepped on his hand and took it away from him.

The manager of the Yale Club woke the staff and gathered them in the big kitchen on the top floor. They knew Isaac Bell as a regular who remembered their names and was generous when the club's no-tipping rule was waived at Christmas. All of them, manager, housekeeper, barman, chambermaids, porters, and front-desk clerk, clearly wanted to be of help when Bell asked, 'Where did the trunk outside my door on the third floor come from?'

No one could answer. It had not been there when the day shift ended at six. A night-shift waiter had noticed it when passing by with room service at eight. The freight-elevator operator had not seen it, but he admitted taking a long dinner between six and eight. Then Matthew, who had stayed at the front door after Bell interviewed him privately, suddenly appeared, saying, 'The new laundress? Mr. Bell. I found her across the street, weeping.'

Bell turned to the housekeeper. 'Mrs. Pierce, who is the laundress?'

'The new girl, Jenny Sullivan. She doesn't live in the house yet.'

'Matthew, could you bring her in?'

Jenny Sullivan was small and dark and trembling with fear. Bell said, 'Sit down, miss.'

She stood rigid by the chair. 'I didn't mean no harm.'

'Don't be afraid, you've –' He reached to comfort her with a gentle hand on her arm. Jenny screamed in pain and shrank back.

'What?' Bell said. 'I'm sorry, I didn't mean to hurt – Mrs. Pierce, could you look after Jenny?'

The kindly housekeeper led the girl away, speaking to her softly.

'I think everyone can go back to bed,' said Bell. 'Good night. Thank you for your help.'

When Mrs. Pierce returned, she had tears in her eyes. 'The girl is beaten black-and-blue from her shoulders to her knees.'

'Did she say who did it?'

'A man named Weeks.'

'Thank you, Mrs. Pierce. Get her to a hospital – not in the district where she lives but the best in the city. I will pay all expenses. Stint on nothing. Here's money for immediate needs.' Bell pressed it in the housekeeper's hand and hurried to his room.

Swiftly, methodically, he cleaned his Browning and replaced the spent shell. Wondering again whether a heavier gun would have stopped Weeks before he could stab Alasdair MacDonald, he took a Colt .45 automatic from his safe. He checked the loads in his derringer and put on his hat. He stuffed the Colt and spare ammunition for both guns in his coat pockets and went down the stairs three at a time.

Matthew recoiled from the expression on his face. 'Are you all right, Mr. Bell?'

'Not that you would frequent the joint, Matthew, but do you know the address of Commodore Tommy's Saloon?'

'I believe it is way far across West 39th, almost to the river. But if I ever did "frequent the joint,"' he added bluntly, 'I would not go alone.'

21

Isaac Bell charged out of the Yale Club. Men who saw him coming moved aside. He crossed Sixth Avenue and Seventh, ignoring the blare of auto horns, and turned downtown on Eighth Avenue. On the nearly deserted sidewalk Bell increased his pace and yet he could not outpace the thundering anger in his head. At West 39th Street he broke into a run.

A police officer in his path, a big man patrolling with a twenty-six-inch nightstick and revolver, looked him over and quietly crossed the street. At Ninth Avenue groups of men and a few women, mostly older, shabbily dressed, with the despairing features of the homeless, had gathered on the streetcar tracks under the El. They were staring up into the dark structure of fan-top columns that supported the overhead train tracks. Bell shouldered through them. Then he stopped short. A man in a sack suit was hanging by his neck from a rope tied to a transverse girder.

An express train on the middle track thundered overhead. As it clattered away and silence descended, someone muttered, 'Looks like the Gophers wanted the Iceman should die slow.'

Bell saw what he meant. They hadn't bound the dead man's hands. His fingers had caught under the noose as if he were still tugging at his throat. His eyes were bulging and his mouth was locked in a terrible grimace. But even wearing the mask of death, he was beyond any doubt the man who had killed Alasdair MacDonald in Camden.

A drunk snickered, 'Maybe the Iceman committed suicide.'

'Yeah,' answered his companion sarcastically. 'And maybe the Pope is dropping by Commodore Tommy's for a beer.'

They laughed. A toothless old woman turned on them. 'Would you mock the dead?'

'He deserves what he got. Evil mug.'

An old man in a slouch hat growled, 'No Gopher ever killed another because he was evil, ya silly bastards. They killed the Iceman because he was getting too big for his britches.'

Isaac Bell shoved past and continued west.

Both were wrong. The Gophers had killed Weeks to break the chain of evidence that connected his boss to the murder in Camden. It was justice of a sort, rough justice. But it hadn't been done for justice, only self-protection. What link was left between Alasdair's killing and the spy who ordered it?

He could feel the cold breath of the river now, and he heard ship horns and the piping of tugs. With Weeks dead, he was no closer to the spy who plotted to kill the minds that imagined Hull 44.

He quickened his pace, then stopped abruptly under a signboard above the first floor of a crumbling red brick tenement so old that it had no fire escapes. Faded white letters on a gray field read 'Commodore Tommy's Saloon.'

The building looked more like a fort than a saloon.

Dim light shone through the barred windows. He heard voices inside. But when he tried the front door, it was locked. Bell jerked the .45 out of his coat, fired four shots in a circle around the knob, and kicked the door open.

He went through it fast, slewed sideways into a dimly lit barroom, and slammed his back hard against the wall. A dozen Gophers scattered, upending tables and crouching behind them.

'I'll shoot the first man with a gun,' said Isaac Bell.

They gaped, staring at him. Eyes flickered at the door, back at him, again at the door. Exchanging surprised glances, the Gopher gangsters registered that Bell was alone and rose menacingly to their feet.

Bell switched the .45 to his left hand and pulled his Browning with his right.

'Everyone's hands where I can see them. Now!'

At the sight of the enraged detective standing against the wall with two guns sweeping the barroom, most dropped weapons and displayed empty hands. Bell aimed at two who didn't. 'Now!' he repeated. 'Or I'll clean out the place.'

Up came an ancient horse pistol, barrel yawning. Bell shot it out of the gangster's hand. The man cried out in pain and astonishment. The other was swinging a heavy coach gun at him, a wide-gauge, double-barreled sawed-off that could cut him in half. Bell threw himself sideways as he triggered the Browning again. Buckshot screeched through the air he had vacated. An errant slug burned a furrow across his left arm with a mule-kick impact that nearly knocked the .45 out of his fist. He rolled across the floor and sprang up, guns ready, but the gangster who had fired the coach gun was sprawled on his back, clutching his shoulder.

'Which one of you skunks is Tommy Thompson?'

'He ain't here, mister.'

Bell had a vague idea that the same rage twisting his face into the expression that cowed them might also be keeping him from thinking straight. He didn't care.

'Where is he?' he shouted.

'At one of his new joints.'

'Where?'

Far beneath the surface of Isaac Bell's conscience, a voice cautioned that he would get himself killed like this. But Bell's fighting voice, always nearest the surface, retorted that no one in the dimly lit barroom could kill him. In a flash, he assessed the contradiction: the fighter saw something the worrier did not. This was too easy. Twelve Gophers, and only two had pulled weapons. By rights, the rest of the gang should still be slinging lead at him. Instead, they were gaping openmouthed and wide-eyed.

'*Where?*'

'Don't know, mister.'

'One of the new joints.'

Fear and confusion in the gangsters' tones made Bell look more closely. Now he noticed that the weapons they had dropped were brass knuckles, saps, and knives. No guns. Then it dawned on him. These were mostly old men, missing teeth, hunched, scarred – the weary down-and-out slum dwellers of Hell's Kitchen where forty was old, fifty ancient.

New joints. That was it. Commodore Tommy Thompson had moved up and left them behind. These sorry devils had been abandoned by their boss and scared out of their wits by an enraged detective blasting open the door and gunning down the only two with the go left in them to fight.

Bell felt a cool calm settle over his mind, and with it an electric clarity.

Change was sweeping the Hell's Kitchen Gophers, and he had a strong hunch what was causing it. The old men saw the softening in his face. One piped, 'Could we put our hands down, mister?'

The tall detective was still too angry to smile, but he came close. 'No,' he said. 'Leave them where I can see them.'

A taxi horn blared in the street.

Bell shot a glance out the door. The taxi was sliding to a halt. Five grim-faced Van Dorn veterans and an up-and-coming young fellow spilled out bearing firearms. They were trailed at a distance by a squad of New York cops on foot. Harry Warren, the gang specialist, was leading the Van Dorns. He had a sawed-off pressed against his leg and a revolver tucked in his waistband. Passing the youngster a wad of cash, he gestured for him to deal with the cops, and assessed the front of Commodore Tommy's with an eye to storming it.

Bell stepped out of the saloon. 'Evening, boys.'

'Isaac! You O.K.?'

'Tip-top. What are you doing here?'

'Your Yale Club doorman telephoned the Knicker-bocker. Sounded real worried, said that you needed a hand.'

'Old Matthew's like a mother hen.'

'What the hell are *you* doing here?'

'Just out for a stroll.'

'Stroll?' They looked up and down the dark and grimy street. '*Stroll?*' They stared at Isaac Bell. 'And I suppose a mosquito drilled that hole in your coat sleeve?' one detective remarked.

'Same one that shot the lock off this door?' asked another.

'And made those Gophers inside hold their hands in the air?' said a third.

Harry Warren beckoned the kid who had just returned. 'Eddie, go tell the cops they should send an ambulance.'

Isaac Bell grinned. 'Might as well call it a night, boys. Thanks for coming out. Harry, if you'd walk me home, I have questions for you.'

Harry handed his shotgun to the boys, shoved his revolver in his coat pocket, and passed Bell a handkerchief. 'You're bleeding.'

Bell stuffed it up his sleeve.

They walked to Ninth Avenue. The cops had cordoned off the area under the El where Weeks was hanging. Firemen were holding ladders for morgue attendants who were trying to cut the body loose.

'So much for connecting the Iceman to Tommy and your foreign spy,' said Harry.

'This connection is precisely what I want to talk to you about,' said Isaac Bell. 'It looks to me like Tommy Thompson is moving up in the world.'

Harry nodded. 'Yeah, I hear talk in the neighborhoods that the Gophers are throwing their weight around.'

'I want you to find out who his new friends are. Five'll get you ten, they will be the connection.'

'You could be onto something. I'll get right to it. Oh, here, they passed me this as we were leaving.' Harry fished in his pockets. 'Wire came in for you from the Philadelphia office.'

They had reached the corner of 42nd Street. Bell stopped under a streetlamp to read the wire.

'Bad news?'

'They got a line on a German sneaking around Camden.'

'Wasn't that a German who did the Bethlehem job?'

'Possibly.'

'What's in Camden?'

'They're launching the battleship *Michigan*.'

22

The spy summoned his German agent with a cryptic note left at his Camden rooming house. They met in Philadelphia in a watchman's shack on a barge tied to the west bank of the Delaware directly across the busy river from the shipyard. Through an ever-moving scrim of tugboats, lighters, ships, ferries, and coal smoke they could see the stern of the *Michigan* thrusting her propellers out the back of the shed that covered her ways. The river was only a half mile wide, and they could hear the steady drumbeat of carpenters pounding wooden wedges.

The ship workers had built a gigantic wooden cradle big enough to carry the 16,000-ton ship down greased rails from her building place on land to her home in the water. Now they were raising the cradle up to her by driving wedges under it. When the wedges pressed the cradle tightly against the hull, they would continue hammering them until the cradle lifted the ship off her building blocks.

The German was glum.

The spy said, 'Listen. What do you hear?'

'They're hammering the wedges.'

The spy had earlier passed close by in a steam launch to observe the scene under the hull, which was painted with a dull red undercoat. The 'hammers' were actually rams, long poles tipped with heavy heads.

'The wedges are thin,' he said. 'How much does each blow raise the cradle?'

'You'd need a micrometer to measure.'

'How many wedges?'

'*Gott in Himmel,* who knows. Hundreds.'

'A thousand?'

'Could be.'

'Could any one wedge raise the cradle under the ship?'

'Impossible.'

'Could any one wedge lift the cradle and the ship off her blocks?'

'Impossible.'

'Every German must do his part, Hans. If one fails, we all fail.'

Hans stared at him with a strange look of detachment. 'I am not a simpleton, *mein Herr.* I understand the principle. It is not the doing that troubles me, but the consequences.'

The spy said, 'I know you're not a simpleton. I am merely trying to help.'

'Thank you, *mein Herr.*'

'Do the detectives frighten you?' he asked, even though he doubted they did.

'No. I can avoid them until the last moment. The pass you had made for me will throw them off. By the time any realize what I am up to, it will be too late to stop me.'

'Do you fear that you will not escape with your life?'

'I would be amazed if I did. Fortunately, I have settled that question in my own mind. That is not what troubles me.'

'Then we are back to the same basic question, Hans. Would you have American warships sink German warships?'

'Maybe it is the waiting that is killing me. No matter where I go I hear them hitting the wedges. Like the ticking clock. Ticktock. Ticktock. Ticking for innocent men who don't know yet that they will die. It's driving me crazy – What is this?'

The spy was pushing money into his hand. He tried to jerk back. 'I don't want money.'

The spy seized his wrist in an astonishingly powerful grip. 'Recreation. Find a girl. She'll make the night go faster.' He stood up abruptly.

'Are you leaving?' Suddenly Hans did look afraid – afraid to be alone with his conscience.

'I'll be nearby. I'll be watching.' The spy smiled reassuringly and slapped him on the shoulder.

'Go find that girl. Enjoy the night. It will be morning before you know it.'

23

Waiters sporting red, white, and blue bow ties spread watercress sandwiches and iced wine in the dignitaries' pavilion. Bartenders, who had been issued similarly patriotic garters for their sleeves, rolled kegs of beer and carts of hard-boiled eggs into the ship workers' tents on the riverbank. A warm breeze drifted through the enormous shed that covered the shipway, sunlight filtered down from glass panels in the roof, and it appeared that half the population of Camden, New Jersey, had turned out to celebrate launching the battleship *Michigan,* whose 16,000 tons were balanced at the high end of a track of greased rails that slanted into the river.

The shed still resounded with steel banging on wood, but the pace of the hammering had slowed. The wedges had lifted the battleship off nearly all her building blocks. But for a last few under her keel and bilges, she rested on the cradle she would ride down the ways.

The ceremonial launching platform surrounding the ship's steel bow was draped with red, white, and blue bunting. A champagne bottle, wrapped in crocheted mesh to keep glass from flying and beribboned in the colors of the flag, waited in a bowl of roses.

The battleship's sponsor, the pretty, dark-haired girl who would christen her, stood by in a striped flannel walking dress and a wide-brimmed *Merry Widow* hat heaped with silk peonies. She was ignoring the fevered instructions of an Assistant Secretary of the Navy – her father – who was warning her not to hold back at the crucial moment but to 'Whack her with all you've got the instant the ship starts to move or it'll be too late.'

Her gaze was fixed on a tall, golden-haired detective in a white suit, whose restless eyes were looking everywhere but at her.

Isaac Bell had not slept in a bed since he arrived in Camden two days ago. He had originally intended to come down with Marion the night before the ceremony and dine in Philadelphia. But that was before the Philadelphia office had sent the urgent wire to New York. Disquieting rumors had begun to drift in concerning a mysterious German bent on disrupting the launch. Detectives assigned to the German immigrant community heard of a recent arrival who claimed to be from Bremen but spoke with a Rostock accent. He kept asking about finding work at New York Ship but had never applied to the company. Several hands had unaccountably lost the gate badges that identified them as employees.

This morning at dawn, Angelo Del Rossi, the frock-coated proprietor of the King Street dance hall where Alasdair MacDonald had been murdered, sought Bell out. He reported that a woman had come to him, distraught and frightened. A German who met the description of the man from Rostock – tall and fair, with troubled eyes – had confessed to the woman, who in turn had confessed to Del Rossi.

'She's a part-time working girl, Isaac, if you know what I mean.'

'I've heard of such arrangements,' Bell assured him. 'What exactly did she say?'

'This German she was with suddenly blurted out something to the effect that the innocent should not die. She asked what he meant. They had been drinking. He fell silent, then blurted some more, as drinkers will, saying that the cause was just, but the methods wrong. Again she asked what he meant. And he broke down and began to weep, and said – and this she claimed to quote exactly – "The dreadnought will fall, but men will die."'

'Do you believe her?'

'She had nothing to gain coming to me, except a clear conscience. She knows men who work in the yard. She doesn't want them to be hurt. She was brave enough to confide in me.'

'I must speak with her,' said Bell.

'She won't talk to you. She doesn't see any difference between private detectives and cops, and she doesn't like cops.'

Bell pulled a gold piece from inside his belt and handed it to the saloonkeeper. 'No cop ever paid her twenty dollars to talk. Give this to her. Tell her I admire her bravery and that I will do nothing to endanger her.' He turned his gaze sharply on Del Rossi. 'You do believe me, Angelo. Do you not?'

'Why do you think I came to you?' said Del Rossi. 'I'll see what I can do.'

'Is it enough money?'

'More than she clears in a week.'

Bell tossed him more gold. 'Here's another week. This is vitally important, Angelo. Thank you.'

Her name was Rose. She had offered no last name when Del Rossi arranged for them to meet in the back of his dance hall, and Bell asked for none. Bold and self-possessed, she repeated everything she had told Del Rossi. Bell kept her talking, probing gently, and she finally added that the German's parting words, as he staggered from the private booth they had rented in a waterfront bar, were, 'It will be done.'

'Would you recognize him if you saw him again?'

'I should think so.'

'How would you like to become a temporary employee of the Van Dorn Detective Agency?'

Now she was cruising the shipyard in a summery white dress and a flowered hat, pretending to be the kid sister of two burly Van Dorn operatives disguised as celebrating steamfitters. A dozen more detectives were prowling the shipyard checking and rechecking the identities of all who were working near the *Michigan,* particularly the carpenters driving the wedges directly under the hull. These men were required to carry special red passes issued by Van Dorn – instead of New York Ship – in case spies had infiltrated the offices of the shipbuilding firm.

The runners who reported to Bell on the platform were chosen for their youthful appearance. Bell had ordered them to be attired like innocuous college boys, in boaters, summer suits, rounded collars, and neckties, so as not to unnecessarily frighten the throng that had come out to greet the new ship.

He had argued strongly for a postponement, but there

was no question of calling the ceremony off. Too much was riding on the launch, Captain Falconer had explained, and every party involved would protest. New York Ship was proud to put *Michigan* in the water just ahead of Cramp's Shipyard's *South Carolina,* which was only weeks behind. The Navy wanted the hull immediately afloat to finish fitting her out. And no one in his cabinet dared inform President Roosevelt of any delay.

The ceremony was scheduled to start exactly at eleven. Captain Falconer had warned Bell that they would launch on time. In less than an hour the dreadnought would either slide uneventfully down the ways or the German saboteur would attack, wreaking a terrible toll on the innocent.

A Marine brass band started playing a Sousa medley, and the launching stand got crowded with hundreds of special guests invited to stand close enough to actually see the champagne bottle crack on the bow. Bell spotted the Secretary of the Interior, three senators, the governor of Michigan, and several members of President Roosevelt's vigorous 'Tennis Cabinet.'

The top bosses of New York Ship trooped up the steps in close company with Admiral Capps, the chief naval constructor. Capps seemed less interested in talking to shipbuilders than to Lady Fiona Abbington-Westlake, the wife of the British Naval Attaché, a beautiful woman with a shiny mane of chestnut hair. Isaac Bell observed her discreetly. The Van Dorn researchers assigned to the Hull 44 spy case had reported that Lady Fiona spent beyond her husband's means. Worse, she was paying blackmail to a Frenchman named Raymond Colbert. No one knew what Colbert had on her, or whether it involved her husband's purloining of French naval secrets.

The German Emperor, Kaiser Wilhelm II, was represented by a saber-scarred military attaché, Lieutenant Julian Von Stroem, recently returned from German East Africa, who was married to an American friend of Dorothy Langner. Suddenly Dorothy herself parted the crowd in her dark mourning clothes. The bright-eyed redheaded girl he had noticed at the Willard Hotel was at her elbow. Katherine Dee, Research had reported, was the daughter of an Irish immigrant who had moved back to Ireland after making his fortune building Catholic schools in Baltimore. Orphaned soon after, Katherine had been convent-educated in Switzerland.

The handsome Ted Whitmark trailed behind them, shaking hands and slapping backs and declaring in a voice that carried to the glass roof, '*Michigan* is going to be one of Uncle Sam's best fighting units.' While Whitmark occasionally played the fool in his private life, gambling and drinking, at least before he met Dorothy, Research had made it clear that he was extremely adept at the business of snagging government contracts.

Typical of the incestuous relationships in the crowd of industrialists, politicians, and diplomats that swirled around the 'New Navy,' he and Dorothy Langner had met at a clambake hosted by Captain Falconer. As Grady Forrer of Van Dorn Research had remarked cynically, 'The easy part was discovering who's in bed with whom; the hard part is calculating why, seeing as how "why" can run the gamut from profit to promotion to espionage to just plain raising hell.'

Bell saw a small smile part Dorothy's lips. He glanced in the direction she was looking and saw the naval architect Farley Kent nod back. Then Kent threw an arm around his guest – Lieutenant Yourkevitch, the Czar's dreadnought architect – and plunged into the crowd as if to get out of the path of Ted and Dorothy. Oblivious, Ted seized an elderly admiral's hand and bellowed, 'Great day for the Navy, sir. Great day for the Navy.'

Dorothy's eyes wheeled Bell's way and locked with his. Bell returned her gaze appraisingly. He had not seen her since the day he had called on her in Washington, though he had, at Van Dorn's urging, reported to her by long-distance telephone that there was strong reason to hope that her father's name would soon be cleared. She had thanked him warmly and said that she hoped she would see him in Camden at the luncheon that would follow the launching. It occurred to Bell that neither Ted Whitmark nor Farley Kent would be pleased by the look she was giving him now.

A warm breath whispered in his ear. 'That's quite a smile for a lady dressed in mourning black.'

Marion Morgan glided behind him and made a beeline for Captain Falconer. He looked heroically splendid in his full-dress white uniform, she thought, or splendidly heroic, his handsome head erect in a high-standing collar, medals arrayed across his broad chest, sword at his trim waist.

'Good morning, Miss Morgan,' Lowell Falconer greeted Marion Morgan heartily. 'Are you enjoying yourself?'

She and Isaac had dined aboard Falconer's yacht the night before. When Bell promised him that Arthur Langner would be completely vindicated of accepting bribes, her pride in her fiancé had spoken legions for her love. Still, Falconer admitted ruefully, he had not been disappointed when Bell had to excuse himself early to oversee another inspection of the ways beneath the ship. After the detective left, their conversation had flowed seamlessly from dreadnought design to moving pictures to naval warfare to the paintings of Henry Reutendahl to Washington politics and Falconer's career. He realized in retrospect that he had told her more about himself than he had intended to.

The Hero of Santiago knew himself well enough to acknowledge that he had fallen half in love with her. But he was completely unaware that the beautiful Miss Morgan was using him for cover as she tracked the head-bowing, hat-tipping passage through the crowd of an elegantly dressed Japanese.

'Why,' she asked Falconer, filling time, 'is the shipbuilder called New York Ship when it's in Camden, New Jersey?'

'That confuses everyone,' Falconer explained with his warmest smile and a devilish glint in his eye. 'Originally, Mr. Morse intended to build his yard on Staten Island, but Camden offered better rail facilities and access to Philadelphia's experienced shipyard workers. Why are you smiling that way, Miss Morgan?'

She said, 'The way you're looking at me, it's a good thing that Isaac is nearby and armed.'

'Well, he ought to be,' Falconer retorted gruffly. 'Anyway, Camden, New Jersey, has the most modern shipyard in the world. When it comes to building dreadnoughts, it is second only to our most important facility at the Brooklyn Navy Yard.'

'And why is that, Captain?' Her quarry was drawing near.

'They embrace a thoroughly modern system. Major parts are prefabricated. Overhead cranes move them around the yard as easily as you'd assemble the ingredients to bake a cake. These sheds cover the ways so bad weather doesn't delay production.'

'They remind me of the glass studios we use to film indoors, though ours are much smaller.'

'Fittings that used to be mounted after launch are applied in the comfort of those covered ways. She'll be launched with her guns already in place.'

'Fascinating.' The man she was watching had stopped to peer through a break in the scaffolding that revealed the ship's long armor belt. 'Captain Falconer? How many men will crew the *Michigan*?'

'Fifty officers. Eight hundred and fifty enlisted.'

She uttered a thought so grim that it shadowed her face. 'That is a terrible number of sailors in one small space if the worst happens and the ship sinks.'

'Modern warships are armored coffins,' Falconer answered far more bluntly than he would with a civilian, but their conversations last night had established an easy trust between them and left him in no doubt of her superior intelligence. 'I saw Russians drown by the thousands fighting the Japs in the Tsushima Strait. Battleships went down in minutes. All but the spotters in the fighting tops and a few men on the bridge were trapped belowdecks.'

'Can I assume that our goal is to build warships that will sink slowly and give men time to get off?'

'The goal for battleships is to keep fighting. That means protecting men, machinery, and guns within a citadel of armor while keeping the ship afloat. The sailors who win stay alive.'

'So today is a happy day, launching such a modern ship.'

Captain Falconer glowered at Marion under his heavy eyebrows. 'Between you and me, miss, thanks to Congress limiting her to 16,000 tons, *Michigan* has eight feet *less* freeboard aft then the old *Connecticut*. She'll be wetter than a whale, and if she ever makes eighteen knots in heavy seas, I'll eat my hat.'

'Obsolete before she is even launched?'

'Doomed to escort slow convoys. But if she ever tangles with a real dreadnought, it better be in calm waters. Hell!' he snorted. 'We should anchor her in San Francisco Bay to greet the Japanese.'

A petite girl wearing a very expensive hat secured to her red hair with Taft-for-President 'Possum Billy' hatpins stepped up. 'Excuse me, Captain Falconer. I'm sure you don't remember me, but I had a wonderful time at a picnic on your yacht.'

Falconer seized the hand that she had offered tentatively. 'I remember you indeed, Miss Dee,' he grinned. 'Had the sun not shone on our clambake, your smile would have made up for it. Marion, this young lady is Miss Katherine Dee. Katherine, say hello to my very good friend Marion Morgan.'

Katherine Dee's big blue eyes got bigger. 'Are you the moving-picture director?' she asked breathlessly.

'Yes, I am.'

'I love *Hot Time in the Old Town Tonight*! I've seen it four times already.'

'Well, thank you very much.'

'Do you ever act in your movies?'

Marion laughed. 'Good Lord, no!'

'Why not?' Captain Falconer interrupted. 'You're a good-looking woman.'

'Thank you, Captain,' Marion said, casting a quick smile at Katherine Dee. 'But good looks don't necessarily show up on film. The camera has its own standards. It prefers certain kinds of features.' Like Katherine Dee's, she thought to herself. For some magical reason the lens and the light tended to favor Katherine's type, with her petite figure, large head, and big eyes.

Almost as if she could read her mind, Katherine said, 'Oh, I wish I could see a movie being made.'

Marion Morgan took a closer look at the girl. She seemed physically strong for one so petite. Strangely so. In fact, behind Katherine's breathless, little-girl manner, Marion sensed something slightly peculiar. But didn't the camera also often transform peculiarities into characteristics that charmed the movie audience? She was tempted to confirm whether this girl indeed had qualities the camera would love, and an invitation was on the tip of her tongue. But there was something about her that made Marion uncomfortable.

Beside her, Marion felt Lowell Falconer plumping up again as he did whenever he saw a pretty girl. The woman approaching was the tall brunette who had been making eyes at Isaac earlier.

Lowell stepped forward and extended his hand.

Marion thought that Dorothy Langner was even more striking than the descriptions she had heard. She thought of a term uttered by her long-widowed father now that he was finally stepping out in late middle age: 'A looker.'

'Dorothy, I am so glad you came,' said Falconer. 'Your father would be very proud to see you here.'

'I'm proud to see his guns. Already mounted. This is a splendid shipyard. You remember Ted Whitmark?'

'Of course,' said Falconer, shaking Whitmark's hand. 'I imagine you'll be a busy fellow when the fleet replenishes at San Francisco. Dorothy, may I present Miss Marion Morgan?'

Marion was aware of being carefully measured as they traded hellos.

'And of course you know Katherine,' Falconer concluded the introductions.

'We came up together on the train,' said Whitmark. 'I hired a private car.'

Marion said, 'Excuse me, Captain Falconer, I see a gentleman Isaac asked me to meet. Nice to meet you, Miss Langner, Mr. Whitmark, Miss Dee.'

The pounding of the wedges suddenly stopped. The ship was fully on her cradle. Isaac Bell headed to the stairs for a final look below.

Dorothy Langner intercepted him at the top of the stairs. 'Mr. Bell, I was hoping to see you.'

She extended her gloved hand, and Bell it took it politely. 'How are you, Miss Langner?'

'Much better since our conversation. Vindicating my father won't bring him back, but it is a comfort, and I am very grateful to you.'

'I am hoping that soon we will have definitive proof, but, as I said, I personally have no doubt that your father was murdered, and we will bring his killer to justice.'

'Whom do you suspect?'

'No one I am prepared to discuss. Mr. Van Dorn will keep you appraised.'

'Isaac – may I call you Isaac?'

'All right, if you want.'

'There is something I told you once. I would like to make it clear.'

'If it's about Mr. Whitmark,' Bell smiled, 'be aware he's headed this way.'

'I will repeat,' she said quietly. 'I am not rushing into anything. And he is leaving for San Francisco.'

It struck Bell that a key difference between Marion and Dorothy was how they regarded men. Dorothy wondered whether she could add one to her list of conquests. Whereas Marion Morgan had no doubt she could conquer and therefore was not inclined to bother. It showed in their smiles. Marion's smile was as engaging as an embrace. Dorothy's was a dare. But Bell could not ignore her desperate fragility, despite her bold manner. It was almost as if she were putting herself forth and asking to be saved from the loss of her father. And he did not believe that Ted Whitmark was the man to do that.

'Bell, isn't it?' Whitmark called loudly as he bustled up.

'Isaac Bell.'

He saw tugboats gathering in the river to take charge of

the hull when she hit the water. 'Excuse me. I'm expected on the ways.'

Yamamoto Kenta had studied photographs of American warship launchings to choose his costume. He could not disguise that he was Japanese. But the less alien his clothes, the farther he could roam the shipyard and the closer he could approach the distinguished guests. Observing his fellow travelers on the train up from Washington, he was proud to see that he had dressed perfectly for the occasion in a pale blue-and-white seersucker suit and a pea green four-in-hand necktie matched by the color of his straw boater's hatband.

At the shipyard in Camden, he doffed the boater repeatedly in polite acknowledgment of ladies, important personages, and older gentlemen. The first person he had run into upon arriving at the remarkably up-to-date Camden shipyard was Captain Lowell Falconer, the Hero of Santiago. They had spoken late last fall at the unveiling of a bronze tablet to commemorate Commodore Thomas Tingey, the first commandant of the Washington Navy Yard. Yamamoto had given Falconer the impression that he had retired from the Japanese Navy holding the rank of lieutenant before returning to his first love, Japanese art. Captain Falconer had given him a cursory tour of the arsenal with the notable exception of the Gun Factory.

This morning, when Yamamoto congratulated Falconer on the imminent launch of America's first dreadnought, Falconer had replied with a wry '*almost* dreadnought' on the assumption – from one sea dog to another – that a former officer of the Japanese Navy would recognize her shortcomings.

Yamamoto touched his brim once again, this time for a tall, striking blond woman.

Unlike the other American ladies who streamed past with chilly nods for 'that puny Asiatic,' as he had heard one murmur to her daughter, she surprised him with a warm smile and the observation that the weather had turned lovely for the launching.

'And for the blooming of the flowers,' said the Japanese spy, who was actually comfortable with American women, having secretly romanced several high-ranking Washington wives who had convinced themselves that a visiting curator of Asian art must be soulfully artistic as well as exotically Asiatic. At his flirtatious remark, he could expect her to either stalk off or move closer.

He was deeply flattered when she chose the latter.

Her eyes were a startling sea-coral green.

Her manner was forthright. 'Neither of us is dressed as a naval officer,' she said. 'What brings *you* here?'

'It is my day off from where I am working at the Smithsonian Institution,' Yamamoto replied. He saw no bulge of a wedding ring under her cotton glove. Probably the daughter of an important official. 'A colleague in the Art Department give me his ticket and a letter of introduction that makes me sound far more important than I am. And you?'

'Art? Are you an artist?'

'Merely a curator. A large collection was given to the Institution. They asked me to catalog a small portion of it – a very small portion,' he added with a self-deprecating smile.

'Do you mean the Freer Collection?'

'Yes! You know of it?'

'My father took me to Mr. Freer's home in Detroit when I was a little girl.'

Yamamoto was not surprised that she had visited the fabulously wealthy manufacturer of railway cars. The social set that swirled around the American's New Navy included the privileged, the well-connected, and the newly rich. This young lady appeared to be of the former. Certainly, her ease of manner and sense of style set her off from the oft-shrill nouveaux. 'What,' he asked her, 'do you recall from that visit?'

Her engaging green eyes seemed to explode with light. 'What stays in my heart are the colors in Ashiyuki Utamaro's woodcuts.'

'The theatrical pieces?'

'Yes! The colors were so vivid yet so subtly united. They made his scrolls seem even more remarkable.'

'His scrolls?'

'The simple black on white of his calligraphy was so . . . so – what is the word – *clear,* as if to imply that color was actually unessential.'

'But Ashiyuki Utamaro made no scrolls.'

Her smile faded. 'Do I misrecall?' She gave a little laugh, an uncomfortable sound that alerted Yamamoto Kenta that all was not well here. 'I was only ten years old,' she said hurriedly. 'But I'm certain I remember – no, I guess I'm wrong. Aren't I the silly one. I'm terribly embarrassed. I must look like a complete ninny to you.'

'Not at all,' Yamamoto replied smoothly while glancing about surreptitiously to see who on the crowded platform was watching them. Nobody he could see. His mind was racing. Had she tried to trick him into revealing gaps in his hastily acquired knowledge of art? Or had she made a genuine mistake? Thank the gods that he had known that Ashiyuki Utamaro had presided over a large printshop and had not been the monastic sort of artist who toiled alone with a few brushes, ink, and rice paper.

She was looking about as if desperate for an excuse to break away. 'I'm afraid I must go,' she said. 'I'm meeting a friend.'

Yamamoto tipped his boater. But she surprised him again. Instead of immediately fleeing, she extended her long, slender cotton-gloved hand, and said, 'We've not been introduced. I enjoyed talking with you. I am Marion Morgan.'

Yamamoto bowed, thoroughly confused by her openness. Perhaps he was paranoid. 'Yamamoto Kenta,' he said, shaking her hand. 'At your service, Miss Morgan. If you ever visit the Smithsonian, please ask for me.'

'Oh, I will,' she said, and strolled away.

The puzzled Japanese spy watched Marion Morgan sail sleek as a cruiser through a billowing sea of flowered hats. Her course converged with that of a woman in a scarlet hat heaped with silk roses. Their brims angled left and right, forming an arch under which they touched cheeks.

Yamamoto felt his jaw go slack. He recognized the woman who greeted Marion Morgan as the mistress of a treacherous French Navy captain who would sell his own mother for a peek at the plans of a hydraulic gyro engine. He felt a strong urge to remove his boater and scratch his head. Was it coincidence that Marion Morgan knew

Dominique Duvall? Or was the beautiful American spying for the perfidious French?

Before he could ponder further, he had to doff his boater to a beautiful lady dressed head to toe in black.

'May I offer my condolences?' he asked Dorothy Langner, whom he had met at the unveiling of the bronze tablet at the Washington Navy Yard shortly before he murdered her father.

A master carpenter in blue-striped overalls served as Isaac Bell's guide when he made his final inspection under the hull. They walked its length twice, up one side and down the other.

The last of the wooden shores bracing the ship had been removed, as had the poppets – the long timbers holding her bow and her stern. Where there had been a dense forest of lumber was a clear view alongside the cradle from front to back. All that remained leaning against the ship were temporary tumbler shores – heavy timbers designed to fall away as she began to slide down the flat rails, which were thickly greased with yellow tallow.

Nearly every keel block supporting the vessel had been removed. The final blocks were assembled from four triangles bolted into single wooden cubes. Carpenters disassembled them by unscrewing the bolts that held them together. As the triangles fell apart, the battleship settled harder on the cradle. Swiftly, they unbolted the bilge blocks, the last holding her, and now *Michigan*'s full weight came on the cradle with an audible sighing of minutely shifting plates and rivets.

'All that's holding her now are the triggers,' the carpenter told Bell. 'Yank them, and off she goes.'

'Do you see anything amiss?' the detective asked.

The carpenter stuck his thumbs in his overalls and peered around with a sharp eye. Foremen were herding workmen off the ways and out of the shed. With the hammering of the wedges finally stopped it was eerily quiet. Bell heard the tugs hooting signals on the river and the murmur of the expectant throng above him on the platform.

'Everything looks right as rain, Mr. Bell.'

'Are you sure?'

'All they've got to do now is bust that bottle.'

'Who is that man with the wedge ram?' Bell pointed at a man who abruptly appeared carrying a long pole over his shoulder.

'That is a mighty brave fellow getting paid extra to poke the trigger if it jams.'

'Do you know him?'

'Bill Strong. My wife's brother's nephew by marriage.'

A steam whistle blew a long, sonorous blast. 'We ought to get out of here, Mr. Bell. There'll be tons of junk falling off her when she moves. If it happens to brain us, folks will say she's an unlucky ship – "launched in blood."'

They retreated toward the stairs that led up to the platform. As they parted at the juncture where the carpenter would join his mates on the riverbank and Bell would continue up to the christening, the tall detective took one last look at the ways, the cradle, and the dull red hull. At the bottom of the ways, where the rails dipped into the water, massive iron chains were heaped in horseshoe loops.

Attached to the ship by drag cables, the chains would help slow her as she slid into the water.

'What is that man doing with the wheelbarrow?'

'Bringing more tallow to grease the ways.'

'Do you know him?'

'Can't say that I do. But here comes one of your men checking him now.'

Bell watched the Van Dorn intercept him. The man with the wheelbarrow showed the bright red pass required to work under the ship. Just as the detective stepped aside, motioning for the man to continue, someone whistled, and the detective ran in that direction. The man lifted the handles of his barrow and wheeled it toward the rails.

'A regular patriot,' said the carpenter.

'What do you mean?'

'Wearing that red, white, and blue bow tie. A regular Uncle Sam, he is. See you later, Mr. Bell. Stop by the workmen's tent. I'll buy you a beer.' He hurried off, chuckling, 'I'm thinking of getting me one of those bow ties for Independence Day. The waiters was wearing them at the boss's tent.'

Bell lingered, studying the man pushing the wheelbarrow toward the back of the ship. A tall man, thin, pale, hair hidden under his cap. He was the only man on the ways except for Bill Strong, who crouched with his ram hundreds of feet away at the bow. Coincidence that he wore a waiter's bow tie? Did he get past the gates pretending to be a waiter until the ways were cleared and it was time to make his move unhindered? His pass had convinced the detective, though. Even at this distance Bell had seen it was the proper color.

He began hastily shoveling globs of tallow out of the barrow onto the flat rail. So hastily, Bell noticed, that it looked more like he was emptying the barrow rather than spreading the grease.

Isaac Bell plunged down the stairs. He ran the length of the ship at a dead run, drawing his Browning.

'Elevate!' he shouted. 'Hands in the air.'

The man whirled around. His eyes were big. He looked frightened.

'Drop the shovel. Put your hands in the air.'

'What is wrong? I showed my red pass.' His accent was German.

'Drop the shovel!'

He was gripping it so tightly that tendons stood like ropes on the backs of his hands.

A hoarse cheer erupted overhead. The German looked up. The ship was trembling. Suddenly it moved. Bell looked up, too, sensing a rush from above. In the corner of his eye he glimpsed a timber thick as railroad crosstie detach from the hull and tumble toward him. He leaped back. It crashed in the space in which he had been standing, knocking his broad-brimmed hat off his head and brushing his shoulder with the force of a runaway horse.

Before Bell could recover his balance, the German swung the shovel with the gritted-teeth determination of a long-ball hitter determined to turn a soft pitch into a home run.

24

The launching platform had begun to shake without warning.

The crowd fell silent.

It suddenly felt as if after three years of building, growing heavier every day as tons of steel were bolted and riveted to tons of steel, the battleship *Michigan* refused to wait a moment longer. No one had touched the electric button that would activate the rams that would release the triggers. But she had moved anyway. An inch. Then another.

'Now!' the Assistant Secretary of the Navy cried shrilly to his daughter.

The girl, more alert than he, was already swinging the bottle.

Glass smashed. Champagne bubbled through the crocheted mesh, and the girl sang out in golden tones, 'I christen thee *Michigan*!'

The hundreds of onlookers on the launching platform cheered. Thousands more on the shore, too far away to see the bottle break or the slow movement of the hull, were alerted by the voices of those on the platform and cheered, too. Tugboats and steamers tooted in the river. On the train tracks behind the shed, a locomotive engineer tied down his whistle. And slowly, very slowly, the battleship began to pick up speed.

Under the ship, the German's shovel smashed Bell's gun out of his hand and caromed off his shoulder. Bell was already thrown off balance by the falling timber. The shovel sent him pinwheeling.

The German jumped back to the wheelbarrow and plunged his hands into its gelatinous cargo, confirming what Bell had seen from the stairs. He had been shoveling tallow onto the ways not only to appear to be innocently performing his job but to expose what he had hidden under the tallow. With a glad cry he pulled out a tightly banded pack of dynamite sticks.

Bell leaped to his feet. He saw no fuse to detonate the explosive, no powdered string to light, which meant that the German must have rigged a percussion cap to detonate on contact when the saboteur smashed it against the cradle. The German's face was churning into a mask of insane triumph as he ran at the cradle holding the dynamite aloft, and Isaac Bell recognized the cold-eyed fearlessness of a fanatic willing to die to set off his bomb.

With every shore and block removed, *Michigan* was balanced precariously as she started down the ways. An explosion would derail the cradle and spill the 16,000-ton battleship on its side, crushing the launching platform and sweeping hundreds to their deaths.

Bell tackled the German. He brought the man down. But the madness that propelled the German to fearlessly face death gave him the strength to wrest free from the detective. The slowly sliding ship still had not left the shed nor reached the water's edge. The German stood up and ran full tilt at its cradle.

Bell had no idea where his Browning had fallen. His hat

had disappeared and with it his derringer. He pulled his knife from his boot, propped erect on one knee, and threw it with a smooth overhand motion. The razor-sharp steel pieced the back of the German's neck. He stopped in his tracks and reached back as if to swat a fly. Grievously wounded, he buckled at the knees. Yet he staggered toward the ship, raising his bomb. But Isaac Bell's knife had cost him more than a few precious seconds. By stopping for an instant, he remained directly in the downward path of another falling timber. It hit the German squarely, crushing his head.

The dynamite fell from his upstretched hand. Isaac Bell was already diving for it. He caught it in both hands before the percussion cap hit the ground and drew it gently to his chest as the long red hull hurtled past.

The ground shook. The drag chains thundered. Smoke poured from the cradle. *Michigan* accelerated out of the shed into the sunlit water, trailing the acrid scent of burning tallow fired by friction and billowing the river into clouds of spray that the sunshine pierced with rainbows.

While every eye in Camden locked on the floating ship, Isaac Bell seized the dead German and stuffed him in the wheelbarrow. The detective who had checked the saboteur's pass came running up, trailed by others. Bell said, 'Get this man in the back door of the morgue before anyone sees him. Shipbuilders are superstitious. We don't want to spoil their party.'

While they covered the body with scrap wood, Bell found his gun and put his hat on his head. A detective handed him his knife, which he sheathed in his boot. 'I'm supposed to take my girl to the luncheon. How do I look?'

'Like somebody ironed your suit with a shovel.'

They took out handkerchiefs and brushed his coat and trousers. 'You ever consider wearing a darker outfit for days like this?'

Marion took one look when Bell entered the pavilion and asked in a low voice, 'Are you all right?'

'Tip-top.'

'You missed the launching.'

'Not entirely,' said Bell. 'How did you get along with Yamamoto Kenta?'

'Mr. Yamamoto,' said Marion Morgan, 'is a phony.'

25

'I laid a trap, and he walked right into it – Isaac! He did not know about Ashiyuki Utamaro's Exile Scrolls.'

'You've got me there. What are Ashiyuki Utamaro's Exile Scrolls?'

'Ashiyuki Utamaro was a famous Japanese woodblock printmaker during the later Edo period. Woodblock artists operate large, complex shops where employees and acolytes do much of the work, tracing, carving, and inking after the master draws the image. They don't do calligraphy scrolls.'

'Why does it matter that Mr. Yamamoto didn't know about something that doesn't exist?'

'Because Ashiyuki Utamaro's Exile Scrolls *do* exist. But they were made secretly, so only real scholars know about them.'

'And you! No wonder you won the first law degree ever granted a woman at Stanford University.'

'I wouldn't know either except my father occasionally bought a Japanese scroll, and I remembered a strange story he told me. I wired him in San Francisco for the details. He wired back a very expensive telegram.

'Ashiyuki Utamaro was at the height of his printmaking career when he got in trouble with the Emperor apparently for making eyes or more at the Emperor's favorite geisha. Only the fact that the Emperor loved Ashiyuki Utamaro's woodcuts saved his life.

'Instead of chopping his head off, or whatever they do to Japanese Lotharios, he banished him to the northernmost cape of the northernmost island of Japan – Hokkaido. For an artist who needed his workshop and staff, it was worse than prison. Then his mistress smuggled in paper, ink, and a brush. And until he died, alone in his tiny little hut, he drew calligraphy scrolls. But no one could admit they existed. His mistress and everyone who helped her visit him would have been executed. They could not be displayed. They could not be sold. Somehow the prints ended up with a dealer in San Francisco, who sold one to my father.'

'Forgive me my skepticism, but it does sound like an art dealer's story,' said Bell.

'Except it is true. Yamamoto Kenta does not know about the Exile Scrolls. Therefore he is no scholar and no curator of Japanese art.'

'Which makes him a spy,' Bell said grimly. 'And a murderer. Well done, my darling. We'll hang him with this.'

The speeches that accompanied the luncheon's toasts were mercifully brief, and the rousing one delivered by Captain Lowell Falconer, Special Inspector of Target Practice, was, in the words of Ted Whitmark, 'a real stem-winder.'

With crackling language and powerful gestures, the Hero of Santiago praised Camden's modern yard, lionized the ship workers, thanked the Congress, commended the chief constructor, and acclaimed the naval architect.

During one of the explosions of applause, Bell whispered to Marion, 'The only thing he hasn't praised is the *Michigan*.'

Marion whispered back, 'You should have heard what he said privately about the *Michigan*. He compared her to a whale. And I don't believe he meant it as a compliment.'

'He did mention that it is barely half the size of Hull 44.'

With a courtly bow in Dorothy's direction, Falconer wound his toast up with a stirring testimonial to Arthur Langner. 'The hero who built *Michigan*'s guns. Finest 12s in the world today. And a harbinger of even better to come. Every man jack in the Navy will miss him.'

Bell glanced at Dorothy. Her face was alight with joy that even a maverick officer like Falconer had said for all to hear that her father was a hero.

'May Arthur Langner rest in peace,' Captain Falconer concluded, 'knowing that his nation sleeps in peace secured by his mighty guns.'

The last bit of business was the presentation by the chairman of New York Ship of a jeweled pendant to the Assistant Secretary of the Navy's quick-moving daughter, who had cracked the champagne over *Michigan*'s bow before the ship got away. Heading for the podium, the savvy industrialist shook hands warmly with a man in an elegant European frock coat, who handed him the pendant. And before he draped it around the young lady's neck, he used the occasion to plug the booming jewelry industry in Camden's sister city of Newark.

Anticipating the crush heading home to New York, Bell had bribed Camden detective Barney George to arrange for a police launch to run him and Marion across the river to Philadelphia, where a police car sped them to the Broad

Street Station. They boarded the New York express and settled into the lounge car with a bottle of champagne to celebrate the safe launching, the thwarting of a saboteur, and the imminent capture of a Japanese spy.

Bell knew that he had been too visible today to take a chance trailing Yamamoto back to Washington. Instead, he put the Japanese under close surveillance by the best shadows Van Dorn could field on short notice, and they were very good indeed.

'What do you think of Falconer?' Bell asked Marion.

'Lowell is a fascinating man,' she answered, adding enigmatically, 'He's torn by what he wants, what he fears, and what he sees.'

'That's mysterious. What does he want?'

'Dreadnoughts.'

'Obviously. What does he fear?'

'Japan.'

'No surprises there. What does he see?'

'The future. The torpedoes and submarines that will put his dreadnoughts out of business.'

'For a man torn, he's mighty sure of himself.'

'He's not that sure. He talked a blue streak about his dreadnoughts. Then suddenly his whole face changed, and he said, "There came a time in the age of chivalry when armor had grown so heavy that knights had to be hoisted onto their horses with cranes. Just about then, along came the crossbow, shooting bolts that pierced armor. An ignorant peasant could be taught how to kill a knight in a single afternoon. And *that*," he said – patting my knee for emphasis – "in our time could be the torpedo or the submarine."'

'Did he happen to mention the airplane flights at Kitty Hawk?'

'Oh, yes. He's been following them closely. The Navy sees their potential for scouting. I asked what if instead of a passenger the airplane carried a torpedo? Lowell turned pale.'

'There was nothing pale about his speech. Did you see those senators beaming?'

'I met your Miss Langner.'

Bell returned her suddenly intense gaze. 'What did you think of her?'

'She's set her cap for you.'

'I applaud her good taste in men. What else did you think of her?'

'I think she's fragile under all that beauty and in need of rescue.'

'That's Ted Whitmark's job. If he's up to it.'

Two cars ahead on the same Pennsylvania Railroad express, the spy, too, headed for New York. What some would call revenge he regarded as a necessary counterattack. Until today the Van Dorn Detective Agency had been more irritant than threat. Until today he had been content to monitor it. But today's defeat of a well-laid plan to destroy the *Michigan* meant that it had to be dealt with. Nothing could be allowed to derail his attack on the Great White Fleet.

When the train arrived in Jersey City, he followed Bell and his fiancée out of the Exchange Place Terminal and watched them drive off in the red Locomobile that a garage attendant had waiting for them with the motor running. He went back inside the terminal, hurried to the ferry house, rode the Pennsylvania Railroad's *St. Louis* across the river to Cortlandt Street, walked a few steps to Greenwich, and boarded the Ninth Avenue El. He got off in Hell's Kitchen and went to Commodore Tommy's Saloon, where Tommy tended to hang out instead of his fancy new joints uptown.

'Brian O'Shay!' The gang boss greeted him effusively. 'Highball?'

'What leads have you got on the Van Dorns?'

'That louse Harry Warren and his boys are nosing around like I told you they would.'

'It's time you broke some heads.'

'Wait a minute. Things are going great. Who needs a war with the Van Dorns?'

'Great?' O'Shay asked sarcastically. 'How great? Like waiting around for the railroads to run you off Eleventh Avenue?'

'I seen that coming,' Tommy retorted, hooking his thumbs in his vest and looking proud as a shopkeeper. 'That's why I hooked up with the Hip Sing.'

Brian O'Shay hid a smile. Who did Tommy Thompson think had sent him the Hip Sing?

'I don't recall the Hip Sing being famous for loving detectives. How long will your Chinamen put up with Van Dorns acting like they own your territory?'

'Why you got to do this, Brian?'

'I'm sending a message.'

'Send a telegram,' Tommy shot back. He laughed. 'Say, that's funny, "Send a telegram." I like that.'

O'Shay took his eye gouge from his vest pocket. Tommy's laughter died in his mouth.

'The purpose of a message, Tommy, is to make the other

man think about what you can do to him.' O'Shay held the gouge to the light, watched it glint on the sharp edges, and slipped it over his thumb. He glanced at Tommy. The gang boss looked away.

'Thinking what you can do, it makes him wonder. Wondering slows him down. The power of wondering, Tommy – make him wonder and you'll come out on top.'

'All right, all right. We'll bust some heads, but I'm not killing any detectives. I don't want no war.'

'Who else do they have poking around other than Harry Warren's boys?'

'The Hip Sing spotted a new Van Dorn poking around Chinatown.'

'New? What do you mean, new. Young?'

'No, no, he's no kid. Out-of-town hard case.'

'New to New York? Why would they bring an out-of-town guy into the city? Doesn't make sense.'

'He's a pal of that son of a bitch Bell.'

'How do you know that?'

'One of the boys saw them working together at the Brooklyn Navy Yard. He's not from New York. It looks like Bell brought him in special.'

'He's the one. Tommy, I want him watched real close.'

'What for?'

'I'm going to send Bell a message. Give him something to wonder about.'

'I'll not have my Gophers kill any Van Dorns,' Tommy repeated stubbornly.

'You let Weeks take a shot at Bell,' O'Shay pointed out.

'The Iceman was different. The Van Dorns would have seen it was personal between Weeks and Bell.'

Brian 'Eyes' O'Shay regarded Tommy Thompson with scorn. 'Don't worry – I'll leave a note on the body saying, "Don't blame Tommy Thompson."'

'Aw, come on, Brian.'

'I'm asking you to watch him.'

Tommy Thompson took another swig from his glass. He glanced at O'Shay's thumb gouge and quickly looked away. 'I don't suppose,' he said petulantly, 'I get any say in this.'

'Follow him. But don't tip your hand.'

'All right. If that's what you want, that's what you get. I'll use the best shadows I got. Kids and cops. No one notices kids and cops. They're always there, like empty beer barrels on the sidewalk.'

'And tell your cops and kids to keep an eye on Bell, too.'

John Scully cruised up the Bowery and into the narrow, twisting streets of Chinatown. Staring at the men's long pigtails and gawking up at the overhead tangle of fire escapes and clotheslines and signs for Chinese restaurants and teahouses, he was disguised as a 'blue jay' – an out-of-town hayseed who was wandering the big city for a good time. He had just appeared to find it in the arms of a skinny streetwalker who had also ventured over from the Bowery when a pair of corner loafers visiting from that same neighborhood flashed a rusty knife and a blackjack and demanded his money.

Scully turned out his pockets. A roll of cash fell to the pavement. They snatched it and ran, never knowing how lucky they were that the ice-blooded detective had not felt sufficiently threatened to spoil his disguise by opening fire with the Browning Vest Pocket tucked in the small of his back.

The woman who had observed the robbery said, 'Don't expect nothin' from me with your empty pockets.'

Scully tugged open some stitches of his coat lining and pulled out an envelope. Peering into it, he said, 'Looky here. Enough left to make both our nights.'

She brightened at the sight of the dough.

'What do you say we get something to drink first?' said Scully, offering a kindness to which she was unaccustomed.

After they were settled in a booth in the back of Mike Callahan's, a dive around the corner on Chatham Square, with a round of whiskey in her and another on the way, he asked casually, 'Say, do you suppose those fellers was Gophers?'

'What? What the hell are go-phers?'

'The men who robbed me. Gophers? Like gangsters.'

'Go-phers? Oh, *Goofers*!' She laughed. 'Mother of Mary, where did you come from?'

'Well, were they?'

'Could be,' she said. 'They've been drifting down from Hell's Kitchen for a couple of months now.'

Scully had heard rumors of this strange news from others. 'What do you mean, a couple of months? Is that unusual?'

'Used to be the Five Pointers would bust their heads. Or they'd be chopped by the Hip Sing. Now they're walking around like they own the place.'

'What is Hip Sing?' Scully asked innocently.

26

'Isaac,' Joseph Van Dorn protested exasperatedly. 'You've got Japs and Germans darned-near red-handed, the French spying on the Great White Fleet, and a Russian practically living in Farley Kent's design loft. Why are you launching a frontal attack on the British Empire? From where I sit, they appear to be the only innocents in this whole tangled spiderweb.'

'Apparently innocent,' Isaac Bell retorted.

With Washington, D.C., Van Dorn Detective Agency operatives shadowing Yamamoto Kenta to determine the extent of the Japanese spy's organization and Harry Warren's boys trawling Hell's Kitchen to get a line on the upward-bound Commodore Tommy Thompson's new connections, Bell decided it was time to confront the Royal Navy.

'The British didn't build the most powerful Navy in the world without keeping a close eye on their rivals. Based on Abbington-Westlake's successes against the French, I'm willing to bet that they're probably pretty good at it.'

'But you've got the Jap dead to rights. Have you considered picking up Yamamoto right now?'

'Before he gets away or does more damage? Of course! But then how do we determine who else he's tied up with?'

'Partners?'

'Maybe partners. Maybe underlings. Maybe a boss.' Bell shook his head. 'It's what we *don't* know that concerns me. Assume that Yamamoto is the spy we think he is. How did he persuade that German to attack the *Michigan*? How did he get him or some other German to attack at Bethlehem Steel? We know, according to the Smithsonian, that he was in Washington the day that poor kid fell off the cliff. Who did Yamamoto get to push him? Who did he send to Newport that almost got Wheeler in his cottage?'

'I presume Wheeler is sleeping safe in the torpedo barracks now?'

'Reluctantly. And his girlfriends are hopping mad. The list goes on and on, Joe. We have to find the connections. How did Yamamoto tie up with a gangster like Weeks in Hell's Kitchen?'

'Borrowed him from Commodore Tommy Thompson.'

'If so, how did a Japanese spy team up with the boss of the Gophers? We don't know.'

'Apparently you knew enough to shoot up his saloon,' Van Dorn observed.

'I was provoked,' Bell replied blandly. 'But you see my point. Who else do we not even know about yet?'

'I see it. I don't like it. But I see it.' Van Dorn shook his big head, stroked his red whiskers, and rubbed his Roman nose. Finally, the founder of the agency granted his chief investigator a small smile. 'So now you want to brace the British Empire?'

'Not their whole empire,' Bell grinned back. 'I'm starting with the Royal Navy.'

'What are you looking for?'

'A leg up.'

Joseph Van Dorn's hooded eyes gleamed with sudden interest. 'Leverage?'

'Yamamoto and his mob may call themselves spies, Joe. But they act like criminals. And we know how to nail criminals.'

'All right. Get to it!'

Isaac Bell went directly to the Brooklyn Bridge and joined Scudder Smith on the pedestrian walkway. It was a bright, sunny morning. Smith had chosen for his watch the comparative darkness of the shade of the bridge's Manhattan pier. Smith was one of the best Van Dorn shadows in New York. A former newspaperman, fired – depending upon who told the story – either for writing the truth or overembroidering it, or for being drunk before noon, he was intimate with every district in the city. He passed Bell his field glasses.

'They've been walking back and forth across the bridge pretending to be tourist snapshot fiends. But somehow their Brownies are always pointed down at the navy yard. And I don't think those are real Brownies inside those Brownie boxes but something with a special lens. The large, round fellow is Abbington-Westlake. The terrific-looking woman is his wife, Lady Fiona.'

'I've seen her. Who's the little guy?'

'Peter Sutherland, retired British Army major. Claims he's traveling to Canada to look over the oil fields.'

The strangely cold spring had persisted into May, and the chilly wind blew hard high over the East River. All three wore topcoats. The woman's had a sable collar that matched her hat, which she was anchoring with one hand against the gusts.

'Looking the oil fields over for what?'

'Last night at dinner Sutherland said, "Oil is the coming fuel for water transportation." Abbington-Westlake being Naval Attaché, you can bet water transportation means dreadnoughts.'

'How'd you happen to overhear it?'

'They thought I was the waiter.'

'I'll take over before they order more pheasant.'

'Want the glasses?'

'No, I'm going to make my move.'

Scudder Smith vanished among the pedestrians crossing to Manhattan.

Bell headed for the make-believe tourists.

Nearing the middle of the span, he gained a clear view of the Brooklyn Navy Yard immediately north of the bridge. He could see all the shipways, even a section of the northernmost that cradled the beginnings of Hull 44. All were open to the weather, markedly different from the closed sheds at New York Ship in Camden. Cantilevered bridge cranes trundled along elevated rails that allowed them to hover directly over the ships under construction. Switch engines moved freight cars laden with steel plate around the yard.

Away from the building area, horse-drawn wagons and auto trucks were delivering daily rations to the warships moored in slips beside the river. Long strings of sailors in white were carrying sacks up gangways. Bell saw a dry dock nearly eight hundred feet long and over a hundred wide. In the middle of the bay was an artificial island containing docks and ways and slips. A ferry shuttled between it and the mainland, and fishing boats and steam lighters moved slowly up and down a crowded channel that ran between the artificial island and a market on the shore.

The trio was still snapping photographs as Bell bore down on them. Emerging suddenly from the stream of Brooklyn-bound pedestrians, he flourished his 3A Folding Pocket Kodak and called out a friendly, 'Say, would you like me to snap all three of you together?'

'No need, old boy,' Abbington-Westlake replied in plummy aristocratic tones. 'Besides, how would we get the film?'

Bell snapped their picture anyway. 'Should I use one of your cameras? You have a lot of them,' Bell said affably.

Suspicion hardened Fiona Abbington-Westlake's attractive features. 'I say!' she exclaimed in an accent that managed to sound clipped and drawled at the same time. 'I've seen you before, somewhere. Quite recently, as a matter of fact. Never forget a face.'

'And in a similar setting,' Isaac Bell replied. 'Last week at New York Ship in Camden, New Jersey.'

Lady Fiona and her husband exchanged glances. The major grew watchful.

Bell said, 'And today we "observe" the New York Navy Yard in Brooklyn. These reversed names must be confusing to tourists.' He raised his camera again. 'Let's see if I can get all of you in the picture with the navy yard right behind you – the way you were snapping it.'

It was Abbington-Westlake's turn to blurt, 'I say!,' and he did arrogantly. 'Who the devil do you think you are? Move along, sir. Move along!'

Bell threw a hard look at 'retired major' Sutherland. 'Drilling for oil in Brooklyn?'

Sutherland allowed himself the abashed smile of a man who'd been caught. But not Abbington-Westlake. The Naval Attaché charged past his companions and blustered at Isaac Bell, 'You'll move along if you know what's good for you. Or I'll call a constable.'

Bell answered quietly. 'A constable is the last person you want to see you here at this moment, Commander. Meet me in the basement bar of the Knickerbocker at six o'clock. Take the entrance from the subway.'

Flummoxed by Bell's use of his rank, Abbington-Westlake transformed himself from arrogant aristocratic naval officer to a type that Bell had known at college – the young man eager to act old and stuffy before his time. 'I'm afraid I don't use the subway, old chap. Rather a plebeian form of transport, don't you think?'

'The subway entrance will let you meet me for a cocktail without the upper crust noticing, "old chap." Six o'clock sharp. Leave your wife and Sutherland. Come alone.'

'And if I don't appear?' Abbington-Westlake huffed.

'I'll come looking for you at the British Embassy.'

The Naval Attaché turned white. Research had assured Bell that he would, because Great Britain's Foreign Office, Military Intelligence, and Naval Intelligence were all highly mistrustful of one another. 'Hold on, sir!' he whispered. 'The game just isn't played that way. One doesn't blunder into one's adversary's embassy shouting secrets.'

'I didn't know there were rules.'

'Gentlemen's rules,' Abbington-Westlake replied with a studied friendly wink. 'You know the drill. Do what we please. But set a good example for the servants and don't frighten the horses.'

Isaac Bell handed him his card. 'I don't follow spy rules. I'm a private detective.'

'A *detective*?' Abbington-Westlake echoed disdainfully.

'We have our own rules. We collar criminals and turn them in to the police.'

'What the devil do —'

'On rare occasion we give criminals a break — but only when they help us collar criminals much, much worse than they are. Six o'clock. And don't forget to bring me something.'

'What?'

'A spy worse than you are,' Isaac Bell smiled coldly. 'Much worse.'

He turned on his heel and walked back toward Manhattan, certain that Abbington-Westlake would report at six as ordered. Descending the stairs from the Brooklyn Bridge walkway, he failed to take note of a one-eyed slum urchin disguised as a newsboy hawking the afternoon *Herald*.

Bell got as far as the subway steps when a sixth sense told him he was being watched.

He passed the subway entrance, crossed Broadway, and turned down the thoroughfare, which was jam-packed with delivery trucks and wagons, buses and streetcars. He paused repeatedly, studied reflections in shopwindows, ducked around moving vehicles, and popped in and out of stores. Did Abbington-Westlake have men backing him up, who had taken up his trail? Or the so-called major? He wouldn't put it past the major. Sutherland looked competent, like a man who'd been in the wars. And it would be wise to remember that the bombastic, vaguely silly demeanor Abbington-Westlake affected should not obscure his espionage successes.

Bell jumped onto a trolley on busy Fulton Street and looked back. No one. He rode the trolley to the river, got off as if heading for the ferry, but suddenly reversed course and boarded the westbound trolley. He disembarked as quickly and swerved into Gold Street. He saw no one. But he still had an intense feeling that he was being stalked.

He entered a crowded oyster house and slipped a dollar to a waiter to let him out the kitchen door into an alley that led him to Platt Street. When he still saw no one following but still sensed it, he plunged deep into the ancient lanes of lower Manhattan – Pearl, Fletcher, Pine, and Nassau.

Try as he might, Bell saw no one following.

He was studying reflections in the showroom window of a manufacturer of assay and diamond scales, having just gone in the front and out the back of the Nassau Café, when he found himself on Maiden Lane – New York's jewelers' district. The upper floors of the four- and five-story cast-iron-fronted buildings that darkened the sky were a beehive of gem cutters, importers, jewelers, goldsmiths, and watchmakers. Below the factories and workrooms, retail jewelry shops lined the sidewalk, their windows gleaming like pirate chests.

As Bell cast a sharp eye up and down the narrow street, his stern visage softened and a quizzical smile began to tug at the corners of his mouth. Most of the men crowding the pavement were around his own age, smartly dressed in topcoats and derbies, but with shoulders sloped and faces bewildered as they blundered in and out of the jewelry shops. Bachelors about to propose marriage, Bell surmised, attempting to seal a momentous decision with the purchase of a valuable gem about which they feared they knew nothing.

Bell's smile got bigger. This was a fine happenstance. Maybe no one had followed him after all. Maybe some 'Higher Being' with a sense of humor had foxed his ordinarily trustworthy sixth sense to send him wandering into lower Manhattan for the express purpose of buying his beautiful fiancée an engagement ring.

Isaac Bell's smile grew less sure as he joined the parade of men pacing the sidewalk and meditating upon the dozens of display windows that glittered with myriad possibilities and infinite choices. Finally, the tall detective took the bull by the horns. He squared his shoulders and strode into the shop that looked the most expensive.

The child who watched Isaac Bell enter the jeweler's shop – a boy who was clean enough not to be chased out of the jewelry district and had a shoeshine box strapped to his back as a disguise – waited to be sure that the Van Dorn had not ducked inside just to give them the slip again. He was the fourth to have trailed their quarry on his circuitous ramble. Eyeing the shadowy silhouettes of Bell and the jeweler through the window, he signaled another boy and passed him the box. 'Take over. I gotta report.'

He ran the few short blocks west into the tenement-and-warehouse district that bounded the North River, darted into the pier-side Hudson Saloon, and made for the free lunch.

'Get outta here!' roared a bartender.

'Commodore!' the shoeshine boy growled back, fearlessly stuffing liverwurst between slabs of stale bread. 'Make it quick!'

'Sorry, kid. Didn't recognize you. This way.' The bartender ushered him into the saloon owner's private office, which had the only telephone in the neighborhood. The owner watched him warily.

'Get out,' said the boy. 'This ain't none of your business.'

The owner locked his desk and left, shaking his head. There was a time when a Hell's Kitchen Gopher ventured downtown into this neighborhood, he'd end up hanging from a lamppost. But that time had ended fast.

The boy telephoned Commodore Tommy's Saloon. They said Tommy wasn't there, but he'd call him right back. That was strange. The boss was always in his saloon. People said Tommy hadn't been outdoors in daylight in years. He stepped out to the free lunch for another sandwich, and when he returned the phone was ringing. Commodore Tommy was mad as hell that he'd been kept waiting. When he got done yelling, the boy told him about Isaac Bell's wander around the city starting from the middle of the Brooklyn Bridge.

'Where is he now?'

'Maiden Lane.'

27

Isaac Bell retreated in complete confusion from the fourth jewelry store he had entered in an hour. He had time for one or two more before heading uptown to grill Abbington-Westlake at the Knickerbocker.

'Shine, sir? Shoeshine?'

'Not a bad idea.'

He leaned his back against the wall and submitted his left boot to the polish-stained fingers of the skinny kid with the wooden box. His mind was reeling. He had been simultaneously informed that a diamond set in platinum was the 'only appropriate stone to make a girl feel properly engaged' and that a large semiprecious gemstone mounted in gold was 'considered most fashionable.' Particularly when compared to a small diamond. Although even a small diamond was an 'acceptable token of betrothal.'

'Other foot, sir.'

Bell removed his throwing knife, palming it, and let the kid polish his right boot.

'Is it always so busy down here?'

'May and June are the bridal months,' the kid answered without looking from the cloth he was whipping so fast it was a blur.

'How much?' Bell asked when the boy was done and his boots gleamed like mirrors.

'A nickel.'

'Here's a dollar.'

'I don't got no change for a buck, mister.'

'Keep it. You did a fine job.'

The kid stared at him. He appeared about to speak.

'What is it?' asked Bell. 'You all right, son?'

The boy opened his mouth. He looked around and suddenly grabbed his box and ran, dodging shoppers, and disappeared around the corner. Bell shrugged, and entered another jewelry store, Solomon Barlowe, a smaller establishment on the ground floor of a five-story, Italianate-style cast-iron-clad building. Barlowe sized him up with piercing brown eyes as shrewd as a police magistrate's.

'I want to buy an engagement ring. I think it should be a diamond.'

'Were you considering a solitaire setting or incluster?'

'Which would you recommend?'

'If expense were an object, of course –'

'Assume it is not,' Bell growled.

'Ah! Well, I can see that you are a man of taste, sir. Let us look at some stones for your approval.' The jeweler unlocked a case and laid a black velvet tray on the counter between them.

Bell whistled amazement. 'I've seen kids shooting marbles smaller than these.'

'We are fortunate in our supplier, sir. We import our own. Ordinarily, I would have more stock to show you, but the bridal months are upon us, and the choice gems have already been snapped up.'

'In other words, buy now before it's too late?'

'Only if you need something immediately. Is your wedding impending?'

'I don't think so,' said Bell. 'We're neither of us children and both rather busy. On the other hand, I would like to nail things down.'

'A large solitaire diamond of a unique hue has a way of doing that, sir. Here, for instance –'

The door opened and a well-dressed gentleman about Bell's age walked into Barlowe's shop flourishing a gold-headed cane studded with gems. He looked vaguely familiar, but the detective could not quite place him. It was rare his memory for faces failed, and he suspected it would be a case of seeing someone completely out of context, as if they had last met in a Wyoming saloon or been seated side by side at a Chicago prizefight. He was clearly not a desperate bachelor. There was nothing of the tentative buyer in his demeanor, which was supported by a confident smile.

'Mr. Riker!' Barlowe exclaimed. 'What a wonderful surprise.' To Bell he said, 'Excuse me, sir. I'll just be a moment.'

'No, no,' said Riker. 'Don't let me interrupt a sale.'

Barlowe said, 'But I was just discussing you with my customer, who is in the market for something special and has a bit of time to look for it.'

He turned to Bell. 'This is the very gentleman I mentioned to you, our gem supplier. Mr. Erhard Riker of Riker and Riker. We're in luck, sir. If Mr. Riker can't find your stone, it doesn't exist. He is the foremost supplier of the finest gemstones in the world.'

'Good Lord, Barlowe,' Riker smiled. 'Your generosity of spirit will mislead your customer into believing I am a miracle worker instead of a simple merchant.'

Riker spoke with an English accent similar to Abbington-Westlake's aristocratic drawl, but the color of his coat suggested to Bell that he was German. It was a Chesterfield, with the traditional black velvet collar. An Englishman's or American's Chesterfield would be cut of a navy or charcoal gray fabric. Riker's was a dark green loden cloth.

Riker removed his gloves, slipped his cane into his left hand, and extended his right. 'Good day, sir. As you have just heard, I am Erhard Riker.'

'Isaac Bell.'

They shook hands. Riker had a strong, firm grip.

'If you would allow me the honor, I will look for the perfect gem for your fiancée. What color are the lady's eyes?'

'Coral-sea green.'

'And her hair?'

'Her hair is blond. Pale as straw.'

'By the smile on your face, I have a picture of her beauty.'

'Multiply it by ten.'

Riker bowed in the European manner. 'In that event, I will find for you a gem that is *almost* her equal.'

'Thank you,' said Bell. 'You are very kind. Have we met before? Your face is familiar.'

'We have not been *introduced* before,' replied Riker. 'But I, too, recognize you. I believe it was at Camden, New Jersey, early this week.'

'At the *Michigan* launching! Of course. Now I remember. You gave the shipyard owner the gift he presented to the young lady who sponsored the battleship.'

'I stood in for one of my Newark clients who decorated the pendant with my gemstones.'

'Well, isn't this a wonderful coincidence?' exclaimed Solomon Barlowe.

'Two coincidences,' Isaac Bell corrected him. 'First, Mr. Riker happened along while I was shopping for a special diamond. Second, it turned out we attended the same ship launching in Camden last Monday.'

'As if written in the stars!' Riker laughed. 'Or should I say diamonds? For what are diamonds but man-size stars? My hunt begins this instant! Do not hesitate to get in touch, Mr. Bell. In New York I stay at the Waldorf-Astoria. The hotel forwards my mail when I travel.'

'You can find me at the Yale Club,' said Bell, and they exchanged cards.

Every Van Dorn, from apprentice to chief investigator, was taught from the first day he went to work that coincidences were presumed guilty until proven innocent. Bell asked Research to look into the gem importers Riker & Riker. Then he turned over his camera, ordered the film to be developed and brought to him immediately, and went down to the hotel's basement lobby, off of which was snugged a quiet, dimly lit bar.

Abbington-Westlake had arrived ahead of him, a good sign that he had frightened the daylights out of the Naval Attaché with his threat to go to the British Embassy.

Bell decided that he would get more out of him now with a milder approach, and he said, 'Thank you for coming.'

He saw immediately it was a mistake. Abbington-Westlake glowered imperiously, and snapped, 'I don't recall being offered a choice in the matter.'

'Your choice of snapshots,' Bell fired back, 'would get you arrested if I were a government agent.'

'No one can arrest me. I have diplomatic immunity.'

'Will your diplomatic immunity bail you out of trouble with your superiors in London?'

Abbington-Westlake's lips shut tightly.

'Of course it won't,' Bell said. 'I'm not a government agent, but I certainly know where to find one. And the last thing you want is for your rivals in the Foreign Office to learn you've been caught with your hand in the cookie jar.'

'See here, old boy, let's not go off half cocked.'

'What did you bring me?'

'I beg your pardon?' Abbington-Westlake stalled.

'*Who* did you bring me? Give me a name. A foreign spy whom I can have arrested instead of you.'

'Old chap, you have an extremely inflated estimate of my powers. I don't *know* anyone to bring you.'

'And you have an extremely inflated estimate of my patience.' Bell glanced around inquiringly. Couples were drinking at the nearly dark tables. Several men stood alone at the bar. Bell said, 'Do you see the gentleman on the right? The one wearing the bowler hat?'

'What about him?'

'Secret Service. Shall I ask him to join us?'

The Englishman wet his lips. 'All right, Bell. Let me tell you what I can. I warn you it is very little.'

'Start small,' said Bell coldly. 'We'll work from there.'

'All right. All right.' He wet his lips again and glanced around. Bell suspected that he was starting a lie. He let the Englishman speak without interruption. After tangling himself in it, he would be more vulnerable to pressure.

'There is a Frenchman named Colbert,' Abbington-Westlake began. 'He trades in arms.'

'Colbert, you say?' God bless the Van Dorn Research boys.

'Raymond Colbert. And while trading arms is hardly a savory enterprise, it is actually a blind for Colbert's sinister deeds . . . You are familiar with the Holland submarine?'

Bell nodded. He'd had Falconer fill him in and borrowed a book.

As the Naval Attaché wove his tale, Isaac Bell was struck with admiration – which he concealed – for Abbington-Westlake's cool nerve. Faced with the threat of exposure, he was turning it into an opportunity to destroy the man who was blackmailing his wife. He rattled on a while about purloined architect drawings and a special gyro to keep the boat on course underwater. Bell let him, until the door opened and a Van Dorn apprentice came in with a large manila envelope. Bell noted approvingly that the kid did not approach until Bell gave him the nod and retreated silently after handing him the envelope.

'As we speak, old boy, Colbert is en route to New York on a Compagnie Générale Transatlantique mail boat. You can nab him the instant she docks at Pier 42. Don't you see?'

Bell opened the envelope and riffled through the prints.

Abbington-Westlake asked acidly, 'Am I boring you, Mr. Bell?'

'Not at all, Commander. I can't recall a more exciting fiction.'

'Fiction? See here –'

Bell passed a print over their table. 'Here is a snapshot of you and the Lady Fiona and the Brooklyn Navy Yard – careful, the paper is a still damp.'

The Englishman sighed, heavily. 'You make it abundantly clear that I am at your mercy.'

'Who is Yamamoto Kenta?'

Bell was gambling that, not unlike bank robbers and confidence men, the spies of the international naval race were aware of their rivals and fellow practitioners. He saw it was true. Even in the dim light, Abbington-Westlake's eyes gleamed as if he suddenly saw a way out of the mess he was in.

'Careful!' Bell warned. 'The instant I hear a breath of fiction this photograph goes to that gentleman of the Secret Service, along with copies to the British Embassy and U.S. Naval Intelligence. Do we understand each other?'

'Yes.'

'What do you know of him?'

'Yamamoto Kenta is a highly decorated Japanese spy. He's been at it for donkey's years. And he is number one at the Black Ocean Society, which acts in the Japs' overseas interests. He was a prime instigator of the Jap infiltration of the Russians' Asiatic Fleet and a prime reason the Japs now occupy Port Arthur. Since the war, he's operated in Europe and made an absolute mockery of Britain's and Germany's attempts to keep secrets in their ship works. He knows more about Krupp than the Kaiser, and more about HMS *Dreadnought* than her own captain.'

'What is he doing here?'

'I don't know.'

'Commander,' Bell said warningly.

'I don't know. I swear I don't know. But I will say one thing.'

'It better be interesting.'

'It is interesting,' Abbington-Westlake shot back confidently. 'It is very interesting because it makes absolutely no sense that a Japanese spy of Yamamoto's caliber is operating here in the United States.'

'Why?'

'The Japs don't want to fight you chaps. Not now. They're not ready. Even though they know you Americans are not ready. It doesn't take a naval genius to rate the Great White Fleet as a joke. But they damned well know that their fleet is not ready either and won't be for many, many years.'

'Then why did Yamamoto come here?'

'I suspect that Yamamoto is playing some sort of double game.'

Bell looked at the Englishman. There was a certain puzzlement in his expression that looked absolutely genuine. 'How do you mean?'

'Yamamoto is working for someone else.'

'Other than the Black Ocean Society?'

'Precisely.'

'Whom?'

'I haven't the foggiest. But it's not for Japan.'

'If you don't know who he is working for, what makes you think it's someone other than the Japanese?'

'Because Yamamoto offered to buy information from me.'

'What information?'

'He suspected that I had information concerning the new French dreadnought. Offered a pretty penny for it. Expense was obviously no object.'

'Did you have the information?'

'That's neither here nor there,' Abbington-Westlake answered opaquely. 'The point is, the Japs don't give a hang about the Frogs, old boy. The French Navy can't fight in the Pacific. They can barely defend the Bay of Biscay.'

'Then what did he want it for?'

'That is the point. That is what I am telling you. Yamamoto intended to sell it to someone who *does* care about the French.'

'Who?'

'Who else but the Germans?'

Bell studied the Englishman's face for a full minute. Then he leaned closer, and said, 'Commander, it is now clear to me that behind a façade of amiable bumbling, you are extremely well informed about your fellow spies. In fact, I suspect you know more about them than the ships you're supposed to be spying on.'

'Welcome to the world of espionage, Mr. Bell,' the Englishman replied cynically. 'May I be the first to congratulate you on your very recent arrival.'

'What Germans?' Bell demanded harshly.

'Well, I can't tell you with any precision, but –'

'You don't believe for one second that the Germans are paying Yamamoto Kenta to spy for them,' Bell cut in. 'Whom do you really suspect?'

Abbington-Westlake shook his head, visibly dismayed. 'No one I have heard of – none of the regulars one bumps into . . . It's as if the Black Knight galloped out of the ether and threw his gauntlet on King Arthur's Roundtable.'

'A freelance,' mused Bell.

28

'A freelance indeed, Mr. Bell. You've hit the nail on the head. But the possibility of a freelance merely raises the larger question.' Abbington-Westlake's round face brightened with relief that he had so intrigued Bell that the tall detective would let him go. 'Whom does the freelance serve?'

'Are freelances commonly used in the spy game?' Bell asked.

'One employs all available resources.'

'Have you ever worked as a freelance?'

Abbington-Westlake smiled disdainfully. 'The Royal Navy *hires* freelances. We don't work for them.'

'I mean you personally – if you need money.'

'I work for His Majesty's Navy. I am not a mercenary.' He stood up. 'And now, Mr. Bell, if you will excuse me, I believe I have paid you for your photograph in equal coin. Agreed?'

'Agreed,' said Bell.

'Good day, sir.'

'Before you go, Commander?'

'What is it?'

'I have been dealing with you in my capacity as a private investigator. As an *American,* however, let me warn you that if I ever again see or hear of you taking photographs of the Brooklyn Navy Yard, or any other shipyard in my country, I will throw your camera off the bridge and you after it.'

Isaac Bell hurried upstairs to the Van Dorn office. A big case kept getting bigger and wider. If Abbington-Westlake was telling the truth – and Bell bet he was – then Yamamoto Kenta was not the head of the spy ring attacking Hull 44 but only another of its many agents. Like the German, and the hired killer Weeks, and whoever threw the young fire-control expert off the cliff. Who was the freelance? And whom did he serve?

Bell knew he was at a crossroads. He had to decide whether to arrest Yamamoto and squeeze what information they could out of him or continue following him in the hope that the Japanese spy would lead them higher up the chain of deceit. There was risk in waiting. How long would it take a seasoned professional like Yamamoto to catch the scent of his stalkers and go to ground?

As Bell strode into the back room, the man on the telephones said, 'Here he is right now, sir, just walked in,' and handed him the middle one. 'The boss.'

'Where?'

'Washington.'

'Yamamoto just hopped the train to New York,' Van Dorn said without preamble. 'Coming your way.'

'Alone?'

'Not if you count three of our men in the same car. And others watching every station the Congressional Limited stops at.'

'I'll watch the railroad ferry. See who he's come to meet.'

Yamamoto Kenta had a choice of three different Pennsylvania Railroad ferries to cross the river from the Jersey City Exchange Place Terminal to Manhattan Island. After disembarking from the Congressional Limited into the enormous glass-ceilinged train shed, he could take a boat to 23rd Street, another to Desbrosses Street near Greenwich Village, or one that would land all the way downtown at Cortlandt Street. There was even a boat to Brooklyn, and another went up the East River to the Bronx. The ferry he chose would depend upon the actions of the Van Dorns following him.

He had spotted two detectives in his railcar. And he suspected that an older man dressed as an Anglican priest had shadowed him several days earlier disguised in the uniform of a Washington, D.C., streetcar conductor. He had considered jumping off the train early at Philadelphia and dodging the Van Dorns watching the platform. But with so many alternatives awaiting him in New York, he saw no need to inconvenience himself by breaking the journey early.

It was after midnight, and the crowd rushing from the train shed was thin, providing less cover than he would have liked. Still, the advantage was his. The detectives did not realize that he knew they had been following him for a week. A thin smile played upon his lips. A natural aptitude for spying? Or simply experience. He'd been at the game before many of the shadows trailing him had been born.

As always, he traveled light, carrying only a small valise. The Black Ocean Society had limitless cash reserves; he could buy extra clothing when he needed it instead of carrying it when a situation like this one demanded he move quickly. His gabardine raincoat was of a tan hue, so pale as to be almost white. His hat was of a similar distinctive color, a finely woven Panama with a dark band.

At the juncture of the train platform and the arrival hall, he saw the Anglican priest forge ahead and signal a tall man whom Yamamoto had last seen in Camden, New Jersey. Frantic research back in Washington – sparked by his discovery that he was being followed – led him to believe that the Van Dorn was the fabled Isaac Bell. Bell had worn a white suit and broad-brimmed hat at the *Michigan* launching. Tonight he was attired like a deckhand in a snug sweater, with a knit watch cap covering his striking golden hair. Yamamoto smiled to himself. Two could play that game.

Swept along by the torrent of passengers and trunk-trundling porters, Yamamoto followed the signs from the arrival hall into the ferry house. A row of ferries waited in their slips – magnificent Tuscan red, smoke-belching, two-deck double-ender behemoths big as dreadnoughts and named for great American cities: *Cincinnati, St. Louis, Pittsburgh, Chicago*. Engines ahead, propellers pushing them tight to their piers, they offered the Japanese spy additional choices of which deck to travel on.

Teams of draft horses, iron shoes clattering, were pulling freight wagons aboard the lower vehicles decks, vast open spaces they shared with autos and trucks. Foot passengers could ride beside them, separated by the bulkheads of flanking passenger cabins that ran the length of the boat.

The main cabins were above. As a first-class passenger, Yamamoto could enjoy the brief river crossing in a private cabin. There was one cordoned off for gentlemen, another for ladies. Or he could stand in the open air where the salty harbor wind would disperse the smoke and cinders.

He chose a ferry not for its destination but for the fact that its deckhands were already closing its scissor gate, blocking any more passengers from boarding.

'Not so fast, Chinkboy!' a burly deckhand shouted in his face.

Yamamoto already had ten dollars in his hand. The man's eyes widened at his good fortune, and he reached for it, shouting, 'Step lively, sir. Step lively.'

Yamamoto slid past him and moved deeper into the boat, heading for the stairs to the upper deck at a rapid clip.

The whistle blew a sharp tenor note. The deck stopped shuddering as the screws holding her in place stopped turning. Then the enormous boat shook from stem to stern as the screws reversed to drive her out of her slip.

Yamamoto reached the ornamentally carved wooden staircase that swept upward in a graceful curve. For the first time, he looked back, a quick glance over his shoulder. He saw Isaac Bell running full speed to the edge of the slip. At the edge, the detective launched himself in the air in an attempt to broad-jump the rapidly widening gap. The Japanese spy waited to confirm that Bell had fallen in the churning water.

Isaac Bell landed gracefully as a gull, strode to the scissor gate, and engaged the deckhands in conversation.

Yamamoto ran up the stairs. He showed his train ticket to enter the first-class gentleman's lounge, headed for the men's room, entered a stall, and closed the door. He turned his tan coat inside out, revealing its black lining. His hatband was formed by multiple layers of tightly wound silk. He unwound it into a long scarf, bent the brims of his Panama downward, and tied it on his head with the scarf. The final touch was packed in his valise. Then all he had to do was wait when the ferry docked until all the men had left the first-class cabin. He had just opened his valise when beneath his feet the rumble of the screws abruptly stopped.

Forward momentum slowed so quickly, he had to brace against the wall. The whistle gave three short blasts. The screws rumbled anew, shaking the deck. And to Yamamoto's horror and disbelief, the giant ferry backed out of the river and into the terminal slip from which it had just emerged.

The loudest of the hundreds of the Pennsylvania Railroad ferry passengers inconvenienced was a United States senator. He roared like an angry lion at the ferry captain, 'What in blue blazes is going on here? I've been traveling all day from Washington and I'm late for a meeting in New York.'

No one dared asked a senator traveling without his wife whom he was meeting at midnight. Even the ferry captain, a veteran North River waterman, was not brave enough to explain that a Van Dorn detective dressed like a deckhand had barged into his wheelhouse and drawn from his wallet a railroad pass unlike any he had ever seen. The document required all employees to accord him privileges of the line that exceeded even that of a senator who voted religiously in favor of legislation the railroads approved. Handwritten and signed and sealed by the president of the line, and witnessed by a federal judge, it superseded all dispatchers. Its only limits were common sense and the rules of safety.

'What did you do to get that pass?' the captain had asked as he hurriedly signaled the engine room *Stop Engines*.

'The president returned a favor,' had said the detective. 'And I always tell the president how kindly I am treated by his employees.'

So the captain told the legislator, 'A mechanical breakdown, Senator.'

'How the devil long are we going to wait here?'

'Everyone is disembarking for the next boat, sir. Let me carry your bag.' The captain seized the senator's valise and led him to the main deck and down the gangway, where cold-faced detectives observed every passenger trooping off.

Isaac Bell stood behind the other Van Dorns, watching over their heads each and every face. The manner that Yamamoto had chosen to get away – jumping aboard at the last instant – made it clear that the shadows had slipped up, and the Japanese spy knew he was being followed. Now it was a chase.

Three hundred eighty passengers, men, women, and sleepy children, shuffled past. Thank the Lord, thought Bell, it was the middle of the night. The boats carried thousands at rush hour.

'That's the last of them.'

'O.K. Now we check every nook and cranny on the boat. He's hiding somewhere.'

A small, elderly woman in a long black dress, a warm shawl, and a straw bonnet tied to her head with a dark scarf boarded a streetcar outside the Jersey City Exchange Place Terminal. It was a slow, stop-and-start ride to the city of Hoboken. The trolley looped around the square at Ferry and River streets, and now her journey moved swiftly as she descended to the first completed of the McAdoo tubes. For a nickel, she boarded an eight-car electric train so new it smelled of paint.

It whisked her under the Hudson River. Ten minutes after boarding, she left the tube train at the first station in New York. The conductors operating the air-powered doors exchanged a glance. The neighborhood at Christopher and Greenwich streets above the beautifully lighted vaulted ceilings of the tube line was nowhere near as pleasant as the subterranean station, particularly at such a late hour. Before they could call a warning, the woman hurried past a pretty florist's shop at the foot of the stairs – closed, with lights still shining on the flowers – and disappeared.

At street level she found a dark square of grimy cobblestones. Warehouses loomed over formerly genteel residences long since partitioned into rooming houses. She drew the attention of a thug who followed her, drawing close as she neared an alley. She whirled suddenly, pressed a small pistol to his forehead, and said in a soft male voice with a slight accent the thug had never heard before, 'I can pay you handsomely to guide me to a clean room where I can spend the night. Or I can pull the trigger. I will let you choose.'

29

'I have a job for Harry Wing and Louis Loh,' said Eyes O'Shay.

'Who?' asked Tommy Thompson, who was beginning to think that he was seeing more of Eyes than he wanted to.

'Your Hip Sing highbinders,' Eyes said impatiently. 'The high-class tong Chinamen you made a hookup with the same day I came back from the dead. Stop playing stupid with me. We've discussed this before.'

'They ain't mine, I told you. I just made a deal with 'em to open some joints.'

'I have a job for them.'

'What do you need me for?'

'I do not want to meet them. I want you to deal with them for me. Do you understand?'

'You don't want them to see your mug.'

'Or hear about me. Not one word, Tommy. Unless you want to spend the rest of your life as a blind man.'

Tommy Thompson had had just about enough. He leaned back in his chair, tipping it up on the two back legs, and said coldly, 'I'm thinking it's time to pick up a gun and blow your brains out, O'Shay.'

Brian O'Shay was on his feet in a flash. He kicked one of the chair legs, splintering it. The gang boss crashed to the floor. At the sounds, which shook the building, Tommy's bouncers charged into the room. They pulled up short.

O'Shay had the boss in a headlock, down on one knee, pointing Tommy's face toward the ceiling, with his gouge scraping his left eye.

'Deal with your floor managers.'

'Get out of here,' Tommy said in a strangled voice.

The bouncers backed out of the room. O'Shay let him go abruptly, dropping the bigger man on his back and rising to brush sawdust from his trousers. 'Here's what I want,' he said conversationally. 'I want you to send Harry Wing and Louis Loh to San Francisco.'

'What's in San Francisco?' Tommy asked sullenly, climbing to his feet and pulling a bottle from his desk.

'The Mare Island Naval Shipyard.'

'What the hell is that?'

'It's a navy yard. Like the Brooklyn Navy Yard. It's where the Great White Fleet ships will re-provision and get their bottoms painted before they sail for Honolulu and Auckland and Japan.'

'Eyes, what the hell are you into now?'

'There's an ammunition magazine in the Mare Island Naval Shipyard. I want Harry Wing and Louis Loh to blow it up.'

'Blow up a navy yard?' Thompson dropped his bottle and jumped to his feet. 'Are you crazy?'

'No.'

Tommy looked around frantically as if cops suddenly had ears pressed to his well-guarded walls. 'What are you telling me this for?'

'Because when the Mare Island magazine blows up, you stand to make more dough than you ever saw in your life.'

248

'How much?'

Eyes told him, and Commodore Tommy sat down, smiling.

Van Dorn detective John Scully continued scouting Chinatown in a variety of disguises. He was a street peddler one day, a ragpicker the next, a drunk sleeping outdoors as a soldier in the 'army of the park benches,' and an official of the city health department, which raised sufficient bribes to keep down expenses. He kept picking up hints about the Gopher Gang moving downtown. Streetwalkers talked wistfully about a high-class gambling hall and opium den that was really choosy about the girls they hired. But a Hip Sing boss's girlfriend personally ran the joint, and she treated you on the level.

'Chinese girls?' asked a wide-eyed Scully, provoking laughter from the women he was standing to drinks on Canal Street.

'There's no China girls in Chinatown.'

'No China girls?'

'They're not allowed to bring them into the country.'

'Where do they get the girls?'

'*Irish* girls. Whaddaya think?'

'The Chinaman's girlfriend is Irish?' Scully asked as if such a combination were beyond his imagination.

One of the women lowered her voice and looked around before she whispered furtively, 'I hear she's a Gopher.'

At that, Scully did not have to pretend a bumpkin's amazement. It was so unusual as to be either impossible or evidence of a strange and dangerous new alliance between Hell's Kitchen and Chinatown.

Scully knew he should report even the hint of a tong-Gopher coalition to headquarters. Or at least confide in Isaac Bell. But his gut and his years of experience told him that he was on the edge of a breakthrough that would solve the Hull 44 case. He felt so close to learning the whole story that he decided to let reporting in ride for another day or so.

Had the Gophers offered the girl as a prize to seal the deal? Or had she initiated it? According to Harry Warren, the Gopher women were often worse criminals than the men – smarter by a long shot and more devious. Whatever the connection was, Detective John Scully regarded it as a personal point of honor to stroll into the Knickerbocker with the whole story instead of a measly piece of a rumor.

A few days later he struck pay dirt.

He was back in blue jay costume. A clumsily tailored sack suit hung loosely on his ample frame. His trouser cuffs barely covered the tops of his unfashionable boots. But the expensive new straw boater purchased from Brooks Brothers on Broadway shading his round face and the gold watch chain glistening on the bulge of his vest sent a clear signal that he was a prosperous candidate to be buncoed.

He went inside a Chinese opera house on Doyers Street, which the newspapers had recently dubbed the 'Bloody Angle' due to the short, crooked street's reputation as a battleground for the warring Hip Sing and On Leong tongs. Somewhere on Doyers, he had heard, was the Hip Sing joint that offered beautiful girls, the purest opium, and a roulette wheel spun by a croupier who knew his business.

The detective had seen enough of opium and roulette to steer clear of the roulette. He had nothing against beautiful girls, and for some reason he could never figure out why they often took a shine to him. And when that happened, the opium only made a good thing better.

When he stepped back out on the street after watching the show for a while, a genuine blue jay was gazing up at an American flag on a pole thrust from a third-story dormer of the opera house. 'Chinese opera?' he asked Scully. 'What's that like?'

'No opera I ever heard,' answered Scully. 'Screeching like they needed their axles oiled. But the costumes and greasepaint are something else. They'll knock your eyes out.'

'Any girls?'

'Hard to tell.'

The blue jay stuck out his hand. 'Tim Holian. Waterbury Brass Works.'

'Jasper Smith. Schenectady Dry Goods,' replied Scully, and then he heard every detective's nightmare.

'Schenectady? Then you sure as heck know my cousin Ed Kelleher. He's president of the Rotary in Schenectady.'

'Not since he ran off with my wife's niece.'

'What? No, there must be some mistake. Ed's a married man.'

'Just thinking about it makes my blood boil. The poor girl is barely fifteen.'

Holian retreated dazedly toward Mott Street. Scully continued loitering between the opera house entrance and a bow window shielded with wire mesh. It didn't take long for a roper to discover him.

'Say, brother, looking for a good time?'

Scully looked him over. Middle-aged, with very few teeth and ragged clothes, former Bowery Boy, no longer the violent sort but perfectly willing to deliver him to those who were if the gaze fixed on his watch chain was any clue. 'What did you have in mind?'

'Want to meet girls?'

Scully pointed toward Mott Street. 'Fellow that was just standing here in a straw hat. He's looking for girls.'

'What about you? Want to see deranged addicts in an opium den?'

'Shove off.'

The roper took his expression as fair warning and headed after the man from Waterbury. Scully continued to loiter.

But so far, no go. He had not learned a damned thing more since he'd parked himself in front of the opera house. Not a sign of customers coming and going. Maybe it was too early. But these places tended to keep the drapes drawn and the game going round the clock. He hung around for another hour but got no sense that he was getting close. Ropers like the one he'd sent packing would never steer him to such a high-class joint. So he kept giving the ropers the shove while he watched to see arriving customers point the way.

An unusual sight caught his eye. Walking quickly, darting anxious glances behind her at a cop who seemed to be following, was a fair-skinned Irish girl carrying a Chinese baby. She was built as solidly as a bricklayer and had the kind of about-to-wink smile in her eye that Scully appreciated. He tipped his hat and made room on the narrow sidewalk as she hurried past toward Mott. Up close, the baby looked not entirely Chinese, not with that tuft of yellow hair crowning its head.

The cop brushed past Scully and caught up with the woman at the angle in Doyers. He peered suspiciously into her blanket. Scully ambled over, suspecting what would happen.

'I'm going have to take you in,' said the cop.

'What the bloody hell for?' asked the mother.

'It's for your own protection. Every white woman married to a Chinese has got to show she was not kidnapped and held captive.'

'Kidnapped? I'm not kidnapped. I'm going shopping to bring supper home for my husband.'

'You'll have to show me your marriage license before I'll believe that.'

'I don't carry it around with me, for God's sake. You know I'm married. You're just giving me a hard time. Expect me to put money in your hand.'

The cop flushed angrily. 'You're coming in,' he said, and took her by the arm.

John Scully shouldered up to him. 'Officer, if we could speak in private?'

'Who are you? Get out of here.'

'Where I come from, money talks,' said Scully, passing the cop the bills he had palmed. The cop turned on his heel and lumbered back toward the Bowery.

'What did you do that for?' She had angry tears in her eyes.

'It seemed like a good idea at the time,' said Scully. 'They bother you much?'

'They do it to all of us who marry Chinamen. As if a girl had no say in who she wanted to marry. They hate that a white woman would marry a Chinese, so they say we did it because we're addicted to opium. What's wrong with marrying a Chinaman? Mine works hard. Comes home at night. He don't drink. He don't beat me. Of course, I'd floor him if he tried. He's a little fellow.'

'Doesn't drink?' asked Scully. 'Does he smoke opium?'

'He comes home for supper,' she smiled. 'I'm his opium.'

Scully took a deep breath, looked around guiltily, and whispered, 'What if a fellow wanted to try to smoke some just to see what it was like?'

'I'd say he's playing with fire.'

'Well, let's say he wanted to take the chance. I'm not from around here. Is there a safe place for a fellow to try it?'

The woman put her hands on her hips and stared him in the face. 'I saw you give that cop much too much. Do you have a lot of money?'

'Yes, ma'am. I've done very well by myself, but it's time I cut loose. I really want to try something new.'

'It's your funeral.'

'Yes, ma'am. That's how I see it. But I'd pay the extra to go to a place where they won't knock me on the head.'

'You're standing right in front of it.' She indicated with a toss of her head the opera house. Scully looked up at the tall windows on the second story.

'In there? I was just in there hearing the opera.'

'There's a place for high rollers upstairs. You can try your opium. And other things.'

'Right here?' Scully scratched his head and pretended to gawk. His detective work had brought him pretty close. But without her, he'd have been looking all week. Just went to show that good deeds were rewarded.

'You go up to the balcony like you was intending to hear the opera. Climb all the way to the back and you'll see a little door. You knock on that, and they'll let you in.'

'Just like that?'

'For Chinese there are only two kinds of people. Strangers outside, family and friends inside.'

'But I'm a stranger.'

'You tell them Sadie sent you and you won't be a stranger.'

Scully smiled. 'So you played with fire?'

'No,' she laughed, and slapped him on the shoulder. 'Go on with you. But I know some of the girls.'

Scully bought another ticket, climbed to the balcony, turned his back on the screeches coming from the stage, climbed to the top, and knocked on the door she'd told him about. He heard a peephole slide open and grinned the unsure grin of a man way off his own territory. The door opened a crack, secured by a strong chain.

'What do you want?' asked a thickset Chinese.

Scully glimpsed a hatchet handle protruding from his tunic. 'Sadie sent me.'

'Ah.' The guard loosed the chain, opened the door, and said solemnly, 'Enter.' He pointed the way up carpeted stairs, and John Scully climbed into air that was dense with sweet-smelling smoke.

At first sight, the Van Dorn detective did not have to feign a country bumpkin's astonishment at the very large space bathed in golden light. It had a canopy ceiling of red cloth, and every inch of the walls was covered in curtains, hanging carpets, and painted silk panels depicting dragons, mountains, and dancing girls. Furnished with elaborate carved wooden furniture and illuminated by colored lanterns, it looked, Scully thought, like his idea of the throne room of a Peking palace, minus the eunuch guards.

Deadly-looking Hip Sing hatchet men dressed in dark business suits stood watch over the faro wheel, the fantan tables, and the pretty girls carrying opium pipes to customers lounging on sofas. The girls, who wore clinging skirts slit high as their knees, were white, though those with dark hair were made up with greasepaint to look Chinese. Like the streetwalkers had told him, genuine Chinese women were scarcer than hens' teeth in Chinatown.

The customers lolling half conscious in the smoke were a mix of yellow and white men. He saw prosperous-looking Chinese merchants, some in traditional Mandarin jackets, others in sack suits and derbies or boaters. The whites included Fifth Avenue swells and wealthy college boys, the sort who relied on their father's checkbooks to clear up their gambling debts. Most interesting of all were a couple of pug-ugly gangsters in tight suits and loud ties that Scully would bet a month's pay were Hell's Kitchen Gophers.

How long had they all been here? He'd stood outside for hours and hadn't seen a single one of them enter. Obviously the joint had another entrance from some street other than Doyers. He'd been waiting outside the back door while they went in the front.

A white man sat up on his couch, clapped his derby on his head, and swung his feet unsteadily to the floor. As he stood, their gazes met. Scully almost dropped his teeth. What in hell was Harry Warren doing here?

Both detectives looked away abruptly.

Had Harry, too, heard the same rumors he had ferreted out? No, Scully recalculated. Harry Warren would have been shadowing the Gophers. That's how he got here. The gang specialist didn't know about the Hip Sing–Gopher alliance yet. He had just followed a Gopher and ended up inside, failing to put two and two together. Scully was miles ahead of Harry and his so-called experts, he thought proudly. Before he was done he'd beat the New York Van Dorns in their own hometown.

Two girls came his way.

One was a shapely dark Irish lass made up like a Chinese. The other was a petite redhead, a dead-swell looker, with blue eyes so bright they flashed in the dim lantern light. She put Scully in mind of Lillian Russell in her leaner years. Although that could be the effect of her enormous hat, with its upswept brim, or a natural reaction to the intoxicating clouds of pungent smoke, or the heavy coating of paint and powder slathered thick as an actress's makeup on a face that didn't need any cosmetics at all.

The redhead dismissed the dark girl with a curt nod.

Scully's pulse quickened. Young as she was, she acted like she might be the madame of the operation. The Hip Sing boss's girlfriend he'd been hunting.

'Welcome to our humble establishment,' she said,

reminding Scully of a Chinese princess on the vaudeville stage. Except her accent was pure Hell's Kitchen. 'How did you happen to find us?'

'Sadie sent me.'

'Sadie does us great honor. What will be your pleasure, sir?'

Scully gaped like a blue jay from the sticks as if overwhelmed by the possibilities. In fact, he *was* a little overwhelmed. She was talking business like any madame worth the name, but she was gazing into his eyes as if offering herself. And *herself,* the dazzled Scully had to admit, was quite a cut above the usual fare.

'Your pleasure?'

'I always wanted to try a little opium.'

She looked disappointed. 'You could get that from your apothecary. Where are you from?'

'Schenectady.'

'Can't a man of your means get opium in a pharmacy?'

'Sort of afraid to at home, if you know what I mean.'

'Of course. I understand. Well, opium it will be. Come with me.'

She took his hand in hers, which was small, strong, and warm. She led him to a couch half hidden by drapes and helped him get comfortable, with his head propped on soft pillows. One of the painted 'Chinese' girls brought a pipe. The redhead said, 'Enjoy yourself. I'll come back later.'

30

'The Gophers got one of my boys,' Harry Warren telephoned Isaac Bell at the Knickerbocker.

'Who?'

'Little Eddie Tobin, the youngster.'

Bell raced to Roosevelt Hospital at 59th and Ninth Avenue.

Harry intercepted him in the hallway. 'I put him in a private room. If the boss won't pay for it, I will.'

'If the boss won't pay, I will,' said Bell. 'How is he?'

'They kicked him in the face with axheads in their boots, cracked his skull with a lead pipe, broke his right arm and both legs.'

'Is he going to make it?'

'The Tobins are Staten Island scowmen – oysters, tugboats, smuggling – so he's a tough kid. Or was. Hard to say how a man comes out of a beating like that. Near as I can tell there were four of them. He didn't stand a chance.'

Bell went into the room and stood with clenched fists over the unconscious detective. His entire head was swathed in thick, white bandages seeping blood. A doctor was sliding a stethoscope incrementally across his chest. A nurse stood by in starched linen. 'Spare no expense,' Bell said. 'I want a nurse with him day and night.'

He rejoined Harry Warren in the hall. 'It's your town, Harry, what are we going to do about this?'

The gang expert hesitated, clearly not happy with the answer he had to deliver. 'One on one they don't mess with Van Dorns. But the Gophers outnumber us by a lot, and if it comes to war, they're fighting on their own territory.'

'It already has come to war,' said Isaac Bell.

'The cops won't be any help. The way the city works, politicians, builders, the church, the cops, and gangsters divide it up. Long as nobody gets so greedy that the reformers take hold, they're not going to bother each other over a private detective getting beat up. So we're on our own. Listen, Isaac, this is odd. It's not Tommy Thompson's way to take on trouble he doesn't have to. Sending a message telling us to back off? You do something like that to a rival gang – the Dusters or the Five Pointers. He knows you don't do that to the Van Dorns. He's as much as admitting he's taking orders from the spy.'

'I want you to send a message back.'

'I can get the word passed to people who will tell him, if that's what you mean.'

'Tell them that Isaac Bell is wiring his old friend Jethro Watt – Chief of the Southern Pacific Railroad Police – asking him to dispatch two hundred yard bulls to New York to guard the Eleventh Avenue freight sidings.'

'Can you do that?'

'Jethro is always spoiling for a fight, and I know for a fact that the railroads are getting fed up with their freight trains being robbed. Tommy Thompson will think twice before he hits a Van Dorn again. The SP's cinder dicks may be the dregs but they're tough as nails, and the only thing they fear is Jethro. Until they get here, none of our

260

boys go alone. Two Van Dorns or more on the job, and careful when they're off duty.'

'Speaking of alone, I bumped into your pal John Scully.'

'Where? I haven't heard from him in weeks.'

'I shadowed a Gopher lieutenant into Chinatown. Dead end. He spent the day smoking opium. Scully wandered into the joint tricked out like a tourist.'

'What was Scully doing?'

'Last I saw, lighting a pipe.'

'Tobacco?' Bell asked, doubting it.

''Fraid not.'

Bell looked at Harry Warren. 'Well, if you could survive it, Scully will, too.'

The transatlantic steamer *Kaiser Wilhem der Gross II* thrust four tall black funnels and two even taller masts into the smoky sky at the edge of Greenwich Village. Her straight bow towered over tugboats, the pier, and fleets of horse-drawn hansom cabs and motor taxis.

'Right here is fine, Dave,' Isaac Bell said into the speaking tube of a brewster green Packard limousine provided by Archie Abbott's wife Lillian's father. The railroad tycoon was unable to meet his beloved daughter's ship, as he was steaming across the continent on his private train – on the trail, Bell assumed, of an independent railroad to fold into his empire. Bell, who had urgent reason to speak with Archie, had offered to stand in for him.

'Pick me up on Jane Street after you get them loaded.'

He stepped out onto the cobblestones and watched the gangway. Not surprisingly, the newlyweds were first off

261

the ship, guided ashore by solicitous purser's mates and followed closely by a pack of newspaper reporters, who would have boarded the ship at Sandy Hook to greet New York's most exciting young couple. More reporters were waiting on the pier. Some had cameras. Others were accompanied by sketch artists.

Bell, who preferred not to see his face on newsstands while investigating in disguise, retreated from the pier and waited on the street of low houses and stables.

Fifteen minutes later the limousine slowed, and he stepped nimbly aboard.

'Sorry about all the hoopla,' the blue-blooded Archibald Angell Abbott IV greeted him, clasping his hand. They had been best friends since boxing for rival colleges. 'All New York is dying to see my blushing bride.'

'I'm not surprised,' said Bell, kissing the beauteous young Lillian warmly on the cheek before he settled on the folding seat that faced the couple. 'Lillian, you look absolutely radiant.'

'Blame my husband,' she laughed, running her fingers through Archie's thick red hair.

When they got to the limestone Hennessy mansion on Park Avenue, Bell and Archie talked in the privacy of the library. 'She's radiant,' said Bell. 'You look beat.'

Archie raised his glass with a shaking hand. 'Revels all night, cathedrals and country-house parties all day, then more revels. One forgets how energetic one was at nineteen.'

'What did you learn on the ship?'

'The Europeans are all looking for a fight,' Archie replied soberly. 'All worried the other guy will throw the first punch.

The British are convinced there will be war with Germany. They know that the German Army is immense, and the German military has the Kaiser's ear. Ear, hell, the Army and the Navy have the Kaiser's heart *and* his blessing!

'The Germans are convinced there will be war with England because England will not tolerate an expanding German Empire. The British know that defeating the German Navy would not guarantee victory, whereas the defeat of the British Navy would spell the end to England's overseas empire. If that weren't enough, the Germans suspect that Russia will attack them to derail a revolution by distracting their peasants with a war. If that happens, the Germans fear, Britain will side with Russia because France is allied with the Russians. So Germany will force Austria and Turkey onto their side. But none of these idiots understand that their alliances will cause a war like no one's ever seen.'

'That bleak?'

'Fortunately for us, none of them want the United States as an enemy.'

'Which is why,' Bell said, 'I wonder if England and Germany are attempting to make the United States think the other is their enemy.'

'That's precisely the kind of byzantine talk I heard on the ship,' said Archie. 'You have an evil mind.'

'I've been hanging around the wrong crowd lately.'

'I thought it was that Yale education,' said Archie, a Princeton man.

'Courting the United States to be their ally, England and Germany could each secretly be maneuvering to make their enemy look like our enemy.'

'What about the Japanese?'

'Captain Falconer claims that anything that loosens the European footholds in the Pacific will embolden the Japanese. They'll stay out of it as long as they can and then side with the winner. Frankly, he seems possessed by a fear of the Japanese. He saw them up close in the Russo-Japanese War, so he thinks he knows them better than most. He insists they're brilliant spies. Anyway, to answer your question, we've had a Jap under surveillance for a week. Unfortunately, he gave us the slip.'

Archie shook his head in mock dismay. 'I go away for one little honeymoon, and the detective business goes to hell. Where do you suppose he is?'

'Last seen on the railroad ferry into New York. We're combing the city. He's the best part of the case. I need him badly.'

'Got the report on Riker and Riker,' Grady Forrer reported when Bell got back to headquarters. 'On your desk.'

Erhard Riker was the son of the founder of Riker & Riker, importers of precious gems and precious metals for the New York and Newark jewelry industries. The younger Riker had expanded the company since taking over seven years ago when his father was killed in Boer War cross fire in South Africa. He shuttled regularly between the United States and Europe on luxury transatlantic ocean liners, favoring the German *Wilhelm der Grosse* and the British *Lusitania,* unlike his father who had patronized older, more staid steamships like the Cunard Line *Umbria* and North German Lloyd's *Havel.*

One fact caught Bell's eye: Riker & Riker maintained its own private protection service both for guarding jewelry shipments and escorting Riker personally when he himself was carrying valuables.

Bell sought out the head of Research. 'Are private guard services common in the gem line?'

'Seem to be with the Europeans,' said Grady Forrer, 'traveling the way they have to.'

'What sort does he hire?'

'Pretty-boy bruisers. The sort you can dress up in fancy duds.'

A receptionist stuck his head in the door. 'Telephone call for you, Mr. Bell. Won't say who he is. English accent.'

Bell recognized the plummy drawl of Commander Abbington-Westlake.

'Shall we have another cocktail, old chap? Perhaps even drink it this time.'

'What for?'

'I have a very interesting surprise for you.'

31

'Police! Police! Don't none of youse move!'

The door from the opera house balcony through which John Scully had entered the Hip Sing opium den crashed open with a loud bang and knocked the heavyset Chinaman guarding it into the wall. The first man through was a helmeted sergeant broad as a draft horse.

The Chinese gambling at the fan-tan table were accustomed to police raids. They moved the quickest. Cards, chips, and paper money went flying in the air as they bolted through a curtain that covered a hidden door. The Hip Sing bouncers scooped the money off the faro table and ran. The white players at the faro wheel ran, too, but when they pawed at other curtains they found blank walls. Girls screamed. Opium smokers looked up.

The redheaded madame ran to Scully's couch. 'Come with me!'

She pulled Scully through another curtain as the cops stormed in swinging their clubs and shouting threats. Scully saw no door in the near darkness, but when she shoved on the wall a narrow panel swung open. They went through, and she hinged it closed and threw heavy bolts shut at the top and bottom. 'Quickly!'

She led him down a steep and narrow stairway barely wide enough for the detective to squeeze his bulk through.

At each landing was another narrow door, which she opened, closed, and bolted behind them.

'Where are we going?' asked Scully.

'The tunnel.'

She unlocked a door with a key. Here was the tunnel, low-ceiled, narrow, and damp. It stretched into darkness. She took a battery light from a hole in the wall and by its flashing beam led them underground for what felt to Scully to be a distance of two city blocks. By the twists and turns and breaks in the walls, he surmised it was actually a right-of-way constructed through a series of connected cellars.

She unlocked another door, took his hand again, and led him up two flights of stairs into the conventionally furnished parlor of an apartment with high windows that offered views of the Chatham Square El station flooded in sunlight.

Scully had been in the dark so long, he found it hard to believe that daylight still existed.

'Thanks for the rescue, ma'am.'

'My name is Katy. Sit down. Relax.'

'Jasper,' said Scully. 'Jasper Smith.'

Katy threw down her bag, reached up, and began removing hatpins.

Scully watched avidly. She was even prettier in the daylight. 'You know,' he laughed. 'If I carried a knife as long as your hatpins, the police would arrest me as a dangerous character.'

She gave him a cute pout. 'A girl can't wear her chapeau all crooked.'

'It doesn't seem to matter if a girl wears a cartwheel or

a little ding-dong affair, she always nails it down with hat-pins long as her arm. I see you are a fellow Republican.'

'Where'd you get that idea?'

Scully reached for the ten-inch steel pin she was removing and held it to the light. The decorative bronze head depicted a possum holding a golf club. '"Billy Possum." That's what we call William Howard Taft.'

'They're trying to make a possum like a teddy bear. But everyone knows that Taft is no Roosevelt.'

She stuck all four pins in a sofa cushion and tossed her hat beside them. Then she struck a pose, with her strong hands on her slim hips. 'Opium is the one pleasure I can't offer you here. Would you settle for a Scotch highball?'

'Among other things,' Scully grinned back.

He watched her mix Scotch and water in tall glasses. Then he clinked his to hers, took a sip, and leaned closer to kiss her on the mouth. She stepped back. 'Let me get comfortable. I've been in these clothes all day.'

Scully searched the room quickly, thoroughly, and silently. He was looking for a rent bill or gas bill that would show whose apartment it was. He had to stop when the El clattered by because he couldn't hear her coming back from the bedroom. It passed, and he looked some more.

'Say, how you doing in there?' he called.

'Hold your horses.'

Scully looked some more. Nothing. Drawers and cabinets were bare as a hotel room. He cast a look down the hall, and opened her purse. Just as he heard the door open, he hit the jackpot. Two railroad tickets for tomorrow's three-thirty p.m. 20th Century Limited – the eighteen-hour excess-fare flyer to Chicago – with connections through to San Francisco. Tickets for Katy and whom? The boss? The Hip Sing boyfriend?

When she found the little thirteen-ounce .25 holstered in the small of his back, she wanted to know what it was doing there.

'Got robbed once carrying the payroll for my clerks. It ain't gonna happen again.'

She seemed to believe him. At least it didn't get in the way of the proceedings. Not until he saw her add the knockout drops to his second highball.

Scully felt suddenly old and blue.

She was so very good at it. She had the patience to wait to dress the second drink so he'd be less likely to taste the bitter chloral hydrate flavor. She hid the vial expertly between the crease of her palm and the fleshy part of her thumb. She crossed her legs as she did it, with a distracting flash of snow-white thighs. Her only failing was her youth. He was too old to be buncoed by a kid.

'Bottoms up,' she smiled.

'Bottoms up,' Scully whispered back. 'You know, I never met a girl quite like you.' Gazing soulfully into her pretty blue eyes, he reached blindly for his glass and knocked it off the table.

Isaac Bell got to the Knickerbocker's cellar bar ten minutes early. Mid-afternoon on a sunny day, it was largely empty, and he saw right away that Abbington-Westlake had not yet arrived. There was one man at the bar, two

269

couples at tables, and a single slight figure seated on the banquette behind the small table where he had sat with the English Naval Attaché in the darkest corner of the room. Immaculately dressed in an old-fashioned frock coat, high-standing collar, and four-in-hand tie, he beckoned, half rising and bowing his head.

Bell approached, wondering if he could believe his eyes.

'Yamamoto Kenta, I presume?'

32

'Mr. Bell, are you familiar with the Nambu Type B?'

'Low-quality, 7-millimeter semiautomatic pistol,' Bell answered tersely. 'Most Japanese officers buy themselves a Browning.'

'I'm a sentimental patriot,' said Yamamoto. 'And it *is* remarkably effective at a range of one small tabletop. Keep your hands where I can see them.'

Bell sat down, laid his big hands on the table, one palm down, one up, and scrutinized a face that gave away nothing.

'How far do you think you will get if you shoot me in a crowded hotel?'

'Considering how far I have gotten from a dozen professional detectives for the past two weeks, pursuit by ordinary citizens drinking in a hotel bar holds few terrors for me. But surely you can guess that I did not lure you here to shoot you, which I could have done late last night as you walked home from this hotel to your club on 44th Street.'

Bell returned a grim smile. 'My congratulations to the Black Ocean Society for teaching their spies the art of invisibility.'

'I accept the compliment,' Yamamoto smiled back. 'In the name of the Empire of Japan.'

'Why does a patriot of the Empire of Japan become the instrument of an English spy's revenge?'

'Don't be put out with Abbington-Westlake. You hurt his pride, which is a dangerous thing to do to an Englishman.'

'Next time I see him, I won't hurt his pride.'

Yamamoto smiled again. 'That is between you and him. Let us remember that you and I are not enemies.'

'You murdered Arthur Langner in the Gun Factory,' Bell shot back coldly. 'That makes us enemies.'

'I did not kill Arthur Langner. Someone else did. An overzealous subordinate. I've taken appropriate measures with him.'

Bell nodded. He saw no profit in challenging that cold-eyed lie until he learned Yamamoto's intention. 'If you didn't murder Langner and we are not enemies, why are you pointing a gun under the table at my belly?'

'To hold your attention while I explain what is going on and what I can do to help you.'

'Why would you want to help me?'

'Because you can help me.'

'You are offering to deal.'

'I am offering to trade.'

'Trade what?'

'The spy who arranged Langner's murder *and* the murder of Lakewood, the fire-control expert, *and* the murder of the turbine expert, MacDonald, *and* the murder of Gordon, the armorer in Bethlehem, *and* the attempt to sabotage the launch of the *Michigan,* which you so ably thwarted.'

'Trade for what?'

'Time for me to disappear.'

Isaac Bell shook his head emphatically. 'That makes no

sense. You've demonstrated that you could disappear already.'

'It is more complicated than simply disappearing. I have my own responsibilities – responsibilities to my country – which have nothing to do with you because we are not enemies. I need to get clean away and leave no tracks to haunt me or embarrass my country.'

Bell thought hard. Yamamoto was confirming what he had suspected – that a spy other than he was the mastermind who had recruited not only the Japanese murderer but the German saboteur and who knew how many others.

Yamamoto spoke urgently. 'Discretion is survival. Defeats, and victories, should be observed quietly, after the fact, at a distance.'

To save his own skin – and who knew for what other motives – Yamamoto would betray the mastermind. As the treacherous Abbington-Westlake had put it so cynically at this same table, 'Welcome to the world of espionage, Mr. Bell.'

'How can I trust you?'

'I will explain two reasons why you should trust me. First, I have not killed you, and I could have. Agreed?'

'You could have tried.'

'Second, here is my pistol. I am passing it to you under the table. Do what you will.'

He handed Bell the pistol, butt first.

'Is the safety on?' asked Bell.

'It is now that it's pointed at me,' replied Yamamoto. 'Now I will stand up. With your permission.'

Bell nodded.

Yamamoto stood up. Bell said, 'I will trust you more after you hand me that second pistol hidden in your side pocket.'

Yamamoto smiled faintly. 'Sharp eyes, Mr. Bell. But in order to deliver the goods, I may need it.'

'In that case,' said Bell, 'take this one, too.'

'Thank you.'

'Good hunting.'

Late that night, Yamamoto Kenta confronted the spy in his Alexandria, Virginia, waterfront warehouse. 'Your plan to attack the Great White Fleet at Mare Island,' he began in the formal, measured phrases of a diplomat, 'is not in the interest of my government.'

It had been raining for two days, and the Potomac River was rising, swelled by the vast watershed that drained thousands of square miles of Maryland, Virginia, West Virginia, Pennsylvania, and Washington, D.C. The powerful current made the floor tremble. The rain drummed on the ancient roof. Leaks dripped into a helmet turned upside down on the spy's desk, splashed on the old searchlight behind him and streamed down its lens.

The spy could not hide his astonishment. 'How did you find out?'

Yamamoto smiled thinly. 'Perhaps it is my "natural aptitude for spying, and a cunning and self-control not found in the West." His smile froze in a hard line, his lips so tight that the spy could see his teeth outlined against them.

'I will not permit this,' the Japanese continued. 'You

will drive a wedge between Japan and the United States at precisely the wrong time.'

'The wedge is already in motion,' the spy said mildly.

'What good would come of it?'

'Depends on your point of view. From the German point of view, embroiling Japan and the United States in conflict would open up opportunities in the Pacific. Nor will Great Britain mourn if the U.S. Navy is forced to concentrate its battleships on its West Coast. They might even seize the opportunity to reoccupy the West Indies.'

'It does nothing for Japan.'

'I have German and British friends willing to pay me for their opportunities.'

'You are even worse than I thought.'

The spy laughed. 'Don't you understand? The international dreadnought race presents splendiferous opportunities to a man with the intestinal fortitude to seize them. The rival nations will pay anything to stop each other. I'm a salesman in a seller's market.'

'You are playing both ends against the middle.'

The spy laughed louder. 'You underestimate me, Yamamoto. I am playing *every* end against the middle. I am building a fortune. What will it cost me to keep you out of my game?'

'I am not a mercenary.'

'Oh, I forgot. You're a patriot.' Idly, he picked up a thick black towel that had been draped over the arm of his chair. 'A gentleman spy with high morals. But a gentleman spy is like a pistol that shoots blanks – good for starting bicycle races, but little else.'

Yamamoto was coldly sure of his position. 'I am not a

gentleman spy. I am a patriot like your father, who served his Kaiser as I serve my Emperor. Neither of us would sell out our country.'

'Will you leave my poor dead father out of this?' the spy asked wearily.

'Your father would understand why I must stop you.' Yamamoto drew from his coat his Nambu semiautomatic pistol, deftly pulled the cocking knob, and pointed the short barrel at the spy's head.

The spy looked at him with a thin smile. 'Are you serious, Kenta? What are you going to do, turn me in to the U.S. Navy? They may have questions for you, too.'

'I am sure they would. Which is why I'm going to turn you over to the Van Dorn Detective Agency.'

'What for?'

'The Van Dorns will hold you until I am safely out of the country. *They* will turn you over to the U.S. Navy.'

The spy shut his eyes. 'You're forgetting one thing. I don't have a country.'

'But I know where you came from, Eyes O'Shay. Mr. Brian "Eyes" O'Shay.'

The spy's eyes popped open. He stared at the towel that he had been raising to his face. It lay in his hands like an offering.

Yamamoto gloated. 'Surprised?'

'I am very surprised,' the spy admitted. 'Brian O'Shay has not been my name for a very long time.'

'I told you, I was playing this game before you were born. Put your hands where I can see them or I'll give the Van Dorns your corpse instead.'

The spy squeezed his eyes shut again. 'You frighten me,

Kenta. I am merely trying to mop the perspiration from my face.' He dabbed his forehead, then pressed the black towel as tightly as he could to his eyes. Hidden at his feet was a thick electrical cable that connected the public-utility main to a knife switch in the open position. The switch's hinged metal lever was poised inches above its jaw. He stomped down on the lever's insulated handle, closing the circuit. A fat blue spark cracked like a pistol shot.

From behind him, the 200,000,000-candlepower searchlight capable of illuminating enemy ships at six miles shot a beam like white fire into Yamamoto's eyes. It was so bright that the spy could see the bones in his hands through his eyelids, the thick towel, and his skin and flesh. It seared Yamamoto's retinas, blinding him. The Japanese spy fell backward, screaming.

The spy kicked the switch open again and waited for the light to fade before he dropped the towel and stood up, blinking at the pink circles spinning before his eyes.

'Navy captains tell me that searchlights fend off destroyers better than guns,' he said conversationally. 'I can report that they work just as well on traitors.'

From his desk drawer, he took a folded copy of the *Washington Post* and removed from it a twelve-inch length of lead pipe. He circled the desk and stepped around the fallen chair. He was only a few inches taller than the tiny Yamamoto, who was writhing on the floor. But he was as strong as three men and he moved with the concentrated purpose of a torpedo.

He raised the lead pipe high and slammed it down on Yamamoto's skull.

One blow was more than enough.

He felt inside Yamamoto's pockets to make sure he carried identification and found in his wallet a letter of introduction to the Smithsonian Institution from a Japanese museum. Perfect. He rummaged about the warehouse until he found a cork lifesaving jacket. He made sure its canvas was still strong, then he worked Yamamoto's arms into it and tied it securely.

He dragged the body to the dock side of the warehouse where the building cantilevered over the Potomac. A wooden lever that stood tall as his shoulders released the trap in the floor. It dropped with a loud bang. The body splashed. On a rain-lashed night like this, the river would sweep it miles away.

He was done here. It was time to leave Washington. He circled the dusty warehouse, tipping over kerosene hurricane lamps that he had placed there for his departure. He circled again, lighting matches and tossing them on the spilled kerosene, and when all was blazing bright orange flames he walked out the door and into the rain.

33

Bell waited all the next day for word from Yamamoto. Every time a telephone rang or a telegraph key clattered, he startled at his desk only to sit back disappointed. Something must have gone wrong. It made no sense that the Japanese spy would betray him. He had appeared voluntarily. He had suggested the trade. As the afternoon wore on, the phones kept ringing and ringing.

Suddenly the agent manning them signaled, and Bell raced across the room.

'Operator just called. Message from Scully.'

'What?'

'All he said was, "Grand Central, three-thirty p.m."'

Bell grabbed his hat. Enigmatic even by Scully's standards, it meant either that Scully turned up something of vital importance or he was in danger. 'Keep listening for Yamamoto. I'll telephone from Grand Central if I can. But soon as Yamamoto reports, send a courier to come looking for me.'

John Scully had decided it was time to bring in Isaac Bell. Truth be told, he admitted to himself as he hunted the public telephone pay station in Grand Central, it was past time. He couldn't find the damned thing. The old railroad station was being torn down and replaced by a vast new terminal,

279

and they kept moving the telephones. Where the telephones had been the last time he used them was a gaping pit that offered a view of track levels descending sixty feet into the ground. When he finally found the telephones, losing ten minutes in the process, he told the operator, 'Van Dorn Detective Agency. Knickerbocker.' A uniformed attendant showed him into one of the wood-paneled booths.

'Good afternoon,' came the dulcet tones of an operator chosen for her beautiful voice and clear head. 'You have reached the Van Dorn Detective Agency. To whom do you wish to speak?'

'Message for Isaac Bell. Tell him Scully said, "Grand Central, three-thirty p.m." Got that? "Grand Central, three-thirty p.m."'

'Yes, Mr. Scully.'

He paid the attendant and hurried toward the track designated for the 20th Century Limited. The terminal was in chaos. Workmen were everywhere, swarming over scaffolds and banging hammers on stone, steel, and marble. Laborers cluttered the hall, wheeling carts and barrows. But at the Limited's temporary gate, beside which a blackboard said CHICAGO, company employees were respectfully checking tickets, and her famous red carpet was already in place leading out onto the platform. It looked like once a passenger got this close to the fabled Chicago express, his troubles were over.

'Jasper! Jasper Smith!'

Little Miss Knockout Drops from the opera house opium den was rushing toward him in an elegant traveling outfit capped by a broad-brimmed *Merry Widow* hat. 'What a wonderful coincidence. Thank God, I found you!'

'How did you know I was here?'

'I didn't. I just saw you. Oh, Jasper, I didn't know if I would ever see you again. You left in such a hurry last night.'

Something was way out of whack. He looked around. Where was her Hip Sing boyfriend? Already on the train? Then he saw cutting through the crowds of hurrying passengers a cigar-delivery cart wheeled by a Chinese. And there were three wagonloads of construction debris hauled by Irish laborers. The cart and wagons were converging on them like wagons circling to fend off the Indians.

'What are you doing here?' he asked her.

'Meeting a train,' she said.

I stood outside that opera house like a sitting duck, thought Scully. Long enough for the Hip Sing to get a line on me.

The Irishmen pulling the wagon were staring at him. Gophers? Or were they watching the pretty girl who was smiling up at him like she meant it?

Or did they tip to me and Harry Warren, recognizing each other inside? The Chinaman wheeling cigars looked his way, expression blank. Tong hatchet man?

The train ticket! She let me find the train ticket. She set me up to be here. Scully reached back for his Vest Pocket pistol. Even the police raid was a phony. Paid the cops to raid so he would run with the girl.

Something whacked him in the head.

A football bounced at his feet, and a big, grinning college boy in coat and tie loped up. 'Sorry, sir, we didn't mean it, just horsing around.'

Saved! Saved by a piece of luck he didn't deserve.

Six strapping, privileged young men skylarking with a ball as they ran to catch a train had scared off the tong and the Gophers. They trooped over, apologizing and offering to shake his hand, and suddenly he and Katy were surrounded inside a scrum. But only when three of the college boys held his arms and little Katy whipped a ten-inch steel hatpin from the *Merry Widow* did Scully realize that little Miss Knockout Drops had completely outfoxed him.

Issac Bell rushed through the crowded construction site. He spotted a mob of people milling around the gate to the 20th Century Limited. A cop was shouting, 'Stand back! Stand back!,' and pleading for a doctor. With an awful feeling he was too late, Bell shoved into the center of the crowd.

The cop tried to stop him.

'Van Dorn!' Bell shouted. 'Is that one of my men?'

'Take a look.'

John Scully lay on his back, his eyes staring wide open, his hands folded over his chest.

'Looks like a heart attack,' said the cop. 'He yours?'

Bell knelt beside him. 'Yes.'

'Sorry, mister. Least he went peaceful. Probably never knew what hit him.'

Isaac Bell spread his hand over Scully's face and gently closed his eyes. 'Sleep tight, my friend.'

A whistle blew. 'All aboard!' Conductors shouted. '20th Century Limited to Chicago. Alllllll aboooooard.'

Scully's hat had fallen under his head. Bell reached for

it to cover his face. His hand came away sticky with warm blood.

'Mother of God,' breathed the cop leaning over his shoulder.

Bell turned Scully's head and saw the shiny brass head of a hatpin sticking out of the soft flesh in the nape of his neck.

'All aboard! All aboard! 20th Century Limited for Chicago. Allllllll aboooooard!'

Bell searched Scully's pockets. Tucked inside his coat was an envelope with his name on it. Bell stood up and tore it open. Printed in block letters was a note from the killer:

EYE FOR AN EYE, BELL.
YOU EARNED WEEKS SO WE WON'T COUNT HIM.
BUT YOU OWE ME FOR THE GERMAN.

'Mr. Bell! Mr. Bell!' A Van Dorn apprentice raced up, breathless. 'Wire from Mr. Van Dorn.'

Bell read it in a glance.

Yamamoto Kenta had been found floating in the Potomac.

All was lost.

The tall detective knelt beside his friend again and resumed methodically searching his pockets. In Scully's vest he found a train ticket for the 20th Century Limited with through connections to San Francisco.

'Boarrrrd! All aboa –'

The conductor's final warning was drowned out by the engineer signaling *Ahead* with a majestic double blast on his whistle. Isaac Bell stood up, thinking furiously. John Scully must have been following a suspected spy or saboteur who was headed to San Francisco, where the Great White Fleet would replenish before crossing the Pacific Ocean.

He spoke sharply to the Van Dorn apprentice, who was staring with wide-open eyes at the fallen detective. 'Look at me, son.'

The boy tore his gaze from Scully.

'There's a lot to be done, and you're the only Van Dorn here who can do it. Round up every witness. Those workmen there, those Chinese fellows with the cart, and these folks hanging about. Someone saw something. This officer will help you, won't you?'

'I'll do what I can,' said the cop dubiously.

Bell pressed money into his hand. 'Hold them here while this young gentleman telephones Van Dorn headquarters for every available agent. On the jump, son! Then straight back here and get to work. Remember, people are glad to talk if you give them the chance.'

The floor shook. The 20th Century Limited was rolling toward Chicago.

Isaac Bell bolted onto the platform, ran the length of the express train's red carpet, and jumped.

The Fleet

34

May 1, 1908
Westbound On The 20th Century Limited

'This calls for a drink,' said the spy.

Some special concoction in honor of Isaac Bell.

Just before the telephone line was disconnected when the 20th Century Limited left Grand Central, Katherine Dee had reported that John Scully had gone to that section of kingdom come set aside for Van Dorn detectives. He cradled the instrument and beckoned an observation-car steward.

'Does your bartender know how to make a Yale cocktail?'

'He sure does, sir.'

'Does he have the Crême Yvette?' the spy asked sternly.

'Of course, sir.'

'Bring me one, then – oh, and bring these gentlemen what they would like, too,' he added, indicating a pair of pink-jowled Chicago businessmen who were glowering indignantly. 'Sorry, gents. I hope I didn't thwart any important last-minute telephone calls.'

The offer of a free drink was mollifying, and one admitted, 'Just calling the office to tell them I'm on the train.'

His friend said, 'Guess they'll figure that out when you don't skulk back in moping that you missed it.'

Traveling men within earshot laughed and repeated the joke to others who hadn't heard it.

'Look! There's a fellow who almost did.'

'He must have jumped!'

'Or flew!'

The spy glanced toward the back of the car. A tall man in a white suit was gliding in from the rear vestibule.

'Maybe he's got no ticket, figuring to ride the rails.'

'There goes the conductor – on him like a terrier.'

'Guard my cocktail,' said the spy. 'I just remembered have to dictate a letter.'

The 20th Century Limited supplied a stenographer free of charge. He moved quickly to the man's portable desk at the head of the observation car, pulled his collar up and his hat low, and sat with his back to the detective.

'How soon will a letter I post leave the train?'

'Forty minutes. It will go off at Harmon when we exchange the electric engine for a steam locomotive.' He reached for an envelope engraved VIA 20TH CENTURY. 'To whom shall I address it, sir?'

'K. C. Dee, Plaza Hotel, New York.'

'They'll have it this evening.' The stenographer addressed the envelope, spread a sheet of 20th Century stationery, and poised his pen.

The train was accelerating up the cut that ran north out of the city. Stone walls cast shadows, darkening the windows, causing the glass to mirror the interior of the crowded car. The spy watched Isaac Bell's pale reflection pass behind him. The conductor trailed solicitously, and was clear that, ticket or no, Bell was a welcome passenger.

'Ready when you are, sir,' prompted the stenographer.

He waited for Bell and the conductor to pass through the vestibule to the next car.

"'My dear K. C. Dee,'" he began. He had miscalculated Bell's reaction to the killing of his fellow detective and underestimated how quickly Van Dorns moved when aroused. Fortunately, he had left Katherine Dee fully prepared to accelerate events. It was simply a matter of unleashing her early.

'Ready, sir?'

'It appears that our customer did not receive our last shipment,' he dictated. 'New paragraph. It is imperative that you make a personal visit to Newport, Rhode Island, tonight to set things straight.'

Isaac Bell had presented Scully's ticket for upper berth number 5 in Pullman car 6 and asked to pay the extra fare for a stateroom. Informed that every available room was sold out, he had produced a railroad pass. It was signed by the president of a rival line, but competing titans accommodated one another's personal whims.

'Of course, Mr. Bell. Fortunately, we do have a company suite empty.'

In the privacy of the rosewood-paneled stateroom, Bell tipped the conductor generously.

'With that special pass, you don't need to tip for good service, Mr. Bell,' said train conductor William Dilber, his hand nonetheless closing like a rattrap around the gold pieces.

Isaac Bell did not need service. He needed an eager associate. He had less than eighteen hours before the 20th Century Limited reached Chicago to find out who killed

Scully. No more passengers would board between New York and Chicago. Except Van Dorn detectives.

'Mr. Dilber, how many passengers is your train carrying?'

'One hundred twenty-seven.'

'One of them is a murderer.'

'A murderer,' the conductor echoed tranquilly. Bell was not surprised. As captain of a crack luxury express train, William Dilber was to remain unflappable in the face of derailments, disgruntled tycoons, and snowbound Pullmans.

'You'll want to see the passenger list, Mr. Bell. Got it right here.'

He unfolded it from his immaculate blue tunic.

'Do you know many of the passengers?'

'Most. We get a lot of regulars. Most from Chicago. Businessmen back and forth to New York.'

'That will help. Could you point out those you don't know?'

The conductor traced name by name with a clean, manicured fingernail. He was indeed familiar with most, for the 20th Century Limited was very much a rolling private club. The costly excess-fare express drew on the tiny minority of passengers who were extremely well off, and the train ran a proscribed route between New York and Chicago that was fully booked and rarely took on passengers at intermediate stations. Bell saw well-known names in business, politics, and industry, and some famous touring actors. He noted the names of those few Dilber didn't know.

'I am particularly interested in foreigners.'

'We've got the usual handful. Here's an Englishman.'

'Arnold Bennett. The writer?'

'I believe he is on a lecture tour. Traveling with these

two Chinamen. Harold Wing and Louis Loh. They are missionary students, from an English seminary, I believe. Mr. Bennett made a point of telling me personally that he's their protector in case anyone gives them trouble. I told him it was all the same to me as long as they pay their fare.'

'Did he say what's he's protecting them from?'

'Remember that murder last month in Philadelphia? The girl, and all that white-slaving talk in the papers? The police are shadowing Chinamen hot and heavy.'

Train conductor Dilber continued down the list. 'I don't know this German gentleman. Herr Shafer. His ticket was booked by the German Embassy.'

Bell, make a note.

'Here's one *I* know,' the detective said. 'Rosania – if he's traveling under his own name. But he can't be – a natty dresser of about forty?'

'That's him. Snappy as a magazine ad.'

'What are you carrying in the express car?'

'The usual stocks and banknotes. Why do you ask?'

'The fellow is a regular wizard with nitroglycerine.'

'A train robber?' the conductor asked less unflappably.

Bell shook his head. 'Not as a rule. Rosania generally favors mansions he can talk his way into to blow the jewelry safes after everyone goes to bed. Master of his craft. He can detonate an explosion in the library that they'll never hear upstairs. But last I knew, he was at Sing Sing State Prison. Don't worry, I'll have a word with him and see what's up.'

'I would appreciate that, sir. Now, this Australian. Something told me he was trouble – not that he did anything, but I overheard him discussing the sale of a gold mine and caught a tone of the bunco man in his palaver.

I'll watch him close in the club car if he joins any of the card games.'

'And here's *another* I know,' Bell said. 'Funny.' Bell pointed at the name.

'Herr Riker. Oh, yes.'

'You know him?'

'The diamond merchant. He's a regular, every couple of months or so. Is he a friend of yours?'

'We met recently. Twice.'

'I believe he is traveling with his bodyguard. Yes, this fellow here. Plimpton. Big bruiser in a Pullman berth. Riker's got his usual stateroom. I reckon there's something locked up in the express car that's Riker's.' He followed down the list. 'No mention of his ward.'

'What ward?'

'Lovely young lady. But, no, she's not listed this trip. Pity.'

'What do you mean?'

'Nothing, sir. I just mean, one of those girls that isn't hard on the eyes.'

'Riker seems young to have a ward.'

'She's just a student – oh, I see what you mean. Don't you doubt it, sir. I see every sort of couple you could imagine on the Limited. Riker and his ward are completely on the up-and-up. Always separate staterooms.'

'Adjoining?' asked Bell, who always booked two staterooms when he traveled with Marion.

'But it's not what you think. You get an eye for this on the 20th Century, Mr. Bell. They're not that sort of couple.'

Bell resolved to check on that. Research had made no mention of a ward.

'What is her name?'

'I only know her as Miss Riker. Maybe he adopted her.'

The train was flying at a clip of sixty miles to the hour, and mileposts were flashing by the windows. But just as he and the conductor were finishing up the passenger list, forty minutes out of New York, Bell felt the engine ease off.

'Harmon,' the conductor explained, checking the time on his Waltham watch. 'We'll exchange the electric for a steamer and then we'll fly, better than four miles in three minutes.'

'I'll have a word with my old nitro acquaintance. Find out what he's got planned for your express car.'

While they changed engines, Bell telegraphed Van Dorn, inquiring about the German, the Australian, the Chinese traveling with Arnold Bennett, and Herr Riker's ward. He also sent a wire to Captain Falconer:

INFORM GUNNER'S DAUGHTER MURDERER DEAD.

A single glimmer of justice in a joyless day. The death of Yamamoto might comfort Dorothy Langner, but it was hardly a victory. The case, already thrown into turmoil by Scully's murder, was completely unhinged by the death of the Japanese spy who had come so close to handing Bell his true quarry.

He climbed back aboard the 20th Century.

The high-wheeled Atlantic 4-4-2 steam locomotive swiftly gathered speed and raced northward along the banks of the Hudson River. Bell walked to the head of the train. The club car was fitted with comfortable lounge chairs. Men were smoking, drinking cocktails, and waiting for their turn with the barber and manicurist.

'Larry Rosania! Fancy meeting you here.'

The jewel thief looked up from a newspaper blazing headlines about the Great White Fleet approaching San Francisco. He peered over the tops of his gold wire-rimmed reading glasses and pretended not to recognize the tall, golden-haired detective in the white suit. His manner was polished, his voice patrician. 'Have we been introduced, sir?'

Bell sat down uninvited. 'Last I heard, my old pals Wally Kisley and Mack Fulton leased long-term lodgings for you at Sing Sing.'

At the mention of Bell's friends, Rosania dropped the façade. 'I was saddened to hear about their demise, Isaac. They were interesting characters and honest detectives in a world short of both.'

'Appreciate the thought. How'd you get out? Blow a hole in the prison wall?'

'Haven't you heard? I got a pardon from the governor. Would you like to see it?'

'Very much so,' said Isaac Bell.

The suave safecracker pulled from his coat a finely tooled wallet. From it he drew an envelope embossed with gold leaf and from the envelope unfolded a sheet of vellum with the seal of the governor of New York State on top and Rosania's name illuminated as if drawn by monks.

'Assuming for the moment that this is not a forgery, do you mind me asking what you did to get this?'

'If I told you, you wouldn't believe me.'

'Try.'

'When I was twelve years old, I helped a little old lady

cross the street. Turned out she was the governor's mother – before he was governor. She never forgot my kindness. I told you you wouldn't believe me.'

'Where are you headed, Larry?'

'Surely you've combed through the passenger list. You know perfectly well that I'm bound for San Francisco.'

'What do you intend to blow up there?'

'I've gone straight, Isaac. I don't do safes anymore.'

'Whatever you're doing, you're doing it well,' Bell observed. 'This train doesn't come cheap.'

'I'll tell you the truth,' said Rosania. 'You won't believe this either, but I met a widow who believes that the sun and the moon rise and set on me. As she inherited more money than I could steal in a lifetime, I am not disabusing her of the thought.'

'Can I inform the train conductor that his express car is safe?'

'Safe as houses. Crime doesn't pay enough. What about you, Isaac? Heading for Chicago headquarters?'

'Actually, I'm looking for someone,' said Bell. 'And I'll bet that even reformed jewel thieves are close observers of fellow passengers on luxury railroad trains. Have you noticed any foreigners I might be interested in?'

'Several. In fact, one right here in this car.'

Rosania nodded toward the back of the club car and lowered his voice. 'There's a German pretending to be a salesman. If he is, he's the nastiest drummer I ever saw.'

'The stiff-necked one who looks like a Prussian officer?' Bell had noticed Shafer on his way into the club car. The German was about thirty years old, expensively dressed, and exuded a fiercely unfriendly chill.

'Would you buy anything from him?'

'Nothing I didn't need. Anyone else?'

'Look out for the carney Australian selling a gold mine.'

'The conductor noticed him, too.'

'There's no fooling a good train conductor.'

'He didn't tip to you.'

'Told you, I've gone straight.'

'Oh, I forgot,' Bell grinned. Then he asked, 'Do you know a gem importer named Erhard Riker?'

'Herr Riker, I never messed with.'

'Why not?'

'For the same reason I would never dream of blowing Joe Van Dorn's safe. Riker's got his own private protection service.'

'What else do you know about him?'

'From my *former* point of view, that was all I needed to know.'

Bell stood up. 'Interesting seeing you, Larry.'

Rosania suddenly looked embarrassed. 'Actually, if you don't mind, I go by Laurence now. The widow likes calling me Laurence. Says it's more refined.'

'How old is this widow?'

'Twenty-eight,' Rosania replied smugly.

'Congratulations.'

As Bell turned away, Rosania called, 'Wait a minute.' Again he lowered his voice. 'Did you see the Chinamen? There's two of them on board.'

'What about them?'

'I wouldn't trust them.'

'I understand they're divinity students,' said Bell.

Laurence Rosania nodded sagely. 'The preacher man is

"The Invisible Man." When I worked the divinity student game, and the old ladies took me home to meet nieces and granddaughters, the gentlemen who owned the mansions looked through me like I was furniture.'

'Thanks for the help,' said Bell, fully intending when the train changed engines at Albany to send Sing Sing's warden a telegram recommending a head count.

He walked back through the club car, eyeing the German. Skillful European tailoring mostly concealed a powerful frame. The man sat bolt upright, erect as a cavalry officer. 'Afternoon,' Bell nodded.

Herr Shafer returned a cold, silent stare, and Bell recalled that Archie had told him that in Kaiser Wilhelm's Germany citizens, both male and female, were required to surrender their train seats to military officers. Try that here, Bell thought, and you'll earn a punch in the snoot. From men *or* women.

He continued toward the back of the train through six Pullman and stateroom cars to the observation car, where passengers were drinking cocktails as the setting sun reddened the sky across the Hudson River. The Chinese divinity students were dressed in identical ill-fitting black suits, each with a bulge indicating a bible near his heart. They sat with a bearded Englishman in tweed whom Bell assumed to be their protector, the journalist and novelist Arnold Bennett.

Bennett was a rugged-looking man with a stocky, powerful build. He appeared a bit younger than Bell had assumed him to be based on the articles he had read in *Harper's Weekly*. He was holding forth to a rapt audience of Chicago businessmen on the pleasures of travel in the United States, and as Bell listened he got the distinct impression that the writer was practicing phrases for his next article.

'Could a man be prouder than to say, "This is the train of trains, and I have my stateroom on it."'

A salesman with a booming voice like Dorothy Langner's Ted Whitmark brayed, 'Finest train in the world, bar none.'

'The Broadway Limited ain't nothing to sneeze at,' remarked his companion.

'Old folks ride the Broadway Limited,' the salesman scoffed. 'The 20th Century's for up-and-up businessmen. That's why Chicago fellows like it so.'

Arnold Bennett corralled the conversation again with practiced ease. 'Your American comforts never cease to amaze. Do you know I can switch the electric fan in my bedchamber to three different speeds? I expect that it will provide through the night a continuous vaudeville entertainment.'

The Chicagoans laughed, slapped their thighs, and shouted to the steward for more drinks. The Chinese men smiled uncertainly, and Isaac Bell wondered how much English they understood. Were the slight young men frightened in the presence of large and boisterous Americans? Or merely shy?

When Bennett flourished a cigarette from his gold case, one student struck a match and the other positioned an ashtray. It looked to Bell like Harold Wing and Louis Loh filled dual roles as wards of the journalist and as manservants.

Approaching Albany, the train crossed the Hudson River on a high trestle bridge that looked down upon brightly lighted steamboats. It halted in the yards. While the New York Central trainmen wheeled the engine away, then coupled on another and a dining car for the evening meal, Isaac Bell sent and collected telegrams. The fresh engine, an Atlantic 4-4-2 with drive wheels even taller than the last, was already rolling when he swung back aboard and locked himself in his stateroom.

In the short time since he had sent his wires from Harmon, Research had not learned anything about the German, the Australian, the Chinese traveling with Arnold Bennett, or Herr Riker's ward. But the Van Dorns who had raced to Grand Central had started piecing together witnesses' accounts of Scully's murder. They had found no one who reported actually seeing the hatpin driven into John Scully's brain. But it appeared that the killing had been coordinated with military precision.

This was now known: A Chinese delivery man bringing cigars to the departing trains reported seeing Scully rush up to the 20th Century platform. He seemed to be looking for someone.

Irish laborers hauling demolition debris said that Scully was talking to a pretty redhead. They were standing very close as if they knew each other well.

The police officer hadn't come along until the crowd had formed. But a traveler from upstate New York had seen a mob of college students surround Scully and the redhead, 'Like he was inside a flying wedge.'

Then they hurried away and Scully was on the floor.

Where did they go?

Every which way, like melted ice.

What did they look like?

College boys.

'They set him up good,' Harry Warren had put it in his telegram to Bell. 'Never knew what hit him.'

Bell, mourning his friend, doubted that. Even the best of men could be tricked, of course, but Scully had been sharp as tacks. John Scully would have known that he had been fooled. Too late to save himself, sadly. But Bell bet that he'd known. If only as he took his last breath.

Harry Warren went on to speculate whether the girl seen with Scully was the same redhead he had seen in the Hip Sing opium den where the detectives had inadvertently bumped into each other. The witnesses' descriptions at Grand Central were too general to know. A pretty redheaded girl, one of a thousand in New York. Five thousand. Ten. But descriptions of her clothing did not jibe with the costume worn by the girl Harry had seen in the Chinatown gambling and drug parlor. Nor had she been wearing thick rouge and paint.

Bell took the spy's taunting note from his pocket and read it again.

EYE FOR AN EYE, BELL.
YOU EARNED WEEKS SO WE WON'T COUNT HIM.
BUT YOU OWED ME FOR THE GERMAN.

The spy was boasting that both Weeks and the German had worked for his ring. Which struck Bell as reckless behavior in a line of business where discretion was survival and victories should be celebrated in the quietest manner. He could not imagine the cool Yamamoto or even the supercilious Abbington-Westlake writing such a note.

The spy also seemed deluded. Did he really believe that Isaac Bell and the entire Van Dorn Agency would ignore his attack? He was practically begging for a counterpunch.

Bell went to the dining car for the second seating.

The tables were arranged in place settings of four and two, and the custom was to be seated wherever there was room. He saw Bennett and his Chinese had an empty chair at their table for four. As earlier in the observation car, the witty writer was regaling nearby tables while his solemn charges sat quietly. The German, Shafer, was eating in stiff silence across from an American drummer who was failing miserably to make conversation. The Australian was at another table for two speaking earnestly with a table mate dressed as if he could afford to buy a gold mine. At another two, Laurence Rosania was deep in conversation with a younger man in an elegant suit.

Bell slipped the diner captain money. 'I would like that empty seat at Mr. Bennett's table.'

But as the captain led him toward the writer's table, Bell heard another diner call out from a table he had just passed.

'Bell! Isaac Bell. I thought that was you.'

The gem merchant Erhard Riker rose from his table, brushing a napkin to his lips and extending his hand. 'Another coincidence, sir? We seem to repeat them. Are you alone? Care to join me?'

The Chinese could wait. The passenger list showed them connecting through to San Francisco, whereas Riker was changing trains in the morning to the Atchison, Topeka and Santa Fe's California Limited.

They shook hands. Riker indicated the empty chair across from him. Bell sat.

'How's our diamond hunt going?'

'I'm closing in on an emerald fit for a queen. Or even a goddess. It should be waiting for us when I get back to New York. We can only pray the lady will like it,' he added with a smile.

'Where are you headed?'

Riker looked around to ensure they weren't overheard. 'San Diego,' he whispered. 'And you?'

'San Francisco. What's in San Diego?'

Again Riker looked around again. 'Pink tourmaline.' He smiled self-disparagingly. 'Forgive my taciturnity. The enemy has spies everywhere.'

'Enemy? What enemy?'

'Tiffany and Company are attempting to corner the tourmaline supply in San Diego because Tz'u-hsi, Dowager Empress of China – an eccentric despot with all the wealth of China at her disposal – loves San Diego's pink tourmaline. Uses it for carvings and buttons and the like. When she fell head over heels for pink tourmaline, she created a whole new market. Tiffany is attempting to seize it.' He lowered his voice further. Bell leaned closer to hear. 'This has created splendid opportunities for an independent gem merchant who is able to snap up the best samples before they do. It's dog-eat-dog in the gem line, Mr. Bell.' He added a wink to his smile, and Bell was not sure whether he was serious.

'I don't know anything about the jewelry business.'

'Surely a detective comes across jewels, if only stolen ones.'

Bell looked at him sharply. 'How did you know I was a detective?'

Riker shrugged. 'When I agree to hunt for a significant

gem, I first investigate whether the client can afford it or is merely wishing he can.'

'Detectives aren't rich.'

'Those who inherit Boston banking fortunes are, Mr. Bell. Forgive me if I seemed to intrude on your privacy, but I think you can understand that gathering information about my customers is a necessary part of doing business. I have a small operation. I can't afford to spend weeks hunting stones for a client who turns out to have eyes bigger than his stomach.'

'I understand,' said Bell. 'I presume you understand why I don't bandy it about?'

'Of course, sir. Your secrets are safe with me. Though I did wonder when I discovered who you are how a successful detective keeps out of the limelight.'

'By avoiding cameras and portraitists.'

'But it would seem that the more criminals you catch the more famous you will be.'

'Hopefully,' said Bell, 'only among criminals behind bars.'

Riker laughed. 'Well said, sir. Come, here I am talking a blue streak. The waiter is hovering. We must order our dinner.'

Behind him, Bell heard Arnold Bennett announcing, 'This is the first time I ever dined *à la carte* on any train. An excellent dinner, well and sympathetically served. The mutton was impeccable.'

'There's an endorsement,' said Riker. 'Perhaps you should have the mutton.'

'I've never met an Englishman who knew a thing about good food,' Bell replied, and asked the waiter, 'Are we still in shad season?'

'Yes, sir! How would you like it cooked?'

'Grilled. And may I reserve some roe for breakfast?'

'It will be a different diner in the morning, sir. Hitched on at Elkhart. But I'll leave some on ice with the Pullman conductor.'

'Make that two portions,' said Riker. 'Shad tonight, shad roe in the morning. What do you say, Bell, shall we share a bottle of Rhine wine?'

After the waiter left them, Bell said, 'Your English is remarkable. As if you have spoken it your entire life.'

Riker laughed. 'They beat English into me at Eton. My father sent me to England for preparatory school. He felt it would help me get on in the business if I could mingle with more than just our German countrymen. But tell me something – speaking of fathers – how did you manage to stay out of your family's banking business?'

Aware from the Van Dorn reports that Riker's father had been killed during the Boer War, Bell answered obliquely in order to draw him out. 'My father was, and still is, very much in charge.' He looked inquiringly at Riker, and the German said, 'I envy you. I had no such choice. My father died in Africa when I was just finishing university. If I had not stepped in, the business would have fallen to pieces.'

'I gathered from the way that jeweler spoke that you've made quite a go of it.'

'My father taught me every trick in the book. And some more he invented himself. Plus, he was well liked in the factories and workshops. His name still opens doors, particularly here in America, in Newark and New York. I would not be surprised to bump into one of his old comrades in San Diego.' He winked again. 'In that event, Tiffany's buyers will be lucky to get out of California with the gold fillings still in their teeth.'

The spy had completely recovered from the initial shock of seeing Bell jump aboard the 20th Century Limited at Grand Central. Katherine Dee would soon be working her wiles in Newport while he would turn the detective's unexpected presence on the train to advantage. He was accustomed to jousting with government agents – British, French, Russian, Japanese – as well as the various naval intelligence officers, including the Americans, and he had a low opinion of their abilities. But a private detective was a new wrinkle that he had come to realize belatedly deserved careful observation before he made a move.

He was glad he had ordered Detective John Scully killed. That shock would take a toll on Isaac Bell, although the tall detective hid it well, striding about the train like he owned it. Should he kill Bell, too? It seemed necessary. The question was, who would replace him? Bell's friend Abbott was back from Europe. An aggressive adversary, too, from what he could gather, though not quite in Bell's league. Would the formidable Joseph Van Dorn himself step in? Or stay above the fray? His was a nationwide agency with a diverse roster. God knows who they had waiting in the shadows.

On the other hand, he thought with a smile, it was unlikely even God knew everyone *he* had waiting in the shadows.

35

'We're still checking on the Chinese traveling with Arnold Bennett. But it will take a while. Same for Shafer, the German. Research can't find anything on him, but like you said, Mr. Bell, it seems odd that the embassy booked tickets for a salesman.'

The Van Dorn agent was reporting hurriedly in the privacy of Bell's stateroom while the train stopped in Syracuse to take on a fresh engine and drop the dining car.

'Sing Sing confirmed Rosania's story.'

Rosania had not taken it on the lam but had been released, as he claimed, by the governor. The self-dubbed Australian gold miner was actually a Canadian con man who usually worked the gold mine game on the western railroads, where he could show the mark worthless claims 'salted' by blasting rock walls with shotgun pellets made of gold.

The locomotive whistle signaled *Ahead*.

'Gotta go!'

Bell said, 'I want you to arrange a long-distance telephone connection with Mr. Van Dorn to our next stop at East Buffalo.'

Two hours later when they stopped to change engines in a brightly lighted, cacophonous rail yard in East Buffalo, a Van Dorn detective was waiting to take Bell to the yardmaster's office. Bell queried him for the latest while the long-distance telephone operators completed the connections.

'Near as we can make out from all the witnesses, Scully was talking to a well-dressed redhead. A football comes flying through the air and hits him on the shoulder. College boys horsing around run up and surround him, apologizing. Someone yells their train is leaving, and they run for it. Scully's lying on his back like he's got a heart attack. Bunch of people crowd around to help. Cop comes along, shouts for a doctor. Then you come running up. Then a kid from the New York office. Then you ran after the Limited, and some woman sees the blood and screams, and then the cop is telling everybody to stay where they are. And pretty soon there's a bunch of Van Dorns running around with notebooks.'

'Where's the redhead?'

'No one knows.'

'Well-dressed, you say?'

'Stylish.'

'Says who? The cop?'

'Says a lady who's a manager at Lord and Taylor, which is a very high-tone dry-goods store in New York City.'

'Not dressed like a floozy?'

'High-tone.'

Just when Bell thought he was going to have to run to catch his train, the telephone finally rang. The connection was thin, the wire noisy. 'Van Dorn here. That you, Isaac? What do you have?'

'We have one report of a redhead wearing the sort of paint, clothes, and hat you'd expect in an opium den, and another of a redhead dressed like a lady, and both were seen with Scully.'

'Was Scully partial to redheads?'

'I don't know,' said Bell. 'All we ever discussed were lawbreakers and firearms. Did they find his gun?'

'Browning Vest Pocket still in the holster.'

Bell shook his head, dismayed that Scully had been thrown so off balance.

'What?' Van Dorn shouted. 'I can't hear you.'

'I still can't imagine anyone catching Scully flat-footed.'

'That's what comes from working alone.'

'Be that as it may –'

'What?'

'Be that as it may, the issue is the spy.'

'Is the spy on that train with you?'

'I don't know yet.'

'What?'

Bell said, 'Tell them to hold on to John Scully's gun for me.'

Joseph Van Dorn heard that clearly. He knew his detectives well. Now and then, he even thought he knew what made them tick. He said, 'It will be waiting for you when you get back to New York.'

'I'll report from Chicago.'

As the 20th Century Limited roared out of East Buffalo with five hundred twenty miles to go to make Chicago by morning, Bell went forward to the club car. He found it empty but for one draw poker game. The Canadian con man pretending to be an Australian gold miner was playing with some older businessmen. He did not look pleased that conductor Dilber was watching closely.

Bell walked to the back of the speeding train. Though it was after midnight, the observation car was crowded with men, talking and drinking. Arnold Bennett, attended by his solemn Chinese, was entertaining a crowd. Shafer the German salesman was deep in conversation with Erhard Riker. Bell got a drink and made himself conspicuous until Riker saw him and waved him over to join them. Riker introduced the German as Herr Shafer. To Bell he said, 'What line did you say you were in, Mr. Bell?'

'Insurance,' he answered, nodding his thanks to Riker for not identifying him as a detective. He sat where he could observe Bennett's Chinese as well.

'Of course,' Riker nodded back, smoothly continuing the ruse. 'I should have remembered. So we're all drummers, or commercial travelers as the English call us. All selling. I supply gems to American jewelers. And Mr. Shafer here represents a line of organs built in Leipzig. Am I right, sir?'

'Correct!' Shafer barked. 'First, I sell. Then the company sends German workman with organs to assemble the pieces. They know best how to put together the best organs.'

'Church organs?' asked Bell.

'Churches, concert halls, stadiums, universities. German organs, you see, are the best organs in the world. Because German music is the best in the world. You see.'

'Do you play the organ?'

'No, no, no, no. I am a simple salesman.'

'How,' asked Isaac Bell, 'did a cavalry officer become a salesman?'

'What? What cavalry officer?' Shafer glanced at Riker, then back at Bell, his expression hardening. 'What do you mean, sir?'

'I couldn't help but notice that your hands are calloused from the reins,' Bell answered mildly. 'And you stand like a soldier. Doesn't he, Riker?'

'And sits like one, too.'

'Ah?' A bright flush rose in Shafer's neck and reddened his face. '*Ja,*' he said. 'Of course. Yes, I was once a soldier, many years ago.' He paused and stared at his powerful hands. 'Of course, I still ride whenever I find the time in this my new occupation as salesman. Excuse me, I will return.' He started to bolt away, paused and caught himself. 'Shall I ask the steward for another round of drinks?'

'Yes,' said Riker, hiding a smile until Shafer had entered the facilities.

'In retrospect,' he said, his smile broadening, 'my father is beginning to seem a wiser and wiser man – as your Mark Twain noted about his. Father was right to school me in England. We Germans are not comfortable in the presence of other nationalities. We boast without considering the effect.'

'Is it common in Germany for Army officers to go into trade?' asked Bell.

'No. But who knows why he left the service? He is far too young to have retired, even on half pay. Perhaps he had to make a living.'

'Perhaps,' said Bell.

'It would appear,' smiled Riker, 'that you are not on holiday. Or are detectives always on the case?'

'Cases tend to blur into each other,' said Bell, wondering whether Riker's statement was a challenge or merely fellow train traveler's comradery. 'For example,' he said, watching closely for Riker's reaction, 'in the course of an unrelated investigation I learned when I boarded the train that you often travel with a young lady who is believed to be your ward.'

'Indeed,' said Riker. 'You learned the truth.'

'You are young to have a ward.'

'I am. But just as I was unable to dodge taking responsibility for my father's firm, so was I not excused from the obligation of caring for an orphan when tragedy struck her family. Happenstance will sneak up on even the most footloose man, Mr. Bell . . . when he least expects it. But I will tell you this: the events we don't plan for are sometimes the best that ever happen to us. The girl brings light into my life where there was darkness.'

'Where is she now?'

'At school. She will graduate in June.' He pointed across the table at Bell. 'I hope you can meet her. This summer she will sail with me to New York. As she was reared in a cloistered manner, I make every effort to broaden her horizons. Meeting a private detective would certainly fall into that territory.'

Bell nodded. 'I look forward to it. What is her name?'

Riker seemed not to hear the question. Or, if he did, chose not to answer it. Instead, he said, 'Equally broadening will be her opportunity to meet a woman who makes moving pictures. Mr. Bell, why do you look surprised? Of course, I know your fiancée makes moving pictures. I already told you, I don't engage in business blindly. I know that you can afford the best, and I know that she will cast a clear eye on the best I have to offer. Together, you present quite a challenge. I only hope that I am up to it.'

Shafer returned. He had splashed water on his face. It had spotted his tie. But he was smiling. 'You are very observant, Mr. Bell. I thought when I removed my uniform I had removed my past. Is that a habit of the insurance man, to notice such discrepancies?'

'When I sell you insurance, I am taking a chance on you,' Bell replied. 'So I suppose I am always on the look-out for risk.'

'Is Herr Shafer a good bet?' asked Riker.

'Men of steady habits are always a good bet. Herr Shafer, I apologize if I seemed to pry.'

'I have nothing to hide!'

'Speaking of hiding,' Riker said, 'the steward appears to be. How the hell does one get a drink around here?'

Bell nodded. A steward came running and took their orders.

Arnold Bennett announced to his Chinese companions, 'Gentlemen, you look sleepy.'

'No, sir. We are very happy.'

'Expect little sleep on a train. Luxuries may abound – tailor's shop, library, manicurist, even fresh and saltwater baths. But unlike in Europe where the best trains start with the stealthiness of a bad habit, I have never slept a full hour in any American sleeper, what with abrupt stops, sudden starts, hootings, and whizzings round sharp corners.'

Laughing Chicagoans protested that that was the price of speed and worth every penny.

Isaac Bell addressed his German companions – Erhard Riker, who seemed so English, even American, and Herr Shafer, who was as Teutonic as Wagnerian opera. 'In the company of not one but two of the Kaiser's subjects, I must ask about the talk of war in Europe.'

'Germany and England are competitors, not enemies,' Riker answered.

'Our nations are evenly balanced,' Shafer added quickly. 'England has more battleships. We have by far the greater

Army – the most modern and advanced, the strongest in the world.'

'Only in those parts of the world that your Army can march to,' Arnold Bennett called from the next table.

'What is that, sir?'

'Our American hosts' Admiral Mahan put it most aptly: "The nation that rules the seas, rules the world." Your Army is worth spit in a bucket if it can't get to where the fight is.'

Shafer turned purple. Veins bulged on his forehead.

Riker cautioned him with a gesture, and answered, 'There is no fight. The talk of war is just talk.'

'Then why do you keep building more warships?' the English writer shot back.

'Why does England?' Riker retorted mildy.

The Chicagoans and the Chinese seminary students swiveled eyeballs between the Germans and the English like spectators at a tennis match. To Isaac Bell's surprise, one of the silent Chinese answered before the writer could.

'England is an island. The English see no choice.'

'Thank you, Louis,' Arnold Bennett said. 'I could not have put it better myself.'

Louis's dark almond eyes grew wide, and he looked down as if embarrassed to have spoken up.

'By that logic,' said Riker, 'Germany has no choice either. German industry and German trade demand a vast fleet of merchant ships to sail our goods across every sea. We must protect our fleet. But, frankly, it is my instinct that sensible businessmen will never go to war.'

Herr Shafer scoffed, 'My countryman is gullible. Businessmen will have no say in it. Britain and Russia conspire to obstruct German growth. France will side with England, too. Thank *Gott* for the Imperial German Army and our Prussian officers.'

'Prussians?' shouted a Chicagoan. 'Prussian officers made my grandfather emigrate to America.'

'Mine, too,' called another, red in the face. 'Thank *"Gott"* they took us out of that hellhole.'

'Socialists,' Shafer commented.

'*Socialists?* I'll show you a Socialist.'

The Chicagoan's friends restrained him.

Shafer took no notice. 'We are besieged by England and England's lackeys.'

Arnold Bennett leaped up, spread his legs in a burly stance, and said, 'I don't at all care for your tone, sir.'

Half the observation car was on their feet by now, gesticulating and shouting. Isaac Bell glanced at Riker who looked back, eyes alight with amusement. 'I guess that answers your question, Mr. Bell. Good night, sir, I'm going to bed ahead of the riot.'

Before he could rise from his chair, Shafer shouted, 'Besieged from without and undermined within by Socialists and Jews.'

Isaac Bell turned cold eyes on Shafer. The German drew back, mumbling, 'Wait. When they finish us off, they'll go after you.'

Isaac Bell drew a deep breath, reminded himself why he was on the train, and answered in a voice that carried through the car. 'After Admiral Mahan demonstrated that sea powers rule the world, he said something to a bigot that I've always admired: "Jesus Christ was a Jew. That makes them good enough for me."'

The shouting stopped. A man laughed. Another said,

'Say, that's a good one. "Good enough for me,"' and the car erupted in laughter.

Shafer clicked his heels. 'Good night, gentlemen.'

Riker watched the cavalryman retreat toward the nearest steward and demand schnapps. 'For a moment there,' he said quietly, 'I thought you were going to floor Herr Shafer.'

Bell looked at the gem merchant. 'You don't miss much, Mr. Riker.'

'I told you. My father taught me every trick in the book. What got you so riled?'

'I will not abide hatred.'

Riker shrugged. 'To answer your question – truthfully – Europe *wants* a war. Monarchists, democrats, merchants, soldiers, and sailors have been at peace too long to know what they're in for.'

'That is too cynical for my taste,' said Isaac Bell.

Riker smiled blandly. 'I'm not a cynic. I'm a realist.'

'What about those sensible businessmen you were talking about?'

'Some will see the profit in war. The rest will be ignored.'

The spy watched Isaac Bell watching his 'suspects':

The detective cannot know whether I am here in this very car.

Or already asleep in my bed.

Or even on the train at all.

Nor can he know who on this train belongs to me.

Get some sleep, Mr. Bell. You're going to need it. Bad news in the morning.

36

'Your shad roe and scrambled eggs, Mr. Bell,' announced the diner steward with a broad smile that faded as he saw the expression on Bell's face change from pleasurable anticipation to rage. Two hours from its destination, the 20th Century Limited had picked up Chicago morning newspapers left by an eastbound express. A crisp edition folded at each place setting greeted the passengers at breakfast.

EXPLOSION IN U.S. NAVY TORPEDO
STATION AT NEWPORT
TWO OFFICERS BLOWN TO ATOMS

NEWPORT, RHODE ISLAND, MAY 15TH. — An explosion that caused death and destruction occurred in the Naval Torpedo Station at Newport. It killed two naval officers and wrecked a production line.

Isaac Bell was stunned. Had he gone in the wrong direction?

'Good morning, Bell! You haven't touched your roe. Has it turned?'

'Morning, Riker. No, it smells fine. Bad news in the paper.'

Riker opened his as he sat. 'Good Lord. What caused it?'

'It doesn't say. Excuse me.' Bell went back to his stateroom.

If not an accident but sabotage, then the spy's reach was as broad as it was vicious. In the course of a single day his ring had executed a traitor in Washington, murdered a detective hot on his trail in New York, and blown up a heavily guarded naval station on the Rhode Island coast.

Isaac Bell set up temporary headquarters in the back of the LaSalle Station luggage room within minutes of the 20th Century steaming into Chicago. Van Dorn detectives from the Palmer House head office had already blanketed the railroad station. They followed his suspects as they scattered.

Larry Rosania promptly vanished. A veteran Chicago detective was reporting embarrassedly when another rushed in. 'Isaac! The Old Man says to telephone long-distance from the stationmaster's private office. And make sure you're alone.'

Bell did so.

Van Dorn asked, 'Are you alone?'

'Yes, sir. Was either of the officers killed Ron Wheeler?'

'No.'

Bell breathed a huge sigh of relief.

'Wheeler snuck off to spend the night with a woman. If he hadn't, he'd be dead, too. It was his people who were killed.'

'Thank the Lord he wasn't. Captain Falconer says he's irreplaceable.'

'Well, here is something else irreplaceable,' Van Dorn

growled. Six hundred miles of copper telephone wire between Chicago and Washington did not diminish the sound of his anger. 'This is not in the newspapers, and it won't ever be – are you still alone there, Isaac?'

'Yes, sir.'

'Listen to me. The Navy has suffered a terrible loss. The explosion started a fire. The fire destroyed their entire arsenal of experimental electric torpedoes that had been imported from England. Wheeler's people had apparently improved their range and accuracy vastly. More important – much more important – Wheeler's people figured out a way to arm the warheads with dynamite. The Navy Secretary told me this morning. He is distraught. So much so, he is threatening to offer the President his resignation. Apparently the use of TNT would have given U.S. torpedoes ten times more power underwater.'

'Can we assume it was not an accident?'

'We have to,' Van Dorn answered flatly. 'And even though the Navy is nominally in charge of guarding their own facility, they are extremely disappointed with Van Dorn Protection Services.'

Isaac Bell said nothing.

'I don't have to explain the consequences of being a government entity's target of blame, deserved or not,' Van Dorn continued. 'And I am not entirely sure what you were doing in Chicago when the spy attacked in Newport.'

This did require an answer, and Bell said, 'The Great White Fleet is about to make landfall at San Francisco. Scully was tracking the spy, or his agents, to San Francisco. Thanks to Scully, I very likely have him in my sights.'

'What do you suppose he intends to do?'

'I don't know yet. But it must involve the fleet, and I am going to stop him before he does it.'

Van Dorn remained silent for a long minute. Bell said nothing. Finally the boss said, 'I hope you know what you're doing, Isaac.'

'He will not pack his bags and go home after Newport. He will attack the fleet.'

Van Dorn said, 'All right. I'll alert Bronson in San Francisco.'

'I already have.'

He went back to the luggage room. Van Dorns reported that Herr Shafer and the Chinese traveling with Arnold Bennett had transferred to the Overland Limited to San Francisco, as their tickets had indicated. 'Their train's leaving, Isaac. If you're going with 'em, you gotta go.'

'I'm going.'

Two strong horses pulled an ice wagon modified with carriage springs and pneumatic tires instead of hard rubber, which made its ride unusually smooth on the rough cobbled streets that slanted down to Newport's waterfront. No one took note in the dim light of the thinly scattered gas lamps that the driver clutching the brake handle cut too slight and boyish a figure to heave hundred-pound blocks of ice onto a fishing dock. And if anyone thought it odd that the driver was singing to her horses,

'You can't remember
what I can't forget,'

in a soft soprano, they kept their opinions to themselves. The seamen of Newport had been smuggling rum, tobacco, slaves, and opium for three hundred years. If a girl wanted to entertain her horses while delivering ice to a boat in the dark, that was her business.

The boat was a rugged, broad-beamed, thirty-foot cat-boat with a stubby mast ahead of a low coach roof. With its gaff-rigged sail that was nearly square, and a centerboard instead of a fixed keel, it was faster than it looked and equally at home in shallow bays and off the coast. A gang of men in slickers and wool watch caps climbed out of the cabin.

While the girl stood watch with her hands buried in her pockets, the men drew the canvas off the ice wagon's cargo, inclined a ramp of planks between the wagon and dock, and gently slid four seventeen-foot-long, cigar-shaped metal tubes down the ramp one by one. They shifted the ramp and slid all four into the boat, and lashed them securely to a cushioned bed of canvas sails.

When they were done, the wide wooden hull squatted low in the water. All but one of the men climbed into the wagon and drove away. The man who stayed raised the sail and untied the mooring lines.

The girl took the tiller and sailed the boat skillfully off the dock and into the night.

That same night – the westbound Overland Limited's first night out of Chicago – reports waiting for Bell at Rock Island, Illinois, confirmed that the gem merchant Riker had indeed boarded the California Limited to San Diego. Still disliking coincidences, Bell wired Horace Bronson, head of the San Francisco office, asking him to assign James Dashwood, a young operative who had proven himself on the Wrecker case, to intercept the California Limited at Los Angeles. Dashwood should see whether Riker actually continued on to San Diego to purchase pink tourmaline gems or changed trains to San Francisco. Regardless, the young detective would trail Riker and observe his subsequent actions. Bell warned Bronson that Riker was traveling with a bodyguard named Plimpton, who would be watching his back.

Then he wired Research back in New York, asking for more information on the death of Riker's father in South Africa and urging Grady Forrer to step up the hunt for information about his ward.

Laurence Rosania's disappearance upon arrival had set off a frantic manhunt. But when Bell reached Des Moines, Iowa, the information was waiting that the retired thief – after giving his Van Dorn shadows the slip out of habit or professional pride – had been written up in the *Chicago Tribune* marriage announcements and was scheduled to steam toward a San Francisco honeymoon in his bride's private car. So much for admonishing youth that crime did not pay, noted the Chicago Van Dorn headquarters.

Herr Shafer, Arnold Bennett, and Bennett's Chinese companions had transferred to the Overland Limited to San Francisco, and it was with them that Bell continued on the journey west, hoping to pick up additional information from Research at the station stops along with what he could detect in their presence.

Then New York wired that Shafer was definitely a German spy.

'Herr Shafer' was an active cavalry officer, still serving as a major in the German Army. His real name was Cornelius Von Nyren. And Von Nyren was expert in land tactics and the use of quickly laid narrow-gauge railroads to supply an army's front lines. Whatever he was spying on in America had nothing to do with Hull 44.

'Formidable on land,' Archie wrote. 'But wouldn't know a dreadnought from a birch-bark canoe.'

37

'Chinese to the back of the line!'

It was the second morning out of Chicago, the Overland Limited drawing near Cheyenne, Wyoming, and something was wrong with the dining car. The corridor in the Pullman behind it backed up with hungry people in line for a breakfast already an hour late.

'You heard me! Chinks, Mongolians, and Asiatics to the back!'

'Stay where you are,' Isaac Bell said to the divinity students.

Arnold Bennett was whirling to their defense. Bell stopped him. 'I'll deal with this.' At last a chance to get to know Arnold Bennett's charges, Harold and Louis. He turned around and faced the bigot who had shouted. The cold anger in Bell's blue eyes, and the unmistakable impression that it was barely contained, caused the man to back away.

'Don't mind him,' the tall detective told the divinity students. 'People get testy when they're hungry. What's your name, young fellow,' he asked, thrusting his hand out. 'I'm Isaac Bell.'

'Harold, Misser Bell. Thank you.'

'Harold what?'

'Harold Wing.'

'And you?'

'Louis Loh.'

'L-e-w Lewis or L-o-u Louis?'

'L-o-u.'

'Pleased to meet you.'

'Little wonder that unpleasant chap is hungry,' growled Arnold Bennett, who was standing first in line. 'The breakfasting accommodation of this particular unit of the Overland Limited was not designed on the same scale as its bedroom accommodation.'

Isaac Bell winked at Louis and Harold, who looked bewildered by Bennett's densely circuitous English. 'Mr. Arnold means that there are more sleeping berths in the Pullmans than chairs in the diner.'

The students nodded with vague smiles.

'They had better open that dining car,' Bennett muttered. 'Before it's put to the sack by ravening hordes.'

'Did you sleep well?' Bell asked Harold and Louis. 'Are you getting used to the motion?'

'Very well, sir,' said Louis.

'Despite,' said Bennett, 'my warning about jerky trains.'

The dining car finally opened for breakfast, and Bell sat with them. The Chinese were silent as sphinxes no matter what Bell said to draw them into conversation while the writer was happy to talk nonstop about everything he saw, read, or overheard. Wing took a small Bible from his coat and read quietly. Loh stared out the window at a land growing green in the spring and speckled with cattle.

Isaac Bell lay in wait for Louis Loh in the corridor outside Arnold Bennett's staterooms.

West of Rawlins, Wyoming, the Overland Limited was increasing speed across the high plateau. The locomotive fireman was pouring on the coal, and at eighty miles an hour the train swayed hard. When Bell saw the Chinese divinity student coming down the corridor, he let the careening train throw him against the smaller man.

'Sorry!'

He steadied himself by holding Loh's lapel. 'Did they issue your pocket pistol at the seminary?'

'What?'

'This bulge is not a Bible.'

The Chinese student appeared to shrivel with embarrassment. 'Oh, no, sir. You are right. It is a gun. It is just that I am afraid. In the West, there is much hatred of Chinese. You saw at the breakfasting car. They think we're all opium addicts or tong gangsters.'

'Do you know how to use that thing?'

They were standing inches apart, Bell leaning close, still holding his lapel, the youth unable to back away. Louis lowered his dark eyes. 'Not really, sir. I guess just point it and pull the trigger – but it is the threat that is important. I would never shoot it.'

'May I see it, please?' Bell asked, extending his open hand.

Louis looked around, confirmed they were still alone, and gingerly drew the pistol from his pocket. Bell took it. 'Top-quality firearm,' he said, surprised that the student had found himself a Colt Pocket Hammerless that looked fresh out of the box. 'Where did you get it?'

'I bought it in New York City.'

'You bought a good one. Where in New York City?'

'A shop near the police headquarters. Downtown.'

Bell made sure the manual safety was on and handed it back. 'You can get hurt waving a gun around you don't know how to use. You might shoot yourself by mistake. Or someone will take it away and do it for you – and get off by claiming self-defense. I would rest easier if you would promise to put it in your suitcase and leave it there.'

'Yes, sir, Misser Bell.'

'If anyone else on the train gives you trouble, just come to me.'

'Please don't tell Mr. Bennett. He wouldn't understand.'

'Why not?'

'He is kind man. He has no idea how cruel people are.'

'Put it in your suitcase, and I won't tell him a thing.'

Louis seized Bell's hand in both of his. 'Thank you, sir. Thank you for understanding.'

Bell's face was a mask. 'Go put it in your suitcase,' he repeated.

The Chinese man hurried down the corridor and through the vestibule to the next car, where Bennett had his adjoining staterooms. Louis turned and waved another grateful thank-you. Bell nodded back as if thinking, What a pious young fellow.

In truth, he was speculating that the boyish-looking missionary students could be tong gangsters. And if that were so, he had to marvel at John Scully's clairvoyance.

No other detective in the Van Dorn Agency could wander alone into Chinatown and two weeks later connect a pair of tong gangsters to the Hull 44 spy ring. He was tempted to clamp cuffs on Louis Loh and Harold Wing and lock them in the baggage car. Except he doubted that Louis and Harold were ringleaders if gangsters at all – and if they were henchmen, he could trail them to their boss.

That the spy recruited tong Chinese was typical of his international reach. It was hard to imagine someone like Abbington-Westlake even thinking about it. That the spy had tricked a famous English novelist into providing cover for his operatives indicated an imagination as intricate as it was diabolical.

'Bet's to you, Whitmark. In or out?'

Ted Whitmark knew full well that he should never stay in a hand of seven-card stud trying to fill an inside straight. The odds were ridiculous. He needed a four. There were only four fours in the deck, one heart, one diamond, one spade, one club. And the four of clubs had already been dealt to a hand across the table, and that man had bet when it fell, suggesting another four hidden in his hole cards. Four fours in a deck, one clearly missing, another likely. The odds were less than ridiculous, they were impossible.

But he had dropped a ton of money into the pot already and he had a feeling his luck was about to change. It had to. His losing streak had started weeks ago in New York, and it was tearing him down. He had lost more on the train to San Francisco, and since he had arrived he had lost nearly every night. One four gone. One or even two likely gone. Sometimes you had to take the bull by the horns and be brave.

'Bet's to you, Whitmark. In or out?'

No more 'Mr.' Whitmark, Ted noticed. Mr. had gone by the boards when he borrowed his third five thousand early in the evening. Sometimes you had to be brave.

'In.'

'It's eight thousand.'

Whitmark shoved his chips in the pot. 'Here's three. And here's my marker.'

'You sure?'

'Deal the cards.'

The man dealing looked across the table not at Ted Whitmark but at the scarred-face owner of the Barbary Coast casino who had been approving the loans. The owner frowned. For a moment, Whitmark felt saved. He could not call if he didn't have the money. He would fold. He could go back to his hotel, sleep, and tomorrow work out a schedule to pay his losses from money the Navy would owe him after he delivered the goods to the Great White Fleet. Or Great White 'Eat,' as one of his rivals had noted approvingly. Fourteen thousand sailors ate a lot of food.

The casino owner nodded.

'Deal the cards.'

The guy with the four caught another four. Whitmark got a nine of clubs, about as ugly a card as he had ever seen. Somebody bet. Somebody called. The fours raised the pot. Ted Whitmark folded.

'You mind showing me your last card after the hand?' he asked of the man to his left.

When it was over and three fours across the table had won, the man to Ted's left, who had received the card Ted would have if he had stayed in, said, 'It was a four. Bet you would have liked that,' he called across the table to the trip fours. 'You would have had *four* fours.'

'I would have liked it, too,' said Ted, and he stumbled to the bar. Before he could raise a glass, the man who owned

328

the casino walked up and said, 'I have a message for you from Tommy Thompson in New York.'

Ted shrank from the man's cold gaze. 'Don't worry,' he mumbled. 'I'll pay you first, soon as I can.'

'Tommy says to pay me. I bought your marker.'

'On top of what I owe you? You're taking a hell of a chance.'

'You'll pay. One way or another.'

'I make a lot of money. I'll get it to you, soon.'

'It's not money I need, Mr. Whitmark. I need a little help, and you're the man to give it to me.'

'If me and you was half as smart as we think we are we'd have tumbled to it a month ago!' John Scully's words thundered through a dream about the Frye Boys.

Isaac Bell shot awake from his first full night's sleep since he had left New York. The berth was tilted forward, and he did not have to look out his stateroom window to know that they had crested the Sierra Nevada and were beginning the descent to the Sacramento Valley. Five hours to San Francisco. He got up and dressed quickly.

Had he missed a bet?

'Days ago,' he muttered to himself.

He had not once questioned the novelist Arnold Bennett's role as Harold's and Louis's protector. What if the opposite had occurred? What if the writer was also a British spy? Like Abbington-Westlake, hiding behind a scrim of upper-crust, above-it-all mannerisms and a witty tongue?

The train pulled into Sacramento. Bell bolted to the telegraph office and sent a wire to New York. Was Bennett

329

the one who recruited the tong hatchet men and dressed them up as divinity students? Talk about hiding in plain sight. For all he knew, Bell realized, Arnold Bennett was the spy himself, the leader of the ring.

Katherine Dee cursed aloud.

Like a sailor, she laughed, giddy on little sleep and lots of dust. Cursing like a sailor. Wind and spray were playing hell with the cocaine she was sniffing from an ivory vial to stay awake on the final night of her voyage from Newport. She could not see the coast, but the thunder of the surf told her she had veered too close.

She had sailed the heavily laden catboat down the southern coast of Long Island, timing her passage from Montauk Point to enter Fire Island Inlet at first light. She steered, unseen except by some fishermen, through the opening in the barrier beach. Once inside, out of the ocean swells, she followed a channel marked with stakes and watched for her landmark on the Long Island shore five miles across the bay. When she spotted it, she crossed the choppy waters of the Great South Bay steering for a white mansion with a red roof. Stakes marked the mouth of a newly dredged creek bulkheaded with creosoted wood.

The catboat glided up the glassy creek.

The boathouse was clad in new cedar shingles. The roof was tall, the opening high enough to accommodate the low mast. Katherine Dee lowered her sail and let the boat drift. She had timed it just right. It stopped close enough for her to toss a looped line around a piling. Pulling on the line, directing her strength with economy, she eased the heavily laden boat stern first into the shadows under the roof.

A man appeared through the back door that opened to the land.

'Where's Jake?'

'He tried to kiss me,' she answered in a distant voice.

'Yeah?' he said, as if to say, You're a girl, what do you expect alone on a boat in the middle of the ocean? 'So where is he?'

She looked him full in the face. 'A shark jumped into the boat and ate him.'

He considered the way her smile stiffened her mouth, the iceberg grimness in her eyes, and the people she knew, and decided that Jake had gotten what he deserved, and he was not at all interested in how it had happened. He held up a wicker basket. 'I brought you supper.'

'Thank you.'

'I brought enough for two. Not knowing that –'

'Good. I'm starving.'

She ate alone. Then she spread her sleeping bag on the canvas cushioning her cargo and slept secure in the thought that Brian O'Shay would be proud of her. The explosion at the torpedo factory had masked the theft of four experimental electric torpedoes that had been imported from England for research. Armed with TNT by the brilliant Ron Wheeler, they were ten times more powerful than the English had made them. And no one at the Newport Naval Torpedo Station realized that they had not been blown to smithereens.

38

'There you are, Bell! Jolly good, we didn't miss saying good-bye.'

Bell was surprised when he reboarded the train as it pulled out of Sacramento on the last ninety-mile leg to San Francisco that Arnold Bennett and the Chinese, who were ticketed through to San Francisco, had their bags packed and in the corridor.

'I thought you were going to San Francisco.'

'Changed our mind, inspired by all these orchards and berry fields.' The train was passing through strawberry fields crowded with fruit pickers in straw hats. 'We're hopping off early at Suisun City. Decided to catch a train to Napa Junction. An old school chum of mine is farming up St. Helena way – started a vineyard, actually, stomping grapes and all that. We'll recover bucolically from the rigors of our travels – splendid as they were – before pressing on to San Francisco. I've a mind to cobble up an article for *Harper's* on the subject while the boys enjoy some fresh air in the country before carrying the Word of God home to China.'

Bell thought fast, envisioning the long, sprawling bays of San Francisco enclosed from the Pacific Ocean by the San Francisco Peninsula and the Marin Peninsula. From Suisun City, the main line continued southwest seventeen miles to the Benicia Ferry that carried the train across the narrow Carquinez Strait to Port Costa. Then the final thirty-mile run beside San Pablo Bay to Oakland Mole, where a passenger ferry crossed San Francisco Bay to the city.

Twenty miles north of the city, up San Francisco Bay and across San Pablo Bay, was the Mare Island Naval Shipyard. It was the U.S. Navy's Brooklyn Navy Yard of America's West Coast, with a long history of building, repairing, and refitting warships and submarines. Napa Junction, connected to Suisan City by a local branch line to the west, was only five miles north of the shipyard.

Bennett and the Chinese would be a short train or electric trolley ride from Mare Island, where the Great White Fleet would put in from its voyage to refit, replenish food and water, and load fresh ammunition from the magazines.

'Isn't that a coincidence?' said Isaac Bell.

'What do you mean?'

'I'm taking that very same train.'

'Where are your bags?'

'I travel light.'

The Overland Limited pulled into Suisun City ten minutes late. The train to Napa Junction was blowing its whistle. Bell snatched a handful of wires waiting for him at the telegraph office and hurried to board. It was a two-coach local, with a gaily striped awning sheltering its back platform. There were a half dozen passengers in the rear car, Arnold Bennett in their midst and starting to tell a story. He interrupted himself to indicate an empty seat. 'Come let us talk you into tromping grapes with us at St. Helena.'

Bell waved the telegrams and headed back to the platform to scan them in private. 'Join you in a minute. Orders from the front office.'

Bennett laughed jovially, calling over his shoulder, 'But you already know they're only instructing you to sell more insurance.'

The train was crossing salt marshes, and the cool, wet wind that swirled under the awning smelled of the sea. The wind rattled the emergency-brake handle that swung from a short rope rhythmically against the wall and buffeted the flimsy yellow telegraph paper.

Research had no word yet from Germany on the identity of the schoolgirl who was Riker's ward – that it was taking so long was proof that Joe Van Dorn was right to expand field offices into Europe.

They *had* unearthed additional details about the death of Erhard Riker's father in South Africa in 1902 during the Boer War. Smuts, the Transvaal leader, had led a sudden raid on the copper-mine railroad from Port Nolloth, where the senior Riker was searching for a rumored deposit of alluvial diamonds. He was taking refuge in a British railroad blockhouse when the Boers attacked with dynamite hand bombs.

The third wire was from James Dashwood.

RIKER ARRIVED LA.

NOW EN ROUTE TO SAN DIEGO.

BODYGUARD PLIMPTON SUSPICIOUS.

JD MISTOOK FOR TIFFANY JEWEL AGENT.

BODYGUARD PERSUADED JD ITINERANT TEMPERANCE SPEAKER.

Bell grinned. Dash had the makings of becoming a character. His grin faded abruptly. The last wire in the stack started with the warning initials YMK.

You must know – Archie Abbott warning that if Bell was not already aware, he should be.

YMK.
ARNOLD BENNETT AT HOME PARIS.

'What?' Bell said aloud. He glanced through the glass in the door, saw the man in tweed who claimed to be Arnold Bennett, and looked back at the telegram.

WRITER NOT – REPEAT NOT – ON OVERLAND
LIMITED.
SF VD AGENTS MEETING TRAIN AT BENICIA FERRY.
WATCH STEP.

It was a stunning revelation, and Isaac Bell rejoiced.

At last he knew for sure who he was hunting. The man who claimed to be Arnold Bennett was in league with the Chinese, probably with their boss, who was likely the man who ordered the redhead to kill Scully when the detective uncovered the Chinatown connection.

At last he held the advantage. They did not know that Bell knew.

'Misser Bell?'

Bell looked up from his telegrams and down a gun barrel.

39

'Louis, I thought we agreed that you would keep that in your suitcase.'

Harold was behind Louis, drawing a weapon from his coat.

'You disappoint me, too, Harold. That is not a Bible. Not even a traditional tong hatchet but a firearm any self-respecting, modern American criminal thug would be proud to carry.'

Louis's English was suddenly accentless, his manner superior.

'Step to the edge of the platform, Mr. Bell, and turn your back to us. Do not draw the pistol you conceal in your shoulder holster. Do not try for the derringer in your hat. Do not consider reaching for the knife in your boot.'

Bell glanced past them through the vestibule door. At the front of the coach, the false Arnold Bennett was holding forth with broad gestures that were having his desired effect of distracting the few people in the car. The wheels were clattering too loudly for Bell to hear their laughter.

'You're unusually observant of sidearms for a divinity student, Louis. But have you considered that witnesses will hear you shoot me?'

'We'll shoot you if you force us to. Then we will shoot the witnesses. I'm sure you've heard that we Asiatics and Mongolians have no regard for human life. *Turn around!*'

Bell looked over his shoulder. The railing was low. The roadbed was disappearing behind the train at fifty miles an hour, a blur of steel rails, iron spikes, stone ballast, and wooden ties. When he turned, they would crack his skull with a gun barrel or plunge a knife in his back and dump him over the railing.

He opened his hand.

The telegrams scattered, twisting and twirling in the buffeting slipstream, and flew in Louis's face like demented finches.

Bell thrust his arms straight up, grabbed the edge of the roof awning, tucked his knees, and kicked a boot at Harold's head. Harold jumped left where Bell wanted him to, clearing a path to the red wooden handle of the train's emergency brake.

Any doubt that they were not divinity students vanished when Bell's hand was an inch from the emergency brake. Louis smashed his gun against Bell's wrist, slamming it away from the brake pull. Unable to bring the train to a crashing halt, Bell ignored the searing pain in his right wrist and punched with his left. It landed with satisfying force, hard enough on Louis's forehead to buckle his knees.

But Harold had recovered. Concentrating his strength and weight like a highly trained fighter, the short, wiry Chinese wielded his gun like a steel club. The barrel smashed into Bell's hat. The thick felt crown and the spring steel band within absorbed some of the blow, but momentum was against him. He saw the awning spin overhead, then the sky, and then he was tumbling over the side rail and falling toward the tracks. Everything seemed to move in slow motion. He saw the railroad ties, the

337

wheels, the truck they carried, and the platform steps. He seized the top step with both hands. His boots hit the ties. For an awful split second he was trying to run backward at fifty miles an hour. Squeezing hard on the steel step, knowing that if his hands slipped he was through, he curled his arms as if doing a chin-up and hauled his feet onto the bottom stop.

Harold's pistol descended in a blur. It seemed to fill the sky. Bell reached past the gun to seize Harold's wrist and yanked with all his might. The tong gangster catapulted over him, flew through the air, and smashed into a telegraph pole, his body bent backward around it like a horseshoe.

Clinging to the steps, Bell reached for his own pistol. Before he could pull it, he felt Louis's automatic pressed to his head. 'Your turn!'

40

Bell braced his feet to jump and cast a lightning-swift glance over the ground racing past. From his precarious perch on the steps he could see farther ahead than Louis. Beside the train was a steep ballast embankment, an endless row of telegraph poles, and a clump of thick trees as deadly as the poles. But far ahead spread an open field dotted with sheep. A barbed-wire fence ran along the track to keep livestock off the rails. He had to clear the fence if he had any hope at all of surviving the jump. But first he needed a five-second reprieve to get to the field.

He shouted into the roaring wind and clattering wheels, 'I will track you down, Louis.'

'If you live, I will cock my ears for the clump of crutches.'

'I will never give up,' Bell said, buying another second. Almost to the grassy field. The slope was steeper than it appeared from the distance.

'Last chance, Bell. Jump!'

Bell bought one more second with 'Never!'

He launched in a desperate dive to clear the fence. Too low. He missed a telegraph pole by feet and a fence post by inches. But the top strand of barbed wire was leaping at his face. The speeding train's slipstream slammed into him. The blast of air lifted his flying body over the wire. He hit the grass face-first like a base runner stealing second, and he tried to tuck arms and legs into a tight ball. He rolled, powerless to avoid any rock or boulder in his path. In the blur of motion there was suddenly something solid right in front of him, and he had no choice but to slam into it.

The shock jolted every fiber in his body. Pain and darkness clamped around his head. He was vaguely aware that his arms and legs had untucked and were flopping like a scarecrow's as he continued rolling on the grass. He hadn't the strength to gather them in again. The darkness deepened. After a while he had the vague impression that he had stopped moving. He heard a drum beat. The ground shook under him. Then the darkness closed in completely, and he lay absolutely still.

At some point the drums ceased. At another, he became aware that the darkness had lifted. His eyes were open, staring at a hazy sky. In his mind he saw a spinning field filled with sheep. His head hurt. The sun had moved an hour's worth to the west. And when he sat up and looked around, he saw a flock of real sheep – unshorn woollies grazing peacefully, all but one a hundred yards away that was struggling to stand.

Bell rubbed his head, then he felt for broken bones and found none. He rose unsteadily and walked toward the sheep to see if he had injured it so badly that he would have to shoot it to put it out of its misery. But, as if inspired by his success, it managed to stand on all fours and limp painfully toward the flock. 'Sorry, pardner,' said Bell. 'Didn't aim to run into you, but I'm glad I did.'

He went looking for his hat.

When he heard a train coming, he climbed up the embankment and planted himself in the middle of the tracks. He stood there, swaying on his feet, until the train stopped with the tip of its engine pilot pressing between his knees. A red-faced engineer stomped to the front of his locomotive and yelled, 'Who the hell do you think you are?'

'Van Dorn agent,' Bell answered. 'On my way to Napa Junction.'

'You think that makes you own the railroad?'

Bell unbuttoned the inner breast pocket of his grass-stained coat and presented the most compelling of the several railroad passes he carried. 'In a manner of speaking, I do.' He staggered to the ladder that led to the cab and climbed aboard.

At Napa Junction, the stationmaster reported, 'The English clergyman and his Chinese missionary took the train north to St. Helena.'

'When's your train to St. Helena.?'

'Northbound leaves at three-oh-three."

'Wait.' Bell steadied himself on the counter. 'What did you say?' Another field of round sheep was spinning in his head. *'Clergyman?'*

'Reverend J. L. Skelton.'

'Not a writer? A journalist?'

'When's the last time you saw a newspaperman wearing one of them white collars?'

'And he went north?' Away from Mare Island.

'North.'

'Did he take the Chinese student with him?'

'I told you. He bought two tickets to Mount Helen.'

'Did you see them both board?'

'Saw them board. Saw the train leave the station. And I can report that it didn't come back.'

'When's your next train south?'

'Train to Vallejo just left.'

Bell looked around. 'What are those tracks?' An electric catenary wire was supported over them. 'Interurban?'

'Napa-Vallejo and Benicia Railroad,' the stationmaster answered, adding with a disdainful sniff, 'the trolley.'

'When's the next trolley to Vallejo?'

'No idea. I don't talk to the competition.'

Bell gave the stationmaster his card and ten dollars. 'If that reverend comes through here again, wire me care of the commandant of Mare Island.'

The stationmaster pocketed half a week's salary, and said, 'I suppose I've never seen you if the reverend asks?'

Bell gave him another ten dollars. 'You took the words right out of my mouth.'

He was waiting at the Interurban tracks, head spinning, when a red, four-seat Stanley Steamer with yellow wheels glided by silently. It looked brand-new but for mud spattered on its brass headlamps.

'Hey!'

Bell ran after it. The driver stopped. When he peeled back his goggles, he looked like a schoolboy playing hooky. Bell guessed that he had 'borrowed' his father's car.

'I'll bet you twenty bucks that thing can't do a mile a minute.'

'You'll lose.'

'It's six miles to Vallejo. I'll bet you twenty bucks you can't get there in six minutes.'

Bell was losing the bet until, two miles from Vallejo, they came squealing around a bend in the road, and the driver stomped on his brakes. The road was blocked by a

342

gang of men who had dug a trench across it to lay a culvert pipe. 'Hey!' yelled the driver. 'How in heck are we supposed to get to Vallejo?'

The foreman, seated in the shade of an umbrella, pointed at a cutoff they had just passed. 'Over the hill.'

The driver looked at Bell. 'That's not fair. I can't do sixty over a hill.'

'We'll work out a handicap,' said Bell. 'I think you're going to win this race.'

The driver poured on the steam, and the Stanley climbed briskly for several hundred feet. They tore across a short plateau and climbed another hundred. At the crest, Bell saw a breathtaking vista. The town of Vallejo lay below, its grid pattern of streets, houses, and shops stopping at the blue waters of San Pablo Bay. To the right, Mare Island was marked by tall steel radio towers like those Bell had seen at the Washington Navy Yard. Ships lay alongside the island. In the distance, he saw columns of black smoke rising behind Point San Pablo, which divided San Francisco Bay from San Pablo Bay.

'Stop your auto,' said Bell.

'I'm losing time.'

Bell handed him twenty dollars. 'You already won.'

A line of white battleships rounded the headland and steamed into view. He knew their silhouettes from the Henry Reutendahl paintings reproduced for months in *Collier's*. The flagship, the three-funnel *Connecticut*, led the column, followed by *Alabama*, with two smoke funnels side by side, then the smaller *Kersage*, with two tall in-line funnels and stacked forward turrets, and *Virginia* taking up the rear.

'Wow!' exclaimed the kid at the wheel. 'Say, where are they going? They're supposed to anchor at the city.'

'Down there,' said Bell. 'Mare Island for maintenance and supplies.'

The kid dropped him on a street of tailors' shops that catered to Navy officers.

'How much to replace my suit of clothes?'

'Those are mighty fine duds, mister. Fifty dollars if you want it fast.'

'A hundred,' said Bell, 'if every man in your shop drops everything and it's done for me in two hours.'

'Done! And we'll get your hat cleaned free of charge.'

'I would like to use your washroom. And then I believe I would like to sit in a chair where I can close my eyes.'

In the mirror over the sink he saw a slight dilation of his pupils that told him he might have suffered a minor concussion. If that was all. 'Thank you, Mr. Sheep.'

He washed his face, sat in a chair, and slept. An hour later he awakened to the rumbling of a seemingly endless line of wagons and trucks heading for Mare Island Pier. Every fourth truck had T. WHITMARK stenciled on the side. Ted was doing well feeding the sailors.

The tailor was as good as his word. Two hours after arriving in Vallejo, Isaac Bell stepped off the ferry *Pinafore* onto the Mare Island Naval Shipyard. U.S. Marines snapped to attention at the gate. Bell showed the pass Joseph Van Dorn had procured from the Navy Secretary.

'Take me to the commandant.'

The commandant had a message for Bell from the Napa Junction railroad station.

'My hosts usually hold the reception after I preach,' said the visiting English clergyman, Reverend J. L. Skelton.

'We do things differently on Mare Island,' said the commandant. 'This way, sir, to your receiving line.'

Gripping the clergyman's elbow, the commandant marched him through a chapel lit by brilliant Tiffany stained-glass windows and flung open the door to the Navy chaplain's office. Behind a sturdy desk, Isaac Bell rose to his full height, immaculate in white.

Skelton turned pale. 'Now, wait, everyone, gentlemen, this is not what you imagine.'

'You were a fake writer on the train,' said Bell. 'Now you're a fake preacher.'

'No, I am truly of the clergy. Well, was . . . Defrocked, you know. Misunderstanding, church funds . . . a young lady . . . Well, you can imagine.'

'Why did you impersonate Arnold Bennett?'

'It presented an opportunity I could not afford to pass up.'

'Opportunity?'

Skelton nodded eagerly. 'I was at the end of my rope. Parties in England had caught up with me in New York. I had to get out of town. The job was tailor-made.'

'Who,' asked Bell, 'gave you the job?'

'Why, Louis Loh, of course. And poor Harold, who I gather is no longer among us.'

'Where is Louis Loh?'

'I'm not entirely sure.'

'You'd better be sure,' roared the commandant. 'Or I'll have it beaten out of you.'

'That won't be necessary,' Bell said. 'I'm sure –'

'Pipe down, sir,' roared the commandant, cutting him off as they had agreed ahead of time. 'This is my shipyard. I'll treat criminals any way I want. Now, where is this Chinaman? Quickly, before I call a bosun.'

'Mr. Bell is right. That won't be necessary. This is all a huge misunderstanding, and –'

'Where is the Chinaman?'

'When I last saw him, he was dressed like a Japanese fruit picker.'

'Fruit picker? What do you mean?'

'Like the fruit pickers we saw from the train at Vaca. You saw them, Bell. There's vast communities of Japanese employed picking fruit. Berries and all . . .'

Bell glanced at the commandant, who nodded that it was true.

'What was he wearing?' Bell asked.

'Straw hat, checkered shirt, dungarees.'

'Were the dungarees overalls? With a bib?'

'Yes. Exactly like a Jap fruit picker.'

Bell exchanged glances with the commandant. 'Do you have fruit trees on Mare Island?'

'Of course not. It's a shipyard. Now, see here, you, you'd better come clean or –'

Bell interrupted. 'Reverend, you have one opportunity not to spend the rest of your life in prison. Answer me very carefully. Where did you see Louis Loh dressed like a fruit picker?'

'On the queue.'

'What queue?'

'The carts queued up for the freight ferry.'

'Was he on a cart?'

'He was driving one, don't you see?'

Bell headed for the door. 'He is disguised as a Japanese farmer delivering fruit?'

'That's what I'm trying to tell you.'

'What kind of fruit?'

'Strawberries.'

'Pass! You lousy Mongolian,' shouted the Marine guarding the entrance to the short road that crossed Mare Island from the ferry dock to the piers, where sailors were streaming up and down gangways carrying provisions into the ships. 'Show your pass!'

'Here, sir,' said Louis Loh, eyes cast downward as he handed over the paper. 'I showed it at the ferry.'

'Show it again here. And if I had my way, Japs wouldn't set foot on Mare Island, pass or no pass.'

'Yes, sir.'

The Marine glowered at the paper, muttering, 'Asiatics driving trucks. Farmers must be getting hard up.' He commenced a slow, deliberate circle around the wagon. He snatched a strawberry from one of the crates and popped it in his mouth. A sergeant marched up. 'What the hell is the delay?'

'Just checking this Jap, sir.'

'You got a hundred wagons lined up. Get it moving.'

'You heard him, you stupid Mongolian. Get out of here.'

He slammed a big hand down on the mule and it jumped ahead, nearly throwing Louis Loh off the wagon. The road, paved with cobblestones, cut in and out of storehouses and machine shops and crossed a railroad track. Where it forked, Louis Loh jerked the reins. The mule, which had been plodding after the other wagons, reluctantly turned.

Loh's heart started pounding. The map he had been given indicated that the magazine was at the end of this road at the water's edge. He rounded a factory building, and there it was, a stone structure a quarter mile ahead, with small barred windows and terra-cotta tile roof. The terra-cotta roof and the splash of blue of San Pablo Bay reminded him of his native city of Canton on the South China coast. Scared as he was, he was suddenly assailed with a powerful dose of homesickness that tore at his resolve. There were so many beautiful things he would never see again.

Wagons were streaming out of the magazine onto a long finger pier, at the end of which lay the gleaming white *Connecticut,* the flagship of the Great White Fleet. He was close. Ahead, he saw the final guard post manned by Marines. He reached under the wagon seat and tugged a string. He imagined he could hear the alarm clock ticking under the strawberries, but in fact it was completely muffled by the barrels of explosives under the fruit. He was close. The only question was, how much closer could he get before they stopped him?

He heard the grinding of a heavy motor and chain drive behind him. It was a stake truck piled high with red-and-white Coca-Cola syrup barrels. Had it followed him by mistake out of the provisioning line? Whatever the reason, its presence made his lone wagon less conspicuous. The truck blared its horn and roared ahead of him. A second later it stopped short, hard rubber tires screeching on the cobblestones. It slid sideways, blocking the road, which had a ditch on either side. There was no way around it, and Loh had already started the timing device that would detonate the explosives.

Louis called, 'Sir, could you please move your truck? I am making delivery.'

Isaac Bell jumped down from the cab, grabbed the mule's bit collar, and said, 'Hello, Louis.'

Louis Loh's fear and homesickness dissolved like windswept fog. Icy clarity replaced it. He reached under the wagon seat and tugged a second cord. This one led forward along the wagon tongue and under the mule's traces. It detonated a strip of firecrackers that went off in a string of rapid explosions. The terrified mule reared violently, throwing Bell to the ground. It plunged blindly into the ditch, dragging the wagon, which overturned, spilling the strawberries and the explosives. The maddened animal broke free and ran, but not before Louis Loh, seeing that all was lost, jumped on its back. Bucking and kicking, it tried to throw Louis Loh, but the agile young Chinese clung tightly, urging it toward the water.

Isaac Bell took off after them, running full tilt over a field that led back toward the narrow strait that separated Mare Island from Vallejo. He saw the mule stop suddenly. Louis Loh was catapulted over its neck. The Chinese rolled across on the grass, flipped to his feet, and ran. Bell followed. Suddenly a massive explosion shook the ground. He looked back. Coca-Cola barrels were flying through the air. The wagon had disappeared and the truck was burning. The Marines at the guard post and the men on the munitions pier ran toward the fire. The *Connecticut* and the stone magazine were both unscathed.

Bell took off after Louis Loh, who was running toward a pier. A launch was tied alongside. A sailor scrambled out of it and tried to stop the Chinese. Louis Loh straight-armed him and dove into the water. When Bell got to the pier, he was swimming toward Vallejo.

Bell ran to the launch. 'Steam up?'

The sailor was still on the pier, dazed. 'Yes, sir.'

Bell cast the fore and aft lines off the bollards.

'Hey, what are you doing, mister?' The sailor scrambled onto the launch and reached for Bell. 'Stop!'

'Can you swim?'

'Sure.'

'Good-bye.'

Bell took his hand and threw him overboard. The tide was pulling the boat from the dock. Bell engaged the propeller and steered around the sailor, who sputtered indignantly, 'What did you do that for? Let me help you.'

The last thing Bell wanted was the Navy's help. The Navy would arrest Louis and hold him in the brig. 'My prisoner,' he said. 'My case.'

The tide swept Louis downstream. Bell followed closely in the launch, ready to rescue him from drowning. But he was a strong swimmer, cutting through the water with a modern front crawl.

In the last hundred yards, Bell drove the launch ashore at a pier and was waiting on the bank, dangling handcuffs, when Louis staggered out of water. The Chinese stood, breathing hard, staring in disbelief at the tall detective, who said, 'Stick out your hands.'

Louis pulled a knife and lunged with surprising speed for a soaking-wet man who had just swum across a racing tide. Bell parried with the cuffs and punched him hard. Louis went down, sufficiently stunned for Bell to cuff his hands behind his back. Bell hauled him to his feet, surprised by how slight he was. Louis couldn't weigh more than one-twenty.

Bell marched him toward the pier where he had tied the launch. It was only four or five miles down the Carquinez Strait from Vallejo to Benicia Point, where, with any luck, he could board a train before the Navy got wise.

But before he could reach the pier, a Mare Island Ferry pulled in and disgorged a mob of ship workers.

'There he is!'

'Get him!'

The workmen had heard the explosion and seen the barrels flying and put two and two together. As they ran toward Bell and Louis Loh, a second group who'd been repairing a trolley siding came running with sledgehammers and iron bars and joined the first. They became a solid mass, blocking the Van Dorn detective and his prisoner from the launch.

The track gang lit an oxyacetylene torch. 'Burn the Jap. To hell with a trial.'

Isaac Bell told the lynch mob, 'You can't burn him, boys.'

'Yeah, why not?'

'He's not a Jap. He's Chinese.'

'They're all Mongolians – Asiatic coolies – they're all in it together.'

'You still can't burn him. He belongs to me.'

'You?' the mob erupted in angry chorus.

'Who the hell are you?'

'There's one of you and a hundred of us!'

'A hundred?' Bell snapped his derringer from his hat and his Browning from his coat and swept the crowd with the muzzles. 'Two shots in my left hand. Seven in my right. You don't have a hundred. You have ninety-one.'

Some in front backed up, slipping between the men behind them, but others replaced them. The new front row edged closer, exchanging glances, seeking a leader. Face unyielding as granite, eyes cold, Bell looked from man to man, watching their eyes.

It would only take one to get brave.

'Who's first? How about you fellows in front?'

'Get him!' yelled a tall man in the second row.

Bell fired the Browning. The man screamed and fell to his knees, clapping both hands to a bloody ear.

41

'Ninety-nine,' said Isaac Bell.

The mob backed away, mumbling sullenly.

A trolley glided up, clanging its bell to chase men off the tracks. Bell dragged Louis Loh onto it.

'You can't get on here,' the operator protested. 'That Jap's all wet!'

Bell shoved the wide mouth of the double-barreled derringer in the trolley driver's face. 'No stops. Straight through to Benicia Terminal.'

Speeding past waiting passengers at the many stops along the way, they pulled up to the Southern Pacific Ferry Slip in ten minutes. Across the mile-wide strait at Port Costa, Bell saw the *Solano,* the largest railway ferryboat in the world, loading a locomotive and a consist of eastbound Overland Limited Pullmans. He dragged Loh to the stationmaster's office, identified himself, purchased stateroom tickets to cross the continent, and sent telegrams. The ferry crossed in nine minutes, tied up, and locked to the tracks. The locomotive pulled the front half of the train onto the apron. A switch engine pushed the rear four cars off the boat. In ten minutes the train was whole again and steaming out of Benicia Terminal.

Bell found his stateroom and handcuffed Louis to the plumbing.

As the transcontinental train sped up the Sacramento

River Valley, Louis Loh finally spoke. 'Where are you taking me?'

'Louis, to which tong do you belong?'

'I am not tong.'

'Why were you trying to make it look like the Japanese blew up the magazine?'

'I will not talk to you.'

'Of course you will. You will tell me everything I want to know about what you were trying to do, why, and who gave you your orders.'

'You do not understand a man like me. I will not talk. Even if you torture me.'

'"That ain't my style,"' Bell quoted from a popular poem.

'"Strike One,' the umpire said,"' Louis Loh shot back smugly, 'I read your "Casey at the Bat."'

'You've told me something already,' Bell replied. 'You just don't know it.'

'What?'

The tall detective fell silent. In fact, Louis Loh had confirmed his suspicion that he was more complicated than a run-of-the-mill tong gangster. He did not believe that the Chinese was the spy himself, but there was more to Loh than today's attempt at Mare Island had revealed.

'You give me a great advantage,' said Loh.

'How is that?'

'By admitting you are not man enough to torture me.'

'Is that the Hip Sing definition of a man?'

'What is Hip Sing?'

'You will tell me.'

'When the tables are turned,' said Louis Loh, 'when you are my prisoner, I will torture you.'

Bell stretched out on the bed and closed his eyes. His head hurt, and sheep were still turning somersaults.

'I will use a chopper, at first,' Loh began. 'A cleaver. Razor-sharp. I will start with your nose . . .' Louis Loh continued to recite lurid descriptions of the horrors he would inflict on Bell until Bell began to snore.

The detective opened his eyes when the train stopped in Sacramento. There was a knock at the stateroom door. Bell admitted two burly Protection Services agents from the Sacramento office. 'Take him to the baggage car, man-acle him hand and foot. One of you stays with him at all times. The other sleeps. I've got a Pullman berth for you. You will never let him out of your sight. You will not dis-tract yourself talking to the train crew. If there is a cut or a bruise on him, you will answer to me. I will look in on you regularly. We will be particularly vigilant whenever the train stops.'

'All the way to New York?'

'We have to change trains at Chicago.'

'Do you think his friends will try to bust him out?'

Bell watched Loh for a reaction and saw none. 'Did you bring shotguns?'

'Autoloads, like you said. And one for you, too.'

'Let them try. All right, Louis. Off you go. Hope you enjoy being luggage for the next five days.'

'You will never make me talk.'

'We'll find a way,' Bell promised.

Luxury train tickets, a suit of 'wealthy English writer' tweed, a gold pocket watch, expensive luggage, and a hundred dollars were all it had cost the spy to hire the defrocked J. L. Skelton to masquerade as Arnold Bennett. So reported Horace Bronson, the head of the San Francisco office, in a wire waiting for Isaac Bell in Ogden. But although threats of a long prison term had frightened him into talking freely, Skelton had no idea why he had been hired to pretend to escort so-called missionary students.

'He swore on a stack of Bibles,' Bronson noted wryly, 'that he did not know why he was then paid another hundred dollars to revert to clergy status and hold a service in the Mare Island chapel. And he denied any knowledge of why Harold Wing and Louis Loh tried to make it look like the Japanese blew up the Mare Island magazine to cripple ships of the Great White Fleet.' Horace Bronson believed him. So did Isaac Bell. The spy was an expert at making others do his dirty work. Like Arthur Langner's big guns, he stayed miles away from the explosion.

The source of the pass that Loh had used to get his wagon aboard the ferry into the navy yard would have been a clue. But the paper itself had burned up in the explosion, along with the wagon and the truck. Even the mule was no help. It had been stolen in Vaca the day before. The guards, who had admitted hundreds of trucks and wagons, could not pinpoint any helpful information about the passes or the wagon load of strawberries they had allowed on the island.

Two days later, when the train was highballing across Illinois, Bell brought Louis Loh a newspaper from Chicago. The tong gangster lay on a fold-down cot in the dark, windowless baggage car with a wrist and ankle handcuffed to the metal frame. The PS operative guarding him was dozing on a stool. 'Get yourself some coffee,' Bell ordered, and when they were alone he showed Louis the newspaper. 'Hot off the press. News from Tokyo.'

'What do I care about Tokyo?'

'The Emperor of Japan has *invited* America's Great White Fleet to make an official visit when it crosses the Pacific.'

The bland mask that Louis Loh habitually wore on his face slipped a hair. Bell detected a minute slumping of his shoulders that broadcast an inner collapse of hope that his failed attack had still somehow provoked a clash between Japan and the United States.

Bell was puzzled. Why did Louis care so? He had already been caught. He was facing prison, if not the hangman, and had lost the money he would have been paid for success. What did he care? Unless he had done it for reasons other than money.

'We can assume, Louis, that His Imperial Majesty would *not* have invited the fleet if you had managed to blow up the Mare Island Naval Shipyard in his name.'

'What do I care about the Emperor of Japan?'

'That is my question. Why would a Chinese tong hatchet man try to inflame U.S.-Japanese antagonism?'

'Go to hell.'

'And for whom? Who did you do it for, Louis?'

Louis Loh smiled mockingly. 'Save your breath. Torture me. Nothing will make me talk.'

'We'll find a way,' Bell promised. 'In New York.'

Heavily armed Chicago Van Dorns backed up by railroad police transferred Louis Loh from the Overland Limited across LaSalle Station to the 20th Century Limited. No one tried to snatch Louis or kill him, which Bell had half expected. He decided to leave him in the care of Protection Services until the 20th Century got to New York. And Bell continued to stay out of Louis's sight at Grand Central, where another squad of Van Dorns put Louis in a truck and drove him to the Brooklyn Navy Yard. Lowell Falconer was on hand to smooth the way for Louis Loh to spend his first night in a Navy brig.

Bell waited for the captain on his turbine yacht. *Dyname* was moored to a navy yard pier, between Hull 44's ways and a huge wooden barge attended by a seagoing tugboat. On the barge, engineers were erecting a cage mast. It was a full-scale rendition of the twelve-to-one scale model that Bell had seen in Farley Kent's design loft.

High overhead, Hull 44's stern filled the blue sky. Hull plating was creeping higher up her frame, and she more and more was taking the shape of a ship. If she became half the fighting ship Falconer had envisioned and Alasdair MacDonald and Arthur Langner had labored to make swift and deadly, Bell thought, then this view of the back of her was one the enemy would never see until their own ships were adrift and on fire.

Falconer came aboard after he got the prisoner settled. He reported that Louis's last words as they clanged the door shut were, 'Tell Isaac Bell I will not talk.'

'He'll talk.'

'I would not count on that,' Falconer cautioned. 'When I was in the Far East, Japs and Chinese virtually eviscerated captured spies. Not a peep.'

The Van Dorn detective and the Navy captain stood on

the foredeck as *Dyname* backed into the East River, her nine propellers spinning with a smoothness that Bell still found eerie.

'There is something more to Louis Loh,' he mused. 'I can't yet put my finger on what makes him different.'

'Strikes me as being fairly low down the totem pole.'

'I don't think so,' said Bell. 'He conducts himself with pride, like a man who has a mission.'

'It's an up-and-down world for the New York gangs,' said Harry Warren, and the handful of Van Dorn detectives who kept track of them nodded solemnly. 'One day they're high-and-mighty, next they're in the gutter.'

The back room of the Knickerbocker headquarters was gray with cigar and cigarette smoke. A bottle of whiskey Isaac Bell had bought was making the rounds.

'Who is in the gutter currently?' he asked.

'The Hudson Dusters, the Marginals, and the Pearl Buttons. The Eastmans are in trouble, what with Monk Eastman at Sing Sing, and making it worse for themselves by continuing to feud with the Five Pointers.'

'They had a wonderful shoot-out under the Third Avenue El the other night,' remarked a detective. 'No one killed, unfortunately.'

'In Chinatown,' Harry continued, 'the Hip Sing are clawing ahead of the On Leongs. On the West Side, Tommy Thompson's Gophers are riding high. Or *were*. The sons of bitches have their hands full since you sicced the railroad police on 'em for ambushing little Eddie Tobin.'

This was met by enthusiastic nods, and a remark in

grudging admiration, 'Those western cinder dicks are about the worst bastards I ever seen.'

'They've got the Gophers so discombobulated that the Hip Sing tong opened a new opium den right in the middle of Gopher Gang territory.'

'Not so fast,' Harry Warren cautioned. 'I saw Gophers in a Hip Sing joint downtown. Where Scully was, Isaac? I got a feeling that something was up between the Hip Sing and Gophers. Maybe Scully did, too.'

A few muttered agreement. They'd heard rumors.

'But none of you can tell me anything about Louis Loh?'

'That don't mean much, Isaac. Chinatown criminals are just plain more secretive.'

'And better organized. Not to mention smarter.'

'And hooked up to Chinatowns throughout the United States and Asia.'

'The international connection is intriguing, this being a spy case,' Bell admitted. 'Except for one big thing. Why send two men from New York all the way across the continent when they could have used local San Francisco Chinatown men who knew the territory?'

No one answered. The detectives sat in uncomfortable silence broken only by the clink of glass and the scrape of a match. Bell looked around the room at Harry's team of veterans. He missed John Scully. Scully had been a wizard in a brain session.

'Why the whole charade on the train?' he demanded. 'It doesn't make sense.'

More silence ensued. Bell asked, 'How's little Eddie doing?'

'Still touch and go.'

'Tell him I'll get up there soon as I can for a visit.'

'Doubt he'll know you're in the room.'

Harry Warren said, 'That's another weird thing, as far as I'm concerned. Why would the Gophers go out on a limb to fire up Van Dorns against them?'

'They're stupid,' a detective answered, and everyone laughed.

'But not that stupid. Like Isaac says about Louis Loh crossing the continent. Beating up the kid didn't make sense. The gangs don't pick fights outside their circle.'

Isaac Bell said, 'You told me it was strange that the Iceman went to Camden.'

Harry nodded vigorously. 'Gophers don't leave home.'

'And you said that Gophers don't send warning messages or take revenge that will bring down the wrath of outsiders. Is it possible that the spy paid them to take revenge, just like he paid killers to go to Camden?'

'Who the hell knows how spies think?'

'I know someone who does,' said Bell.

Commander Abbington-Westlake sauntered out of the Harvard Club, where he had wrangled a free honorary membership, and signaled for a cab with a languid wave. A red Darracq gasoline taxi zipped past a man hailing it outside the New York Yacht Club and stopped for the portly Englishman.

'Hey, that's my cab!'

'Apparently not,' Abbington-Westlake drawled as he stepped into the Darracq. 'Smartly now, driver, before that disgruntled yachtsman catches up.'

The cab sped off. Abbington-Westlake gave an upper Fifth Avenue address and settled in for the ride. At 59th, the cab suddenly swerved into Central Park. He rapped his stick on the window.

'No, no, no, I'm not some tourist you take around the park. If I wanted to drive out of my way through the park, I would have instructed you to go out of the way through the park. Return to Fifth Avenue immediately!'

The driver slammed on the brakes, throwing Abbington-Westlake off his seat. When he recovered, he found himself glaring into the cold eyes of a grim-visaged Isaac Bell.

'I warn you, Bell, I have friends who will come to my aid.'

'I will not deliver a well-deserved punch in your nose for selling me down the river to Yamamoto Kenta *if* you answer a question.'

'Was that you who killed Yamamoto?' the English spy asked fearfully.

'He died in Washington. I was in New York.'

'Did you order his death?'

'I am not one of you,' said Bell.

'What is your question?'

'Whoever this freelance spy is, I believe he is acting strangely. Look at this.'

He showed Abbington-Westlake the note. 'He left this on the body of my detective. Why would he do such a thing?'

The Englishman read it in a glance. 'Appears to be sending you a message.'

'Would you?'

'One does not indulge in childish exercises.'

'Would you kill my man for revenge?'

'One does not indulge in the luxury of revenge.'

362

'Would you do it as a threat? Believing it would stop me?'

'He should have killed you, that would put a stop to it.'

'Would you?'

Abbington-Westlake smiled. 'I would suggest that successful spies are invisible spies. Ideally, one copies a secret plan rather than stealing it so one's enemy never knows that his secret was stolen. Similarly, if an enemy must die, it should seem to be an accident. Falling debris at a work site might crush a man without raising suspicion. A hatpin piercing his brain is a red flag.'

'The hatpin was not in the newspapers,' Bell said coldly.

'One reads between the lines,' the Englishman retorted. 'As I told you at the Knickerbocker, welcome to the world of espionage, Mr. Bell. You've learned a lot already. You know in your gut that the freelance spy is not first and foremost a spy.'

'He doesn't think like a spy,' said Bell. 'He thinks like a gangster.'

'Then who better to catch a gangster than a detective? Good day, sir. May I wish you happy hunting?' He climbed out of the cab and walked toward Fifth Avenue.

Bell hurried back to the Hotel Knickerbocker and corralled Archie Abbott.

'Get up to the Newport Torpedo Factory.'

'The Boston boys are already –'

'I want you. I'm getting a strange feeling about that attack.'

'What kind of feeling?'

'What if it wasn't sabotage? What if it was a robbery? Stay there until you discover what they took.'

He walked Archie to the train at Grand Central and returned to the office, deep in thought. Abbington-Westlake had confirmed his suspicions. The spy *was* first and foremost a gangster. But he couldn't be Commodore Tommy. The Gopher had lived and fought within the narrow confines of Hell's Kitchen his whole life. The answer must lie with Louis Loh. He could be the tong. He could even be the spy. Perhaps that was what he had noticed was different about Louis: he acted like he had a purpose. It was time to put the question to him.

Bell collected Louis Loh from the Brooklyn Navy Yard brig late at night and handcuffed his wrists behind his back.

Loh's first surprise came when instead of putting him in a truck or an auto, Bell walked him toward the river. They waited at the water's edge. Hull 44 loomed behind them. The wind carried the sounds of ship engines, slatting sails, whistles, and horns. Blacked out but for running lights, Lowell Falconer's turbine yacht *Dyname* approached in near silence.

Deckhands guided Bell and his prisoner aboard without speaking a word. The yacht backed into the river and headed downstream. It went under the Brooklyn Bridge and passed the Battery and picked up speed on the Upper Bay.

'If you're planning to throw me overboard,' Louis Loh said, 'remember I know how to swim.'

'Wearing those manacles?'

'I assumed you would remove them, being above torture.'

The helmsman increased speed to thirty knots. Bell took Loh into the darkened cabin, where they sat in silence

364

sheltered from the wind and spray. *Dyname* crossed the Lower Bay. Bell saw the lightship flash by the porthole. When *Dyname*'s bow rose to the first Atlantic comber, Louis Loh asked, 'Where are you taking me?'

'To sea.'

'How far to sea?'

'About fifty miles.'

'That will take all night.'

'Not on this ship.'

The helmsman opened her up. An hour passed. The turbines slowed, and the yacht settled down. Suddenly it bumped hard against something and stopped. Bell took Louis's arm, checked that he hadn't jimmied open the cuffs, and led him out on deck. Silent deckhands helped them onto the wooden deck of a barge. Then *Dyname* wheeled about and raced off. In minutes, all to be seen of her was the fiery discharge from her stack, and soon she vanished into the night.

'Now what?' asked Louis Loh. Creamy whitecaps shone in the starlight. The barge rolled with the movement of the sea.

'Now we climb.'

'Climb? Climb what?'

'This mast.'

Bell directed Louis's gaze up the cage mast. The airy structure rose so high that its swaying top seemed to brush the stars. 'What is this? Where are we?'

'We're on a target barge anchored in the U.S. Navy Atlantic Firing Range. Test engineers have erected on the barge this one-hundred-twenty-five-foot cage mast, the latest development in dreadnought spotting masts.'

Bell climbed two rungs, unlocked Louis's right cuff, and locked it around his own ankle.

'Ready? Here we go.'

'Where?'

'Up these ladders. When I raise my leg, you raise your arm.'

'Why?'

'There's a test scheduled for dawn to see how the cage mast fares in battle conditions when bombarded by 12-inch guns. Any spy worth his salt would give his eye-teeth to watch. Let's go.'

It was a long climb to the spotting top, but neither man was breathing hard when they reached the platform. 'You are in excellent condition, Louis.' Bell removed the cuff from his ankle and locked it to the tubing that formed the mast.

'Now what?'

'Wait for dawn.'

A cold wind sprang up. The mast swayed as it sighed around the tubing.

At first light, the silhouette of a battleship took shape on the horizon.

'New Hampshire,' said Bell. 'You recognize her, I'm sure, by her three funnels and old-fashioned ram bow. You will recall that she carries 7- and 8-inch guns in addition to four 12s. Any minute now.'

The battleship emitted a red flash. A five-hundred-pound shell roared past like a freight train. Louis ducked. 'What?' he screamed. 'What?' Now the sound of the gun rumbled their way.

Another flash. Another shell roared closer.

'They'll have the range soon!' Bell told Louis Loh.

The 12-inch gun flashed red. A shell struck in a shower of sparks fifty feet below. The mast shook. Louis Loh cried, 'You're a madman.'

'They say this helix design is remarkably strong,' Bell replied.

More shells roared by. When another hit, Louis covered his face.

Soon there was enough light in the sky for Bell to read his gold watch. 'A few more single shots. Then they're scheduled to blast salvos. Before they finish up with full broadsides.'

'All right. All right. I admit I am tong.'

'You're more than tong,' Isaac Bell replied coldly. He was rewarded by an expression of surprise on Louis's ordinarily immobile face.

'What do you mean?'

'Sun-tzu on the art of war. If I may quote your countryman: "Be so subtle that you are invisible."'

'I don't know what you mean.'

'You told me on the train, "They think we're all opium addicts or tong gangsters." You sounded like a man with a broader point of view. Who are you really?'

A salvo thundered. Two shells ripped through the structure. Still it stood, but it was swinging side to side.

'I am not tong.'

'You just told me you are. Which is it?'

'I am not a gangster.'

'Stop telling me what you aren't and start telling me what you are.'

'I am Tongmenghui.'

367

'What is Tongmenghui?'

'Chinese Revolutionary Alliance. We are a secret resistance movement. We pledge our lives to revive Chinese society.'

'Explain,' said Isaac Bell.

In a rush of words, Louis Loh admitted that he was a fervent Chinese Nationalist plotting to overthrow the corrupt Empress. 'She is strangling China. England, Germany, all Europe, even the U.S., feed on China's dying body.'

'If you are a revolutionist, what are you doing in America?'

'Dreadnought battleships. China must build a modern fleet to fend off colonial invaders.'

'By blowing up the Great White fleet in San Francisco?'

'That wasn't for China! That was for him.'

'"Him"? Who are you talking about?'

With a fearful glance at the *New Hampshire,* Loh said, 'There is a man – a spy – who pays. Not in money but in valuable information about other nations' dreadnoughts. We, Harold Wing and me, pass it along to Chinese naval architects.'

'And you pay for it by doing his bidding.'

'Exactly, sir. Can we go down now?'

Bell knew this was a major breakthrough in the case. This was the freelance whom Yamamoto had tried to betray in exchange for a clean escape. Louis had gotten him close again.

'You are working for *three* masters. The Chinese Navy. Your Tongmenghui resistance movement. And the spy who paid you to attack the magazine at Mare Island. Who is he?'

Another freight train of a shell roared by. The structure trembled.

'I don't know who he is.'

'Who is your intermediary? How does he give you orders and information?'

'Mailboxes. He sent information, orders, and money for expenses in mailboxes.' Loh ducked another shell. 'Please, let us go down.'

Across the water, sparkling in the first rays of sunlight, all the *New Hampshire*'s guns traversed toward the cage mast. 'Here comes a broadside,' said Bell.

'You must believe me.'

Bell said, 'I feel a certain affection for you, Louis. You held off shooting me until I jumped from the train.'

Louis Loh stared at the battleship. 'I was not sparing your life. I didn't have the guts to pull the trigger.'

'I'm tempted to let you down, Louis. But you haven't told me all you know. I don't believe that everything came in the mail.'

Louis Loh cast another fearful gaze at the white battleship and broke down completely. 'It was Commodore Tommy Thompson who told us to attack the magazine at Mare Island.'

'How did you hook up with the Gopher Gang?'

'The spy bribed the Hip Sing to allow us to approach Commodore Tommy Thompson in their name, pretending we were tong.'

Bell handed Louis Loh a snowy white handkerchief. 'Wave this.'

He led Loh down the mast. When they reached the

barge, apoplectic Test Range officers raced up in a boat. 'How did you —'

'Thought you'd never stop shooting. We were getting hungry up there.'

'I don't believe for a moment that Commodore Tommy is the spy,' Isaac Bell told Joseph Van Dorn. 'But I'm willing to bet Tommy's got a good idea who he is.'

'He better,' said Van Dorn. 'Raiding his territory is costing a carload of money for the cops and some very expensive favors to keep Tammany Hall from protesting.' The tall detective and his broad-chested boss were overseeing preparations for the raid from inside a Marmon parked across from Commodore Tommy's Saloon on West 39th Street.

'But the railroads will love us,' said Bell, and the boss conceded that several rail tycoons had already thanked him personally for cutting back the worst depredations of the Gopher Gang. 'Looking at the bright side, after this the spy's ring will be a lot smaller.'

'I'm not counting on that,' said Isaac Bell, mindful of learning about the explosion at the Newport Torpedo Factory while on the train to San Francisco.

A dozen railroad cops led the attack, battering down the saloon door, breaking up the furniture, smashing bottles, and staving in beer kegs. Shots rang within. Harry Warren's boys, standing by with handcuffs, marched a dozen Gophers into a Police Department paddy wagon.

'Tommy's holed up in the cellar with a bullet hole in his arm,' Harry reported to Bell and Van Dorn. 'He's all alone. He may listen to reason.'

Bell went first, down wooden steps into a damp cellar. Tommy Thompson was slumped in a chair like a mountain brought low by an earthquake. He had a pistol in his hand. He opened his eyes, looked up blearily at Bell's weapon pointed at his head, and let his pistol fall to the earthen floor.

'I'm Isaac Bell.'

'What's wrong with the Van Dorns?' Tommy was indignant. 'It's always been live and let live. Pay the cops, stay out of each other's business. We got a whole system at work here, and a bunch of private dicks screw it up.'

'Is that why you put one of my boys in the hospital?' Bell asked coldly.

'That wasn't my idea!' Tommy protested.

'Wasn't your idea?' Bell retorted. 'Who ramrods the Gophers?'

'It weren't my idea,' Tommy repeated sullenly.

'You're asking me to believe that the famous Commodore Tommy Thompson, who's killed off every rival to command the toughest gang in New York, takes orders from someone else?'

Resentment boiled behind Tommy's tough façade. Bell played on it, laughing, 'Maybe you are telling the truth. Maybe you are just a saloonkeeper.'

'Goddammit!' Tommy Thompson erupted. He tried to get out of the chair. The tall detective restrained him with a warning gesture. 'Commodore Tommy don't take orders from no one.'

Bell called out, and Harry Warren and two of his men trooped down the stairs. 'Tommy says it wasn't his idea to beat up little Eddie Tobin. Some fellow made him do it.'

'Some fellow?' Harry echoed scornfully. 'Did this "some fellow" who ordered you to beat up a Van Dorn happen to be the same fellow who ordered you to send Louis Loh and Harold Wing to blow up the magazine at Mare Island?'

'He didn't order me. He paid me. There's a difference.'

'Who?' Bell demanded.

'Bastard, left me to stick around and face the music.'

'*Who?*'

'Goddamned Eyes O'Shay. That's who.'

'Eyes O'Shay?' Harry Warren echoed incredulously. 'You take us for jackasses? Eyes O'Shay is dead fifteen years.'

'No he ain't.'

'Harry,' Bell snapped. 'Who is Eyes O'Shay?'

'Gopher kid, years ago. Vicious piece of work. A comer, 'til he disappeared.'

'I heard talk he was back,' muttered one of Harry's detectives. 'I didn't believe it.'

'I still don't.'

'I do,' said Isaac Bell. 'The spy's been acting like a gangster all along.'

A Streak of God

42

Isaac Bell asked, 'Why did they call him Eyes?'

'If you got in a fight with him, he'd gouge your eye out,' said Tommy Thompson. 'He fit a copper pick over his thumbnail. Now it's made of stainless steel.'

'I imagine,' said Bell, 'he didn't get in many fights.'

'Not once word got around,' Tommy agreed.

'Other than that, what is he like?'

Tommy Thompson said, 'If I'm going sit here yapping, I want a drink.'

Bell nodded. The Van Dorns produced an array of hip flasks. Tommy took long pulls from a couple and wiped his mouth with his bloody sleeve. 'Other than gouging eyes, what's Brian O'Shay like? He's like he always was. A guy who can see around a corner.'

'Would you call him a natural leader?'

'A what?'

'A leader. Like you. You run your own gang. Is he that kind of a man?'

'All I know is he's thinking all the time. Always ahead of you. Eyes could see inside of people.'

'If you're telling us the truth, Tommy, that O'Shay is not dead, where is he?'

The gang leader swore he did not know.

'What name does he go by?'

'He didn't say.'

'What does he look like?'

'He looks like anybody. Clerk in a store, guy owns a bank, bartender. I hardly recognized him. Duded up like a Fifth Avenue swell.'

'Big man?'

'No. A little guy.'

'Compared to you, Tommy, most guys are little. How tall is he?'

'Five-eight. Built like a fireplug. Strongest little guy I ever saw.'

Bell continued conversationally, 'He didn't need the gouge to win a fight, did he?'

'No,' said Tommy, taking another slug of whiskey. 'He just liked doing it.'

'Surely after he reappeared out of nowhere and paid you all that money, you had him followed.'

'I sent Paddy the Rat after him. Little bastard came back short one eye.'

Bell looked at one of the detectives, who was nodding agreement. 'Yeah, I seen Paddy wearing a patch.'

'Disappeared, just like when we was kids. Vanished into thin air that time, too. Never thought we'd see him again. Thought he got thrown in the river.'

'By whom?' asked Bell.

The gang leader shrugged.

Harry Warren said, 'A lot of people thought you were the one who threw him in the river, Tommy.'

'Yeah, well a lot of people thought wrong. I used to think Billy Collins done it. 'Til Eyes came back.'

Bell glanced at Harry Warren.

'Dope addict,' Harry said. 'Haven't heard his name in years. Billy Collins ran with Eyes and Tommy. They made quite the trio. Remember, Tommy? Rolling drunks, robbing pushcarts, selling dope, beatin' up anybody got in their way. O'Shay was the worst, worse than the Commodore here, even worse than Billy Collins. Tommy was sweetness and light compared to those two. The last anybody expected was Tommy taking over the Gophers. Except you got lucky, Tommy, didn't you? Eyes disappeared, and Billy got the habit.'

Isaac Bell asked, 'Tommy, why did you think Billy Collins threw Eyes in the river?'

'Because the last night I ever saw Eyes, they was drinking together.'

'And today you have no idea where O'Shay is?'

'Just like always. He vanished into thin air.'

'Where is Billy Collins?'

The wounded gang leader shrugged, winced, and took another pull on a flask. 'Where do hop fiends go? Under a rock. In a sewer.'

43

Ten miles off Fire Island, a barrier beach between Long Island and the Atlantic Ocean, fifty miles from New York, three vessels converged. The light of day started to slip over the western horizon, and stars took shape in the east. Atlantic Ocean swells were bunching up on the shallow continental shelf. Neither captain of the larger vessels – a 4,000-ton steam freighter with a tall funnel and two king posts, and an oceangoing tugboat hipped up to a three-track railcar barge – was pleased with the prospect of getting close enough to transfer cargo in such choppy seas, particularly with the wind shifting fitfully from sea to shore. When they saw that the third vessel, a broad-beamed little catboat powered only by sail, was steered by a petite redheaded girl, they began snarling at their helmsmen.

It looked like the rendezvous would end before it started. Then the girl took advantage of a shifty gust to bring her craft about so smartly that the steamer's mate said, 'She's a seaman,' and Eyes O'Shay said to the tugboat captain, 'Don't lose your nerve. We can always throw you overboard and run the boat ourselves.'

He spotted Rafe Engels waving from the steamer's bridge wing.

Rafe Engels was a gunrunner wanted by the British Special Irish Branch for arming rebels of the Irish Republican Brotherhood, and by the Czar's secret police for supplying Russian revolutionists. O'Shay had first met him on the *Wilhelm der Grosse*. They had danced carefully around each other, and again on the *Lusitania*, probing warily at the kindred spirit they each sensed behind the other's elaborate disguise. There were differences: the gunrunner, always on the rebels' side, was an idealist, the spy was not. But over the years they had worked out several trades. This exchange of torpedoes for a submarine would be their biggest.

'Where's the Holland?' O'Shay called across the water.

'Under you!'

O'Shay peered into the waves. The water started bubbling like a boiling pot. Something dark and stealthy took shape under the bubbles. A round turret of armor steel emerged from the white froth. And then, quite suddenly, a glistening hull parted the sea. It was one hundred feet long and menacing as a reef.

A hinged cover opened on top of the turret. A bearded man thrust his head and shoulders into the air, looked around, and climbed out. He was Hunt Hatch, at one time the Holland Company's chief trials captain, now on the run from Special Irish Branch. His crew followed him out, one after another, until five Republican Brotherhood fighters who had pledged their lives to win Home Rule for Ireland were standing on the deck, blinking in the light and breathing deeply of the air.

'Treat them well,' Engels had demanded as they clasped hands cementing their deal. 'They are brave men.'

'Like my own family,' O'Shay had promised.

All had served as Royal Navy submariners. All had ended up in British prisons. All hated England. They dreamed, O'Shay knew, that when the Americans discovered that the submarine and its electric torpedoes were from England, it would appear that England had instigated an attack to cripple American battleship production. They dreamed that when war engulfed Europe, angry Americans would not side with England. Then Germany would defeat England, and Ireland would be free.

A lovely dream, thought the spy. It would serve no one better than Eyes O'Shay.

'There is your submarine torpedo boat,' Engels called from across it. 'Where are my Wheeler torpedoes?'

Eyes O'Shay pointed at the sailboat.

Engels bowed. 'I see the fair Katherine. Hallooo, my beauty,' he hailed through cupped hands. 'I did not recognize you out of your sumptuous gowns. But I see no torpedoes.'

'Under her,' said O'Shay. 'Four Wheeler Mark 14s. Two for you. Two for me.'

Engels gestured. The steamer's seamen swung a cargo boom out from her king post. 'Come alongside, Katherine. I'll take two torpedoes – and maybe you, too, if no one is looking.'

As Katherine effected the difficult maneuver and Engels's crew snaked the torpedoes out of the catboat, they heard a rumble like distant thunder. O'Shay watched the submarine's crew coolly assess what the noise really meant and the distance from which it was coming.

'U.S. Navy's Sandy Hook Test Range,' he called down to them. 'Don't worry. It's far away.'

'Sixty thousand yards,' Hunt Hatch called back, and a man added, 'Ten-inchers, and some 12s.'

O'Shay nodded his satisfaction. The Irish rebels who would crew his submarine knew their business.

It may not have looked like a fair trade, the submarine being six or seven times longer than the torpedoes and capable of independent action. But the Holland, though considerably elongated and modified by the English from its original design, was fully five years old and outstripped by rapid advances in underwater warfare. The Mark 14s were Ron Wheeler's latest.

Each man had what he wanted. Engels was steaming away with two of the most advanced torpedoes in the world to sell to the highest bidder. And the Holland and the two torpedoes that the tug and barge crews were wrestling out of the sailboat and into the submarine made a deadly combination. The Brooklyn Navy Yard would never know what hit it.

44

Jimmy Richards's and Marv Gordon's Dutch uncle, Donald Darbee, sailed them six miles across the Upper Bay in his oyster scow, a flat-bottomed boat with a square bow and a powerful auxiliary gasoline motor he only used when chasing or running from something. Jimmy and Marv knew every watery inch of the Port of New York, but neither of the enormous young men had ever set foot on Manhattan Island despite many a night poking around Manhattan piers for items that had fallen off. Uncle Donny recalled going ashore in 1890 to rescue a fellow Staten Islander from the cops.

As they approached the Battery, a Harbor Squad policeman on a launch tied to Pier A called his roundsman up on deck. 'Looks like we're being invaded.'

Roundsman O'Riordan cast a jaundiced eye on the Staten Island scowmen. 'Watch 'em, closely,' he ordered, hoping they were not up to no good. Arresting a gang of muscle-bound oyster tongers would cost broken arms and busted teeth on both sides.

'How do we get to the Roosevelt Hospital at 59th Street?' called the shaggy oldster at the helm.

'If you got a nickel, take the Ninth Avenue El.'

'We got a nickel.'

Jimmy Richards and Marv Gordon paid their nickels and rode to 59th Street, staring at tall buildings and crowds of people they could scarcely believe, many of whom stared back at them. Wandering the huge hospital wards, they finally asked directions from a pretty Irish nurse and found their way to a private room with only one bed. The patient in the bed was completely wrapped in bandages, and they would never have recognized Cousin Eddie Tobin except that hanging on a clothes tree was the snappy suit of clothes that the Van Dorns had staked Eddie when they hired him to apprentice last winter.

A tall, yellow-haired dude, lean as wire rope, was bending over him, holding a glass so Eddie could drink from a straw. When he saw them in the doorway, his eyes turned gray as a nor'easter, and a big hand slid inside his coat where he could keep a pistol, if he was the sort to pack one and he looked like he was.

'May I help you gentlemen?'

Jimmy and Marv instinctively raised their hands. 'Is that little Eddie Tobin? We're his cousins come to visit.'

'Eddie? Do you know these fellows?'

The bandaged head was already craning painfully toward them. It nodded, and they heard little Eddie croak, 'Family.'

The blue-gray eyes turned a warmer shade. 'Come on in, boys.'

'Fancy digs,' said Jimmy. 'We looked in the ward. They sent us up here.'

'Mr. Bell paid for it.'

Isaac Bell offered his hand and shook their horny mitts. 'Everyone chipped in. Van Dorns look out for their own. I'm Isaac Bell.'

'Jimmy Richards. This here's Marv Gordon.'

'I'll leave you boys to your visit. Eddie, I'll see you soon.'

Richards lumbered out after him into the hall. 'How's he doing, Mr. Bell?'

'Better than we hoped. He's a tough kid. It's going to take a while, but the docs are saying he'll come out of it in pretty good shape. But I have to warn you, he won't win any beauty contests.'

'Who did it? We'll straighten them out.'

'We've already straightened them out,' said Bell. 'It's a Van Dorn fight, and your cousin is a Van Dorn.'

Richards didn't like it. 'None of us was happy when Eddie joined the law.'

Isaac Bell smiled. 'The law does not like their appellation given to private detectives.'

'Whatever you say, bub. We appreciate what you're doing for him. You ever need a church burned down or someone drowned, Eddie knows how to find us.'

Isaac Bell was poring through the noon reports from the squads hunting for Billy Collins when Archie Abbott telephoned from Grand Central. 'Just got off the train. Something is missing from the Newport Torpedo Factory.'

'What?'

'Is the Old Man still in town?'

'Mr. Van Dorn's in his office.'

'Why don't you meet me downstairs?'

'Downstairs' meant privacy in the Hotel Knickerbocker's cellar bar. Ten minutes later, they were hunched over a dark table. Archie beckoned the waiter. 'You might want a drink before we report to the boss. I certainly do.'

'What's missing?'

'Four electric torpedoes imported from England.'

The waiter approached. Bell waved him off.

'I thought everything burned up in the fire.'

'So did the Navy. They loaded all the junk on a barge to dump it offshore. I said to this Wheeler character, "Why don't we count torpedoes?" Long story short, we went through the debris with a fine-tooth comb and tallied four missing electrics.'

Bell stared at his old friend. 'By any chance were they the ones armed with TNT?'

'Wheeler is certain that those with TNT warheads are the ones missing.'

'Do you agree?'

'He had serial numbers. We found them on the remains of the cowlings. Found them all except those four – they'd been set aside for a torpedo boat to fire on the Test Range. It would have been too much of a coincidence if they'd been the only ones blown completely to smithereens.'

'And you're sure the explosion wasn't an accident?'

'I talked to the Navy – found an Annapolis man I knew at prep school. Our specialist confirmed. Riley from Boston, you know him. There is no doubt.'

'They are the Holy Grail of torpedoes,' Bell said, grimly. 'Fast, long-range, silent propulsion married to immensely more powerful warheads.'

'The spy got the best. The only good news is that Wheeler can make more of them. The English are livid. They won't sell us any more, but I learned that Ron Wheeler and his boys already started making unauthorized copies for the Navy. In the meantime, the spy got himself the latest British propulsion armed with the latest American warheads – priceless secrets to sell to the highest bidder.'

'Or deadly weapons to attack.'

'Attack? How would he fire them?' asked Archie. 'Even a spy as cunning as this one can't get his hands on a battleship.'

Isaac Bell said, 'I would not put it past him to acquire a small torpedo boat.'

The old friends locked gazes. The laughter fled Archie's green eyes. Bell's blue turned dark as stone. He and Joseph Van Dorn had already blanketed Captain Falconer's key engineers with protection. And Van Dorn operatives had infiltrated the Brooklyn Navy Yard workforce. But they both knew that neither the arrest of the Chinese spy nor that of the head of the Gopher Gang would stop Eyes O'Shay. The spy would easily rebuild his fluid organization. And with the Great White Fleet beyond his reach at sea, he would resume his attacks on future American battleships.

'We better talk to Mr. Van Dorn.'

'What are you going to tell him?'

'We need manpower to track down those torpedoes. He's got to convince the Navy, Coast Guard, and the police Harbor Squads in every city with a battleship yard – Camden, Philadelphia; Quincy, Fore River, Massachusetts; Bath Iron Works, Maine; Brooklyn – that the threat is deadly. Then I'm going repeat what I've been telling him all along. This is, first and foremost, a murder case. It will take old-fashioned detective work to hang Eyes O'Shay. We'll start with Billy Collins.'

Isaac Bell left the Hotel Knickerbocker by the kitchen door. He dipped his fingers in a vat of used beef fat waiting to be picked up by the rendering plant and rubbed it into his hair. In the alley, down-on-their-luck men were waiting on the breadline. He astonished one, who despaired of raising a nickel to flop indoors on this chilly night that threatened rain, by offering five dollars for his battered slouch hat. Offered the same amount, a man almost as tall as the detective parted eagerly with his ragged coat.

Bell palmed a rusty revolver with three slugs in it and shifted it from his trousers into the coat. He pulled the hat low over his brow, worked his golden hair under it, and buttoned the coat to his chin. Then he shoved his hands in his pockets, bowed his head, and stepped out of the alley onto Broadway. A cop told him to move along.

For the fifth time in five days, he wandered Hell's Kitchen.

He was learning its rhythms, where and when the slum blocks were busy, the streets rumbling with wagons and trucks, the sidewalks crowded, as men streamed into saloons, women into churches, and children roamed, ignoring mothers shouting from tenement windows. He had previously wandered from Ninth Avenue to the river and from the Pennsylvania Railroad Station construction site at 33rd to the 60th Street rail yards. But he hadn't found the 'hop fiend,' Billy Collins, who might lead him to Eyes O'Shay.

So today Isaac Bell was taking a different tack.

As part of his disguise, he limped, left foot dragging slightly, scuffing the shine off his boots as he crossed curbs and streetcar tracks. A coal truck backing to a cellar chute blocked the sidewalk. Bell trailed his fingers along its sooty side and stroked his mustache. He repeated the exercise when he passed an ash can, still warm, and ran his fingers through the hair that escaped from the slouch hat. He inspected his reflection in a window. His eyes glittered too brightly in a worn face. He cast his gaze downward, plucked a clump of straw out of the gutter, and rubbed it to his sleeves until it appeared that he had slept in his coat. They never look a dirty man in the face, Scully taught the apprentices.

He kept checking his image in windows, which, as he headed toward the river, got smaller and dirtier. He knelt beside an empty barrel standing in a puddle outside a saloon, pretended to tie his shoe, and continued on, his trousers smelling of stale beer. The deeper into the slum he wandered, the more slowly he walked, the lower he stooped – a weary, aimless man lost in the crowds.

A young tough wearing a tight suit and red derby blocked his path. 'What do you got for me, Gramps? Come on! Hand it over.'

Isaac Bell resisted the impulse to floor him, dug deep in his coat, and surrendered a nickel.

The tough shoved past.

'Wait!' Bell called.

'What?' The tough spun around. 'What? What do want?'

'Do you know a fellow named Billy Collins?'

The tough hung a blank expression on his face. 'Who?'

He was a kid, Bell realized, barely into his teens. An infant when Tommy Thompson and Billy Collins were running with Eyes O'Shay.

'Billy Collins. Tall, skinny fellow. Ginger hair. Maybe turning gray.'

'Never heard of him.'

'Skin and bones,' Bell said, repeating what Harry Warren and his boys had speculated the opium and morphine addict would look like after all these years. They knew he was still alive, or had been within the week. 'Probably missing teeth.'

'Where you from, Gramps?'

'Chicago.'

'Yeah, well there's a lot of guys around here got no teeth. You're next.' He raised a bony fist. 'Get out of here! Run, old man. Run.'

Bell said, 'Billy Collins used to run with Tommy Thompson and Eyes O'Shay when they were kids.'

The thug backed up a step. 'You with the Gophers?'

'I'm just looking for Billy Collins.'

'Yeah, well, you're not the only one.' He hurried away, calling over his shoulder, 'Everybody's asking about him.'

They should be, Bell thought. Considering what it was costing the agency. In addition to Harry Warren's boys and Harry's informants, he had two hundred railroad cops asking the same question every time they slugged it out with Gophers attempting to rob freight cars. Bell kept asking himself, Where does a hop fiend hide? Where does he sleep? Where does he eat? Where does he get his dope? How come no one saw him in a district where everyone knew everyone?

There had been sightings near Collins's known dens, several by a coal pocket that replenished locomotive tenders in the 38th Street yards, twice around an abandoned caboose at 60th Street. Picked men were watching both. And Bell had a feeling he himself had actually glimpsed

Collins through a wind-spun swirl of locomotive smoke – a rail-thin figure had flitted between freight cars, and Bell had run full tilt after him only to find smoke.

Since then, the one man who might know where O'Shay disappeared to fifteen years ago hadn't shown up at either den. On the plus side, they'd had enough reports to know he was alive, and he was unlikely to leave Hell's Kitchen.

Eyes O'Shay's location was another story. Everyone over the age of thirty had heard the name. No one had seen him in fifteen years. Some people had heard he was back. No one admitted to laying eyes on him. But Bell knew a man described by Tommy Thompson as 'duded up like a Fifth Avenue swell' could sleep and eat anywhere he chose.

45

'Taxicab, sir?' the Waldorf-Astoria's doorman asked of a hotel guest stepping out in a top hat and loden green frock coat.

'I will promenade,' said Eyes O'Shay.

Wielding a jewel-headed walking stick, he strolled up Fifth Avenue, pausing like a tourist to admire mansions and peering into shopwindows. When he was reasonably sure that he wasn't being followed, he entered St. Patrick's Cathedral through the great Gothic arch in front. In the nave, he genuflected with the ease of a daily habit, dropped coins in the poor box, and lighted candles. Then he threw back his head and reflected upon the stained glass in the rose window, imitating the proud gaze of a parishioner who had contributed handsomely to the installation fund.

Since Isaac Bell nailed Tommy Thompson, he had to assume that every Van Dorn in New York, plus two hundred railway police, and the Devil himself knew how many paid informants, were hunting him, or soon would be. He exited the cathedral out the back, through the boardwalks and scaffolding where brick and stone masons were building the Lady Chapel, and strode onto Madison Avenue.

He headed up Madison, still watching his back, turned onto 55th, and stopped in the St. Regis Hotel. He had a drink in the bar and chatted with the bartender, whom he always tipped lavishly, while he watched the lobby. Then he tipped a bellboy to let him out the service entrance.

Moments later, he walked into the Plaza Hotel. He stopped at the Palm Court in the middle of the ground floor. The people seated around small tables for the elaborate afternoon tea were mothers with children, aunts and nieces, and here and there an older gentleman enthralled by a daughter. The maître d' bowed low.

'Your usual table, Herr Riker?'

'Thank you.'

Herr Riker's usual table let him watch the lobby in two directions while screening himself with a jungle of potted palms that would have given Dr. Livingstone and Henry Stanley pause.

'Will your ward be joining you, sir?'

'It is my fond hope,' he replied with a courtly smile. 'Tell your waiter that we will have only sweets at our table. None of those little sandwiches. Only cakes and cream.'

'Of course, Herr Riker. As always, Herr Riker.'

Katherine was late, as usual, and he used the time to rehearse for what he knew would be a difficult discussion. He felt as ready as he could be when she stepped off the elevator. Her tea gown was a cloud of blue silk that matched her eyes and complemented her hair.

O'Shay rose as she approached his table, taking her gloved hands in his and saying, 'You are the prettiest girl, Miss Dee.'

'Thank you, Herr Riker.'

Katherine Dee smiled and dimpled. But when she sat, she looked him full in the face in her direct way, and said,

'You look very serious – ward-and-guardian serious. What are you up to, Brian?'

'Self-annointed "good warriors" who fight "good wars" accuse me with deep disdain of being a mercenary. I take it as a testament to my intelligence. Because for a mercenary the war is over when he says it is over. He retires a victor.'

'I hope you've ordered whiskey instead of tea,' she said.

O'Shay smiled. 'Yes, I know I'm bloviating. I am attempting to tell you that we are in the endgame, dearest.'

'What do you mean?'

'It is time to vanish. We will go out – and lay our future – with a bang they'll never forget.'

'Where?'

'Where they will treat us like gold.'

'Oh, not Germany!'

'Of course Germany. What democracy would take us in?'

'We could go to Russia?'

'Russia is a powder keg waiting for a match. I am not about to take you out of the frying pan into a revolution.'

'Oh, Brian.'

'We will live like kings. And queens. We will be very rich, and we will marry you to royalty . . . What is it? Why are you crying?'

'I'm not crying,' she said, her blue eyes brimming.

'What is the matter?'

'I don't want to marry a prince.'

'Would you settle for a Prussian noble with a thousand-year-old castle?'

'Stop it!'

'I have one in mind. He is handsome, remarkably bright, considering his lineage, and surprisingly gentle. His mother could prove tiresome, but there is a stable teeming with Arabian horses and a lovely summer place on the Baltic where a girl could sail to her heart's content. Even practice for the Olympic yachting event . . . Why are you crying?'

Katherine Dee put both small hands on the table and spoke in a clear, even voice. 'I want to marry *you*.'

'Dear, dear Katherine. That would be like a marrying your own brother.'

'I don't care. Besides, you're not my brother. You only act like one.'

'I am your guardian,' he said. 'I have pledged that no one will ever hurt you.'

'What do you think you're doing now?'

'Stop this silliness about marrying me. You know I love you. But not that way.'

Tears hovered on her lashes like diamonds.

He passed her a handkerchief. 'Dry your eyes. We have work to do.'

She dabbed, lifting her tears onto the linen. 'I thought we were leaving.'

'Leaving with a bang requires work.'

'What am I supposed to do?' she asked sullenly.

'I can't let Isaac Bell get in my way this time.'

'Why don't I kill him?'

O'Shay nodded thoughtfully. Katherine was lethal, a finely tuned machine unencumbered by remorse or regret. But every machine had its physical limits. 'You would only get hurt. Bell is too much like me, a man not easily killed.

No, I won't have you risk trying to kill him. But I do want him distracted.'

'Do you want me to seduce him?' asked Katherine. She flinched from the sudden fury distorting O'Shay's face.

'Have I ever asked you to do such a thing?'

'No.'

'Would I ever ask you?'

'No.'

'It destroys me that you could say such a thing.'

'I am sorry, Brian. I didn't think.' She reached for his hand. He pulled away, his normally bland face red, his lips compressed in a hard line, his eyes wintery.

'Brian, I am not exactly a schoolgirl.'

'Whatever seductions you allow yourself are your business,' he said coldly. 'I have ensured that you possess the means and manner to indulge yourself as only privileged women can. Society will never tell you what you can do and not do. But I want it clearly understood that I would never use you that way.'

'What way? As a seductress? Or an indulgence?'

'Young lady, you are beginning to annoy me.'

Katherine Dee ignored the very dangerous tone in his voice because she knew he was too careful to break up the furniture in the Palm Court. 'Stop calling me that. You're only ten years older than I am.'

'Twelve. And mine are old years, while I have moved heaven and earth to make yours young years.'

Waiters bustled up. Ward and guardian sat in stony silence until the cakes were spread and tea poured.

'How do you want me to distract him?' When he started talking that way there was nothing to do but go along.

'The fiancée is the key.'

'She is suspicious of me.'

'How do you mean?' O'Shay asked sharply.

'At the *Michigan* launching, when I tried to get close, she pulled back. She senses something in me that frightens her.'

'Perhaps she is psychical,' said O'Shay, 'and reads your mind.'

An expression as desolate as it was wise transformed Katherine Dee's pretty face into a lifeless mask of ancient marble. 'She reads my heart.'

46

'Your fiancée is calling on the telephone, Mr. Bell.'

The tall Van Dorn detective was standing over his desk in the Knickerbocker, impatiently sifting reports for some decent news on the whereabouts of Eyes O'Shay or the stolen torpedoes before he hit the streets hunting Billy Collins again.

'This is a nice surprise.'

'I'm across the street at Hammerstein's Victoria Theatre,' said Marion Morgan.

'Are you all right?' She didn't sound all right. Her voice was tight with tension.

'Could you stop by when you have a moment?'

'I'll be right there.'

'They'll let you in the stage door.'

Bell ran down the Knickerbocker's grand staircase three steps at a time and set off a blast of horns, bells, and angry shouts as he ran through the moving wall of autos, streetcars, and horse carts that blocked Broadway. Sixty seconds after dropping the telephone, he pounded on the Victoria's stage door.

'Miss Morgan is waiting for you in the house, Mr. Bell. Through there. Go in quietly, please. They're rehearsing.'

A high-speed, rhythmic tapping echoed from the stage, and when he flung open the door he was surprised to discover that the source of all the noise was a small boy and a tall girl dancing in shoes with wooden soles. He exhaled in relief when he saw Marion sitting alone, safe and sound, in the eighth row of the partially darkened empty house. She pressed a finger to her lips. Bell glided up the aisle and sat beside her, and she took his hand, and whispered, 'Oh, my darling, I'm so glad you're here.'

'What happened?'

'I'll tell you in a minute. They're almost done.'

The orchestra, which had been waiting silently, burst into a crescendo, and the dance was over. The children were instantly surrounded by the director, the stage manager, costumers, and their mother.

'Aren't they wonderful? I found them on the Orpheum Circuit in San Francisco. The top vaudeville circuit. I've persuaded their mother to let them appear in my new movie.'

'What happened to your movie about the bank robbers?'

'The detective's girlfriend caught them.'

'I suspected she would. What's wrong? You don't sound yourself. What happened?'

'I'm not sure. I may be silly, but it seemed sensible to call you. Did you ever meet Katherine Dee?'

'She's a friend of Dorothy Langner. I've seen her at a distance. I've not met her.'

'Lowell introduced her to me at the *Michigan* launching. She hinted that she would like to come out to the movie studio. It was on the tip of my tongue to invite her. She looks like she might be one of those creatures the camera is so fond of – you know, as I've told you, the large head, fine features, slight torso. Like that boy you just saw dancing.'

Bell glanced at the stage. 'He looks like a praying mantis.'

'Yes, the narrow head, the big, luminous eyes. Wait 'til you see him smile.'

'I gather you did not invite Katherine Dee. What changed your mind?'

'She's very strange.'

'How?'

'Call it what you will. Intuition. Instinct. Something about her does not ring true.'

'Never deny a gut feeling,' said Bell. 'You can always change your mind later.'

'Thank you, darling. I do feel a little silly, and yet . . . when I was away in San Francisco, she came out to see me in Fort Lee. Uninvited. She just showed up. And now she just showed up again this morning.'

'What did she say?'

'I didn't give her a chance. I was rushing to the ferry to see these children and their mother, who is also their manager and very ambitious. I just waved and kept going. She called out something about offering to give me a lift. I think she had a car waiting. I just kept moving and hopped the ferry. Isaac, I'm sure I'm being silly. I mean, Lowell Falconer knows her. He didn't seem to think she was strange. On the other hand, I doubt anyone in a skirt would be strange to Lowell.'

'Who told you she had shown up when you were in San Francisco?'

'Mademoiselle Duvall.'

'What did she think of Katherine?'

'I think she sensed what I sensed, though not as strongly.

Strange people often show up at the studio. The movies tug at them. They imagine all sorts of fantastical futures for themselves. But Katherine Dee is different. She's obviously well-off and well-bred.'

'She's an orphan.'

'Oh, my Lord! I didn't realize. Maybe she does need the work.'

'Her father left her a fortune.'

'How do you know?'

'We've investigated everyone in the Hull 44 set.'

'So I'm probably imagining things.'

'Better safe than sorry. I'll have Research dig deeper.'

'Come meet the children . . . Fred, say hello to my fiancé, Mr. Bell.'

'Hello, Mr. Bell,' Fred mumbled, staring at his shoes. He was a shy little guy, seven or eight.

'Hello, Fred. When I came in, I heard you dancing so fast I thought it was a machine gun.'

'Did you?' He looked up and studied Bell with a warm smile.

'How's Miss Morgan treating you?'

'Oh, she's very nice.'

'I agree.'

'And this is Adele,' said Marion. The girl was buoyant, several years older, and did not need any coaxing. 'Are you really Miss Morgan's fiancé?'

'I'm the lucky man.'

'I'll say you are!'

'I'll say you're very wise. What's the movie about?'

Adele looked surprised when little Fred answered for her. 'Child dancers are captured by Indians.'

'What's it called?'

'*The Lesson*. The kids teach the Indians a new dance and they let them go.'

'Sounds uplifting. I look forward to seeing it. Pleased to meet you, Fred.' He shook his little hand again. 'Pleased to meet you, Adele.' He shook hers.

Marion said, 'I'll see you in the morning, children,' and called to their mother, 'Eight o'clock call, Mrs. Astaire.'

They stood alone at the back of the house.

Bell said, 'When you get back to Fort Lee tomorrow morning, you will see someone you know dressed like an Indian. Give him a part that will keep him near you at all times.'

'Archie Abbott?'

'He's the only man I would trust with your life, other than Joe Van Dorn. But no one would ever believe that Mr. Van Dorn dressed up like an Indian was looking for an acting job in your movie. Whereas Archie would have been an actor if his mother had not forbidden it. Until we can be sure that Katherine Dee means no harm, Archie will watch over you at work during the day. At night, I want you to stay at the Knickerbocker.'

'An unmarried lady alone in a respectable hotel? What will the house detective say?'

'If he knows what's good for him, he'll say, "Good night, Mr. Bell. Sleep tight."'

Isaac Bell went back into the streets. He felt he was getting close, so close that he carried sandwiches in his coat pockets assuming that a man living as on the edge as Billy

Collins would be glad of a meal. There had been two more sightings. Both were on Ninth Avenue near where it ended abruptly at 33rd Street by the huge hole in the ground they were excavating for the Pennsylvania Terminal rail yard.

He went to the construction site, shabbily dressed, and watched for the tall, thin silhouette he had seen in the coal pocket. An entire district of the city – six acres of houses, apartments, shops, and churches – had vanished. Ninth Avenue crossed the gigantic hole on stiltlike temporary shoring girders that held up two streetcar lines, the road-bed, and a trestle for pedestrians. Propped high above it, Ninth Avenue Elevated locals and expresses still ran, rumbling across the gaping hole like giant airplanes made of iron and steel.

A steam whistle blew day's end. A thousand workmen climbed out of the pit and hurried home into the city. When they had gone, Bell climbed in, down ladders and temporary wooden stairs, past the severed ends of gas mains, cast-iron water mains, electrical conduits, and brick sewers. Twenty-four feet down, he encountered a steel viaduct partially constructed – underpinning, he had been told, for Ninth Avenue and the buildings around it. He descended through it into darkness lighted by pinpricks of electric work lamps.

Sixty feet below the surface, he found the floor of the pit. It was a field of stone rubble, dynamited granite, criss-crossed by narrow-gauge rails for the cars that hauled debris out and material in and forested with wide columns that carried the viaduct. Through its frame he could see blue electrical sparks arcing as the El trains thundered across the sky.

Bell explored for an hour, keeping an eye peeled for night watchmen. He tripped repeatedly on the uneven ground. The third time he fell, he smelled something sweet and discovered a gnawed apple core. Poking around, he found a man's den – a crumpled blanket, more apple cores, and chicken bones. He settled down to wait, sitting on the ground, still as ice, moving only when he had to stretch his limbs to stay agile and then only when the Els clattering overhead masked his movements.

He was not alone. Rats scuttled, a dog barked, and from hundreds of feet away in the dark he heard an argument between two hobos, which ended with a heavy *thump* and a groan drowned out by a passing El. It got quieter as the night wore on and the El trains ran less frequently. Someone lit a bonfire on the edge of the hole at 33rd Street, which sent flickers and shadows dancing on pillars, girders, and rough-hewn stone walls.

A voice whispered in Bell's ear.

'It's like church in here.'

47

Isaac Bell moved only his eyes.

By the flickering firelight, he saw a long, bony face with a vacant smile. The man was dressed in rags. His hands were empty, his eyes were puffy as if he had just woken, and Bell surmised that he had been nearby all along sleeping soundlessly. Now he was staring with wondering eyes up at the steel skeleton of the viaduct, and Bell saw what he meant by church. The interlocking girders, the dark sky speckled with stars, and the bonfire light conspired to form the image of a medieval cathedral lit by candles.

'Hello, Billy.'

'Huh?'

'You are Billy Collins?'

'Yeah. How'd you know?'

'You used to run with Eyes O'Shay.'

'Yeah . . . Poor Eyes . . . How'd you know?'

'Tommy told me.'

'Fat bastard. You a friend of his?'

'No.'

'Me neither.'

Though he was about Bell's age, Billy Collins looked ancient. His hair was gray, his nose was dripping, and now his puffy eyes began leaking tears.

'You Tommy's friend?' he asked again angrily.

'What did Tommy do to Eyes?' Bell asked.

'Tommy do to Eyes? Are you kidding? That fat bastard? Couldn't do Eyes on his best day. You a friend of Tommy?'

'No. What happened to Eyes?'

'I don't know.'

'They said you were with him.'

'Yeah. So?'

'So what happened?'

Billy closed his eyes, and murmured, 'One of these days, I'm going to get back to doing trains.'

'What do you mean, Billy?' Bell asked.

'There's good money doing trains, you get the right freight. Good money. I used to be rich doing trains. Then they got my little girl, and all of a sudden I couldn't do 'em anymore.' He looked at Bell, the firelight making his eyes look as mad as the tone of his voice. 'Got jobs once. You know that?'

'No, I didn't know that, Billy. What sort of jobs?'

'Got jobs. Sceneshifter in a theater. Once I was a stable-man. I even worked as a dummy boy.'

'What is a dummy boy?' Bell asked.

'Railroad signalman. Eleventh Avenue. I rode a horse ahead of the train. It's the law in New York. You can't run a train on Eleventh Avenue without a guy on a horse. Only time the law ever gave me a job. I didn't stick it.'

He started coughing. Consumption, Bell thought. The man is dying.

'Are you hungry, Billy?'

'Naw. I don't get hungry.'

'Try this.' Bell handed him a sandwich. Billy Collins sniffed, held it near his mouth, and said, 'You a friend of Tommy?'

'What did Tommy do to Eyes?'

'Nothing. Told you. Tommy couldn't do Eyes. Nobody could do Eyes. Except that old man.'

'Old man?'

'Hard old man.'

'You mean his father?'

'*Father?* Eyes didn't have no father. The old man. He's what got us. Got us good.'

'What old man?'

'On Clarkson.'

'Clarkson Street?' Bell asked. 'Downtown?'

'The *Umbria* was sailing for Liverpool.'

The Cunard liner. One of the old ones. 'When?'

'That night.'

'When Eyes disappeared?'

'When we was kids,' Billy answered dreamily. He lay back and gazed up at the frame for the viaduct.

'The *Umbria*?' Bell prompted. 'The steamship? The Cunard liner?'

'We seen this old man. He was rushing to Pier 40 like he's late. Not even looking where he was going. We couldn't believe our luck. We was down on Clarkson Street looking for drunk sailors to roll. Instead, here comes a rich old man in a rich green coat and sparkling rings on his fingers who could pay one hundred fifty dollars for his steamship ticket. It was dark and pouring down rain, not a soul on Clarkson. Eyes clipped on his thumb gouge in case he gave us trouble. We pounced like cats on our rich rat. Brian went to tear his rings from his fingers. I figured to find a wallet bulging with money in his fancy coat . . .'

'What happened?'

406

'He pulled a sword out of his cane.'

Billy Collins turned his gaze on Bell, his eyes wide with wonder. 'A *sword*. We were so drunk, we couldn't hardly get out of our own way. The old man swings his sword. I dodged it. He floored me with the cane. Tough old man, knew his business. Set me up. I dodged right into his cane. Heard a noise like dynamite going off inside my head. Then I was gone.'

Billy Collins sniffed the sandwich again and stared at it.

'Then what happened?' asked Bell.

'I woke up in the gutter, soaking wet and freezing cold.'

'What about Eyes?'

'Brian O'Shay was gone, and I never seen him again.'

'Did the old man kill Eyes O'Shay?'

'I didn't see no blood.'

'Could the rain have washed the blood away?'

Collins begins to weep. 'Vanished into thin air. Just like my little girl. Except she wasn't hurting nobody. But Eyes and me, we sure as hell was trying.'

'What if I told you Eyes came back?'

'I rather you told me my little girl came back.'

'From where?'

'I don't know. Tiny little thing.'

'Your child?'

'Child? I got no child . . . Eyes came back, I heard.'

'Yes, he did. Tommy saw him.'

'Didn't come to see me . . . But who the hell would?' He closed his eyes and began to snore. The sandwich fell from his fingers.

'Billy.' Isaac Bell shook him awake. 'Who was the old man?'

'Rich old guy in a green coat.' He slipped toward sleep again.

'Billy!'

'Leave me be.'

'Who was your little girl?'

Billy Collins screwed his eyes shut. 'No one knows. No one remembers. Except the priest.'

'Which priest?'

'Father Jack.'

'What church?'

'St. Michael's.'

After Bell left him, Billy Collins dreamed that a dog clamped its jaws around his foot. He kicked it with his other foot. The dog grew a second head and bit down on that foot, too. He awoke in terror. A figure was hunched over his feet, working at his laces. A goddamned hobo who wouldn't have dared touch him in the old days was trying to steal his shoes.

'Hey!'

The hobo tugged harder. Billy sat up and tried to punch him in the head. The hobo dropped his shoe, picked up a broken board, and hit him. Billy saw stars. Stunned, he was vaguely aware that the guy was winding up with the board to hit him again. He knew the guy would hit him hard, but he couldn't move.

Steel flashed. A knife materialized out of nowhere. The hobo screamed and fell back, holding his face. The knife flashed again. Another scream, and the hobo scrambled away on all fours, clambered to his feet, and ran for his life.

Billy sank back. Hell of a dream. Everything was strange. Now he smelled perfume. It made him smile. He opened his eyes. A woman was kneeling over him, her hair brushing his face. Like an angel. It seemed he had died.

She leaned very close, so close he could feel her warm breath, and whispered, 'What did you tell the detective, Billy?'

48

'The lady of the house is not a fortune-teller,' Eyes O'Shay assured the anxious captain of his Holland submarine torpedo boat.

Hunt Hatch was not assured. 'There's signs all over the house advertising that Madame Nettie tells fortunes. She'll have customers in and out all hours of the day and night. You've put us in a parlous situation keeping us here, O'Shay. I won't stand for it.'

'The fortune-telling is a blind. She doesn't tell fortunes.'

'What's it a blind for?'

'A counterfeit ring.'

'Counterfeiters. Are you crazy, man?'

'They're the last people in Bayonne who would complain to the cops. That's why I put you here. And the woman who cooks your meals escaped from state prison. She won't tell anyone either. Besides, they can't see your boat from the houses. It's screened by the barge.'

A mowed lawn spread from the counterfeiters' frame house at the foot of Lord Street to the Kill Van Kull. The Kill was a narrow, deepwater channel between Staten Island and Bayonne. The barge was moored on the bank.

The Holland was under the barge. Its turret was accessible through an inside well. It was less than four miles from New York's Upper Bay, and from there a clear five-mile run to the Brooklyn Navy Yard.

Hunt Hatch was not appeased. 'Even if *they* can't, the Kill is swarming with oyster catchers. I see them in their scows. They come right up to the barge.'

'They're Staten Islanders,' O'Shay answered patiently. 'They're not looking for you. They're looking to steal something.'

He gestured at the hills a thousand feet across the narrow strait. 'Staten Island became part of New York City ten years ago. But the Staten Island scowmen haven't heard the news. They're the same coal pirates, smugglers, and thieves they've always been. I promise you, they don't talk to the cops either.'

'I say we attack now and get it over with.'

'We attack,' O'Shay said quietly, 'the moment I say we attack.'

'I am not risking life and freedom to get caught on your whims. I am captain of the ship, and I say we attack now before someone stumbles upon where we've hid the bloody thing.'

O'Shay stepped closer. He raised a hand as if to strike the captain. Hatch quickly lifted both hands, one to block the blow, one to counterpunch. He exposed his belly. By then O'Shay was flicking open a Butterfly-messer with his other hand. He slid the long knife under Hatch's sternum, plunged it to the hilt, jerked the razor-sharp blade down with all his might, and stepped back quickly before the intestines spilling out could stain his clothes.

The captain clutched at them, gasping with horror. His knees buckled. He fell on the rug. 'But who will run the Holland?' he whispered.

'I've just promoted your first mate.'

'This is the newest church building I have ever been in,' Isaac Bell told Father Jack Mulrooney.

The Church of St. Michael smelled of paint, shellac, and cement. The windows gleamed and the stones were fresh, unblemished by soot.

'We've just moved in,' said Father Jack. 'The parishioners are pinching themselves wondering can it be true. In actual fact, the only way that the Pennsylvania Railroad Company could remove us from 31st Street to build the terminal yards without bringing the wrath of God – not to mention Tammany Hall and His Grace the Cardinal – down on their heads was to build us a brand-new church, rectory, convent, and school.'

Bell said, 'I am a private detective, Father, with the Van Dorn Agency. I would like to ask you some questions about people who used to live in your parish.'

'If you want to talk, you must walk. I have my rounds, and you will see that our people live in less bright places than their new church. Come along.' He set off with a surprisingly springy step for a man his age, turned a corner, and plunged into a neighborhood that felt miles, not yards, from his brand-new church.

'You've served here long, Father?'

'Since the Draft Riots.'

'That's forty-five years ago.'

'Some things have changed in the district, most have not. We are still poor.'

The priest entered a tenement with an elaborate carved stone portal and started up a steep flight of rickety stairs.

He was breathing hard by the third floor. At the sixth, he paused to catch his breath, and when the wheezing stopped he knocked on a door, and called, 'Good morning! It is Father Jack.'

A girl with a baby in her arms opened the door. 'Thank you for coming, Father.'

'And how is your mother?'

'Not good, Father, not good at all.'

He left Bell in the front room. A single window that looked onto a yard crisscrossed with clotheslines in the shade admitted the stench of a privy six stories below. Bell folded a wad of dollar bills in his hand and slipped it to the girl as they left.

At the bottom of the stairs, Father Jack caught his breath again. 'Who are you inquiring about?'

'Brian O'Shay and Billy Collins.'

'Brian's long gone from here.'

'Fifteen years, I've been told.'

'If God ever blessed this district, it was the day O'Shay disappeared. I would never say such a thing lightly, but Brian O'Shay was Satan's right-hand man.'

'I've heard he's back.'

'I've heard rumors,' the priest said bleakly, and he led Bell back into the street.

'I saw Billy Collins last night.'

Father Jack stopped and looked at the tall detective with sudden respect. 'Did you really? Down in the hole?'

'You know he's there?'

'Billy has, shall we say, hit bottom. Where else would he go?'

'Who is his little girl?'

413

'His little girl?'

'He kept referring to his little girl. But he claimed he had no children.'

'That's a dubious claim considering the youth he led. In those years, it was rare I baptized a carroty-topped infant and didn't wonder if Billy was the father.'

'I wondered if his hair was red. It seemed mostly gray in the dim light.'

'Though I suppose,' Father Jack added with a thin smile, 'Billy could claim with a certain degree of truth that he is not *aware* he had any children. It would have been an unusually brave girl who would have named him the father. Still, I see his point. Whoring and drunk since he was twelve years old, what would he remember?'

'He was adamant he had no children.'

'That would make the little girl his sister.'

'Of course. He weeps for her.'

'I'm sure he does.'

'What happened to her?' Bell asked.

'Wait for me here,' the priest said. 'I'll only be a moment.' He entered a building and came out shortly. As they continued along the block, Father Jack said, 'There are wicked men living in this community who live by stealing from poor, ignorant people. They'll steal their money, and if they have no money they will steal their drink. If they have no drink, they'll steal their children. Whatever the wicked can sell or use themselves. The child was kidnapped.'

'Billy's sister?'

'Snatched from the street – no more than five years old – and never seen again. Surely she courses through Billy's brain when he injects the morphine. Where was he when she was stolen? Where was he *ever* when the poor babe was needful? He looks back now and loves the *idea* of that wee child. More than he ever loved the child herself.'

The old priest shook his head in anger and disgust. 'When I think of the nights I prayed for that child . . . and all the children like her.'

Bell waited, sensing a natural ebullience in the old man that would rise to the surface. And it did after a while. His expression brightened.

'In truth, it was Brian O'Shay who cared for that little girl.'

'Eyes O'Shay?'

'He looked after her when Billy and his shiftless parents were drunk.' Father Jack lowered his voice. 'They say that O'Shay beat her father to death for sins against the child only the Devil could imagine. She was the only soul Brian O'Shay ever loved. It was a blessing that he never knew what happened to her.'

'Could Brian O'Shay have kidnapped her?'

'Never in this life! Even if he weren't long gone to Hell.'

'But what if he was not killed when he vanished? What if he came back? Could he have kidnapped her?'

'He would never hurt her,' said the priest.

'Evil men do evil, Father. You've told me how wicked he was.'

'Even the most wicked man has a streak of God in him.' The priest took Bell's arm. 'If you remember that, you will be a better detective. And a better man. That wee child was Brian O'Shay's streak of God.'

'Was her name Katherine?'

Father Jack looked at him curiously.

'Why do you say that?'

'I don't really know. But I'm asking you, was it?'

Father Jack started to answer. A pistol shot cracked from a tenement roof. The priest tumbled to the pavement. A second shot drilled the space Bell had occupied an instant before. He was already rolling across the sidewalk, drawing his Browning, snapping to his knees, raising his weapon to fire.

But all he could see were women and children screaming from their windows that their priest was murdered.

'I want a direct telephone connection to the chief of the Baltimore office now!' Isaac Bell shouted as he stalked into Van Dorn headquarters. 'Tell him to have his Katherine Dee file on his desk.'

It took an hour for Baltimore to telephone back. 'Bell? Sorry I took so long. Raining like hell again, half the city's flooded. You'll get yours, it's another nor'easter.'

'I want to know exactly who Katherine Dee is and I want to know now.'

'Well, as we reported, her father went back to Ireland with a boatload of dough he made building schools for the diocese and took her with him.'

'I know that already. And when he died, she went to a convent school in Switzerland. What school?'

'Let me go through this while we're talking. I've got it right here in front of me. The boys have brought it up-to-date since we sent our last report to New York ... Takes so long back and forth to Dublin ... Let's see here ... Well, I'll be. No, no, no, that can't be.'

'What?'

'Some damned fool got confused. Says the daughter died, too. That can't be. We've got records of her at the school. Mr. Bell, let me get back to you on this.'

'Immediately,' said Bell, and hung up.

Archie walked in, still ruddy-faced with Indian war paint. 'You look like death, Isaac.'

'Where's Marion?'

'Upstairs.' Bell had rented a suite for the days she was in New York. 'We got rained out again. Are you O.K.? What happened to you?'

'A priest was gunned down in front of my eyes. For talking to me.'

'The spy?'

'Who else? The block was swarming with cops, but he got clean away.'

An apprentice approached the grim-faced detectives warily. 'Messenger left this at Reception, Mr. Bell.'

Bell tore it open. On Waldorf-Astoria stationery Erhard Riker had written:

FOUND IT!
PERFECTION FOR THE PERFECT
FIANCÉE!!

I'll be at Solomon Barlowe's Jewelry Shop around three o'clock with a brilliant emerald, if this finds you in New York.

Best wishes,

Erhard Riker

49

Bell threw Riker's note on the desk.

Archie picked it up and read it. 'The ring for fair Marion?'

'It'll keep.'

'Go.'

'I'm waiting to hear from Baltimore.'

Archie said, 'Take an hour. Cool off. I'll talk to Baltimore if they call before you're back. Say, why don't you take Marion with you? All this rain is making her stir-crazy. She's raving about going to California to shoot movies in the sunshine. Neglecting to explain where she'd find the actors. Go! Let some steam off. You found Collins. You've got two hundred men looking for O'Shay. And the Navy and Harbor Squad hunting torpedoes. I'll cover for you.'

Bell stood up. 'Just an hour. Back soon.'

'If she likes it, steal an extra ten minutes to buy her a glass of champagne.'

They took the subway downtown and walked rain-swept streets to Maiden Lane. Barlowe's shop cast a warm glow into the dreary afternoon. 'Are you sure you want to do this?' Marion asked as they neared the door.

'What do you mean?'

'Once you slip a ring on a girl's finger, it's pretty hard to get out of it.'

They were holding hands. Bell pulled her close. Her eyes were bright with laughter. Rain and mist gilded the wisps of hair that escaped her hat. 'Houdini couldn't get out of this one,' he said, and kissed her on the mouth. 'Not that he'd want to.'

They entered the shop.

Erhard Riker and Solomon Barlowe were bent over the counter, each with a jeweler's loupe screwed in his eye. Riker looked up, smiling. He extended his hand to Bell, and said to Marion, 'I am afraid that you taxed your fiancé's powers of observation. Try as he might – and I assure you he tried mightily – he was hard put to convey the fullness of your beauty.'

Marion said, 'You tax my power of speech. Thank you.'

Riker bowed over Marion's hand, kissed it, and stepped back, smoothing his mustache and slipping his thumb into his vest pocket. Barlowe whispered to Bell, 'It is most unusual, sir, for a gentleman to show the ring to his fiancée before he has purchased it.'

'Miss Morgan is a most unusual fiancée.'

Something *ticked* against the window. On the sidewalk, ignoring the rain, laughing young men in black derbies were batting a badminton shuttlecock with their hands.

'You should call a constable before they break the glass,' said Riker.

Solomon Barlowe shrugged. 'College boys. This summer, they'll meet girls. Next spring, they'll be buying engagement rings.'

'Here is the making of yours, Miss Morgan,' said Riker. He drew a slim leather case from his pocket, opened it, and removed a folded sheet of white paper. Opening the paper, he let slide onto a demonstration panel of white velvet an emerald – flawless, fiery, and filled with life.

The jeweler Solomon Barlowe gasped.

Isaac Bell thought it shimmered like a green flame.

Marion Morgan said, 'It is certainly very bright.'

'Mr. Barlowe proposes setting it in a simple Art Nouveau ring,' said Erhard Riker.

'I have prepared some sketches,' said Barlowe.

Isaac Bell watched Marion study the emerald. He said, 'I have the impression you do not love it.'

'My dear, I will wear anything you like.'

'But you would prefer something else.'

'It's very beautiful. But since you ask, I would prefer a softer green – rich yet quiet, like the loden green of Mr. Riker's coat. Is there such a gem, Mr. Riker?'

'There is a blue-gray shade of tourmaline found in Brazil. It is very rare. And extremely difficult to cut.'

Marion grinned at Bell. 'It would be less expensive to buy me a nice loden coat like Mr. Riker's . . .' Her voice trailed off. She was about to ask, Isaac, what's the matter? Instead, she moved instinctively closer to him.

Bell was staring at Riker's coat. 'A rich green coat,' he said softly. 'An old man in a rich green coat with rings on his fingers.' He fixed a cold gaze on Riker's gem-studded cane.

'I've always admired that cane of yours, Herr Riker.'

'It was a gift from my father.'

'May I see it?'

Riker tossed it to Bell. Bell weighed it in his hands, testing its balance and heft. He closed one hand around the gold-and-gem head, twisted it with a flick of his wrists, and drew out a gleaming sword.

Erhard Riker shrugged. 'One cannot be too careful in my business.'

Bell held the blade to the light. It was honed so sharply that no light gleamed on the edge. He hefted the cane, the scabbard that had held it. 'Heavy. You wouldn't even need the sword. You could floor a man with this.'

Bell watched Riker eye him warily as if he were wondering whether he had heard Bell correctly or was just taking his measure. Wondering, Do I have to fight? At last Riker spoke. '*Two men,* if you were faster than you looked.'

'And if the men were drunk,' Bell said, moving swiftly to shield Marion. It was suddenly clear to both men that they were discussing the night that Eyes O'Shay and Billy Collins had tried to rob the senior Mr. Riker.

Riker answered in a conversational voice, although his eyes were focused as hard on Bell's as Bell's were on his.

'I awakened,' he said, 'in a first-class cabin on the high seas. The old man was tough as nails. But kind to me. Anything I wanted was mine for the asking. The food on that ship was like what I had heard people say that Diamond Jim Brady ate. Beefsteaks, oysters, roast ducks, wine from crystal glasses. I felt like I had arrived in Heaven. Of course, I wondered what did he want back for all that? But all he ever asked was that I go to school and learn to be a gentleman. He sent me to public school in England, and the finest universities in Germany.'

'Why didn't Mr. Riker leave you in the gutter with Billy Collins?'

'You've spoken with Billy? Of course. How is he?'

'Still in the gutter. Why didn't Riker leave you there?'

'He was grieving for his son who had died of influenza. He wanted another.'

'And you were available.'

'I was *garbage*. I could barely read. But he saw something in me no one else could see.'

'And you repaid him by becoming a murderer and a spy.'

'I repaid him,' Riker said, his shoulders squared, his head held high.

'You're proud of being a murderer and a spy?' Isaac Bell asked scornfully.

'You're a privileged child, Isaac Bell. There are things you can never know. I repaid him. I say it with pride.'

'I say with equal pride that I arrest you for murder, Brian O'Shay.'

Katherine Dee darted through the curtain that screened the back room, slid her arm around Marion's throat, and pressed her thumb to Marion's eye.

50

'Brian taught me this trick for my twelfth birthday. He even gave me my own gouge. It's made of pure gold, see?' The sharpened metal fit her thumb like a claw.

'Stay perfectly still,' Bell told Marion. 'Do not struggle. Mr. O'Shay has the upper hand.'

'Obey your fiancé,' said Katherine Dee.

Eyes O'Shay said, 'To answer your question, Bell, one of the ways I repaid the old man's kindness was by rescuing Katherine as he had rescued me. Katherine is educated, accomplished, and free. No one can hurt her.'

'Educated, accomplished, free, and lethal,' said Bell.

With her other hand Katherine drew a pistol.

'Another birthday present?'

'Give Brian his sword, Mr. Bell, before your fiancée is blinded and I shoot you.'

Bell flicked the sword haft at O'Shay. As he expected, the spy was too sharp to fall for that trick. O'Shay caught it coolly without his eyes leaving Bell's. But when he started to sheathe it, he glanced down to make sure the tip went into the sheath instead of piercing his hand. Bell was waiting for that split second of distraction. He kicked with lightning speed.

The sharp toe of his boot struck Katherine Dee's ulnar nerve, which was drawn tightly over her flexed elbow. She cried out in startled pain and could not prevent her hand

423

from opening convulsively. Her thumb splayed away from Marion's eye.

But the gouge remained attached.

Marion tried to pull away from the smaller woman. Katherine whipped the gouge back at her face. Bell had his derringer in his hand by then and was squeezing the trigger. O'Shay screamed a piercing 'No!' and smashed his cane down on Bell's arm. The gunshot was deafening in the confined space. Solomon Barlowe dove to the floor. Marion cried out, and Bell thought he had shot her. But it was Katherine Dee who fell.

O'Shay grabbed the girl under one powerful arm and flung the door open. Bell lunged for them. He tripped over Solomon Barlowe. By the time he had hurled himself through the door, he saw O'Shay pushing Katherine into a Packard driven by a uniformed chauffeur. Gunmen in black derbies stepped from behind the car and from doorways, aiming pistols.

'Marion, get down!' Bell roared. The pretty-boy bruisers of Riker & Riker's private protection agency unleashed a scathing hail of gunfire. Wild ricochets smashed glass and blasted stone dust from the walls and diamonds from the window display. Pedestrians dropped to the sidewalk. Bell fired back as fast as he could pull the trigger. He heard the Packard roar away. He fired again, emptying his Browning. The big car screeched around a corner and crashed into something. But when the lead stopped flying and he galloped after it, the Packard was smoldering against a lamppost, and O'Shay, Katherine Dee, and their gunmen had gotten away. Bell ran back into the jewelry shop, his heart in his throat. Solomon Barlowe was groaning and holding his leg. Marion was on the floor behind the counter, eyes wide open.

Alive!

He knelt beside her. 'Are you hit?'

She ran a hand over her face. Her skin was dead white. 'I don't think so,' she said in a small voice.

'Are you all right?'

'Where are they?'

'Got away. Don't worry. They won't get far.'

She was clenching something in her tightly closed fist, which she now pressed to her chest.

'What is that?'

Slowly, painfully, she forced her fingers to open. Nestled in her palm was the emerald, green and mysterious as the eye of a cat.

'I thought you didn't like it,' Bell said.

Marion's beautiful eyes roved across the broken glass and the walls pocked with bullet holes. 'I'm not even scratched. Neither are you. It's our lucky charm.'

'The entire Newark fine-jewelry industry is in shock,' said Morris Weintraub, the stocky, white-haired patrician owner of Newark, New Jersey's largest belt-buckle factory. 'I've been buying gemstones from Riker and Riker since the Civil War. Back when there was only one Riker.'

'Did you know that Erhard Riker was adopted?'

'You don't say? No, I didn't.' Weintraub gazed across a sea of workbenches where jewelers labored in pure north light streaming through tall windows A speculative smile played on his lips, and he stroked his chin. 'That explains a lot.'

'What do you mean?' asked Bell.

'He was such a nice man.'

'The father?'

'No! His father was a cold bastard.'

Bell exchanged incredulous glances with Archie Abbott. The factory owner noticed. 'I am a Jew,' he explained. 'I know when a man dislikes me because I am a Jew. The father hid his hatred in order to conduct business, but hatred seeps out. He could not hide it completely. The son did not hate me. He was not so European as the old man.'

Bell and Archie exchanged another look. Weintraub said, 'I mean, he *acted* like a good man. He was a gentleman in business and kindly in person. He is one of the very few people I buy from who I would invite into my own home. Not a man who would shoot up a jewelry shop on Maiden Lane. Not a bigot like his father.'

Archie said, 'So I suppose you were not that upset when his father was killed in South Africa.'

'Nor was I surprised.'

'I beg your pardon?' asked Archie, and Isaac Bell said sharply, 'What do you mean by that?'

'I used to joke to my wife, "Herr Riker is a German agent."'

'What made you say that?'

'He couldn't resist boasting to me of his travels. But I noticed over many years that somehow his trips always led him to where Germany was making trouble. In 1870, he just happened to be in Alsace-Lorraine when the Franco-Prussian War broke out. He was on the island of Samoa in 'eighty-one when the United States, England, and Germany instigated their civil war. He was in Zanzibar when Germany stole her so-called East African Protectorate. He was in China when Germany took Tsingtao, and in South Africa when the Kaiser egged on the Boers fighting England.'

'Where,' Archie noted, 'he was killed.'

'In an engagement led by General Smuts himself,' said Isaac Bell. 'If he wasn't a German spy, he was a master of coincidence. Thank you, Mr. Weintraub. You have been very helpful.'

On their way back to New York, Bell told Archie, 'When I accused O'Shay of repaying the man who adopted him by becoming a murderer and a spy, he answered that rescuing Katherine from Hell's Kitchen was "one" of the ways he repaid him. He said, "I say it with pride." I realize now that he was bragging that he followed in his adopted father's footsteps.'

'If the father who adopted him was a spy, does that mean that Riker-O'Shay spies for Germany? He was born in America. He was adopted by a German father. He attended public school in England and university in Germany. Where are his loyalties?'

'He's a gangster,' said Bell. 'He has no loyalties.'

'Where can he go now that he's exposed?'

'Anywhere they'll take him in. But not before he commits a final crime to benefit the nation that will protect a criminal.'

'Using those torpedoes,' said Archie.

'Against what?' wondered Bell.

Ted Whitmark was waiting in the Van Dorn reception room when Bell got back to the Knickerbocker. He was holding his hat on his knees and could not meet Bell's eye as he asked, 'Is there someplace private we can talk, Mr. Bell?'

'Come on in,' Bell said, noting that Whitmark's Harvard College tie was askew, his shoes scuffed, and his trousers in need of a pressing. He led him to his desk and moved a chair alongside so they could sit close and not be overheard. Whitmark sat, worrying his hands, gnawing his lip.

'How is Dorothy?' Bell asked to put him at ease.

'Well . . . she's one of the things I want to talk about. But I'll get to the main event first, if you don't mind.'

'Not at all.'

'You see, I, uh, I play cards. Often . . .'

'You gamble.'

'Yes. I gamble. And sometimes I gamble too much. I'll hit a losing streak and, before I know it, I'm in over my head. All I'm trying to do is win back some of my losses, but sometimes it only gets worse.'

'Are you in a losing streak at the moment?' Bell asked.

'It looks that way. Yes, you could say that.' Again he fell silent.

'Can I assume that Dorothy is upset with this?'

'Well, yes, but that's the least of it. I've been something of a fool. I've done several really stupid things. I thought I'd learned my lesson in San Francisco.'

'What happened in San Francisco?'

'I dodged a bullet out there, thanks to you.'

'What do you mean?' Bell asked, suddenly alert to a situation more serious than he had assumed.

'I mean when you stopped that cart from blowing up

428

the Mare Island magazine, you saved my life. There would have been lot of innocent folks killed, and they would have been on my head.'

'Explain,' Bell said tersely.

'I gave them the pass and paperwork to get into the Mare Island Naval Shipyard.'

'Why?'

'I owed so much money. They were going to kill me.'

'Who?'

'Well, Commodore Tommy Thompson at first. Here in New York. Then he sold my debt to a guy who had a casino in the Barbary Coast and I lost more out there and he was going to kill me. He said they'd do it slow. But all I had to do to get out of it was give him one of my wagon passes and my company invoices and show 'em the ropes and everything. I know what you're thinking, that I allowed a saboteur onto the base, but I didn't realize that was what they wanted. I thought it was about them landing a big contract. I thought they were doing it for the money.'

'You *hoped* they were doing it for the money,' Isaac Bell retorted coldly.

Ted Whitmark hung his head. When he finally looked up again, he had tears in his eyes. 'That's what I hoped this time, too. But I'm scared it isn't, and something tells me this time will be worse.'

The intercommunicating phone on Bell's desk rang. He snatched it up. 'What?'

'There's a lady out here to see you and the gent you're with. Miss Dorothy Langner. Should I let her in?'

'No. Tell her I'll be out there shortly.' He hung up. 'Continue, Ted. What has happened this time?'

'They want me to turn over one of my trucks going into the Brooklyn Navy Yard.'

'Who?'

'This smooth guy named O'Shay. I heard somebody call him Eyes. Must be his nickname. Do you know who I mean?'

'When do they want the truck?'

'Tomorrow. When the *New Hampshire* is loading food and munitions. She just finished her shakedown, and she'll be ferrying a Marine Expeditionary Regiment to Panama to keep the Canal Zone election peaceful. My New York outfit got the provisions contract.'

'How big a truck?'

'The biggest.'

'Big enough to carry a couple of torpedoes?'

Whitmark chewed his lip. 'Oh, God. Is that what they want it for?'

The door from the reception room opened, and Harry Warren walked in. Bell was turning back to Ted Whitmark when a sudden motion at the door caught his eye and he saw Dorothy Langner in a black sheath dress and black feathered hat slip through it right behind Harry Warren, who said, 'Help you, ma'am?'

'I'm looking for Isaac Bell,' she said in her clear, musical voice. 'There he is, I see him.' She rushed toward Bell's desk, reaching into her handbag.

Whitmark jumped to his feet. 'Hello, Dorothy. Told you I'd talk to Bell. This'll square us, won't it?'

Dorothy Langner searched his face. Then she looked at Bell. 'Hello, Isaac. Is there someplace I could talk to Ted for a moment, in private?' Her beautiful silvery eyes were blank, and Bell had the eeriest sensation that she was blind. But she couldn't be blind, she had just marched in under her own steam.

'I believe that Mr. Van Dorn's office is empty. I'm sure he won't mind.'

He guided them into Van Dorn's office, closed the door, and stood close to it listening. He heard Whitmark repeat, 'This will square us, won't it?'

'Nothing will square us.'

'Dorothy?' asked Ted. 'What are you doing?'

The answer was the sharp crack of a gunshot. Bell threw open the door. Ted Whitmark lay on his back, blood pouring from his skull. Dorothy Langner dropped the nickel pistol she was holding onto Whitmark's chest, and said to Isaac Bell, 'He killed my father.'

'Yamamoto Kenta killed your father.'

'Ted didn't set the bomb, but he's been passing information about Father's work on Hull 44.'

'Did Ted tell you that?'

'He tried to get rid of his guilt confessing to me.'

Harry Warren rushed in, gun drawn, and knelt by the body. Then he grabbed Van Dorn's telephone. 'She missed,' he told Bell, and said to the operator, 'Get a doctor.'

'How badly is he hurt?' asked Bell.

'She only creased him. It's his scalp that's bleeding so much.'

'He won't die?'

'Not from this. In fact, I think he's starting to wake up.'

'She didn't shoot him,' said Bell.

'What?'

'Ted Whitmark tried to kill himself. She grabbed the gun. She saved his life.'

431

Harry Warren had wise, old eyes. 'Tell me why he tried to kill himself, Isaac.'

'He's a traitor. He just confessed to me that he's been passing information to the spy.'

Harry Warren looked Bell full in the face, and said, 'It appears that Miss Langner saved the louse's life.'

The Hotel Knickerbocker's house doctor rushed in with his bag trailed by bellhops lugging a stretcher. 'Stand back, everybody. Please stand back.'

Bell led Dorothy to his desk. 'Sit down.' He beckoned an apprentice. 'Please bring the lady a glass of water.'

'Why did you do that?' Dorothy whispered.

'I would not have if you had succeeded in murdering him. But since you didn't, I think you've been through enough without adding police charges to your misery.'

'Will the police believe it?'

'If Ted goes along with it. And I imagine he will. Now, tell me everything he told you.'

'He lost a lot of money gambling last fall in Washington. Someone in the game offered to lend him money. In exchange, he talked to Yamamoto.' She shook her head in anger and bitterness. 'He still doesn't realize that that man must have set him up to lose.'

'He told me it was bad luck,' said Bell. 'Go on.'

'The same thing happened this spring in New York and then out in San Francisco. Now it's happened again. This time, he finally realized the enormity of what he was doing. Or so he claimed. I think he was trying to get me to come back. I told him we were through. He found out about someone I've been seeing.'

'Farley Kent.'

'Of course you know,' she said wearily. 'Van Dorns never give up. When Ted found out about Farley, I think he realized that nothing in his entire life had any truth to it. He got religion. He was probably hoping I'd be waiting when he got out of jail. Or weeping when they hung him for treason.'

'Shooting him must have disabused him of that notion,' Bell observed.

She smiled. 'I'm not sure how I feel right now about not killing him. I meant to. I can't believe I missed. I was so close.'

'In my experience,' said Bell, 'people who miss a sure shot wanted to miss. Murder does not come easily to most.'

'I wish I had killed him.'

'You would hang for it.'

'I wouldn't care.'

'Where would that leave Farley Kent?'

'Farley would –' she started to say but stopped abruptly.

Bell smiled gently. 'You were about to say that Farley would understand, but you realize that is not so.'

She hung her head. 'Farley would be devastated.'

'I've seen Farley at work. He strikes me as your sort of man. He loves his work. Do you love him?'

'Yes, I do.'

'May I have a man escort you to the Brooklyn Navy Yard?'

She stood up. 'Thank you. I know the way.'

Bell walked her to the door. 'You made this case, Dorothy, when you vowed to clear your father's name. No one has done more to save his and Farley's work on

433

Hull 44. Thanks to you, we discovered the spy, and you can rest assured we will get him.'

'Did Ted tell you anything that helps?'

Bell answered carefully, 'He believes that he did. Tell me, how did Ted happen to find out about Farley Kent?'

'A letter from a busybody signed "A friend." Why are you smiling, Isaac?'

'The spy is getting desperate,' was all Bell would say, but he had a powerful feeling that O'Shay had tricked Ted Whitmark into passing him false information. The spy wanted Bell to believe that he would attack from the land when in fact he intended to attack, somehow, from the water.

Dorothy kissed his cheek and hurried down the grand stairway.

'Mr. Bell,' said the front-desk man, 'Knickerbocker house dick calling for you.'

51

'Got some unsavory types at the front door,' the Hotel Knickerbocker's house detective reported. 'Claim they want to talk to you, Mr. Bell.'

'What are their names?'

'There's a hairy oldster says he doesn't have a name, and I'm inclined to believe him. The young ones call themselves Jimmy Richards and Marv Gordon.'

'Send 'em up.'

'They don't look right for the lobby, if you know what I mean.'

'Understood. But they're little Eddie Tobin's cousins, so they're coming in the front door. Tell the manager I authorized it. You walk with them so they don't frighten the ladies.'

'O.K., Mr. Bell,' the house dick answered dubiously.

The Staten Island scowmen Richards and Gordon introduced their older companion, who had lanky gray hair and the squint lines from a lifetime on the water, as 'Uncle Donny Darbee, who sailed us over.'

'What's up, boys?'

'You still looking for torpedoes?'

'Where did you hear that?'

'The Navy and the Coast Guard and the Harbor Squad are swarming like mosquitoes,' said Richards.

'Searching every pier in the port,' said Gordon.

'Making it hard to do business,' muttered Uncle Donny.

'Have you seen the torpedoes?' Bell asked.

'Nope.'

'What do you know about them?'

'Nothing,' said Richards.

'Except you're looking for them,' said Gordon.

'Nothing at all? Then what did you come to see me about?'

'We was wondering if you was interested in the Holland.'

'What Holland?'

'Biggest Holland we ever saw.'

'A Holland *submarine*?'

'Yup,' chorused the Staten Island scowmen.

'Where?'

'Kill Van Kull.'

'Over on the Bayonne side.'

'Hold on, boys. If you've seen a submarine out in the open, it must belong to the Navy.'

'It's hid. Under a car float.'

'Uncle Donny found it last night when the cops was chasing him.'

'Been watching that barge for days,' said Uncle Donny Darbee.

Isaac Bell questioned them sharply.

Harbor cops hunting coal pirates had noticed Uncle Donny and his two friends following a coal barge in an oyster scow. Uncle Donny had declined to let the police board it for inspection. Pistol shots were exchanged. The cops had boarded anyway. Uncle Donny and his friends had jumped into the Kill and swum for shore.

Darbee's friends were caught, but the old man swam for a car float that he had been eyeing for several days because the barge was tied up all by itself, unattended, and was carrying a pair of freight cars that might contain cargo. Tiring in the cold water as he hid in the shadow of the overhanging prow, the old man had begun to sink only to step on something solid where it was too deep to stand. When the cops gave up, Jimmy and Marv, who had been watching from the Staten Island side, had rescued their Dutch uncle in another oyster boat. Then they took a closer look at the barge. Under it, they saw the outline of a submarine.

'Bigger than the Navy Holland. Same boat, but it looks like they added on a chunk at each end.'

'Uncle Donny knows the Holland,' Jimmy Richards explained. 'He took us off Brooklyn to watch the Navy tests. When was that?'

'In 1903. She made fifteen knots with her conning turret out of the water. And six submerged.'

Bell reached for the telephone. 'So you have good reason to believe that you saw a submarine.'

'Want to come see it?' asked Marv Gordon.

'Yes.'

'Told you he would,' said Uncle Donny.

Isaac Bell telephoned the New York Police Harbor Squad, rounded up Archie Abbott and Harry Warren, and grabbed a golf bag. The Ninth Avenue Elevated express whisked the Van Dorns and the scowmen to the Battery at the southern tip of Manhattan in ten minutes. A forty-foot Harbor Squad launch had its steam up at Pier A.

'Don't touch anything,' the captain warned the Staten Islanders as they trooped warily aboard. He did not want to tow Donald Darbee's scow, which was moored nearby, but Bell insisted and slipped him twenty dollars 'for your crew.'

'Never thought I'd be on one of these,' muttered old Darbee as they churned away from the pier.

A water cop muttered back, 'Except in handcuffs.'

Bell said to Archie and Harry, 'If there's no submarine in the Kill Van Kull, we're going to end up in a cross fire.'

'You really think we're going to find one, Isaac?'

'I believe they *think* they saw a submarine. And a submarine would make those torpedoes a much deadlier affair than a surface torpedo boat. Nonetheless, I will believe a submarine when I see one.'

The Harbor Squad launch plowed across the Upper Bay, threading a swift course through ferries, tugs, barges, and oceangoing schooners and steamers. A thunderous whistle announced the New York arrival of an Atlantic liner passing through the Verrazano Narrows. Tugboats meeting her piped replies. A steady stream of car floats carried freight trains between New Jersey, Manhattan, Brooklyn, and the East River.

The police boat steered into the crooked channel of water between Staten Island and New Jersey known as the Kill Van Kull. Bell estimated it was a thousand feet wide, about the same as the narrow arm of the Carquines Strait where he had captured Louis Loh swimming from Mare Island. To his left rose the hills of Staten Island. The city of Bayonne spread to his right. Docks, warehouses, boatyards, and residences lined the banks. Fou miles down the waterway, Richards and Gordon said, 'There she is!'

The car float stood by itself, tied to the shore beside the flat green back lawn of a large frame house in a district of similar dwellings. It was an old New Jersey Central barge of the three-track type, short and wide, with a boxcar on the nearside tracks and a tall gondola on the inside. The middle track appeared to be empty, though the men on the police launch could not see the space between the two cars.

'What submarine?' asked the Harbor Squad captain.

'Under it,' growled Donald Darbee. 'They cut a well in the middle of the barge for the conning turret.'

'You saw that?'

'No. But how else could they get in and out?'

The launch captain glowered at Isaac Bell. 'Mr. Bell, I predict that my boss is going to be talking to your boss, and neither of us is going to be very happy about it.'

'Let's get closer,' said Bell.

'There isn't enough water there for a Holland submarine.'

'It's plenty deep,' Donald Darbee retorted quietly. 'The tide scours the bank on this side.'

The helmsman called for *Dead Slow*, and drew within fifty feet.

The Van Dorns, the scowmen, and the harbor police peered into the murky water. The launch drifted closer to the car float.

'Lot of mud stirred up,' Darbee muttered worriedly.

'Our propeller's stirring it,' said the captain. 'Told you it's too shallow.' To the helmsman he barked, 'Back off before we run aground.'

Darbee said, 'There's thirty feet of water here if there's an inch.'

'Then what's causing that mud?'

'That's what I'm wondering.'

'So am I,' said Isaac Bell, peering into the water. Bubbles were rising from the murk and hissing on the surface.

52

'Back away!' Isaac Bell shouted. 'Back! Full Astern.'

The helmsman and the engineer had quick reflexes. They reversed the engine in an instant. The propeller churned backward. Smoke and steam shot from the short stack. The boat stopped. But before it could gather way in reverse, a gray malevolent form rose swiftly under it.

'Grab ahold!'

Bell saw a pipe emerge just ahead of the launch – the periscope, a tube of angled mirrors, the submarine's eye. A squat round turret broke the surface, the conning tower, rimmed with handrails. Then a mighty blow from underneath smashed into the bottom of the police launch and pushed its forty-foot hull out of the water. Its keel shattered with a loud crack of splitting wood, and still the police boat rose, lifted by a powerful steel hull that broke the surface like a maddened sperm whale.

The police launch fell onto its side, spilling Van Dorns, cops, and scowmen into the Kill.

Bell jumped onto the steel hull and waded through waist-deep water to the conning tower. He grabbed the handrails that surrounded the hatch on top and reached for a wheel that would open the hatch.

'Look out, Isaac!' Archie Abbott yelled. 'He's going under!'

Ignoring Archie and the water that was suddenly

climbing up his chest, Bell threw his weight on the wheel. For a second, it wouldn't budge. Then he thought he felt it move. Salt water rushed over his shoulders, his mouth, his nose, his eyes. Suddenly the submarine was surging ahead. He held the wheel as long as he could, still struggling to open it, but the force of the rushing water ripped it from his hands. The hull raced under him, and he realized, too late, that the propeller driving it was about to cut him to pieces.

He pushed off desperately with both boots and swam with all his strength. The water rushing past the hull sucked him back. He felt the hull sliding under him. Something hit him hard. It threw him aside and drove him deep. A powerful thrust of turbulence tumbled him deeper. Slammed about in the submarine's propeller wash, he realized that he had been struck by cowling that protected the propeller and, in this instance, protected him, too, from the thrashing blades.

He fought to the surface, saw the conning turret racing up the Kill Van Kull, and swam after it. Behind him, Archie was helping Harry Warren climb onto the muddy bank, Richards and Gordon and the engineer were holding ropes dangling from the barge, and the police captain clung to his overturned launch. 'Telephone for help!' the captain yelled, and two cops staggered toward the frame house.

Donald Darbee was climbing onto his oyster scow, which had broken free of the sinking launch.

'Uncle Donny!' Bell shouted over his shoulder as he swam after the submarine. 'Pick me up.'

Darbee's gasoline motor clattered, spewing blue smoke

The submarine kept submerging. The top of the turret and the periscope tube were all that remained above the surface. The handrails around it, the periscope, and the hatch wheel Bell had tried to open left a wake up the channel, splashing like a mobile fountain.

Darbee's scow came alongside, and Bell climbed on, rolling over the low gunnel onto the flat deck. 'After him!'

Darbee shoved his throttle forward. The motor got louder, the wooden boat trembled, and the old man muttered, 'What do we do with him when we catch him?'

Bell heard gunfire crackling behind him. The cops running to the frame house to telephone for help dove behind shrubs. Pistol fire raked the lawn from every window in the house.

'Counterfeiters live there,' Uncle Darbee explained.

'Faster!' said Bell.

He jumped onto the square forward deck.

'Get me alongside of the turret.'

The mostly submerged Holland was headed toward the Upper Bay at six knots. Darbee fiddled with his motor. The noise deepened to an insistent growl, and the oyster scow doubled her speed. It halved the distance to the splashing handrails, halved it again, and pulled past the backwash of the submarine's enormous propeller. Bell braced to jump to the conning tower. The wooden boat surged alongside. He could sense more than actually see the steel hull beneath the surface. He braced to jump, targeting the periscope tube, gambling that the thin tube was strong enough to hold him until he got a grip on the rails.

The Holland submarine disappeared.

One moment, the turret was just ahead of him. The

next, it was gone, deep in the water. Bell could see trailing bubbles and the ripples from the propeller, but there was nothing to jump onto anymore, no turret, no rails, no periscope.

'Slow down,' Bell called to Darbee. 'Follow his wake.'

Darbee throttled back to match the submarine's six-knot speed.

Bell stood on the foredeck, watching the rhythmic swirls of propeller wash and signaling the old man when to nudge his tiller to the left or right. How the underwater ship was navigating its course was a mystery that was solved after they had gone half a mile. Shortly before the submarine reached the next bend in the channel, its periscope suddenly emerged from the water, and the submarine changed course.

The spy had plotted their route out of the Kill Van Kull by noting the time that would elapse between each turn. Bell signaled a similar change and the oyster scow turned with it. The periscope stayed above water. It swiveled around until its glass eye was facing him.

'Stop engine!' Bell shouted.

The oyster boat's speed dropped as it drifted on momentum. Bell watched for signs that the Holland would back up or even turn around to ram them. But it held its course and pulled ahead of the scow, still showing its periscope.

'Darbee, did the test Holland you watched have a torpedo tube in back?'

'No,' Darbee answered to Bell's relief, until he added, 'I heard talk they might add one.'

'I can't imagine he'd waste an entire torpedo on us.'

'Suppose not.'

'Speed up. Get closer.'

Ahead, the Kill took a sharp turn. The periscope swiveled around, and the unseen helmsman steered through it. Bell signaled for the oyster boat to accelerate. He drew within twenty yards of the stubby tube and the swirling propeller wash. But the water ahead was turning choppy as the Kill spread into the Upper Bay.

Staten Island and Bayonne fell behind. A chilly breeze cut through Bell's wet clothes, and waves began curling over the periscope. Enormous bubbles burst on the surface, and he realized that the Holland was forcing air out of its floatation tanks and admitting water to descend deeper. The periscope dropped from sight. The windswept waves of the Upper Bay obliterated the swirling wake.

'He's gone,' said Darbee.

Bell searched hopelessly. Three miles across the bay sprawled the dockyards of Brooklyn and beyond them low green hills. To his left, four or five miles to the northwest, Bell saw the tall buildings of lower Manhattan and the elegantly draped cables of the Brooklyn Bridge spanning the East River.

'Do you know where Catherine Slip is?'

Darbee swung his tiller. 'What do you want there?'

'Dyname,' Bell answered. The fastest ship in New York, equipped with a telephone and a radio telegraph, and commanded by a high-ranking naval hero who could move quickly to rally the Navy against the spy's submarine and radio the *New Hampshire* to rig torpedo nets before entering the port.

Darbee gave him a canvas pea jacket that smelled of mold. Bell stripped off his wet coat and shirt, dried out his

Browning, and poured water out of his boots. The over-powered oyster scow covered the five miles to the Brooklyn Bridge in twenty minutes. But as they passed under the bridge, Bell's heart sank. The battleship *New Hampshire* had already landed. It was moored to the pier closest to the way that held Hull 44. If 44 was O'Shay's target, they were a pair of sitting ducks. Explosions on the floating ship would set the entire navy yard afire.

To Isaac Bell's relief, *Dyname* was at Catherine Slip.

He jumped from the oyster scow onto the nearest ladder, climbed onto the pier, crossed her gangway, and shoved through the door to *Dyname*'s main cabin. Captain Falconer was seated on the green leather banquette flanked by two of his yacht's crewmen.

'Falconer. They've got a submarine.'

'So I am told,' said the Hero of Santiago with a grim nod at three Riker & Riker Protection Service gunmen who were covering the cabin with pistols and a sawed-off shotgun. Bell recognized the bodyguard, Plimpton, who had accompanied Herr Riker on the 20th Century Limited. Plimpton said, 'You're all wet, Mr. Bell, and you've lost your hat.'

53

'Hello, Plimpton.'

'Hands up.'

'Where's O'Shay?'

'In the air!'

'Tell your boss that I owe him for an excellent emerald and I'm looking forward to paying him in person.'

'Now!'

'Do it, Bell,' Falconer said. 'They've already shot my lieutenant and my engineer.'

Isaac Bell raised his hands, having stalled long enough to rate the opposition. Plimpton held a semiautomatic German Navy Luger like he knew his business. But the pretty-boy bruisers flanking him were out of their league. The elder, gingerly toting a sawed-off 20-gauge Remington, might pass for a small-town bank guard. The younger gripped his revolver like a bouncer in a YMCA. They were not on Falconer's yacht due to a well-thought-out plan, Bell surmised. Something had gone wrong.

What had drawn them at the last moment to *Dyname*? Escape on the fastest ship in the harbor after O'Shay unleashed his torpedoes? But *Dyname* hadn't the range to cross the Atlantic Ocean. Surely O'Shay had intended to take a liner to Europe, traveling with Katherine Dee under assumed names, or had booked secret passage on a freighter.

She was what went wrong, Bell realized. Katherine was wounded.

'Is the girl aboard?' he asked Falconer.

'She needs a doctor!' the boy with the shotgun blurted.

'Shut up, Bruce!' Plimpton growled.

'I'm aboard,' said Katherine Dee. She staggered up the companionway from Falconer's private cabin. Disheveled, pale, and feverish, she looked like a child shaken from a deep sleep. Except for the hatred on her face. 'Thanks to you,' she said bitterly to Bell. 'You're ruining everything.' She had held tight to her pistol when he had shot her in Barlowe's jewelry shop. She raised it with a trembling hand and aimed it at him.

'Miss Dee!' said Bruce. 'You shouldn't be on your feet.'

'She needs a doctor,' said Bell.

'That's what I've been saying. Mr. Plimpton, she's got to have a doctor.'

'Shut up, Bruce,' said Plimpton. 'She'll have a doctor as soon as we get out of this mess.'

Hands in the air, boxed in by O'Shay's gunmen, the tall detective searched her eyes, seeking some advantage, even as he braced for the bullet. He saw no mercy, no hesitation, only the deep, deep weariness of a person with a mortal wound. But she intended to kill him before she died. As she had killed Grover Lakewood and Father Jack and who knew how many others for Eyes O'Shay. How long before she passed out? Where, he wondered, was her 'streak of God'?

'Did you know,' he asked, 'that Father Jack prayed for you?'

'A lot of good his prayers did. It was Brian O'Shay who saved me.'

448

'What did Brian save you for? To hurl Grover Lake-wood to his death? To shoot the priest?'

'Just like you shot me.'

'No,' said Bell. 'I shot you to save the woman I love.'

'I love Brian. I will do anything for him.'

Bell recalled the words of train conductor Dilber on the 20th Century Limited. *'Riker and his ward are completely on the up-and-up. Always separate staterooms.'*

And O'Shay himself, speaking as Riker, had said, 'The girl brings light into my life where there was darkness.'

'And what will Brian be for you?'

'He saved me.'

'Fifteen years ago. What will he do for the rest of your life, Katherine? Keep you pure?'

Her hand shook violently. 'You –' Her breath came hoarsely.

'You kill to please him, and he keeps you pure? Is that how it works? Father Jack was right to pray for you.'

'Why?' she wailed.

'He knew in his heart, in his soul, that Brian O'Shay couldn't save you.'

'And God could?'

'So the priest believed. With all his heart.'

Katherine lowered the gun. Her eyes rolled back in her head. The gun slipped from her fingers, and she folded to the deck as if she were a puppet whose strings had been cut.

'Plimpton, damn you!' Bruce shouted. 'She'll die without a doctor.' He gestured emphatically with his pistol.

Like a viper striking reflexively at movement, Plimpton shot Bruce between the eyes and whirled back to the blur

449

of motion that was Isaac Bell. The bodyguard had committed a fatal error.

Bell fired his Browning twice. Plimpton first, then the remaining gunman. As the gunman pitched forward, his shotgun went off, the report deafening in the confined space of the yacht's cabin. A swath of pellets tore under the banquette into the legs of Lowell Falconer and his crew.

Bell was wrapping a tourniquet above Falconer's knee when Donald Darbee stuck a cautious head in the door. 'Thought you'd want to know, Mr. Bell, the Holland is passing under the Brooklyn Bridge.'

54

'Surface!' shouted Dick Condon, the first mate whom Eyes O'Shay had put in command of his Holland submarine after he murdered Captain Hatch.

'No!' O'Shay countermanded the order. 'Stay down. They'll see us.'

'The tide is killing us,' the frightened Irish rebel shouted back. 'The current is running four knots. We only make six knots on electric! We have to surface to use the gasoline engine.'

O'Shay gripped Condon's shoulder. The panic in the man's voice was scaring the men who were operating the ballasting and trimming tanks and preparing to fire the torpedo, which was precisely why he had decided to sail with the submarine. Someone had to keep a clear head. 'Six? Four? Who cares? We're two knots faster.'

'No, Mr. O'Shay. Only directly into the tide. When I turn broadside to line up a torpedo, we'll be swept away.'

'Try it!' O'Shay demanded. 'Take the chance.'

Dick Condon switched the vertical rudder to hand control from the less fine compressed-air steering and moved it cautiously. The deck tilted under their feet. Then the East River caught the hundred-foot submarine with the fury of a shark tearing into a weak swimmer. The men in the small dark space smashed into pipes, conduits, valves, and air hoses as the boat was tumbled.

'Surface!' Condon's voice rose to a scream.

'No.'

'I must put the conning tower in the air, sir. It doesn't matter, Mr. O'Shay,' he pleaded. 'We can shoot better on the surface. The first torpedo is already loaded. We can fire, submerge, let the current sweep us down again while we reload, and return to the surface. You'll get what you want, sir. And if anyone sees us, they'll see it's a British ship. Just like we want. Please, sir. You must listen to reason or all is lost.'

O'Shay shoved him from the periscope and looked for himself.

The river surface was wild, an ever-moving crazy quilt of tumbling waves. Spray obscured the glass. Just as it cleared, a wave curled over it, blacking it out. The boat lurched violently. Suddenly the periscope stood free of the jumbled water, and O'Shay saw that they were nearly abreast of the navy yard.

The *New Hampshire* was just where he wanted it. He could not have positioned the long white hull better himself. But the submarine was slipping backward even though the propeller was thrashing and the electric motor smelled like it was burning up.

'All right,' O'Shay conceded. 'Attack on the surface.'

'Reduce to half speed!' Condon ordered. The motor stopped straining, and the boat stopped shaking. He watched through the periscope, controlling their drift with skillful twists of the horizontal and vertical rudders. 'Prepare to surface.'

'What's that noise?'

The Royal Navy veterans exchanged puzzled glances.

'Is something wrong with the motor?' asked O'Shay.

'No, no, no. It's in the water.'

The crew stood still, ears cocked to a strange, high-pitched whine that grew louder and shriller by the second.

'A ship?'

Condon spun the periscope, searching the river. The engineer voiced what his shipmates were thinking.

'It doesn't sound like any ship I ever heard.'

'Down!' Condon shouted. 'Take her down.'

'Where did he go?' Lowell Falconer gasped. To Isaac Bell's astonishment, the bloodied Navy captain had dragged himself topside, where Bell was driving *Dyname* toward the Brooklyn Bridge at thirty knots.

'Dead ahead,' said Isaac Bell. He had one hand on the steam lever, the other gripped the helm. 'Is that tourniquet doing its job?' he asked, not taking his eyes from the river.

'I'd be dead if it weren't,' Falconer snapped through gritted teeth. He was white from loss of blood, and Bell doubted he would be conscious much longer. The effort to climb the few steps to the bridge must have been herculean. 'Who's in the engine room?' Falconer asked.

'Uncle Darbee claims he was coal stoker on the Staten Island Ferry, and assistant engineer when the regular fellow got drunk.'

'*Dyname* burns oil.'

'He figured that out when he couldn't find a shovel. We've got plenty of steam.'

'I don't see the Holland.'

'It's gone up and down. I saw the periscope a moment ago. There!'

The stubby conning tower broke the surface. The hull itself emerged briefly and rolled back under.

'Tide's battering him,' muttered Falconer. 'It's ebbing under a full moon.'

'Good,' said Bell. 'We need all the help we can get.'

Dyname streaked through the patch of roiled water. The submarine was nowhere to be seen. Falconer tugged at Bell's sleeve, whispering urgently, 'He's some sort of A-Class Royal Navy Holland – triple our tonnage. Look out, if he surfaces. He'll be faster on his main engine.' With that warning, the captain slid unconscious to the deck. Bell throttled back and turned the speeding yacht around until it was pointing upstream again. He was several hundred yards beyond the Brooklyn Bridge now, scanning the water in the failing light.

A ferryboat pulled abruptly from its Pine Street Pier, cut off a big Bronx-bound Pennsylvania Railroad ferry, and raced up the East River. Their wakes combined to render vast stretches of water too choppy for Bell to distinguish the periscope from breaking seas. He drove into the chop and circled. Suddenly he saw it far ahead. It had trailed behind the ferries, masked by them, and was pulling abreast of the navy yard.

The Holland submarine burst from the water, revealing her conning tower and the full hundred feet of her hull. Blue smoke spewed. Gasoline exhaust, Bell realized, from her powerful main engine. On the surface now, she was a full-fledged torpedo boat, quick and nimble.

But vulnerable.

Bell shoved the steam lever forward, seizing this precious chance to ram her. But even as the steel yacht gathered speed, the long Holland heeled into a tight turn and pointed straight at *Dyname*. Her bow reared. Bell saw the dark maw of an open bow tube. From it leaped a Mark 14 Wheeler torpedo.

55

The torpedo submerged.

Isaac Bell could only guess whether to steer left or right. He could not see the torpedo bearing down on him underwater. Nor whether it was veering left or right. Whatever wake it trailed was erased by the heavy chop. *Dyname* was one hundred feet long and ten feet wide. The instant he turned, he would present a bigger target broadside. If he guessed wrong, the TNT warhead would blow the yacht to pieces. O'Shay would submerge to reload at leisure and continue his attack.

Bell steered straight ahead.

The Holland saw him coming. It began to submerge. But it was descending too slowly to escape the knife-thin steel hull bearing down on it at nearly forty knots. It turned abruptly to the right, Isaac Bell's left. He still could not see the torpedo's wake, nor any trail of bubbles. 'Hang on, Uncle Danny!' he shouted down the voice pipe, and turned left to ram.

A flash of light and an explosion behind him told Bell he had guessed correctly. Had he not counterpunched, the torpedo would have sunk him. Instead, it had detonated against an impervious stone pier of the Brooklyn Bridge, and he was close enough to the Holland to see its rivets. He braced for the impact by pressing hard against the helm the second before she hit the submarine just behind its

456

conning tower. At the speed *Dyname* was traveling, Bell expected to shear through the Holland and cut it in half. But he had miscalculated. With her sharp bow lifting from the water as her nine propellers churned, the yacht rode up onto the Holland's hull, perched across it, then slid off with a screech of tearing steel and shearing rivets.

Dyname's propellers were still spinning, and they pushed the yacht hundreds of yards from the collision before he could stop them. The Holland had vanished, submerged or sunk, he could not tell. Then Uncle Donny poked his head up to report, 'Water's coming in.'

'Can you give me steam?'

'Not for long,' the old man answered. Bell circled the site of the collision. He could feel the water weighing down *Dyname*'s hull.

Seven minutes after the Holland submerged, it reappeared a short distance away.

Bell steered to ram again. The yacht resisted the helm. He could barely coax her into a turn. Suddenly the Holland's conning-tower hatch flipped open. Four men scrambled out and jumped into the river. The tidal current swept them under the bridge. None were Eyes O'Shay, and the Holland was circling, pointing slowly but inexorably toward the four-hundred-fifty-foot hull of the *New Hampshire*. At a range of less than four hundred yards, the spy could not miss.

Bell wrestled with the helm and forced the stricken yacht on a course to ram. He shoved the steam lever to flank speed. There was no response. He yelled down the voice pipe. 'Give me everything you can, and get out before she sinks!'

Whatever the old man managed in the engine room caused the yacht to lumber ahead fitfully. Bell steered at the Holland, which had stopped in place, low in the water, with the East River waves lapping the rim of its open hatch. The thrashing propeller held it against the tide. Its bow was completing its turn, lining its torpedo tube up with the *New Hampshire*.

Isaac Bell drove *Dyname* into the submarine. The vessels lurched together like bloodied, bare-knuckle prizefighters staggering through their final round. The yacht bumped the heavier submarine slightly off its course and scraped alongside. As the effect of the impact receded and the submarine resumed lining up its torpedo, Bell glimpsed through the open hatch Eyes O'Shay's hands manipulating the rudder wheels.

He jumped down from the bridge, dove over *Dyname*'s rails onto the submarine, and plunged through the hatch.

56

The detective rammed through the hatch like a pile driver. His boots smashed down on O'Shay's shoulders. The spy lost his grip on the rudders. Hurtled into the control room below, he sprawled on the deck. Bell landed on his feet.

The stench of bleach – poisonous chlorine gas mixed from saltwater leaks and battery acid – burned his nostrils and stung his eyes. Half blinded, he caught a blurry glimpse of a cramped space, a fraction of a boxing ring, with a curved ribbed ceiling so low he had to crouch and walled in by bulkheads bristling with piping, valves, and gauges.

O'Shay leaped up and charged.

Isaac Bell met the spy with a hard right. O'Shay blocked it and counterpunched, landing a fist that knocked the tall detective sideways. Bell slammed into the bulkhead, seared his arm on a white-hot pipe, bounced off the sharp rim of a rudder indicator, raked his scalp on the compass protruding from the ceiling, and threw another right.

The spy blocked him again with a left arm as strong as it was quick and blasted back with a counterpunch deadlier than the first. It caught Bell in his ribs with the force to hurl him back against the hot pipes. His boots skidded on the wet deck, and he fell.

The stink of chlorine was much stronger low down, the gas being heavier than air, and as Bell inhaled it he felt a burning pain in his throat and the sensation that he was suffocating. He heard O'Shay grunt with effort. The spy was launching a kick at his head.

Bell dodged all but the man's heel, which tore across his temple, and rolled to his feet. Gasping to draw breaths of marginally cleaner air, he circled the spy. They were more evenly matched than Bell had supposed. He had a longer reach, but O'Shay was easily as strong as he and as fast. Bell's extra height was a distinct disadvantage in the confined space.

Again he threw a right, a feint this time, and when O'Shay executed another lightning-fast block and counterpunch the tall detective was ready to hit him with a powerful left that rocked the spy's head back.

'Lucky hit,' O'Shay taunted.

'Counterpunching is all you ever learned in Hell's Kitchen,' Bell shot back.

'Not all,' said O'Shay. He slipped his thumb into his vest and brought it out again, armed with a razor-sharp stainless-steel eye gouge.

Bell moved in, throwing combinations. He landed most, but it was like a punching a heavy workout bag. O'Shay never staggered but merely absorbed the powerhouse blows while he waited for his chance. When it came, he took it, sinking a gut-wrenching blow into Bell's body.

It doubled the detective over. Before Bell could pull back, O'Shay closed in on him with blinding speed and circled his neck with his powerful right arm.

Isaac Bell found himself trapped in a headlock. His left arm was pinned between their bodies. With his right, he tried to reach the knife in his boot. But O'Shay's thumb gouge was arced toward his eye. Bell surrendered all thoughts of his knife and seized O'Shay's wrist.

He realized instantly that he had never grappled with a stronger man. Even as he held his wrist with all his might, O'Shay forced the razor-sharp gouge closer and closer to Bell's face until it pierced the skin and began crawling cross his cheek, plowing a fine red furrow toward his eye. All the while, O'Shay's right arm was squeezing harder and harder around his throat, cutting off air to his burning lungs and blood to his brain. He heard a roaring in his ears. White flashes stormed before his eyes. His sight began to fade, his grip on O'Shay's wrist loosened.

He tried to free his left arm. O'Shay shifted slightly to keep it pinned.

Head trapped, bent low, Bell suddenly saw that he was now partially behind O'Shay. He slammed his knee into the back of O'Shay's knee. It buckled. O'Shay pitched forward. Bell wedged his shoulder under him and rose like a piston.

He flipped O'Shay up and yanked down, slamming the spy to the deck with bone-shaking force. The powerful O'Shay kept hold of Bell's head, took a deep breath of air, and pulled the detective down with him into the heavier concentration of the suffocating gas. But Bell's left arm was no longer pinned between them. He slammed his elbow into O'Shay's nose, cracking bone. Still O'Shay choked him, still the gouge raked at his eye.

Suddenly cold water cascaded down on the fighting men, sending fresh clouds of chlorine up from the massive battery under the deck. The submarine was heeling, the river spilling through the hatch. Bell pushed out with long legs, found a foothold, and forced O'Shay's head against the bulkhead lined with hot pipes. O'Shay tried to writhe away. Bell held fast. Even sharper than the stench of chlorine was the stink of burning hair, and at last O'Shay's grip loosened. Bell pulled out of it, dodged a vicious slash of the gouge, and punched out repeatedly as waves poured in.

Bell struggled to stand, kicked free of O'Shay's grasping hands, and climbed out of the hatch. He saw lights converging. Launches were setting out from the Brooklyn Navy Yard and lowering from the *New Hampshire*. The submarine was sinking, engine still roaring, propeller still fighting the current. A wave tumbled over the hatch and swept Bell to the back of the submarine. He kicked off from the propeller shield, just missing the blades, and was thrown behind by its wash.

O'Shay climbed out of the hatch, retching from the chlorine. He dove after Bell, his face a mask of hatred. 'I'll kill you.'

The Holland's propeller dragged him into its spinning blades.

The river current whisked his torso past Bell. The gangster's head raced after it, glaring at the detective, until the river yanked it under.

The Holland submarine rolled quite suddenly on its side and slid beneath the waves. Isaac Bell thought he was next. He battled to stay afloat, but he was weakened by cold and rendered breathless by the poison gas. A wave curled over him, and his mind suddenly filled with his memory of the day he met Marion and the floor had trembled beneath his feet. His eyes were playing tricks on him. Her thick, lustrous hair was piled atop her head. One long, narrow strand fell nearly to her waist. She looked dainty but strong as a willow, and she was reaching for him.

She gripped his hand. He tightened his own grip and pulled himself to the surface. He looked up into the grinning face of a bearded sailor.

The next Isaac Bell knew, he was sprawled on his back in the bottom of a wooden boat. Beside him lay Captain Lowell Falconer. The Hero of Santiago looked as beat-up as Bell felt, but his eyes were bright.

'You'll be O.K., Bell. They're taking us into sick bay.'

It hurt to talk and was hard to breathe. His throat was burning. 'Better warn the salvage boys that the Holland has a live Wheeler Mark 14 still in its tube.'

'Still in its tube, thanks to you.'

The launch bumped against a dock.

'What are those lights?' asked Bell. The sky was white with them.

'Hull 44 is going to double shifts.'

'Good.'

'"Good"?' Lowell Falconer echoed. 'The most you can say for yourself is "good"?'

Isaac Bell thought hard. Then he grinned. 'Sorry about your yacht.'

On Distant Service

Ten Years Later
North Sea, German Coast

Fog blinded the German soldiers hunting the American spy.

Oozing from the Friesland peat bogs into the morning air, it crowded under the trees and covered the flat ground. It was supposed to last until the sun burned it off midmorning. But it grew thin early when a salt wind from the North Sea roamed ashore. Isaac Bell saw the daylight penetrate, revealing fields crisscrossed by ditches, trees stationed along fence lines, and in the distance a boathouse by a canal. A boat would come in handy now.

Bell saw his own face on a wanted poster nailed to the boathouse.

He had to hand it to the Kaiser's military intelligence. Three days after he had come ashore, the German Army had plastered his image on every tree and barn between Berlin and the coast. One thousand Marks reward, five and a half thousand dollars, a fortune on either side of the Atlantic. The grim-faced fugitive on the *Steckbrief* bore his general likeness. Though they had no photograph, only the account of a sentry at the Wilhelmshaven Naval Station U-boat yard, the sketch artist had captured the determined set of his chin and lips and the hard, lean look of a man more muscle than flesh. Thankfully, the written description of blond hair and mustache and blue eyes fit most men in the Saxon region. Though few stood as tall.

With the United States now fighting Germany in the World War, his clothes – a ragbag mix of uniform parts – and the crutch he carried as a wounded veteran, guaranteed he'd be shot as a spy if they caught him. Nor could he expect any mercy for the map he had drawn of the new U-boat yard that serviced the latest submarines – immensely more powerful than the old Holland, and heavily armed – that were suddenly and unexpectedly winning the war for Germany. The map that was useless until he delivered it to America's Sixth Battle Squadron steaming offshore.

The canal was narrow, and the rushes planted on both sides to protect the banks from wakes tended to hold the fog. He rowed two miles to Wilhelmshaven, abandoning the boat to evade naval station sentries and stealing another. The fog continued cooperating, after a fashion, at the harbor, still fitful, thinning for moments, then thickened by clouds of coal smoke from a hundred warships.

It was low tide. The entrance to the harbor was shallow, and Wilhelmshaven was crowded with funnels and masts of the High Seas Fleet's cruisers, battle cruisers, and dreadnoughts waiting for high water. But shallow-draft torpedo boats could leave, which meant that Bell's escape vessel had to be small enough to operate by himself and very fast, which eliminated tugboats, lighters, launches, and fishing scows.

Intelligence supplied by a Van Dorn who had gone underground when war had closed the Berlin office pinpointed a captured Italian-built MAS fifty-foot armed motorboat. Bell had spotted it on the way in and it was still there, in the grimy shadow of a dreadnought.

He prayed for more fog, and his prayer was answered so quickly that he had only a moment to get a compass fix on the MAS before every vessel in the harbor was buried to its mast tops. He rowed, repeatedly checking the compass on the seat beside him, and tried to judge the current. But to strike a fifty-foot target in a quarter mile was impossible, and the first he knew how far he had missed by was when he banged into the armored side of the dreadnought.

The vague looming of 12-inch guns overhead indicated he was near its bow, and he quietly paddled alongside until he found the MAS. He boarded, confirmed it was unmanned, and untied all but one line. Then he inspected the motors, a pair of the sort of beautifully compact gasoline engines he expected of the Italians. He figured out how to start them, got their fuel pumps primed, and released the last line. Using one of the oars, he paddled it slowly away from the dreadnought and waited for the sun to start burning off the fog. At the moment he could see and be seen, he started the engines, each of which was as a loud as his old Locomobile.

By the time he reached the narrow mouth of the harbor, the Germans knew something was up, if not exactly what. The confusion and still-murky fog bought him a few precious moments, and by the time individuals began firing rifles at him he was thundering across the water at nearly thirty knots. He streaked past some picketboats, drawing more fire, some of it remarkably accurate. Four miles beyond the sea buoy, he looked back. The fog was thinning, little thicker than a haze, and through it he saw columns of smoke – three or four torpedo boats coming after him with 4-inch guns on their bows.

The farther he got from the coast, the rougher the seas, which slowed him. The torpedo boats began to gain. At three miles, they opened fire, and all that saved him was the fact that the fifty-foot MAS was a minuscule target. At two miles, the shells began coming uncomfortably close, and Bell began to zigzag, which made the MAS even harder to hit but slowed his passage, and soon the torpedo boats were close enough for him to see the men working the bow guns.

He peered ahead, straining to see smoke or the tall, fuzzy pillar of a cage mast.

A four-inch shell cut the air with an earsplitting shriek and splashed ahead of him. The fog was gone now. There were patches of blue in the sky. He could see the lead torpedo boat clearly and two behind it. Another shell screeched very close by. He saw it splash beside him and bounce like a skipping stone.

The sky ahead turned blue, and it was suddenly divided vertically by a column of smoke as if split by a dark sword. He heard the rapid booming of quick-firing 5-inch guns. Shells streaked over him. Splashes straddled the lead torpedo boat, and all three sheared around and fled for the coast.

Now Bell saw his savior steaming toward him. At his and its combined speeds, it was only minutes before he recognized the familiar cage masts, radio antennas, and 14-inch guns of the 27,000-ton battleship USS *New York*.

Within minutes, Bell had been hoisted to her main deck. Sailors escorted him to the base of a cage mast. He presented his map to the commander of the Sixth Squadron, a broadly grinning Rear Admiral Lowell Falconer, who seized it with his maimed hand, scanned it eagerly, and issued orders.

Bell said, 'I'll give the range boys a hand sorting out landmarks.'

A sailor half his age offered to help him climb the mast.

'Thanks,' said Bell. 'I've been on one of these before.'

The *New York*'s 14-inch guns, designed by Arthur Langner, were mounted on special turrets that had been perfected by Langner's acolytes. They could be elevated to extraordinary angles, vastly increasing the guns' range. A fire-control system pioneered by Grover Lakewood's team calculated the distance to the U-boat yard. Salvos thundered. High-explosive shells soared toward the distant coast.

By now, the tide had risen. German battle cruisers came boiling out of the harbor. They were fast and heavily gunned, but their armor was no match for the battleship *New York*'s, and they kept their distance until a brace of full-scale German dreadnoughts appeared next on the horizon. The sailors flanking Bell in the spotting top exchanged anxious glances.

The German dreadnoughts drew closer. The American kept bombarding its target.

At last, mountains of smoke marked the ruins of the U-boat yard.

Falconer ordered what he described to Bell as a 'prudent withdrawal.'

The German ships fired at extreme range, but the shells fell short and they were too late. With her original reciprocating engines replaced by the latest model MacDonald turbines, the *New York* left them in her wake.

As the American dreadnought steamed for the harbor of Scapa Flow in the Orkney Islands north of Scotland, Admiral Falconer invited Isaac Bell up to his private cabin just under the bridge. The U.S. Navy was dry, alcohol forbidden, but Bell had brought a flask, and they raised a glass to victory.

'This is one escapade that won't appear in the history books,' Falconer told Bell, adding with a laugh that jealous British admirals would want Bell shot for upstaging them.

'Assure them,' smiled Bell, 'that private detectives serve privately.'

A ship's carpenter knocked at the door and came in with a mallet and steel chisels. Falconer pointed at the builder's plate, which read:

USS NEW YORK
Brooklyn Navy Yard

'Loosen that for me.'

'Yes, sir, Admiral!'

The carpenter chiseled around it, and when it was loose enough to pry from the bulkhead Falconer dismissed him. Alone with Isaac Bell, he peeled it away. Underneath it, raised characters welded to the steel read:

Hull 44

A week later, Isaac Bell stepped off the train from Scotland and strode from Euston Station into London streets that looked weary from a long, long war.

The tall detective turned his face from a newsreel camera and dodged a horse-drawn mail van. He paused to admire a red 1911 Rolls-Royce Lawton Limousine. Its elegant lines were marred by a floppy gas bag on its roof. The limousine had been converted to burn coal gas, thanks to the oil shortage caused by U-boats sinking tankers.

The Rolls-Royce stopped in front of him.

The elderly chauffeur, too old to fight in the trenches, climbed down, saluted Isaac Bell, and opened the door to the passenger compartment. A beautiful woman with straw-blond hair, an hourglass figure, and sea-coral green eyes addressed him in a voice brimming with joy and relief.

'We are so lucky you made it back.'

She patted the seat beside her.

An emerald glowed on her ring finger, mysterious as the eye of a cat.

He just wanted a decent book to read ...

Not too much to ask, is it? It was in 1935 when Allen Lane, Managing Director of Bodley Head Publishers, stood on a platform at Exeter railway station looking for something good to read on his journey back to London. His choice was limited to popular magazines and poor-quality paperbacks – the same choice faced every day by the vast majority of readers, few of whom could afford hardbacks. Lane's disappointment and subsequent anger at the range of books generally available led him to found a company – and change the world.

'We believed in the existence in this country of a vast reading public for intelligent books at a low price, and staked everything on it'
Sir Allen Lane, 1902–1970, founder of Penguin Books

The quality paperback had arrived – and not just in bookshops. Lane was adamant that his Penguins should appear in chain stores and tobacconists, and should cost no more than a packet of cigarettes.

Reading habits (and cigarette prices) have changed since 1935, but Penguin still believes in publishing the best books for everybody to enjoy. We still believe that good design costs no more than bad design, and we still believe that quality books published passionately and responsibly make the world a better place.

So wherever you see the little bird – whether it's on a piece of prize-winning literary fiction or a celebrity autobiography, political tour de force or historical masterpiece, a serial-killer thriller, reference book, world classic or a piece of pure escapism – you can bet that it represents the very best that the genre has to offer.

Whatever you like to read – trust Penguin.